The Canary Girls

Rosie Archer was born in Gosport, Hampshire, where she still lives. She has had a variety of jobs including waitress, fruit picker, barmaid, shop assistant and market trader selling second-hand books. Rosie has had many short stories published in women's magazines. *The Canary Girls* is her second novel, the sequel to *The Munitions Girls.*

Also by Rosie Archer

The Munitions Girls

The Canary Girls

ROSIE ARCHER

Quercus

First published in Great Britain in 2015 by

Quercus Publishing Ltd
Carmelite House
50 Victoria Embankment
London EC4Y 0DZ

An Hachette UK company

A CIP catalogue record for this book is available from the British Library

PB ISBN 978 1 84866 496 8
EBOOK ISBN 978 1 78429 155 6

10 9 8 7 6 5 4 3 2 1

Typeset by CC Book Production

Printed and bound in Great Britain by Clays Ltd, St Ives plc

For Phoebe – through you I see the future.

Chapter One

1944

'Leave her alone!' Rita shouted, grabbing Jack's fingers and prising them away from Em's soft flesh. His nails left bloody indents in his wife's skin as his grip slid away. 'I'll get Blackie to sort you out if ever you mark her again!'

Em, freed, had fallen sobbing in a heap alongside the overturned wheelchair that still held Jack. He was struggling to stop himself sliding onto the living-room floor. Jack's thick, brawny arms and iron grasp weren't quick enough and he cursed his useless lower limbs, courtesy of the war. One leg had been shot away, the other amputated to the knee.

'I'll get you for this, Rita Brown!' There was venom in his voice and hate in his eyes as he glared helplessly up at her. 'You got no call to come between husband and wife.'

Breathless, Rita stared at him as a shudder of fear rushed through her. He was trying to scare her with his words. How could he possibly 'get her' for helping Em? She turned away from him without answering, not wanting him to take out more of his anger on Em later on.

'Shush, Dad.' Lizzie, his daughter, galvanized now into action, pulled the chair into a vertical position. 'Rita, look after me mum.' Her arms slid around Jack's back and chest and she hauled him into the wheelchair. Then she was pushing the protesting, angry man along the narrow passage towards the kitchen at the back of the house, exertion leaving behind her a sweet waft of lily-of-the-valley perfume. Rita, now kneeling on the threadbare carpet, her arms about Em, breathed a sigh of relief that Jack had been removed.

'Thank you, Rita. Dunno what would have happened if you hadn't come calling for me. His legs may be wasted but he's got the strength of ten men in his hands,' the older woman said, her voice muffled in the woollen folds of Rita's best work jumper.

'Lizzie would have stepped in,' whispered Rita. 'It's what she's come home for, to keep an eye on you when Jack's moods get the better of him.' She took her handkerchief from her sleeve and began drying her friend's tears. Em's face was puffy and her cheeks smudged with mascara.

Em sniffed again, her eyes holding Rita's. 'She's torn between us. She remembers her dad as he used to be, the gentlest of men, not the broken wreck this blasted war has made him.' She finished the job of wiping her face with the hem of her flowered pinny.

Then she looked towards the open doorway, almost, thought Rita, as though she was scared to speak her mind when her husband was within earshot. 'Waking in a trench with your dead mates all around you is bound to change a man's thinking,' she added. Many of her friends' boyfriends or husbands had joined the services full of hope, only to be killed in action or return disabled in mind or body, shadows of the men who had gone bravely to war.

Em had told her that Jack, too, had wanted to die when he'd been shipped home from France, a broken man.

The clatter of Lizzie's high heels along the worn lino in the passage heralded her return to the front room. 'Thanks, Rita,' she said. Her face darkened as she looked down at the pair of them. 'I should have done more.' She put up a hand and smoothed back the strands of shoulder-length dark hair that had escaped the pins securing it. Rita thought how pretty Lizzie was, with her flawless skin and slim figure.

Lizzie knelt down beside her mother and Rita. 'You all right, Mum?' Gently she lifted her mother's arm to examine the bloodied skin.

'Never mind me,' Em said, pulling away from her daughter's scrutiny. Rita knew she hated fuss. 'Has he calmed down now?' She used Rita's shoulder to help her stand up. Rita scrambled to her feet and brushed her skirt down, smoothing out the creases. She knew this wasn't the first time Jack had hurt Em and it certainly wouldn't be the last. But to discuss it was a waste of time and Em wouldn't thank her for it. Instead she looked at the wooden-cased clock on the mantelpiece and said, 'We got to get to work, you two. The bloody TNT won't jump into the shells by itself.'

Em nodded, but said to Lizzie, 'What's he up to now?' She glanced fearfully towards the kitchen.

'I left Dad with his paper.' Lizzie was staring again at the marks on her mother's skin. 'You all right to go in today?'

Em worked at Gosport's Priddy's Hard. A steady hand and a calm demeanour were requisites of the dangerous job. 'Tough as old boots, me,' she said.

The clock chimed. If they hurried they could still make their shift at the munitions yard.

Em said, 'I'll just put something on this. Won't do to

get any of those chemicals in it.' She meant the materials used in the detonators they handled. The lead azide, which looked like caster sugar, or fulminate of mercury – both seemed harmless enough but they were toxic and could cause injuries during the filling process. A third chemical, tetryl, which was highly sensitive, caused many complaints, including yellowing of the skin and hair, which gave the workers their nickname – the canary girls. It also caused explosions and accidents.

'Dab of iodine first, I think,' Em said, 'and a bandage.' She smiled then, her face lighting up. 'Don't worry, you two. I'm the overseer at Priddy's and you can't start work until I get there.'

'That's all right for you,' Lizzie broke in, 'but I'm in the office and there's a different set of rules for us lot.'

'I'm only joking, my girl.' Em shook her head. 'All the same, we'd better not take advantage. England needs all the shells and bombs we can fill to fix old Hitler and his box of tricks.'

Em left the room, ample hips swaying, untying her pinny as she went.

Rita asked, 'What started him off this time?'

Lizzie sighed. 'Yesterday night Mum was late in because she queued for bread at Roy's bakery. Apparently there was a line right up to the park gates, but she'd heard Roy had managed a double bake so she waited. Dad got it into his head she was meeting someone after work.'

'Didn't you tell him where she was? You usually go home together, don't you?' Rita often walked with them but last night she'd gone straight round to Blackie's house.

'He refused to believe me, Rita, said I was making excuses for her.'

Rita tutted, then walked to the mirror over the fireplace and stared at her reflection. The mirror was so high she had to stand on tiptoe. Only a tall man could have nailed it to the wall, she thought. Glossy hair waved down one side of her face, hiding the scar that ran from beneath her eye to her chin. She'd got so used to looking at it she no longer really saw it. The blast at the armaments yard had resulted in a lengthy hospital stay and several skin-grafting operations. At first she'd thought she'd never get over it and wished she'd died in the blast. But she'd had good friends, and a wonderful nurse at the East Grinstead Hospital had pulled her through those dark times. The Plastic Surgery and Burns Unit had given her back her looks and, more importantly, her confidence. But it had taken her a long time to realize that there was more to life than a pretty face.

Rita and Lizzie were so alike, apart from the scar, that

they were often mistaken for sisters. Rita didn't mind: she would have liked the kindly Em for a mother. 'I suppose your dad being the way he is makes him even more jealous,' Rita said. 'It don't give him any excuses for knocking your mum about, though.' She checked her lip colour and pursed her mouth. She could do with a new lipstick but there wasn't any to be had in the shops. She wondered if Blackie could get one for her. He had a lock-up that was bursting with goods to sell on at huge profits. When she'd asked him where the gear came from he'd told her he had 'business' with the American forces who had set up stores at Southampton, near the docks. But he wouldn't tell her any more than that. She'd been going out with him for a couple of months now. Blackie was dark, curly-haired, good-looking and fun to be with. And in these days of austerity a bit of fun didn't hurt anyone.

It was a hard decision she'd made, when she was whole again, to return to work at Priddy's. The wages were good. As a shop assistant, she could expect to take home around thirty-two shillings and sixpence a week, but Priddy's paid her as much as four pounds – and she could earn more when she put in extra hours. No, Rita didn't intend that Hitler should destroy her life. On the contrary she was working twice as hard filling shells in an effort to destroy him.

'Would you really have told Blackie Bristow?' Lizzie asked, shaking Rita out of her reverie. She'd put on her coat and tied a knitted scarf around her neck, tucking it inside her coat for extra warmth.

'I dunno. Blackie knows a lot of hard men. Maybe it'd frighten Jack into leaving her alone for a while.'

'Dad really hates you,' said Lizzie, looking around for her gloves. 'He says you take up time from me mum that could be spent on him.' She looked at the clock. 'In half an hour his mate Mickey'll come along to take him down to the Alma for a beer. No doubt your ears'll be burning as he moans on to Mickey about you.' She smiled at Rita. 'I don't see you got any cause to worry about his threat, though.'

Rita imagined the band of wounded warriors drinking their pints, if the pub had any beer, Jack swearing about Em and herself. She felt sorry that Jack's life had come to this, when once upon a time he'd had so much to look forward to. 'Your dad thinks nasty thoughts because it wasn't only his legs that got damaged.' Rita ran her fingers through her hair, then tightened the belt on her coat.

Lizzie gave her a hasty hug. 'Thanks again for being here.'

Footsteps in the passage announced Em's return. Rita saw she had her old blue coat on and her zip-up boots to ward off the January cold. She was carrying two battered Oxo tins containing her and Lizzie's lunches and a carrier bag in her other hand.

Em passed the bag to Lizzie. 'Take the flasks, love. If you ask me, it's about time a big place like Priddy's had a tea wagon or a canteen to save us all bringing in our own food and drink.'

'Yeah, an' pigs might fly,' said Rita. She liked tea breaks, when the women nattered about their families and, of course, the war. Nearly all the workers took in packed lunches and flasks.

There was no sound from Jack in the kitchen as the front door slammed behind them, and Rita, Lizzie and Em strode off arm in arm, up the street, the cold wind reddening their cheeks.

'You sure you're all right, Em?' Rita went on carefully filling the two-pound shell case with the dangerous powder. When it reached the required level the powder had to be tamped down and the shell set back on the conveyor-belt. It was exacting work and grains of powder floated in the air, clinging to their skin and hair. Picric acid drops and toluene vapour caused the nausea and skin irritation that many of the girls suffered from, so spilled grains had to be cleared up immediately.

One careless mistake tamping down a shell could send the whole workroom to kingdom come, and Em's shaking hand as she wrote on her clipboard proved to Rita that her friend was in no fit state to take over on the line should she be needed there.

Sometimes Em handled the tiny detonators: she had to pick each one up, usually half the size of an aspirin tablet, with tweezers, and one little slip could prove fatal.

'Jack's antics shook me up more than I thought.' It was almost as though she had heard Rita's thought. 'Don't worry, I'm not going on the line. I'm glad we got the day off tomorrow, though,' she continued, 'Me and Jack can maybe have a bit of a talk.'

At lunchtime Lizzie came down from the offices to sit with her mother and her friends, but Em was still shaken up. She spoke hardly a word to Rita or her other mate, Gladys, Rita's landlady. The four of them huddled together on chairs, eating their sandwiches and drinking tea from their flasks. The colours of the factory women's uniforms showed which areas they worked in, but they were also for protection. Any hair that wasn't covered by the turban they all wore eventually turned the colour of a canary's feathers.

Around the walls of the room posters advised the girls to 'Be Like Dad, Keep Mum', 'Come Into the Factories' and Rita's favourite, 'You Give Us the Fire and We'll Give 'Em Hell', with its picture of an airman standing in the cockpit of his plane.

Like many of the other workers, the four friends had decided today it was too cold to venture out into the fresh air of the yard. Besides, changing their clothes and shoes, then being searched for cigarettes, matches or any object that might cause a spark and set off an explosion took valuable time off their lunch break. Leaving the premises also meant being searched for stolen materials.

Because of the secret nature of their work the women's leisure time at Priddy's was accounted for, including trips to the lavatory. Officials handed out information only when it was necessary. In fact, the women knew nothing of what went on in other parts of the factory.

Em, as overseer, knew a little more than her friends but her loyalty to Priddy's meant that she kept her mouth closed and her ears open.

All the same, safety at work was paramount. It had been Rita's own carelessness that had resulted in the explosion that had put her in hospital. Rita knew how lucky she was to be alive and how fortunate it was that no one else had been hurt in the fire. Priddy's didn't need another accident.

Em had only picked at her food, Rita noticed. She'd

rolled up her sleeves and the hem of the bandage was just visible.

'The train's loaded up,' said Gladys, breaking into Rita's thoughts with a dig in her ribs. Her turban had slipped and her bright lipstick had leaked into the small lines around her mouth.

Outside the window Rita could see the railway that ferried materials and the filled shell cases to various stations to be lifted aboard carriers or ships for transport elsewhere. Across the yard, an American destroyer was moored at Portsmouth Dockyard. The stretch of water between Portsmouth and Gosport, its sister town, was filled with boats. Along the shore at Hardway, building work was taking place, but it was all very hush-hush. She smiled: the ferry that travelled between Gosport and Portsmouth looked like a small black beetle scuttling across the water. She drank some thick brown tea. 'Funny how thousands of men and women can work in this backwater and not be seen either by road or air, isn't it?'

'That's because, although we're close to the sea, we're not in the heart of Gosport. Also, the roofs here are all painted green to blend in with the surrounding trees and countryside,' replied Gladys. Rita noted that Gladys hadn't pencilled her eyebrows evenly. She decided not to say anything. After all, eyebrows were sisters, not twins, as Gladys kept telling her.

'Have we got any bread at home?' The last of this morning's loaf, except for a tiny crust, had gone into their Spam sandwiches for lunch.

Gladys frowned. 'I asked Pixie to queue for us today.'

Pixie was Gladys's daughter and lived next door at number twelve, Alma Street. Since her return to Gosport from the hospital, Rita had lodged with Gladys.

'I poked the last bit of the crust into the canary's cage,' said Rita. 'It was so hard I thought he might think it was a bit of cuttlefish bone!'

'So that's where it went. I was going to damp it down to soften it up a bit,' said Gladys. 'It would have tasted all right with a dollop of jam on it.' Gladys looked wistful. 'Lovely jam and tins of peaches your Blackie brought round the other night. A rare treat they was.' Gladys poked her in the ribs again. 'I wish I 'ad a lovely boy like him to take me around . . .'

'Come off it! You've had more men than I've had hot dinners!' Rita giggled.

Gladys had been quite a girl when she was younger. But she didn't like to be reminded of it, for that period of her life had been painful.

'Yeah! Well, not all those men were as generous as your Blackie,' said Gladys.

Rita gave her a knowing look. It was time to change the subject.

Gladys turned away. 'Now there's a man to set all our hearts aflutter,' she exclaimed.

Rita noticed all the women's heads swivel in one direction. 'Rupert Scrivenor's definitely a sight for sore eyes,' she admitted.

The tall, slim, blond man was walking between the lines, stopping to look here and there at the workers' tools. Every so often he'd pause to make a note on the clipboard he was carrying.

'He's a better manager than the last one,' said Gladys. 'An' he keeps his hands to 'imself.'

The previous manager had been well known for touching up the women. He'd also forced himself on Doris, Em's other, childlike, daughter, and fathered a child with her. His wife, an extremely well-off and educated woman, had lessened Em's burden by becoming a foster-parent to both Doris and her baby. Eliza Slaughter was able to secure their future in a way Em never could, and Em looked forward to the letters and photos she regularly received, showing how happy her daughter now was.

The arrival of Rupert Scrivenor, with his impeccable

manners and college accent, had made all the women go weak at the knees, especially when he stopped to talk to them, which he often did, never forgetting a name or the job a particular woman did. No boiler-suit for him, Scrivenor favoured an immaculate white shirt with his cufflinks just peeping below the sleeves of his dark suits.

'He's a proper gent,' said Gladys. 'Just like Ronald Colman off the films. Without his moustache, of course,' she added. 'I wonder what it would be like to be dancing in his arms.'

Blackie loved dancing and showing Rita off. Just for a moment she imagined being held by Rupert Scrivenor as they waltzed in a ballroom with gold and crystal chandeliers and velvet sofas to relax on when they were tired of dancing.

Rita saw Gladys give a wistful glance in Rupert Scrivenor's direction, as did Lizzie.

'He's not for the likes of us,' Em said, as he left the room.

'Besides, he might be married.' Gladys sighed loudly, and all of the women laughed.

'I'd run off with him any day,' quipped Lizzie, screwing the lid back onto her flask.

'If you did, how would I manage without your money?'

Em's voice was serious. 'Don't forget, I'm the only breadwinner in our house.'

'But surely Lizzie's money helps?' Rita couldn't help asking.

'It does now. But how long will she stay at home?' Her mother spoke as though Lizzie was no longer sitting with them.

An ear-splitting siren rent the air. The women jumped to attention and, leaving their sandwich tins behind, walked and half-ran towards the exit, hurrying to evacuate the building.

'A daylight raid?' Em's voice showed little emotion. She had pushed her uneaten food back into the Oxo tin and now threaded her way through the women to the loudspeaker at her desk in the corner. Her voice came over loud and clear: 'Keep calm. Stop what you're doing and form an orderly queue for the exit doors. I repeat, keep calm.'

Rita felt proud of her. Em showed no sign of her earlier anxiety and was taking charge, showing them all that she was at ease with the situation. Now the telephone beside her on the desk rang and Em picked up the receiver, listening attentively.

The women quietened as she said, 'It's a dogfight. No need to panic. Take your time.'

Once outside in the fresh air Rita grabbed Gladys's hand and ran for cover in the nearby woodland. Workers sped in all directions like ants.

'One day someone's going to get killed and they'll wish they'd never stored the bloody TNT in the air-raid shelters,' puffed Gladys. She pushed back her turban as she sat down heavily on the freezing ground beneath a large tree. 'Did you see where Em and Lizzie went?'

'Lizzie would have waited for her mum to check the women out.'

'Maybe they're still inside.' Gladys looked worried.

'I'd rather be out here where I can see what's going on,' Rita said.

Already the air was filled the smell of cordite. She put a hand across her forehead to shield her eyes as she looked heavenwards. Planes were chasing each other in a wild sky battle. In the weak sunshine they glittered, caught in the rays of the sun, then darkened as they danced madly through the black smoke issuing from the tail of one.

Anti-aircraft fire rattled from the ground as Spitfires pursued a posse of German fighters. Rita covered her ears to shut out the noise.

'He's got 'im, Rita!' Gladys shrilled.

A German plane, smoke belching, flew unevenly

seawards towards Portsdown Hill. Black clouds curled like a smoky ribbon in the sky. Rita counted four enemy aircraft. She watched as the plane dipped and spun, falling ever nearer the earth. Suddenly she was filled with sorrow for the pilot, who would surely die. 'When will this damn war ever end?'

The remaining three German planes seemed to lose interest and began to fly northwards. The Spitfires followed in a dangerous game of chase.

'The Germans wanted to hit the dockyard. Put ships out of action,' said Gladys. 'But our boys stopped them, didn't they?'

Rita looked at the trees, their branches still covered with frost. She was cold and shivered. Yes, the German planes had been frightened away, but at what cost? 'We'd better get back to the workshops,' she said, as the all-clear sounded. The sky was empty now, except for the tumbling waves of smoke growing ever thinner. She looked towards the red-brick buildings at the side of the creek that fed into the strip of sea. Now all the fighters had gone, a strange silence filled the air. 'I reckon they'll send us home early,' she said. 'We're all wrung out like wet dishcloths. Anyway, the next shift's due in soon.'

Returning to the workshop meant another search procedure. There'd been no time for any of them to change into their own clothing before they'd rushed for safety. Em stood outside with her clipboard, her daughter next to her. 'It's too late to get back to work. The next shift will be fresher,' she said. 'What about you, Lizzie? You coming home?'

Lizzie frowned. 'No such luck. I've got to go back upstairs. I can't blow up the bloody factory by making a mistake in a ledger, can I?'

Rita almost smiled, but then she remembered the pilot who wouldn't make it home to his loved ones. So what if he was a German? Someone at home would mourn him.

One by one the girls were searched, then changed into their own clothes. The smell of perfume mixed with sweat filled the air. The dogfight was the main topic of conversation as they put away their overalls and footwear in their lockers.

'Cheer up, Rita,' said Gladys as, together, they walked towards the main gate. 'Look who's waiting for you. You go on ahead – I've got a bit of shopping to do, if there's anything left in the blasted shops.'

Rita squeezed her friend's arm, then ran towards the gate.

His trilby hat was set at a jaunty angle and his face lit up with a smile as soon as he saw her. He raised a hand in greeting, his dark overcoat slung rakishly across his shoulders over a well-cut suit. Rita spotted his black Humber parked in the background. Her spirits rose. Waving at the man on gate duty, who was supposed to check the workers in and out, she tumbled into Blackie's waiting arms. He smelled of Brylcreem and lemon-scented cologne.

'I saw the tail end of the kerfuffle and guessed they'd let you off a few minutes early. We did well to get that bugger.' His dark eyes twinkled mischievously as he smoothed her hair back from her face. 'You all right, love?'

When she nodded, he said, 'It's good you have the weekend off. Let's get you back to your place, then. I'm taking you to a dance at a hotel in Stratford-upon-Avon.'

Chapter Two

His jacket was slung over the back of the kitchen chair and he sat with his long legs stretched out in front of him. Blackie was good-looking and he knew it. A half-drunk cup of tea was on the table in front of him and Gladys was hovering like a demented bluebottle.

She'd been queuing at the butcher's and had come away with bacon – there was more fat and rind than pork – and a few sausages. Rita was trying to get the last of her ruby-red lipstick from the tube, sitting at the table with a square of mirror propped in front of a half-full bottle of milk.

'Why are you bothering with that stub when I've got something here for you?' Blackie held out both fists. 'Choose a hand.'

'You never got me a new lipstick?' Her heart began to race. Make-up had vanished from the shops.

'Pick a hand, give me a kiss, and if you're lucky I'll give it to you.' His eyes were twinkling. He waved both fists provocatively in front of her. Gladys was laughing.

Rita got up and went round to him, throwing her arms about his neck. Her lips found his. When she came up for air he let the gift topple into her hand. Lipstick was like gold dust. Quickly she twisted the base and the colour rose up, the brightest of reds to complement her dark hair. In a flash she was back in front of the mirror, admiring her lips as she outlined them. 'Thank you,' she murmured.

'And I suppose you also want some nylons.' He had given Gladys a pair of DuPont stockings as soon as she returned home with her shopping. Now he foraged in the inside pocket of his suit jacket and passed a couple of boxes across the table.

Rita grabbed them and laughed. 'How on earth can I get ready if you keep giving me presents?' But she loved his generosity. It was clear that the things he gave her were from 'under the counter', but Rita told herself that the whole country had suffered enough from the war shortages and Blackie's gifts were her just desserts for loving him. After all, if he owned a sweet shop he would give her chocolates, were there any to be had. If he owned a fishmonger's she'd expect kippers for breakfast.

So, the fact that he dealt in black-market goods meant she was entitled to the odd perk that came her way.

'Hurry up, Rita. I'd like to be on the road before dark.' He pushed his chair back with a clatter, hauled his jacket on and went outside to the lavatory at the bottom of the garden.

As soon as the door closed behind him Gladys said, 'You got a good man there. I've said it before an' I'll say it again. You keep him to yourself because you'll never go short all the time he's around.'

'I know he loves me, but sometimes I get the strangest feeling that he wants more from me than I'm able to give.'

'What d'you mean?' Gladys had begun collecting the dirty cups but she paused.

'I know you'll think I'm being silly and should be grateful that a man like Blackie could love me, with this scar an' all, but it's something I can't put me finger on.'

Gladys's eyes flashed. 'That scar don't mean a thing. How many times have I told you? He cares about you for you.'

Rita had no chance to protest because Blackie's footsteps sounded on the icy concrete path outside the scullery door. He came in, bringing a blast of cold air with him. 'Come on, girl, we ain't got all day.' He rubbed his hands together, then blew on them. 'It's going to be cold tonight.'

Rita got up from the table, gathered her make-up together and slipped it into a little cloth bag with a draw-string top. She glanced at her holdall, ready packed with overnight clothes. Gladys reached out her arms and Rita fell into them, kissing her goodbye. 'I'll be back in time for work on Monday,' she said, looking at Blackie for confirmation. He nodded.

In the narrow hall she put on her black wool coat, a present from Blackie, and her court shoes.

'You look lovely,' said Gladys. 'Have a good time.'

Rita peered back up the hall towards the warm kitchen, with the black-leaded range, the sash window hung with blackout curtains and the table surrounded by four chairs. It was only a terraced house, but Gladys made it homely and she would always be grateful to her.

Blackie held her holdall as they stepped out into the vicious cold. His dark Humber, large and gleaming, was parked at the kerb. He opened the back door and pulled out a brown carrier bag that had been sitting beside a large box on the back seat. 'Forgot to bring these in, Glad.' He was grinning at her. 'Just a few tins of stuff off the American lads. I hope you ain't too proud to take them.'

Gladys was overjoyed, and proved it by lunging at Blackie and throwing her arms around him. 'God bless you, you're a good 'un.'

He shrugged her off, threw Rita's holdall into the back, then went round and settled Rita into the passenger seat. She glanced up into the sky. It was like black velvet pierced with diamonds.

'Get back indoors, Glad, you'll catch your death of cold,' Blackie advised. But Gladys stood on the doorstep, smiling and waving as the car glided down the icy street.

Being January, the nights were long but frost glittered in the dulled headlights, making the road seem brighter.

'Where were you this afternoon when the Spitfires were defending us?' Rita asked, gazing at Blackie's silhouette in the darkness of the car.

He put his hand on her knee. 'Already on my way to surprise you. When the siren went, I dashed into the air-raid shelter at Clarence Road. Luckily the dogfight was only a skirmish. I was amazed when the all-clear sounded so quickly. Still, if it's time to go and your number's up . . .'

Rita didn't like the way he was talking. 'One of those German boys won't make it.'

'Then his time had come, Rita. Anyway, we're going to have fun and not think about the awfulness of this war.' Rita hated the way he was dismissing a person's life as if the man, even though he was a German, was of no account. Blackie was almost always interested first in himself, then in the few people he cared about or, Rita thought, who were of use to him. Sometimes she wondered how he'd got under her skin. He was a live wire, fun to be with and made her feel wanted. What more could any girl ask for? Especially when you never knew if a bomb was going to fall from the sky and end everything. Now he gave her a quick grin. 'You want to see what's in that box in the back?'

Rita leaned over the leather seat. The box was already open so she was able to lift out a smaller one. She sat down again, examining it. 'It's a cigar box,' she said. She ran her fingers over the picture on the top. 'Where's it come from?' The smell of tobacco was strong in the confined space of the car.

'That's a Cuban box – I reckon they make the best cigars in the world.'

Rita didn't know anyone who smoked cigars, although Winston Churchill was hardly ever seen without a fat one in his mouth.

'Open it.' He looked sideways at her and laughed, a dark curl falling over his forehead.

She flipped back the lid and was amazed to find

miniature workings inside. She turned it over in her hands 'What is it?'

'A radio set.'

Rita looked at it closely. 'But it's so small!'

'Well, it doesn't have the strength of a long-range model where you can gather worldwide signals. It's a cigar-box radio. It doesn't need electricity or batteries. It's run by a crystal that acts as a semi-conductor for audio radio waves . . .'

'Stop, stop,' cried Rita. 'I'm out of my depth with all that talk. But is this tiny thing really a wireless?'

'Sure is. Straight from the States. After the war they'll be on sale everywhere for about six pounds each . . .'

Rita gasped. 'That's a lot of money.'

'But people will buy them.'

'So how come you've got it now?' She didn't really need to ask. Blackie could lay his hands on anything for someone who paid enough.

'I got contacts. I make money.'

'You mean they're black-market?'

'It's never worried you before.'

'It doesn't worry me now,' Rita said, returning the wireless to the large box. But as she settled back into the depths of the leather seat she wondered if that was true.

*

Rita awoke as the car drove over Clopton Bridge and up into Bridge Street. Blackie parked outside the colonnaded front of the Red Horse Hotel at Stratford-upon-Avon.

'Come on, sleepyhead.' Gently, he shook her shoulder. Then he was out of the car, had opened her door and was bending down, smiling at her. 'It's late. Let's get you into a proper bed.'

The pavement was slippery with fresh snow and Rita was glad to get inside the lobby of the hotel. Subdued music came from behind closed oak doors beyond the reception desk. The air smelled of polish mixed with cigarette smoke. A uniformed boy came towards them, a grin on his cheeky face, and picked up her bag.

Blackie spoke to the chatty girl behind the desk and she handed him a key after signing them in. She had obviously taken a shine to Blackie, for she smiled and simpered while constantly patting her blonde victory roll.

Rita wondered idly if Blackie had entered them in the ledger as a married couple. Probably, she thought. Although the young woman, who was still smiling like a simpleton at Blackie, didn't look the sort to be shocked by an unwed couple sharing a room. There was a war on, after all.

Her heels dug into the thick red carpet as she and

Blackie followed the boy carrying their luggage into the lift, then upstairs to their room. Blackie tipped him and received an even cheekier smile, along with a small bow.

Rita had accompanied Blackie to this hotel before. The girl at the desk was new but she remembered the laughing lad and his red hair. Straight away Rita went to the window and looked out into the cold night. There was a row of shops and a restaurant opposite in Bridge Street.

She yawned. 'I'm shattered,' she said.

Blackie came over and put his arms around her. He bent his lips to her ear, his breath warm on her face. 'I have to go out for a while . . .'

'Oh, Blackie!' It had been just the same the last time they'd come here. They'd hardly got inside the room before he left her alone, disappearing for a couple of hours.

'You have a bath, ring down for anything you want, and I'll be back before you're asleep. I promise I won't be long.'

If he was away as long as he had been the previous time, she'd be well in the land of dreams when he returned, Rita thought. 'Dare I ask where you're off to?'

His mouth nuzzled her ear. 'A place called Ettington. We could have gone there before coming here but

I guessed you were worn out after working all day. Newbold on Stour isn't far. I promise I won't be long.' He began trailing kisses down her neck to her shoulder, pulling her coat aside so he could get to her skin. 'It's just a bit of business, love.'

Rita looked at the white cotton pillows above the dark blue quilt. The bed was *so* inviting. As was the thought of the claw-foot bath in the en-suite bathroom. She was very fond of her room at Gladys's house but coming to these posh places with Blackie made her feel special. A long, leisurely bath with water tumbling from chrome taps was so much better than lugging buckets of hot water from the scullery copper to the tin tub in front of the fire at home. 'All right,' she said. 'I suppose you'll be offloading those radios.'

'Ask no questions and I'll tell you no lies,' he said. He found her lips and kissed her hungrily.

Rita clung to him, her senses reeling as his hands roved over her body. She could feel her nipples hardening at his touch. Then he pulled away from her. The disappointment was almost more than she could bear.

'When I get back we'll continue where we've left off,' he said. He was breathing hard. The glitter in his eyes showed he knew quite well the effect he'd had on her. 'If I don't push you away, I'll never get my errand done.'

He stared into her eyes then gave her a quick kiss on the tip of her nose.

Rita stepped back and sighed. He knew just how to get her going. She hadn't been a virgin when she'd met Blackie at a dance in Gosport's Connaught Hall, and it wasn't long before she discovered that he knew his way around the art of making love. It was something he was very proficient at. Sometimes she had only to look at him to want him – when he sat in the driving seat of his car staring at the road ahead, just a glance at his profile had warmth spreading through her. Often he'd turn and smile lazily, as though he was aware of what she was thinking. Then he'd put his hand on her knee and its heat made her want him even more.

Blackie gave her a quick cuddle. 'In my bag you'll find another present.'

'How will I know it's for me?'

'You just will when you see it.' He smiled, then turned towards the door. 'Would you like me to ask the staff to bring you something to eat or drink?' He moved towards a cupboard and opened it. There were several bottles of beer inside with two glass tumblers. 'No shorts, I'm afraid. But I could send you up a gin and orange . . .'

'Pot of tea. That's what I really fancy.'

He bowed. 'Your wish is my command.' Then he was gone, the door closing softly behind him.

Rita went back to the window, careful not to let the light shine from the room into the street. Frost coated the road and the few cars outside the hotel. People couldn't drive much – the lack of petrol put paid to outings. Blackie never seemed to worry about that, though. Then she saw him. He looked up, clearly expecting her to be there, waved and was gone.

Rita lifted Blackie's leather holdall on to the bed and opened it. She began draping his two silk shirts on the hangers in the heavy oak wardrobe and putting his underwear in the drawers. After leaving his toothbrush and shaving tackle in the bathroom she was interrupted by a knock on the door.

Rita opened it to find a young woman holding a silver tray. She bustled into the room with the tea. Rita thought she should give her a tip. Blushing furiously she fumbled in her handbag but all she had were two pound notes and a halfpenny.

'I'm sorry,' she said. 'I've nothing suitable to give you.' Her face brightened. 'When my – my husband gets back I'll make sure . . .'

'Madam, it's not necessary to tip us every time we do something for you.'

As the girl left, Rita realized there was a huge gulf between herself and Blackie in that he knew how to deal with people and she didn't. She often wondered why he wanted her when so many prettier women hankered after him. She shook herself out of her reverie and poured tea into the thin china cup. Sugar lumps! She'd given up sugar when it became rationed. Rita went into the bathroom for some sheets of toilet paper to wrap them. Gladys would love them. 'Waste not, want not,' she murmured to herself.

Looking at Blackie's bag, she remembered she hadn't finished unpacking for him. The black satin nightdress made her gasp with pleasure. It was floor-length, fish-tailed, and fitted at the bust with tiny straps over the shoulders. Her heart was singing as she held the luxurious material to her cheek, breathing in its scented newness.

After she'd unpacked her own holdall, she luxuriated in a bath. She had switched on the wireless and Frank Sinatra was crooning softly. When she got into bed, though, she felt sad. Why was she alone in a hotel room when she could have been with Gladys, sitting in front of the fire, making toast and gossiping?

Then she remembered the big dance being held at the hotel the next evening. And Rita loved dancing.

She'd hung her black dress in the wardrobe. She thought about the government relaxing the restrictions on clothing coupons with the promises of more material for new suits and clothing, but you needed money as well to buy clothes – if you could get them. Rita was always remodelling her dresses.

She had bought bias binding and stitched it around the short sleeves and down the front of the dress, then pressed the box pleats. She'd also had her favourite sling-back shoes resoled. The suede was a little scuffed but she'd buffed it as best she could. Pixie had said she looked lovely in her make-do-and-mend outfit.

Snug between the crisp white cotton sheets, she let her thoughts run to Gladys's daughter.

Pixie lived next door in Alma Street with Bob, who owned a couple of market stalls. He was a bit of a wheeler and dealer, like Blackie, but unlike Blackie he stayed on the right side of the law. Rita wondered when her friend was going to tell her about the baby she was expecting. As far as Rita knew, Gladys hadn't been told either, but both women could see in Pixie's face that a child was on the way. She, like Gladys, had reckoned Pixie hadn't shared her news because she wasn't married to Bob. It was bad enough being looked down upon because she was living with a man when she already had a child by another man, let alone that Pixie was now expecting a child with Bob.

Pixie was mother to young Sadie, whose father had been an American sailor: he had drowned when his ship was hit by a torpedo from an enemy submarine. Bob loved the bones of Pixie. He'd waited in the background until Pixie's grief faded. The American, Cal, had been her great love, but Bob was a hardworking bear of a man, dark-haired, honest and a wonderful father to Sadie. He had known Pixie was worth waiting for. He'd set his heart on her and now they were a family.

By the time Rita had finished her tea and allowed herself to think again about Blackie, she was asleep.

'I didn't mean to wake you, darling.' Blackie's breath was warm as he nuzzled into her neck. He was still cold from being outside but she could smell the freshness of soap; he'd washed before coming to bed.

'Mmm, did you finish your business?'

His arm snaked around her waist, pulling her towards him. 'I did, and made a nice little profit. On the dressing-table there's a few notes for you to shop with while I meet another mate in the morning.'

Now he was kissing her shoulders and running his hands over the satin nightdress, making her body tingle.

She wanted to be cross with him for telling her he was going to leave her again in the morning, but his actions were forcing her to forgive him. 'I thought we came away to be together,' she whispered.

'And what are we now if it isn't together? Give us a kiss.'

Rita never could be cross with Blackie for long. She put her arms about his neck. 'Do you want me?' she asked. She knew he did. She moved her hand down, touching the strong muscles of his thighs.

He was watching her, a hungry look in his dark eyes.

Gently he raised her body so he could slip inside her. Slowly he began to move and her arms went tighter about him, feeling the chill of his skin disappear as they warmed each other. His hands and fingers probed and were soon replaced by his mouth. And Rita lay back, allowing him to bring her pleasure in ways she'd never experienced before. Sky-rockets were exploding in her head as he brought her to a peak. She stifled a scream as he thrust into her because she was drowning in the waves of passion. And then he was crying out her name. His whole being moving deeper and deeper until she couldn't tell where her body stopped and his began.

Then he was spent, again crying her name as he fell

against her, holding her tightly as though he wanted her never to leave him.

After a while he lifted himself on to one elbow and looked down at her.

'If that's what I get for one nightdress, I'll buy two next time.'

She reached up and kissed his stubbly cheek. 'Thank you,' she said. She felt as though she was floating somewhere in space.

'What for?' He looked puzzled.

'Everything.' She pushed her face towards him and kissed him quickly on the lips.

'You're a lovely woman,' he said. Then he added, 'I'm going to get a drink. You want something?'

Rita shook her head and watched as he slipped out of bed and moved towards the cabinet containing the bottles of beer. He opened one and drank. He had a lovely body, she thought. He was strong-shouldered, broad-chested, his flat stomach tapering to well-muscled legs. 'Back in Gosport I was worried you'd get a hit this afternoon,' he murmured, sitting beside her on the bed. 'The bomb factory must be on Hitler's wanted list.'

'We're well disguised,' she said. 'Though the girls did run for cover.' She laughed. 'Fat lot of good that would do if the place got a direct hit. We'd never stand a chance.'

'Have you found out what's going on with all the building work at Elson on the foreshore? There's a lot of forces types working down there.'

'I couldn't tell you even if I did know.'

'What happened to "the head that shares the pillow shares the secrets"? Anyone would think I was on the other side.' He chuckled. 'You've been watching too many espionage pictures at the Criterion.'

He drank from the bottle thirstily. His smile had dropped. 'I heard Priddy's is stepping up production. Something's going on.'

'I dare say you're right,' Rita said. She was fed up with all his talk of war and the factory. Blackie's interest got on her nerves. She wanted to sleep again, cuddling up to him. 'Come on back to bed.'

Blackie set down the empty bottle on the bedside table and got in beside her. 'I made a good choice with that nightie,' he said. His eyes were warm, so deep that she wanted to drown in them. 'But take it off now.'

Chapter Three

Rita stared at the gold earrings. They were like tiny threepenny bits that glittered on the bed of black velvet. In her handbag were the notes that Blackie had given her.

Ten minutes later she walked from the jeweller's onto the icy street, wearing the earrings, her sleepers in tissue paper. She was to meet Blackie at two for a late lunch at the restaurant opposite the Red Horse, the Top of the Town.

He hadn't begged her to accompany him, and she hadn't asked where he was going. He'd already told her it was business. After a leisurely hotel breakfast, she'd put on her black coat and decided on a sightseeing tour of Stratford-upon-Avon. She'd looked in the myriad of tiny shops in the narrow cobbled streets the last time she was there.

It was much quieter than Gosport, with a definite

village feel about it. There was a market in Henley Street, like Gosport's, and she enjoyed wandering past the colourful stalls. She walked over Clopton Bridge along the side of the river and for a while sat watching the canal boats moored in the basin and the swans, which seemed unconcerned about the freezing water. There were quite a few American soldiers about and a few had whistled at her.

She almost plucked up the courage to pause for a drink in the White Swan, or the Mucky Duck, as it was known locally. But she couldn't bring herself to open the door to look inside the noisy bar. She laughed at herself. She could go into the Fox in Gosport alone because the manager, Sam, was a good friend, but the idea that women who entered pubs on their own were not nice women clung to her.

The air beside the overhanging willows on the banks of the Avon was sweet and crisp and her shoes crunched on the light covering of snow. Even the trees glistened with a silvery frost that the pale sun couldn't warm away. When a cold wind rose, Rita decided she would go back to the hotel, order tea or coffee, charge it to the room, as Blackie had instructed, and wait in the warmth of the lobby.

Later, as she sat nursing a cup of tea, her coat beside

her on a velvet sofa, she watched the lights and banners being erected, then chairs and small tables carried into the ballroom for the night's festivities. It was all very exciting to think she and Blackie would be behind those dark oak doors enjoying themselves tonight. The staff laughed and joked as they went about their business and Rita was content, watching the customers pay their bills and new customers signing in.

She was eager for Blackie to see her earrings, the very first gold jewellery she had ever owned. Every so often she couldn't resist fingering them or taking a look at herself in the mirrored pillars that dotted the lobby. Through the windows she had a good view of the ground-floor entrance to the Top of the Town up a steep flight of steps.

Blackie's car glided to a standstill on the other side of the road. The street door of the restaurant opened and out stepped a small, foreign-looking man, who shook Blackie's hand and began arguing with him. He must have been waiting for Blackie to arrive, Rita thought. The argument became heated, the small man shaking his fist while Blackie frowned and tried to calm him down. She noted that Blackie was keeping his temper in check as he remonstrated with the other.

Rita decided to wait before she crossed the road to

greet him. He might not be at ease with her witnessing a row in the street. People were stopping to stare.

Then Blackie, ignoring the crowd and the man, went up the steps, pushed open the restaurant's door and was lost to her view.

The man was angry, still swearing and waving his arms as he followed Blackie. The onlookers dispersed. Rita drained her tea, put on her coat and smiled at the receptionist, who had also noticed the altercation.

The stairs to the restaurant were well lit. At the top, swing doors opened to reveal Blackie sitting in their usual booth, stirring a cup of coffee. He smiled as she entered, stood up to take her coat and hung it on the coat-stand.

'Charles,' he called, 'I'd like to order.' He kissed her, handed her a menu, then sat opposite her, staring through the wide window that looked down over the street. 'Order whatever you like.' He was very calm and Rita could almost believe the scene she'd just witnessed below in the street hadn't happened.

'I'll just have a salad, if they've got the makings,' Rita said. Blackie ordered a pork chop. The young man who wrote down their order looked about ready for call-up into the services. There were only four kinds of men left in the country: old men, very young ones, members of foreign forces and those who had been wounded in combat.

'Why aren't you in the forces?'

Blackie laughed out loud. 'I often wonder what's going through your head,' he said. 'I'm not medically fit. I've a hearing defect. Nothing would give me greater satisfaction than to sort some of those bastards out. So I do the best I can, the best way I can.' His eyes roved over her face. Then he said, 'There's something different about you.'

Rita preened. She pushed back her hair and showed him the earrings.

'Did I pay for them?' A huge grin split his face. 'You look lovely,' he said. Then, 'Excuse me, love, I'll just go into the kitchens. I need to talk with a friend.'

The man who'd argued with him? she wondered.

Blackie left the table and walked to the end of the dining room, disappearing through a door she supposed led into the kitchen. She looked about her. There were very few diners and the place was run down. There were full ashtrays on the tables and spilled food on the cloths. Rita began to wish she'd stayed at the hotel.

The waiter returned with the food. He wasn't surprised to find her alone but seemed undecided about leaving it. 'My friend'll soon be back so you can put his plate down.'

Rita had no idea if she was telling the truth but decided she wouldn't eat until Blackie returned. Her salad looked unappetising.

Then she heard loud voices and a door slammed. Blackie walked quickly up the aisle towards their table, the foreign man in hot pursuit.

He touched Blackie on the shoulder. Blackie turned back to him and held out a hand. The man reluctantly slid his fingers into his jacket pocket and took out a roll of money. Blackie, without counting it, put it away. The man shook his hand vigorously. Whatever had upset him seemed forgotten. Rita wondered what it was all about but Blackie probably wouldn't tell her the truth if she asked. Besides, it really was none of her business. He sat down opposite her.

They stared at their lunch with distaste, and Blackie frowned when he saw her prodding a dried-up slice of beetroot.

He picked up a fork and moved the incinerated chop. 'This is awful. Even restaurants can't get hold of decent food,' he said, pushing his plate to the centre of the table. Rita felt again as though the scene between Blackie and the foreign man had been a figment of her imagination. 'Let's go shopping, then back to the hotel for something to eat.' He took her hand. 'I'll show you how much I've missed you before we go and dance the night away. I really do need to make up for leaving you alone so much.'

Without a word, Rita got up, took her coat from the coat-stand and put it on. She picked up her bag and turned to Blackie as he was throwing a couple of notes onto the table.

Blackie pushed open the heavy doors, they walked down the steps and, once more, were in the street.

He turned her to face him and tucked her collar up around her throat. 'You mustn't catch cold,' he whispered. 'You mean the world to me.' He pressed her towards him. His musky maleness enveloped her. Then, holding her hand tightly so she wouldn't slip on the ice, he led her along Bridge Street. He obviously had no intention of talking about the previous events and Rita decided that, if he didn't want her to know what had been going on, it was all right with her.

There were a few intrepid shoppers about. Rita admired the Tudor buildings and smiled to herself at the furtive glances the women gave Blackie. He looked good in his long wool coat with his trilby tipped back on his glossy hair. At a high-class dress shop he stopped and said, 'I reckon we might find something in here.'

'I don't think . . .' Rita began to protest.

Blackie ignored her, pulled her inside into the warmth

and swaggered up to the young assistant standing near the till. He whispered something that made the girl smile. Rita could see he had charmed her. The girl went out to the back of the shop and he squeezed Rita's hand.

Within minutes the girl returned with several dresses hanging over her arm. She held up a grey one towards Rita, then quickly discarded it. Rita wasn't disappointed: she didn't like grey and knew it wasn't the best colour for her.

'Go and try them on,' Blackie said, taking the remaining dresses from the assistant. 'And, for God's sake, don't worry about money or coupons.'

She didn't feel like arguing with him.

In the cubicle she fell in love with a red dress that clung to her like a second skin. She was doing up the buttons when the assistant opened the cubicle curtain and asked if she could help. Rita could tell by the look on the woman's face that the dress suited her. She said, 'It feels gorgeous.' Nevertheless she took it off and handed it back to the girl, glad that she was wearing silk underwear, courtesy of Blackie, instead of her usual well-washed and greying white cotton.

The black dress had a long swathe of silk that caressed her hips then fell to the floor. 'I like them both,' confessed Rita. The girl nodded, as she fiddled with hooks and eyes while exuding a flowery perfume that was sweet but not sickly.

Rita caught sight of the price tag as she slipped it off. She'd have to work a lot of overtime at Priddy's to afford it and, no doubt, the red one was just as expensive. The girl took both dresses and left her.

Rita, in her own clothes, pushed back the curtain. Blackie was flirting with the young assistant but he came over, smiling broadly, and asked, 'Which is your favourite?'

'They both looked lovely,' the girl interrupted. Rita agreed.

'Then we'll have both,' Blackie said. Rita opened her mouth to remonstrate but he said, 'Don't argue.' He took money from his wallet, paid the assistant, then whispered to Rita, 'Let's go back to the hotel and you can show me how much you like them.'

Rita stood on tiptoe to kiss him. 'Thank you,' she murmured. The girl looked quite envious as she packed the dresses into flat boxes.

Blackie put both boxes under one arm and escorted her from the shop, having given the assistant one last killer smile. Outside, flakes of snow floated down to the pavement.

She decided whatever Blackie was mixed up in *didn't*

concern her. Especially when at any moment a stray bomb could blow them all sky high.

Rita stood in front of the full-length mirror. The black dress reminded her of a film star's so she'd pinned back her long wavy hair on one side of her face so that the rest cascaded over one cheek. The gold earrings flashed in the light.

Blackie wore a dark suit with a waistcoat and his shoes were polished to perfection. She knew all the women would be drooling as soon as they saw him enter the ballroom. He came up beside her and put his arms around her waist, looking at her in the mirror's reflection. 'We make a superb couple, don't we?'

She had to admit they looked good together. Rita twisted round and kissed him lightly on the lips. They'd spent the rest of the afternoon in bed after eating in the hotel's restaurant. Blackie had called the food inventive. The menu had had quite a few items 'unavailable' but the dishes they'd finally chosen had pleased him. Split-pea soup followed by corned-beef fritters that he'd put away with relish. Rita's Scottish vegetable and meat pudding was a little low on meat but extremely tasty. Both had enjoyed the spiced mixed-fruit roll.

'The Germans should use us in their quest to breed an

Aryan race,' he said thoughtfully, admiring their reflections in the mirror.

'Hitler only wants blondes,' Rita replied. She picked up a bottle of Evening in Paris and touched her wrists and cleavage with it. 'So that's both of us out. Though I read somewhere that he's already chosen many young children to join his so-called "purification" scheme.'

'The Fountain of Life Society. Martin Bormann's idea,' said Blackie. He adjusted his tie, although it didn't need it. 'They want blowing up with one of their own *Vergeltungswaffen*,' he added.

'What the hell is one of them when it's at home?'

'They're the new V-1 flying bombs that we're about to be bombarded with. Much more effective than anything we have at present. Or have you been working on something at Priddy's to blow those bastards into the next world?'

'I work on an assembly line. I'm not an office girl who knows what's going on there. I fill bombs with TNT. Anyway, how come you know so much about what's in store for us?'

'I keep my ear to the ground,' he said softly, and winked at her.

Rita didn't want to carry on with the conversation, which had started that afternoon after they'd made love.

She picked up the hairbrush and pulled it through the back of her hair.

'Your hair shines like conkers,' he said, taking the brush away from her and putting it down on the dressing-table. 'Come on, let's dance and enjoy ourselves.'

'Let's Face the Music and Dance' and the sound of happy voices greeted her as Blackie swung open the heavy doors to the ballroom. Bandsmen in dark suits were on a podium and the room smelled of perfume and food.

'You didn't tell me it was a dinner dance,' she said. A waiter showed them to their reserved table. Going out with Blackie meant eating well, she thought. Already today she'd had better food than during the whole of the past week.

'Only the best for you, my love. I believe the singer is excellent. Do you want to order food first or dance?'

Rita felt if she ate anything else she would burst but she didn't get a chance to say anything as the vocalist entered from the wings near the band and began to sing. She was blonde with her hair pinned high and a silver dress that clung to every curve.

'Just the type for the Fountain of Life Society,' said Blackie, with a wicked smile. Beneath the table Rita kicked him.

When the singer had finished 'You'll Never Know' Rita clapped, along with the other diners. She was glad she hadn't insisted on wearing the dress she'd brought with her from home. She would have looked out of place among all the glitter in the hotel's ballroom. She and Blackie had been to other dances at the Red Horse but this was by far the most glamorous. He pulled her up to dance and they waltzed.

'You're so very lovely,' Blackie said. 'And I'm glad you like to dance,' he whispered. Next came the Lindy Hop and Rita forgot everything that cluttered her mind, her job, the war. Everything paled beside the beat of the music. In Blackie's arms she was whirling with the rhythm, the moment and the handsome man who cared about her.

'I know it's only a register office do but I want you to be there.'

'Well, Pixie, you can hardly get married in church, can you?'

Rita had popped next door to tell her friend about her trip to Stratford. Pixie had news of her own. She and Bob were going to marry and Rita was almost crying with happiness for her.

'Oh, Rita, is it as obvious as all that?' Pixie frowned, looking down at her bump, which was definitely making itself known. 'I haven't told anyone except Bob and Mum.' Of course she didn't want the whole of Gosport to know she was expecting again without the benefit of a wedding ring.

'You didn't need to. We all guessed. Sadie's going to have a little brother or sister and I couldn't be happier for you. You've been with Bob for ages. It was a dead cert he wanted to marry you so why bother with rubbers?' She saw Pixie blush. 'Besides, it's only fair he should have a child of his own.' Rita picked up Pixie's hand and her engagement ring glittered. 'I reckon with the right dress not too many people'll guess there's a littl'un on the way. But is this what you want?'

Rita was remembering how much Pixie had loved the American, Cal. Pixie had almost lost her senses over him when he hadn't replied to her letters while he was away at sea. When she found out he'd died, presumed drowned, Bob had been the mainstay of Pixie's life and had waited patiently, his love for Pixie never wavering. Rita, Bob and Gladys had eventually discovered that Cal's ship, the destroyer USS *Bristol*, had been torpedoed by a German submarine.

Pixie smoothed back her blonde hair, which had fallen across her green eyes. 'Bob's a good man and a wonderful father to my Sadie. I couldn't ask for more.'

Rita, satisfied, picked up the teapot and poured out two more cups of tea. She stirred in the milk, then glanced around the room. It was practically identical to the one next door where she lived with Gladys. The kitchen window looked out over a long, thin garden and the scullery was in between. The furnishings were brightened by the colourful rag rugs that Pixie loved making. Pixie was a good mother. Rita wondered if she'd be a good mother, if and when she fell for a kiddie. So far, although she never took precautions – she knew she should – her periods were quite regular.

'Who else knows you're planning to marry?' Rita asked.

'You're the third person.' Pixie looked smug. 'Both Bob and Mum are thrilled about the baby but worried about me wanting a do.'

'You've got to celebrate,' said Rita. 'I'll ask Blackie! He can get hold of anything. We'll need food and—'

Pixie frowned. 'As long as it doesn't cost the earth,' she said. 'Bob's stalls make money but not a fortune.'

Rita realized she was getting carried away. 'Don't worry, I've got a bit of money put by and it could be our wedding present to you.'

'You're very kind but be careful. You know Bob's a bit funny about Blackie and his dealings.' Pixie finished her tea. 'I'd thought about going back to Priddy's for a while to get extra money but Bob won't hear of it.'

'I should think not. Remember how ill you got working

there? I reckon your liver was about to give up the ghost when you was pouring liquid TNT. You was yellow all over. You don't want anything to happen to this baby, do you?'

Pixie shook her head. 'Do you reckon Blackie might help, then?'

Rita didn't answer. She was already thinking of the lovely food they could cook if only Blackie could get hold of the ingredients. 'Band!' she exclaimed next. 'We need a band so we can dance afterwards.'

'And a hall. What about Sloane Stanley Hall near the Criterion cinema?'

Rita could see Pixie was just as excited as she was. She thought about the hall down the road where they sometimes held jumble sales. It was large, wooden, bright and airy. A few decorations . . . She raised a hand and smoothed back Pixie's blonde hair, which had tumbled forward again. 'I'm so happy for you. You've got everything I want!' Then she became flustered. 'I don't mean I want Bob! Just a home, children, someone to love who loves me in return.'

'You've got Blackie.' Pixie was laughing now. 'Some women would scratch your eyes out to get to him.'

Rita thought of his lovemaking, his lavish presents. But she couldn't quite see him being a husband and father. Did she *really* love him?

Chapter Four

Lizzie scrunched up the letter and threw it into the flames. 'If he thinks I'm going back to his mother's house he's got another think coming, Mum.' She bent down and put a couple of precious lumps of coal on the sitting-room fire. She wiped her hands on her pinny and stood up, staring at Em, who was sitting in an armchair, knitting. The wool was crinkled, salvaged from a jumper Em had bought at a jumble sale.

It had been restful sitting together listening to the wireless, thought Lizzie, until she'd read the letter from Maurice. She ran her fingers through her long hair, which she'd just washed. Her dad was in his wheelchair next to the stove in the kitchen, reading. He rarely stayed in the same room as her mother. Said he didn't want to share space with a wanton whore, but if he needed anything, he expected to be waited on when he called.

'What if he comes here?' Em put down her needles and flexed her fingers.

'I'll tell him to his face.' Lizzie's voice rose as she remembered how the old woman had bullied her. 'In fact, I wouldn't put it past his mother to have made him write that letter just so she could have me at her beck and call again. You don't know how glad I was when you suggested I come home.'

Em got up and went to the door. 'You should have come sooner. I'm going to make a cup of tea. You want a bit of seed cake to go with it?'

Tears welled in Lizzie's eyes. 'Oh, Mum, yes, please.' Her mother had never understood why she hadn't upped and left Maurice before. But Lizzie had thought things would change. Besides, she wasn't one to admit she might have made a mistake.

When the door had closed behind Em, Lizzie poked at the pieces of burning paper, willing them to disappear. Maurice had seemed such a kind boy when she'd met him in the Dive café in the town. He was on the thin side with wispy, fair hair and freckles and lovely clean hands with long fingers. He worked at the tax office and wasn't eligible for call-up: he had a heart condition because he'd had rheumatic fever as a child.

Lizzie had missed her bus and there was a half-hour

wait for the next so she'd decided on a cup of tea and a currant bun in the café opposite the ferry gardens. The proprietor had already margarined her bun and poured her tea from the large urn when she'd discovered she didn't have enough money to pay for it. Maurice, sitting just inside the open doorway, had galloped to her rescue, like a knight on a white charger. He'd invited her to sit down with him and that was how it had started.

Now Em bustled in with a tray and a smile. 'I made a cup for your dad even though he tried to pick an argument.' Her face went white. 'You don't think Maurice really will come here and cause a scene, do you?'

Lizzie took the tray from her and put it on the table near the wireless. 'Not unless his mum tells him to come and beg my forgiveness so I can go back to being her skivvy.' Her mother looked horrified. 'Oh, don't you worry, the one good thing about Maurice is that he's utterly spineless. He'd have to get someone else to bang the top off an egg!'

Em laughed. It was good to see her smile, thought Lizzie. She was glad she'd finally seen sense and broken away from the mean-spirited woman who had nearly become her mother-in-law. Part of the reason for her return, though, was to stop her father attacking her mother.

'Was she very awful?' Em poured the tea into the china cups.

Lizzie took a deep breath of her mother's perfume: lilac, mixed with baking. 'It sort of crept up so I didn't notice. When Maurice suggested we moved in with her, I liked the idea of living in that big Georgian house in Stubbington. She said we could live there rent-free, if I did some of the chores, as it was too much for her on her own. She said it would give us a chance to save some money to get married.'

'Em!' Her father's loud voice carried through from the kitchen. 'C'mon in here, you whore!'

Her mother sighed. 'Best go and see what he wants,' she said. 'I expect it's another bit of cake, and I know perfectly well he can reach the cake tin.'

Lizzie listened to her father's raised voice. He never seemed to speak to her mother in a civil tone. She listened in case he was about to pull one of his tricks, like overturning the wheelchair so he could hurt his wife when she tried to help him upright again. Sometimes Em wasn't quick enough to dodge his flying fists. It wasn't long before Lizzie heard her slippered feet coming back down the hall.

'What did I tell you? More cake. I gave him a big slice. Let's hope it shuts him up.' A cloud crossed her face.

'I'm sorry, love, I shouldn't talk to you about him like that. After all, he is your dad. And you must excuse his language. He can't get over what happened between me and Sam so he takes every chance he can to remind me of it.'

'I'm under no illusions now about what he can be like, don't you worry about that. He and Maurice's mum would have made a fine pair. You know I hadn't been in that woman's house five minutes before I saw the place hadn't been top-and-bottomed for years. So I set to and had a spring-clean. Did she thank me? No, she moaned all the time about me moving her ornaments and not putting them back in their right places. She even accused me of stealing a china shepherdess. What would I want her fairground tat for?' Lizzie brushed crumbs from her skirt.

'Didn't Maurice say anything?'

'He told me she was getting old and forgetful and needed to be cherished. Well, at first I thought that was sweet. Surely, if he looked after her like he did, always running after her, getting her the paper, getting her glasses, he'd look after me too. That's what I thought.'

'Sorry to say this, love, but he sounds a bit of a pansy.' Em put her hand to her mouth. 'Sorry, I shouldn't have said that.'

'If you're asking was I sleeping with him, the answer's no. He put me in a room of my own, all dusty velvet curtains and stuff that had once belonged to his sister.' Lizzie's eyes hardened. 'I had to clean it before I could use it. It hadn't been touched for ages.'

'Where was she, then? The sister, I mean.' Em sipped her tea.

'She was in the army and didn't even come home when she had leave. I suppose that should have told me something.' She looked wistful. 'Maurice wasn't one for showing his feelings.'

Em threw back her head and laughed. 'Give me a bit of hanky-panky any day! Life's too short!'

Unexpectedly Lizzie laughed too. While her dad had been away at war Em had fallen in love with the manager, Sam Owen, of the Fox, although as far as Lizzie knew, there had been no hanky-panky.

'I never saw you happier than when you was with Sam, but Dad was away fighting for his country. It wasn't very fair of you, Mum.'

Em looked at her and Lizzie saw her eyes glisten with fresh tears. 'Whoops, that's me told off! But as God is my witness, even though your dad is a bugger to me, I've not been anywhere near Sam since your dad's been home and I never will. Even if he knocks me black and blue, he'll never be able to say I didn't do my duty by him.' Em felt it was disloyal to remind Lizzie that her father had had an affair that had resulted in a child while he was fighting in Italy, though Jack had no problems reminding Em often that she had turned to Sam for solace.

Lizzie put her arms around her mother. 'I don't know why you don't leave Dad. Sam hankers for you, always asks after you, you know.' Anyone could see the man cared for her.

'That's as maybe. But this house was my mother's and I was brought up in it. I'm not giving it to your dad for him and his cronies. Besides, where would I go? I wouldn't give people the satisfaction of moving in with Sam, even though I know he'd take me like a shot. I've got a bit of pride left, our Lizzie. Anyway, you never did tell me why you finally left Maurice to come home. It was to be a buffer between me and your dad but that wasn't the whole reason, was it?'

Lizzie shook her head. 'Him and his mother asked me to put some money into the kitty. By then I was looking after that big house and his mother at the same time as working in the offices of the estate agent in the square.'

'No wonder you started getting so skinny,' said Em. She took the last mouthful of her cake. 'Why ever didn't you come home and say something?' She brushed cake crumbs off her wraparound pinny into her cupped hand and threw them on the fire.

'How could I moan about my life when there are people getting blown to bits almost every day?' Lizzie stopped talking and stared at the fire. She thought of Maurice playing the piano, or sitting by the fire with his nose in a book. She'd loved him, then. He was so intelligent – he could talk on any subject – and what was she? Just a common Gosport girl. She remembered the night the tax office had taken a hit. Maurice had gone into work the next day to find the place a pile of rubble. Luckily no one was hurt but he had been left without a job. Then he'd spent more time than ever with his mother. 'Besides, whenever Maurice asked me to do something for his mother he said it in such a way that it was hard for me to refuse,' Lizzie said.

'That's called "wheedling"!'

Lizzie sighed. 'I took over the cooking and naturally it was my money that kept us afloat. All the money we'd saved together had gone. I'd still have been breaking my back for them if I hadn't overheard his mother one afternoon when I'd finished work early. The front door was ajar and I went in. As I walked up the passage, I heard her say, "Get the stupid bitch to pay for the piano tuning. She could get an evening job. Your dad's insurance money stays in my wardrobe."'

Lizzie hushed her mum, who had opened her mouth to speak.

'I crept away back to the front door, opened it, slammed it shut, yelled out, "I'm home!", went down the garden to the lavatory and cried my eyes out. When I got back indoors, Maurice kissed me on the forehead and asked why I was so pale. I said I'd had a hard day and was cold. Then I made tea and afterwards, as it was a Friday, Maurice's mum went round to see her friend. It was a dark evening so Maurice went with her. As soon as they'd gone I went into her room and searched her wardrobe. What did I find? A shoebox full of five-pound notes.'

'Gosh,' said Em. 'Did you take back what was yours?'

'No! I'm not a thief. I went and packed up my stuff and came home. I know you'd asked me to come and see you before, and when I saw how horrible Dad was being to you I wished I'd got here sooner. I'm so sorry, Mum.' Her tears flowed. She fell into Em's arms.

'There, there.' Em patted her back as she had when Lizzie was small. 'Out there somewhere is a man who'll love you like you ought to be loved. You're well rid of Maurice and his mother. So what was in the letter?' She was looking at the remnants in the fireplace.

Lizzie sniffed. 'Maurice's mother is ill. He sounds confused, angry. He wants to see me.'

'Will you go?'

Lizzie shook her head. 'He was always pleading her frailty to get me to do jobs she simply didn't want to do. No, I'm not going to him and I'm pretty sure he won't come here after me.'

'Are you positive you won't go and see them both?' Em persisted.

Lizzie saw she looked worried. 'I'd rather stick wasps up my bum,' she said.

The next morning Lizzie awoke to the sound of raised voices. She quickly pulled on her dressing-gown and ran downstairs. In the kitchen her mother was standing by the sink and slices of bread were on the floor. Em was shaking. Her father was settling himself into his wheelchair. His face was grim.

'For God's sake, leave her alone!'

Lizzie could see her mother was scared stiff.

'So we've woken young Lizzie, have we?' Jack said, with a smirk.

'What's the matter, Mum?' Lizzie ignored her father's sarcasm and went across to her mother. Apart from her breathing, which was laboured, she seemed all right, but her whole body was shaking.

'All I wanted was a kiss. Is that too much to ask of me own wife? Or is it only pub landlords she likes kissing?'

Her father wheeled himself towards them and Em immediately stepped away.

'You deliberately turned the chair over so you could bite me when I helped you up.' Em had found her voice.

'Ah, you're telling tales, Em, my love. There's not a mark on you. It was a kiss I wanted. I'm not made of stone, woman.'

'Go in the other room and let me see to breakfast, Mum.' Lizzie turned her mother towards the hallway and gave her a gentle push. Then she put the kettle on the gas, which popped and sizzled.

'Not got that mate of yours to protect your mother this morning, have you?'

Her father wheeled himself right up close to her. Lizzie saw he needed a shave and definitely a wash. He smelled rank. Sometimes she was sure he went dirty purposely, waiting until someone mentioned it.

'If you mean Rita, why would she want to stop you being *loving* towards Mum?'

'That dark-haired bitch'll get her comeuppance.'

Lizzie picked up the bread and put it on the grill for toast. There was no sense in wasting it, she thought. She didn't know or care what he meant by his warning so she ignored him.

*

At six that evening Lizzie stood waiting outside the building where her mother worked. She shivered in her thick wool coat, and her boots were caked with the ground frost that hadn't thawed all day. The buzzer had already gone, so she knew it wouldn't be long before Em came out of the hut.

'Where's your coat?' Her mother was wrapped in an old brown blanket.

Em sighed. 'I spilled an urn of water on it this morning. Don't ask me why. I wasn't thinking properly. It's hanging near the pot-bellied stove in the changing room.' She shrugged. 'I got this off the nurse. Me coat's still wet through. The next shift's overseer'll watch it for me, and in the morning it should be dry enough for me to wear.'

The episode that morning had upset her mother, making her less careful than she'd normally be. 'Oh, Mum.' She took off her own coat and put it round Em, letting the blanket fall away. 'We'll do a swap,' she said. 'Don't argue, I won't hear of it.'

The women were pouring out of the building now, calling goodnight to each other and to Em, as they passed. The new shift was coming in and Lizzie was eager to get home and out of the bitter cold.

Rita joined them, laughing at some joke one of the girls had shared with her.

'What on earth have you got on? Oh, you've swapped.' Rita pulled Lizzie to one side. 'Her own coat's a mess. Like a drowned rat she looked. Your mother's been in a state all day, Lizzie. You got problems at home again?' She didn't wait for Lizzie to answer. 'I know this morning when I was at your house I said I'd have me tea with you, but would you mind if I went out with Blackie instead?' She glanced towards the gate. 'At lunch break a message was passed to me that he'd meet me tonight.' Lizzie nodded. She was shivering. 'You don't mind, do you?' She glanced towards the gates again.

Lizzie could see she wanted to go. 'Course not,' she said.

'Let's do another swap.' Rita took off her belted black coat and prised the old blanket from Lizzie's hands. 'Blackie's got the car. You take my coat. No arguments, I won't need it tonight, an' tomorrow I'll wear me heavy raincoat. I got to hurry – we're going to Fareham.' Throwing her coat at Lizzie, she ran ahead and out of the main gate, waving at Huey the gatekeeper.

'That girl's a bloody marvel,' said Em, as they joined the crowd and walked towards the gates. For good measure Lizzie had put the blanket across her mother's shoulders like a shawl to keep her doubly warm.

When they got in, Lizzie lit the fire in the sitting room.

Her father wasn't in his usual place by the warm stove in the kitchen so she guessed he was with his cronies in the Queen's Hotel bar, just around the corner. When he wasn't about, the house was so much more peaceful.

'Why don't you have a wash and get to bed?' she said to Em. Her mother looked worn out. 'I can get tea ready.'

After taking Em a cup of tea and giving her a copy of *Woman's Weekly* to read, Lizzie peeled the potatoes and saw to the vegetables. There was a dish in the oven with half a Woolton pie left in it. It was made of vegetables and meat extract, with a potato-and-flour topping, so they'd certainly be eating a meatless dinner tonight. War made everyone more inventive about what they could cook and eat when they were short of rations.

Fed up with hearing about Hitler and his bombing conquests on the wireless, Lizzie went upstairs to her mother, who was dozing, her spectacles almost falling off her nose. 'I'm taking Rita's coat back,' she said. 'I know she won't be in but Gladys will be there and I might even pop in to Pixie's and have a chat about the wedding.' It was common knowledge now, the celebrations for Pixie and Bob. 'There's a small fire in the sitting room and dinner's ready – it only needs switching on. I won't be long. I fancy an early night meself,' she said. 'Dad's still out.'

Lizzie shouted 'Goodbye!' as she left the house, and heard a muffled answer. She wore Rita's coat as it was nicer than her old green gabardine raincoat, which was draped over her arm as she went out into the cold.

She heard a muffled cough but, though she looked along the street, she couldn't see anyone.

There were a few stationary vehicles in the road: the lack of petrol meant cars were more often parked than driven. Their bodywork and roofs were white with frost. Lizzie found her woollen gloves in her own coat pocket and put them on. The quickest way to Gladys's house in Alma Street was to walk down King's Road and then cut through the allotments. A railway line intersected the dark wooded area, but two sets of gates allowed access across the lines. It was very dark but the whiteness of the frost helped to make the night brighter

Near the railway lines she felt suddenly as though she wasn't alone. She told herself not to be so stupid. She wasn't normally afraid of the dark. The feeling persisted. She was sure someone was following her. But when she stopped and listened for footsteps there weren't any. A bat flew out of a tree and made her jump. With her heart banging away nineteen to the dozen, she told herself not to be so silly: it was more dangerous working at Priddy's than walking Gosport's back alleys in the dark.

She opened the swing gate and walked across the lines, then continued past the scrapyard into Moreland Road. In a few moments she would be on the main Forton Road where people would be waiting for buses and queuing for the Criterion cinema. It wasn't far to Alma Street now, and when she reached Gladys's house there'd be a nice cuppa waiting.

But first she had to navigate the waste-ground next to the church. A bomb, just weeks ago, had torn down the houses that had stood there. Lizzie picked her way across the rubble. Oh, how she wished this awful feeling of being followed would go away.

A voice called softly, 'Rita!'

Lizzie turned, but before she could see who was behind her she was hit on the side of the head. 'Aghh!'

A haze obscured her view but she summoned the strength to scream again.

The darkness of St John's Church loomed as she felt her knees give way. A second blow missed her head but hit her shoulder. Off balance now, she fell among the rubble.

'Aghh! Please! Don't!' She managed to get the sounds out but whole sentences wouldn't come and she couldn't focus to see who or what had hit her.

'This'll teach you to mind your own business.' The

voice was cold, measured and low. A foot connected with her as she lay on the ground.

'Don't . . .' Her voice was weak.

'Leave 'er!' It was a different voice. Another man. 'That's enough! We're to teach her a lesson, not kill the bitch!' The voice faded as Lizzie fought consciousness. Her shoulder hurt too much to use her arm to push against the heavy hand that turned her face upwards. A huge brick was beneath her back, digging into her, but she couldn't move, couldn't see, couldn't think clearly. Lizzie was forcing herself to stay awake. Tears filled her eyes. Her thoughts were jumbled. Was her head cut? Was it raining? Everything was fading away . . .

'I'm giving her something to remember.' The voice was close.

Then her coat was pulled open, buttons and belt scattering, and she felt the cold air hit her skin as her skirt was torn away. She heard and felt the material of her knickers rip. She had to stop them, stop them, or . . . She could smell cigars. It hurt to try to push away the heavy weight on top of her.

A voice close to her ear whispered, 'I like a bit of spirit.'

Lizzie blacked out.

*

When Lizzie opened her eyes she could hear voices. She struggled to a sitting position. Her back seemed cut in two by something sharp. Through blurred eyes and with the help of the whiteness from the frost she could make out shapes, people walking down the road. She put her hand to her head and winced. She could see the darkness on her fingers. Was it blood?

Her legs were cold. One of her boots was missing. She saw something white on the stones – her knickers. She felt the stickiness between her thighs, the ache between her legs. *She had been raped.*

More voices were coming through the darkness. People were coming out of the cinema. Lizzie had no idea how long she had lain there on the ground.

Crying now, she reached over and picked up her white cotton knickers and, standing unsteadily, managed to put them on. They were torn. Now she was crying because they wouldn't pull up. Every bone in her body hurt, her head most of all, but determinedly she picked up her boot and hauled it on. Her back felt as though a knife had entered her skin. Bending over, she vomited on the rubble. Then she wiped her mouth on her sleeve, suddenly remembering she was wearing Rita's coat. She looked around. There was her raincoat.

Breathing heavily, she staggered a few steps and picked

it up, stopping herself falling forward on to the rubble. Voices, a man's and a woman's, animated, were getting closer. A couple were using the bomb site as a short cut to Moreland Road. She didn't want anyone to see her like this. She pulled Rita's coat around her. Feeling for the belt, she tied it as best she could.

It hurt to stand up straight and pained her even more to force herself to walk over the rough ground towards the main road.

The couple who had been giggling and talking went silent as she passed them. The smell of cigarettes hung momentarily in the air.

Out on the main road, Lizzie walked unsteadily past the chip shop, breathing in the fatty smells. On the corner of Reed's Place she doubled over and spewed into the gutter, looking furtively around in case anyone had seen her. She wiped her face using her glove.

She managed to quicken her pace as she reached Alma Street, where she banged on the door with the shiny knocker.

When Gladys opened the door, Lizzie fell into her arms.

Chapter Five

Lizzie was trying to roll the garter over a thick lisle stocking. 'You're not going to work today! Are you stupid?' Em pushed her daughter back onto the bed to stop her dressing herself.

'I've got to pretend last night never happened. If I let it get the better of me I'll be done for. Got to act normal or people will start talking about me.' She looked at her mother through swollen eyes. 'How long d'you think it can be kept a secret?' She stood up again.

A piece of toast fell off the small plate on the bed and landed on the floor. Em looked at it, then back at Lizzie. 'Get undressed and get back in bed. I'm staying home today as well.'

'Mum, we can't afford to—'

It was as though all Em's pent-up passion couldn't be kept back any longer. 'Bugger the money! You mean more to me than the cash for a bag of bloody spuds. Let your father sort out his disabled pay. Let him put something towards the housekeeping for once. You're not going anywhere in that state.' She snatched Lizzie's stockings from her. Then she took a bottle from the drawer in the bedside table and shook out a couple of tablets. She handed them to Lizzie. 'Swallow these,' she said, passing her a glass of water. 'You should rest.'

'Was he in last night?' Lizzie's voice was quiet. She had it in her mind that her father had had something to do with the attack. She'd slept very little. Memories were surfacing in her mind.

'Whatever are you suggesting?' Em stared at her, and it was as though she'd read her daughter's mind. 'I know he said he'd get even with Rita but it was *you* that was hurt, his own daughter. I don't for one minute think he'd harm you.'

'Look, Mum.' Lizzie grabbed her mother's hand, forcing her to sit beside her on the bed. 'The bloke called me Rita. I was wearing her coat. We look alike – a lot of people have said so. What if Rita was supposed to be knocked about? "That'll teach you to mind your own business" – that's what one of them said before he . . . before he . . .' A fresh flood of tears took over.

Em clasped her daughter to her. 'That bang on your

head could have done any amount of damage. You said yourself most of the time you was fighting to stay awake.' She bent forward, examining Lizzie's skull. Lizzie flinched as her fingers gently explored the area. 'The blood's stopped seeping through the bandage.' Em had bathed Lizzie last night as soon as Bob had brought her home in his van. Gladys had come, too, and dressed the wound on her head. There were no bandages, so Em had torn up a clean pillowcase and Gladys had used that. 'I'm the overseer and I'm saying you're not fit to work today.' She pushed Lizzie away and spoke clearly to get her message over.

Lizzie couldn't help herself. More tears ran down her cheeks. 'You'll get the sack if you don't go in.'

'Oh no I won't. Rita's going to talk to Mr Scrivenor and I'm sure he'll understand.'

Lizzie abandoned the garter and lay back on the bed. Her mother was right: she couldn't even put on her stockings, let alone concentrate on adding up numbers. 'All right, Mum, you win,' she murmured. Her body ached all over and she could still smell the sour aroma of cigars. Her stomach lurched. She turned over and put her face into the freshly laundered pillowcase.

'Dad scares me – I'm frightened of him,' she said eventually.

'Well, you got no reason to be.' Em shook her head. 'When I told him what had happened to you he cried like a baby. He went out after that and he still hasn't come home.' She tried to wipe Lizzie's tear-stained face with the bottom of her pinny. 'He's been gone all night. Round one of his mates, no doubt, or trying to find out who would do such a terrible thing to you. I'm beginning to think he can't face you, his little girl, being hurt like that.' She smiled at Lizzie. 'You know what it's like, dads and their daughters.'

Lizzie was glad that only she and her mother were in the house.

'Of course, it's possible it was a random attack, except for them saying Rita's name.' Em paused. 'Maybe your Maurice got his mates to teach you a lesson because you left him.'

'He's not got the nerve, Mum.' Lizzie was quite sure of that.

'When a bloke's refused the one thing he wants, he can change into a beast.' Em stroked Lizzie's hair. Lizzie could see how upset she was, but her mother was trying hard to keep cheerful for her sake. 'Anyway, love, you get some sleep and I'll arrange a doctor's appointment.' Last night Lizzie had emphatically refused Bob's offer to take her to the War Memorial Hospital's casualty department, even though Em had pleaded with her.

'No!' Lizzie had shouted. 'No! I don't want anyone else knowing!'

'Doctors don't tell. And what if—'

'If there's anything to worry about, I'll deal with it. I can trust Pixie and Bob not to gossip.' Lizzie thought about Gladys and how she'd comforted her as she'd collapsed on her doorstep, then run next door to get Bob to drive her home. 'Gladys won't say anything on the line today – she promised. And I don't want Mr Scrivenor feeling sorry for me.'

'Rita will have had a word with the boss by now, but I'm sure it'll be kept hush-hush.'

Lizzie relaxed. 'Good,' she said. Her eyes closed. The tablets her mother had given her were working and she was suddenly very, very sleepy.

Rita sat up in Blackie's double bed. She'd just woken after spending the afternoon in his arms. Downstairs she could hear cups rattling. She smiled and snuggled down again beneath the soft sheets. She thought of Lizzie. Gladys had told her about the attack. Well, one thing was for certain: she didn't want to wear that coat ever again. Blackie had said he'd get her another. But that poor, poor girl, she must be feeling terrible. What an awful thing to happen to her.

There was a knock on the front door. This was one

of the things she hated about staying at Blackie's house in Avenue Road. There was always someone coming to the house during the day and quite often at night as well. Now she could hear voices and again the banging of the door as it was closed and reopened. Something was unloaded into the hallway. Blackie and someone else exchanged conversation that she couldn't properly hear.

For a simple, well-furnished three-bedroomed house it was chock-a-block with boxes and packages.

After a while, she heard the front door close and footsteps treading up the wooden stairs. The bedroom door opened and Blackie entered with a tray containing tea, a boiled egg, thinly sliced buttered bread and a plate of chocolate biscuits.

Rita grinned at him. His hair was sticking up in all directions, his eyes were bright and he had a smile a mile wide.

'Chocolate biscuits, I don't believe it! And a whole egg to myself?'

He set the tray on the bedside table. His smile grew even wider. 'Wait until you see what I've got downstairs.'

Rita munched a slice of bread with real butter on it. Their frenzied lovemaking had left her ravenous. 'I'm more than happy with this,' she said, waving her hand over the tray. 'You are lovely.'

'You'll take ages eating that and I can't wait any longer!' He pushed the tray aside and pulled her from the bed. He made her go before him down the steep stairs, then pushed her towards the opened boxes. There were four large crates. 'Look inside.'

Rita pulled back a flap and gasped. Flour, sugar, dried fruit, tinned fruit, tinned meat, dried milk, dried egg powder. As she moved the foodstuffs around, a fruity smell rose from the packets. 'This is for Pixie's wedding breakfast, isn't it?'

'A mate of mine owes me a favour so he's just brought it down from Southampton.'

'This is from the American stores there?'

He nodded. 'They've got plenty, they can get plenty. I think it's about time some of our – or, rather, Pixie and Bob's – mates got a good feed to help win this bloody war.'

Rita got up from where she'd been kneeling on the carpet and threw herself into his arms. 'There's only one thing.' She looked up into his still smiling face. 'I'm worried Bob won't accept it. I know he doesn't mind a few tricks to get decent stuff for his stalls. Like so-called 'fire damaged' stock. And buying furniture from bombed-out places. Nothing really against the law, mind, and he'd never steal a thing in case the tax man finds out—'

Blackie interrupted, 'The Americans have a nice little racket going and I'm privileged to be part of it. I promise you there'll be no come-back on Bob. What do you think?'

'If we take this to Gladys's house and start baking, Gladys will love you for ever more. Bob'll be happy if Pixie's happy, and she'll be over the moon because she won't refuse a wedding gift. They've got a bit put by, but Bob won't break into it as it's for Sadie and the new baby. Most of the money he makes goes back into the two stalls he runs with Marlene.'

Blackie looked confused. 'Marlene?'

'Don't tell me you haven't noticed Marlene. She's got the most fantastic russet hair.'

'Ah,' he said. 'The woman who looks like an angel?'

Rita dug him in the ribs. 'You're the angel for doing this for Pixie and Bob.' She pulled his head down and covered his lips with a kiss. She knew it was going on a fraction too long for his tongue became insistent and she felt his hardness against her body. 'Come back to bed an' I'll wipe that picture of Marlene from your mind,' she said, leading him back upstairs.

'You're a right little spitfire when you get going,' he said, stepping out of his trousers and leaving them on the floor. 'Spitting fire like them new bombs the Germans are making. Priddy's ought to be retaliating and making even bigger and more lethal bombs. Or maybe they are.' Blackie sat on the side of the bed, watching Rita take off her nightdress. 'I worry a lot about you, working on untested bomb materials. You're not, are you?'

'Not as far as I know,' said Rita. 'But, then, I'm only one of the workers. I just do as I'm told.' She opened her arms. 'Come here. Let me show you how thankful I am for the lovely present you've got for my very best friend's wedding buffet.'

'I wish it was me getting married.' Gladys went all wistful and stopped rolling out the pastry with the milk bottle she was using. She was covered with flour – even had some in her hair. Rita threw a juicy sultana from the cake mixture she was beating, and it caught Gladys on the cheek. 'Oy! That might be soft but it hurts.' Gladys rubbed her face, leaving more white streaks.

'Bit like you, then,' said Pixie, laughing. 'Soft and hurts easily.' She bent down, opened the oven door and took out a tray of sausage rolls. Hot air belched out. The tops were browned to perfection. Their meaty smell filled the kitchen. Rita passed her a homemade oven mitt.

'They look delicious,' Marlene enthused. ' I haven't had a proper sausage roll for years, and I know what's in those. Certainly not the sawdust we get from the butcher.' Her eyes sparkled wickedly. 'Do you think we could have one for working so hard?'

'I could do with one, and a nice cup of tea.' Rita looked at the sideboard, which was overflowing with food in various dishes they had borrowed for the occasion. 'I ain't seen so much proper grub for ages.'

'It's all down to your Blackie.' Lizzie's voice was small and wistful. 'I wish I had someone like him to look after me.'

The room full of chattering women went suddenly quiet. Rita had begged Lizzie to join in the baking marathon at Gladys's house, hoping it might cheer her up. It was working, but slowly. Rita found it difficult to talk to her. Lizzie was like a snail that had gone deep into its shell and didn't want to come out. Although she was now back at work she was quiet and subdued, and cringed whenever she heard a man's raised voice.

'How to kill a conversation with one sentence,' said Marlene. Her hair was tied back with a cotton scarf. 'You're not the only one without a good bloke,' she added.

Rita felt like slapping her. Though Marlene didn't seem to have much luck with men.

'Marlene!' Pixie chided her. 'If you got nothing better to say or do, put the kettle on.'

Marlene went over to Lizzie and put an arm round her. 'I'm sorry. But you got such a lot going for you, a good job, loving friends and them fantastic shoes you pinched from under my nose at that jumble sale we went to last Saturday.'

Lizzie gave a sudden smile. 'They are rather swish, aren't they? Betty Grable had a pair just like them in *Springtime in the Rockies*.' Her eyes opened wide. 'I wish I had my legs valued at a million dollars like her.'

'Yours would be worth half a crown!' Em shouted across the room.

The girls laughed, and Lizzie poked her tongue out at her mother. Em laughed louder than ever. 'Go next door, love, and make us some tea. We ain't got room to swing a cat while we're baking in this house.'

Marlene's mum, Beth, was next door minding all the children. Rita had decided that if the women were to be really busy preparing food for the wedding in three days' time someone had to keep the little ones out from under their feet. As soon as Lizzie had gone, Em pulled Rita through the scullery and into the garden.

Her face went red and she bit her lip, then blurted out, 'Look, I don't know how to say this, Rita, but I believe my old man was behind Lizzie's rape. It all went wrong. I'm sure it was meant to be you what got hurt. He's been acting so strange lately and has hardly been in the house since that night. But I've said to Lizzie it couldn't have been him.'

Rita stared at her. 'It's been weighing me down too. Of course it was your Jack's fault. You think I'm stupid? The man's so demented he's dangerous. He hates you caring about me.'

'Rita, if Lizzie believed her own father was that evil, she'd have it playing on her mind all her life. God knows what damage that would do.'

Rita frowned. 'So?'

'I want you to help me persuade Lizzie it wasn't him. That she was simply in the wrong place at the wrong time.'

Rita thought for a while. 'I can't ignore it, Em. What if he has another go?'

'No, no!'

'Come on, Em,' Rita was pleading, 'Jack's plan went wrong the first time. Next time he'll make sure it works. But I'm not waiting for him to hurt me. I promise I'll do everything I can to keep the truth, or what I think's the truth, away from Lizzie, for your sake and hers. I'll go along with what Lizzie wants and not involve the police.'

Em was staring into her eyes. 'I love you like you was me own daughter. Thank you.' She put her arms around

Rita, who could feel her shaking with the effort it had taken to ask for help.

The radio was blaring out and their friends were singing 'Oh What A Beautiful Morning'.

'Listen to that,' said Rita, 'It's like a cat's choir.' They smiled at each other.

'Well, it's back to work for all of us tomorrow and tonight the men are going to give us a hand to decorate the hall. Pixie deserves the best we can do for her. He's a good man, her Bob.' Em smoothed back her hair.

'Do you think she would have been as happy if she'd been with that American, Cal?'

'She nearly lost her mind over him. I think she might have been looking forward to being a GI bride and going to live in Ohio with him after the war, but Fate stepped in,' said Rita. 'Sometimes I think it's good we can't look into the future.'

'This conversation's gettin' a bit deep for me,' said Em. 'Let's go in and have a cup of tea with the others. I'm spittin' feathers 'ere.'

Chapter Six

'There's a big advertisement in the *Evening News* for more workers at Priddy's Hard.' Blackie was flicking through the local paper.

'Fancy you bringing that paper with you when we're off enjoying ourselves.' He looked up at her from his armchair in their usual room at the Red Horse hotel.

Rita was sitting in front of the dressing-table mirror trying to tame her hair. When Blackie had gone off in the car today she'd wandered around the shops feeling queasy and lightheaded. His car had been packed with boxes, which, like the cigar-box radios, wouldn't be returning with him. That was the way he was, the way he made his living, she surmised. She knew she shouldn't have left the hotel without eating breakfast, but she'd woken up feeling sick and couldn't face a meal.

She was glad when Blackie had told her he was going

off alone for a couple of hours. In a tiny jeweller's she'd bought two tortoiseshell barrettes. They were very pretty and quite expensive. Tonight she planned on putting up her hair in a victory roll. The sickness had now disappeared and she was looking forward to the dancing.

'Hitler's been after the Royal Arsenal at Woolwich again. Surely the man must know that only bomb cases, cartridge cases and guns are being produced there now.'

Rita sometimes thought Blackie never listened to a word she said and he was always on about the war. 'I expect there's research. There's always research. The government needs the Royal Arsenal.'

'I've got a friend who works there,' said Blackie. 'He says Priddy's knows what's what.'

'Not a friend like that foreign bloke from the Top of the Town you usually have an argument with?'

Blackie stared at her. She could see he was putting a jigsaw puzzle together in his head. He rattled the paper so that the pages crackled. 'Can't argue with someone who threw himself off Clopton Bridge, can I?'

Rita was stunned. 'When was this?' Her voice was soft and she'd gone very cold.

'Sometime during the past week, so I was told.'

Despite the ravages of the bombing that killed

countless people, it was a shock to know someone who had committed suicide. 'I'm sorry,' she said.

'Don't be. He was a bad payer. I had to squeeze every last penny from him. Good riddance, I say.'

Nevertheless she knew he wouldn't have told her if it hadn't been on his mind. 'Let's not talk about it any more,' she said. She went over to Blackie, took the newspaper out of his hands and threw it on the floor. 'And stop quizzing me about work, when it's Saturday night and soon we'll be dancing our socks off. I want to relax and forget about the war.'

'All right. You are a very moody woman, Rita Brown. Do you know that?' Blackie's mouth went into a hard thin line.

Rita couldn't help herself. Lizzie's rape had been on her mind ever since it had happened. She kept thinking about the poor girl and how it might, perhaps should, have been her.

The tears came thick and fast, and Blackie enfolded her in his arms. 'What's the matter, love? I didn't mean to be cross with you for telling me to stop talking about the war. But it is all around us.'

'Oh, Blackie, I'm not usually so tetchy but I feel as though I want to go to bed and sleep for years.' She stared up at his concerned face. Even though he needed a shave he was still beautiful. 'I have to tell you.' So far she'd kept the secret from him, but it was all so upsetting she really did need to talk to someone.

'Lizzie was raped.' The words tumbled over themselves. His face went white. A frown creased his forehead. 'It could have been me – in fact, it *should* have been me.'

'*What?*'

The whole story came out. He listened carefully as she told him about the exchange of coats and that Jack had been present in the morning when Em had invited her back to their house for her tea.

'But I came to Priddy's and picked you up,' Blackie said.

Rita nodded. 'If Jack had arranged for someone to follow me, that someone wouldn't know I wasn't at their house. In my coat, in the dark, Lizzie could easily be mistaken for me.' She rubbed her eyes. 'Trouble is, I had a lot to ponder on today when you left me on my own to go and see your friends.' Fresh tears fell. 'It's been going round and round in my head.'

'There, there, cry it out, my love.' Blackie was holding her so close it was as if their hearts were beating together. After a while, he said, 'A bloke whose mind is so deranged that he thinks you take his wife's attention away from him is never going to give up. Someone's got to protect you.'

For a long time he didn't speak. When he did, he said quietly, 'Leave it with me.'

She drew away from him. 'He's fought for his country. This bloody war has a lot to answer for.'

He cupped his hand beneath her chin and stared into her eyes. 'I'm aware of that. But don't think I haven't noticed you looking a bit peaky lately. You sure that's all you need to tell me?'

Rita nodded. 'This is a secret. I promised I wouldn't talk about what happened to Lizzie. She doesn't want everyone to know.'

'I'm marvellous at keeping secrets,' he whispered.

Rita reached out and took his hand in hers. Blackie was good at making her feel special. Moving towards each other, their lips met. Blackie caressed her. Then, when he, too, was naked, they clung together, as though afraid to let anything come between them. He whispered her name until slowly, then more feverishly, they became one.

Afterwards, his hand lazily stroking Rita's thigh, he said, 'You know I've fallen in love with you?' He turned his face towards her. 'Do you have any regrets about being with me?'

'No,' said Rita. He was unlike any other man she had known. He had the utter confidence of someone who'd learned to stand on his own feet from a very early age. He never spoke to her about his past or the family he might have had or left behind. The one thing she was sure of was that this war had been his stepping-stone to making money. But although he said he loved her, she also had the feeling that his love was a 'here and now' thing. Should she decide to move on, it wouldn't break his heart.

Later, dancing to the music in the ballroom and feeling much better for having shared the secret with him, she relaxed. Confiding had halved her fears that she might be attacked. She hoped Lizzie would get over the dreadful thing that had happened to her. Being back at work had helped, but Lizzie had lost her sparkle and went out of her way to avoid men.

Perhaps the forthcoming wedding and dancing might help to bring a smile to her unhappy face.

Blackie moved up behind the wheelchair as it trundled along the pavement on Forton Road. The smell of piss was almost disguised by the strong aroma of Barbasol on the freshly shaved Jack.

A few people stared at Blackie. He knew he cut a fine figure in his long dark overcoat, pressed suit and Homburg. It was a sunny day, cold and clear, and at last buds were beginning to appear on the trees. An army lorry overtook the people walking along the pavement.

There were so many forces vehicles parked on the roads at Elson and near the shoreline that people had become friendly with the men and often shared their homes and meals with them. An air of excitement hovered over Gosport as the work on the beaches went on. Tarmac and iron strengthened the cement slipways leading into the sea off Hardway. Artificial harbours were being built at points all around the south coast. Blackie had discovered they were designed to take up to two thousand, maybe more, vehicles a day, or around twelve thousand tons of equipment, to be towed across the Channel. He'd found out they were called Mulberry harbours. Gosport was like a huge building site. Troops were everywhere, their vehicles squeezed into any available parking space.

Blackie knew the people of Gosport had grasped that something momentous was going to happen, but no one knew what it was – the operation was top secret. Rumours were rife but one thing was certain: Hitler wouldn't like it.

Blackie stared ahead at the scruffy man firmly handling his wheelchair. They were approaching Ferrol Road.

Blackie knew he mustn't cause a scene. The White Swan public house on the corner was busy: he could smell the scent of beer drifting through the pub's open door. Any disturbance and he might find the drinkers emerging and nosing about to see what was going on. He moved up close to the handles and pushed the chair off its course.

'What the fu—'

'Shut up, old man. We're off for a little walk.'

Jack's face paled as he twisted around to see who was pushing him. He tried to show he was unafraid by giving Blackie a broken-toothed grin.

'Blackie, me ol' mate, nice to see you.' His flat cap was on crooked and he was tieless. A dirty mark showed around the neckline of his worn shirt. Blackie knew how fastidious Em was – Rita had told him often enough – so he guessed the man couldn't be bothered to keep himself clean.

'Shut the fuck up, Jackie boy.' Blackie's voice was soft but menacing. He didn't want a scene in the street or to have people pushing their noses into his affairs and spoiling everything he'd worked for these past few years. Rita was as necessary to him as food and water. He was getting nearer to what he wanted from her. The more he showed he cared about her, the more malleable she would become. And this war-torn stinking husk of a bloke mustn't be allowed to wreck that.

Blackie looked ahead to where the pavement narrowed near the fishermen's cottages, then widened where Hitler's bombs had recently destroyed homes. It was a long road, full of mismatched houses and gaps where brambles and old mattresses bloomed. Military ground that contained gasometers lay close by. There was no doubt that the huge storage tanks were on Hitler's bombers' lists; those and the heavily disguised armaments factory, of course.

At the end of the road there was a slipway. A footbridge spanned the creek and led to the armaments buildings. But Blackie pushed the chair towards the near-derelict boatyard. Vessels in various stages of repair were on stilts out of the water and only a few men mooched around, one walking a dog.

'Where are we going?'

Blackie could almost smell the man's fear, along with the muddy stench of oil and dead fish. He bumped the chair along a narrow wooden jetty. There was barely room for the wheels and he had a tight grip on the handles to stop the chair sliding into the water. An out-of-commission ferry boat, *Vadne*, was moored alongside a rotting wooden jetty.

'This is where we stop. Nice view, isn't it?' Fresh piss from Jack mingled with the stench all around them. Blackie knew the man was shit-scared. He smiled to him self. 'You had a hard time during this war, didn't you, mate?'

Jack nodded. He couldn't twist around far enough to talk to Blackie, so Blackie moved in front of him. The chair slipped forward.

'Ow! Put the bleedin' brake on!'

'I was about to say the same to you, Jack.' Blackie was very calm. 'You put the brake on the way you treat your family. After all, it all went wrong, didn't it? It was *my girl*, Rita, who was supposed to get hurt, wasn't it? Now you got to live with the fact you was responsible for a dirty great bloke gettin' at your little girl . . .'

'Stop it, stop it!' Jack tried to cover his ears.

Blackie, his foot now under the wheel, stopped the chair rolling into the water. 'You ain't going to hurt no one any more, are you?'

Jack shook his head. Blackie slipped his foot away from the tyre and the wheelchair crept even further forward towards the murky depths.

'No! No!'

Blackie pulled the wheelchair back. It lurched and creaked. Jack clung to the armrests, his fingers and knuckles white. Now he was crying. 'I don't want to die in the water. I can't swim no more.'

'You survived a trench . . . Be a bit of a shame for you to fall into the creek here and drown, wouldn't it?'

Blackie held on to the chair's handles, lifting the

back so the man was sliding forward again. Jack's strangled scream mingled with the noise of a flock of gulls squawking overhead.

He pulled the chair level. Jack slumped back. He was breathing heavily and the wet stain on his trousers was easily visible.

'Who were the men involved?'

Without hesitation the names came from Jack.

'I guess you'll leave my Rita alone now?'

'Yes, oh, yes.'

'Then I'll leave you alone.'

Blackie turned and walked away. He didn't look back. How the man would turn round and get out from such a confined, narrow place without tumbling into the water was no concern of his.

'You don't look very happy. Sure you don't want to cheer yourself up and come to the wedding reception? Blackie's got beer. God knows how he's managed it but you might enjoy yourself for once.'

Em was wiping down the kitchen table. The wireless was playing Glenn Miller music and she was humming along with it. Jack had been quite amenable these past few days. He'd even thanked her for the sausage rolls she'd brought home from the baking session.

'I don't want to be in the same room as that man Blackie. And what would I do? Dance the Gay bloody Gordons?'

Em decided not to push it. *She* didn't want to be in the same room with Jack, let alone go to the wedding party with him, but it was her wifely duty to ask. Now when people wanted to know where he was, she could truthfully say he wasn't up to it.

He'd arrived home the day before yesterday in a filthy mood. Nothing new there, of course, but he hadn't told her why his clothes were dirtier than usual. He hadn't said a word all that night, and he hadn't gone out with his cronies after she'd helped him with a bath in front of the fire. When he'd asked her to put the water on in the copper she'd been terrified he would use the bath and her nearness to hurt her. Amazingly, he'd been solicitous of her and grateful. Since then he'd been quiet, and once or twice he had even spoken to her kindly. Lizzie, he ignored.

Pixie had invited Sam Owen from the Fox to the do at the Sloane Stanley Hall.

Just to think of seeing him again brought a smile to Em's lips.

As though reading her thoughts, Jack said, 'And you'd better behave yourself there.' He was thoughtful. 'You could end up in a heap like a couple of my mates.

Found yesterday they was. Come out from the Green Dragon and was jumped on down Daisy Lane, near the allotments.'

Em faced him. 'Wouldn't be the blokes that hurt Lizzie, would they?' Rita had confessed she'd told Blackie about Lizzie. Em guessed he wouldn't allow Rita to worry about anything, if he could help it.

The colour drained from his face. 'I don't know what you're talking about,' he said. He turned his wheelchair away from her so that she was confronted by his back.

'You keep it that way, Jack. I don't want to tell my daughter her own father was responsible for putting her through hell.'

Em started wiping the stove. A sound caused her to look at Jack. His shoulders were heaving. She went back to rubbing grease from the oven door. She didn't have it in her heart to comfort him for what he'd done to her child. When she turned to him again, he'd left the kitchen.

Pixie was blooming. Rita and Gladys had tried their hardest to drape and pleat the soft cream parachute-silk dress made especially for that afternoon's wedding. Bob had got hold of some cream lace from a fellow market trader and left the rest up to the women.

'I look like a cream puff.' Pixie took off the pearl headdress Em had lent her and shook out her blonde hair, which had grown considerably since she'd been at home looking after Sadie and being a 'wife' to Bob. Rita saw her glance across the hall to where the men were gathered around a table set with bottles of drink. 'He really is my husband, now,' Pixie said fondly, as Bob threw back his head and laughed with his market mates.

'He loves the bones of you,' said Rita. 'And all pregnant women feel like cream puffs whether or not they're wearing a flowing wedding dress. You look lovely.'

'How d'you know how pregnant women feel? You've never had a baby!'

Rita frowned. Never *had* a baby was right. But she was certain now that she'd missed a period. And no one was more regular with her monthlies than she was. She'd spent sleepless nights thinking about the reasons for her sickness and tiredness and come to the only conclusion possible. She was pregnant with Blackie's baby.

The band was playing a medley and couples in the Sloane Stanley Hall were laughing and dancing to 'Mairzy Doats'. White and pink decorations festooned the ceiling and walls. A huge cake stood on a table at the back, with two small figures on top representing a married couple. Edie Squires had loaned them to Pixie: she had saved them from her own wedding, which had taken place during the Great War.

Blackie had carried the cake from Southampton in the back of his car. He was most apologetic that it was only a sponge concoction, but Pixie had been over the moon with it. All the women were good bakers, especially Em, but no one had cake tins suitable for such a large cake. The long table groaned with the weight of all the cooking the women had done.

Pixie squeezed Rita's hand. 'Thank you,' she said. 'You made all this possible, you and Blackie. You're a friend in a million.'

'Oh, shut up!' Rita could see Bob weaving his way through the dancers. 'Your old man's coming over. Think he wants you to dance.'

'Doesn't that sound lovely? My old man, my husband!' Pixie's eyes were moist.

'Tell me that in twenty years' time,' said Rita. 'When the shine's rubbed off!'

'Bloody misery,' laughed Pixie, as Bob swept her away. Rita noticed the head of his buttonhole flower had come adrift, leaving a stalk pinned to his best dark suit. She had to admit he was a looker. Suddenly tears welled in her eyes. For a moment she envied Pixie her little girl, Sadie, who was dancing around in her frilly pink dress.

She also envied Pixie the baby she was carrying, and her marriage to the man she loved. She was even covetous of the notebooks Pixie was forever scribbling in.

She couldn't imagine Blackie in the role of father and husband. But then, neither could she imagine herself married to him. He was lovely to have a good time with but something stopped her wanting it to go on for ever.

Across the hall Lizzie was chatting to Blackie. Rita had had to persuade her to come to the reception. She and Pixie had pleaded with her, knowing that the music and dancing would bring her out of herself. She didn't look as if she'd needed that persuasion now . . .

She wore a green dress that might have been sprayed on. Blackie was listening earnestly to her, and every so often he'd throw back his head and laugh. Lizzie laid her hand on his arm and he put down his pint glass, then led her onto the dance floor, where she cuddled up to him. There wasn't room for a matchstick between their two bodies.

'Don't be cross with her. She's beginning to come out of the death wish she had after the . . .' Em couldn't finish the sentence. Sam Owen, in a checked suit more appropriate to a race meeting than a wedding, had his arm around her shoulders. It was obvious he was besotted with her. Rita wondered if the barmaids at the Fox were missing their manager tonight. It would be a quiet evening in the bar without Sam and his bawdy jokes.

'Don't worry, I'm not the jealous sort, Em.' Funnily enough she was telling the truth. Blackie bought her love. She liked the clothes and jewellery but it was a bit like eating steak every night and wanting mince. She glanced across the floor and saw Lizzie's head had fallen onto Blackie's broad shoulder. The girl's dark hair glinted and shone in the harsh electric light. Blackie looked up, as though suddenly aware that he was being watched, and let go of Lizzie's hand to wave at Rita. He mouthed, 'Next dance?' She nodded and smiled at him.

The smell of perfume mixed with sweat and food was making Rita feel sick. She moved towards the back door and lifted the bar. Outside there was an elm tree, with a large branch low enough to sit on. She heard giggling, and then, 'Stop it!' It was Gladys's voice. There was the sound of rustling branches, then a man was saying, 'Go on, you know you want to. Can't be a born-again virgin all your life, Glad.'

Rita coughed loudly, not because she had a tickle in her throat but because it was quite obvious Gladys and her partner had no idea she was there. She didn't want to eavesdrop on them. She was glad the snow had gone, and that the bushes and trees were showing green buds. She had even spotted daffodils blooming on waste-ground. God, but it was cold tonight, she thought, even though she was wearing a warm dress she'd altered especially for the occasion. She hadn't wanted to wear the expensive clothes Blackie had showered on her, not when her friends couldn't afford such luxuries.

Gladys moved into the light from the corner she'd been hiding in, and pulled out a thin man in a cardigan. He was clearly older than she was and had combed what remained of his hair over the top of his bald head. Long strands had come adrift to fall either side of his narrow bespectacled face.

The man was moving from one foot to the other. He looked embarrassed.

'You got no one to worry about except yourself, now that Pixie's safely married, Gladys,' said Rita.

'Too true, love. This is me landlord, Siddy!'

The man smiled shyly and Rita shook his outstretched hand. 'Course it is. I've seen you at the house a few times.'

'I've known Glad for years,' he said. He had a moustache that was reminiscent of Clark Gable's but much, much thinner.

'You don't have to make excuses,' Rita said. 'Certainly not to me.'

In the moonlight, Gladys was looking lovely, in a form-fitting dress, which enhanced her sizeable breasts, and she was wearing the red peep-toe shoes that Rita coveted. Gladys loved shoes, especially high heels.

'I'm not coming home tonight,' she said. 'Since the happy couple are off to Brighton for a few days, I thought I'd take the opportunity of going off for a bit meself.' She paused. 'Not on me own. Siddy here knows of a nice little pub at Littlehampton.'

Rita bent forward and kissed the older woman on the cheek. Gladys had been a bit of a girl in the past and loved the attention of men. She didn't always choose the right ones, but she had Pixie and her family living next door, Rita as her lodger, and she worked hard at Priddy's. Why shouldn't she spend some time with Siddy? He seemed harmless and was willing to give Gladys a bit of fun.

'You bring her home safe and sound,' she said to him, then went back into the crowded hall where the warmth and music welcomed her. The food was just about to be eaten.

Near the table a man was filling his plate. It was Jed Ward, a friend of Blackie's. He smiled guiltily as if he thought he was taking too much, then helped himself to another slice of ham. Rita wondered who had invited him. Probably Blackie. Perhaps he had helped Blackie set the hall up, and if so, he deserved to be here, didn't he?

Everyone still seemed to be having a grand time. Kiddies were running in and out amongst the dancers. Elderly relatives were nursing plates of food and glasses of stout. The girls from the armaments yard were giggly with the drink they'd had and blokes were standing around eyeing them up. In the far corner Marlene was wearing a black dress, her glorious red hair trailing in waves down her back. She was talking to a handsome older man with blond hair and a well-cut suit. Rita wanted to join them but it was obvious they were interested only in each other.

Some of the market traders were singing an old London song, 'Knees Up, Mother Brown', with half the words missing, and a couple of old dears who lived in Alma Street were showing their bloomers as they kicked up their legs.

The bandsmen were sitting down with plates on their laps and pints beneath their seats.

Rita felt the tears rising. She felt *so* alone.

She looked around the hall for Blackie but couldn't see him.

A rush of sickness overtook her and she ran for the lavatory outside. The cold air hit her cheeks, making her shudder. Morning sickness, evening sickness, it was the baby. Why, oh why hadn't she taken precautions? Blackie was so urgent with his lovemaking that her concerns were quite swept away by passion.

After the bile had receded she wiped her face with her handkerchief. This baby was going to complicate things. She'd have to stop work. Pregnant women often experienced breathing problems, asthma and nausea while working with the picric acid at the bomb factories. It was a well-known fact that illness and skin problems were higher in munitions factories than they were in any other occupation. Maybe the baby growing inside her would have something wrong with it. Maybe she would lose her job when her condition was discovered and then how would she manage to pay Gladys the rent?

Rita thought, too, about all the time she'd spent in hospital with the scarring when, through her own foolishness, she'd caused a fire at Priddy's. She was so lucky to have been given a second chance, in work and life. But what had she done? Messed it all up by allowing herself to become pregnant.

And then there was Blackie. How would he take the news? Supposing he was happy about her pregnancy? He'd want her to stop work immediately. She'd *have* to take money off him. Rita shivered. She already felt like a kept woman.

How did she *really* feel about the small being growing inside her?

She didn't want it.

She didn't want Blackie.

She'd had enough of hanging around waiting for him to finish his 'business'. Of wondering about the bad things that happened to Blackie's friends, like the foreign man who'd committed suicide . . . if it was suicide. She was fed up with his unnatural interest in the war. He said that the longer the war lasted the more money he would make. But that didn't sound right. Ordinary people wanted the war to end so they could get back to a normal life. And that was what Rita wanted, an ordinary, normal life.

But what about the baby? Rita loved kiddies. The feel of chubby arms around her neck. A baby's milky smell after it had been fed and bathed. In a different time, a different place, she could love this being growing inside her. She could watch her child take its first steps. Tears rose and she gulped them away. She mustn't feel sentimental. *She mustn't!*

She went back into the hall, where the band had continued playing. People were up and dancing. Laughter and merriment filled the smoky air, and she knew she wouldn't be missed.

She picked up her coat from the back of the chair where she'd left it. The clearing of the hall and the taking down of the bunting was up to the market lot, as Pixie's friends had done the cooking. She wouldn't be needed any more tonight.

Outside in the bitter cold she tied the coat belt tightly around her. She looked back briefly and noted the blackout curtains were all in place. It was only the noise seeping out from the wooden building that showed something was going on in the Sloane Stanley Hall.

She walked across the bomb site, careful of the pot-holes, until Forton Road and Hutfield's garage came into view. The sky was black with stars twinkling like jewels in the night sky. Over the road and up the street, the pavement slippery now with dampness, she hurried, until she reached the door of number fourteen and pulled the string with the key tied to it through the letterbox.

Inside, the house was warm: the range hadn't gone out. After taking off her coat, Rita put some coal on the fire, just a knob or two as they were low on fuel. She went into the scullery and lit the gas under the kettle. On the table the canary was awake and chirping, jumping excitedly from his swing to the bars of the cage.

'Hello, little one,' she said, hunting in the sideboard drawer where his rations were kept. She found a piece of cuttlefish bone. 'That's a lovely song you're singing. Do you ever get lonely, like me?' She poked the cuttlebone through the bars, then filled the bird's water dish. All the while the yellow canary sang its little heart out.

Rita made herself a pot of tea. There were so many questions going around in her head that she had no answers for.

After a strip wash to get rid of the smell of cigarettes and stale air that clung to her, she put on a clean white nightdress she'd left warming over the fender and went upstairs to her room.

Brighton was Pixie and Bob's destination and Gladys was going to Littlehampton with Siddy. Apart from the canary, Rita was alone and would be undisturbed. She knew exactly what she had to do. She took a metal coat hanger from the nail on the back of her bedroom door, then pulled off her pretty dress, which she folded and put on her dressing-table. Carefully Rita bent the metal hanger into a more manageable shape.

Legs apart, she inserted it.

Chapter Seven

'Move around and face me.' Rita opened her eyes at the sharpness of the voice and immediately scrunched them shut as the pain gripped her stomach and wrung it inside out. Something wet and cold was pressed to her forehead, soaking up the hot sweat that poured from her. 'You stupid, stupid girl,' came the voice, sharper now.

She was hauled into a sitting position, then rolled over as, simultaneously, the sheet was pulled from beneath her. She was folded like a hairpin, then lifted, and a sheet that smelled as rubbery as her gas mask was spread beneath her. Her mind begged whoever was doing this to leave her alone. Another sheet was pushed below her fragile body and she couldn't help herself as she fell back like a floppy rag doll, the wet rag falling from her head. Still the manhandling went on.

'Lift your arms.' It was Em's voice.

Rita did as she was told even though her arms felt like lead. Her clammy nightdress was peeled from her body and thrown to the floor while a second flannel, warm this time, was rubbed first across her face, then her breasts. Then another flannel was wiped down her body, legs and in between her thighs. A rolled-up towel was shoved between her legs. 'Can you hear me?' Rita tried to answer but her mouth felt as if it was full of cotton wool, and she wrinkled her nose at the metallic smell that was all around her.

There was a lull in the ministrations: Em had left the room. Rita realized she was in her own bedroom. She felt cleaner, fresher. Vaguely she noted the clatter of shoes going downstairs. She faded.

'I'm not leaving here until you've drunk some of this.' A cup's rim was beneath her nose, at her lips. Rita opened her mouth, drank. And choked.

'Sweet!' The word sounded clearer.

'Sugar helps. Drink some more.'

She didn't like the harsh way Em was talking. She was supposed to be her friend, wasn't she? Rita tried again and this time managed to keep down whatever it was.

'Good girl!' She opened her eyes to see Em, her hair looking like a scarecrow's, and her eyes full of worry.

Rita said, 'I'm cold.'

Em said, 'And thank Christ for that. You've been sweating like a furnace, tossing and turning, and now I've run out of nighties for you. You've got one of Gladys's on.'

Rita raised a smile at the frilly red concoction.

She slid back onto the pillow, Em looming over her.

'The bleeding's under control now. Why did you do it, love? I thought I was going to lose you.' Em burst into tears and fell upon Rita's chest, her arms tight about her. After a while she composed herself and sat back, parking her ample bottom on the chair at the side of the bed. 'Why?'

Could she tell Em? Would Em understand?

'I wanted an end to it. The baby.' Her mouth was full of strange strangled sounds. Why was it so hard for her to get those words out?

'Blackie's?' Em's face was close to Rita's mouth.

She nodded. The sharp pain in her stomach reminded her. 'Is it . . . is it . . .?'

'Yes, and it nearly took you with it.' Em leaned back on the chair. 'I knew you wouldn't have thanked me for fetching an ambulance, even if one had been available. We had another raid while you was out of it. And I guessed Blackie would be the last person you'd want witnessing all this.'

Tears rose unbidden in Rita's eyes. 'I'm sorry.'

'So you bloody well ought to be!' Em's temper flashed. 'I thought you was a bleedin' goner!' She fumbled in her pinny's pocket, found a handkerchief and dabbed at Rita's leaking eyes. 'You can stop all that nonsense. You'll be all right now. It's a good thing I've learned a few things in me time on this earth.'

Em patted the sheets around Rita. 'You ain't the first an' you won't be the last to have a kiddie out of wedlock and try to get rid of it.' She paused. 'Mind you, if that sweating an' bleeding hadn't stopped I'd have had to get you up the War Memorial somehow. Can't take no chances like that ever again.' Her eyes were pleading. 'You scared me stiff.'

'Is it really all gone?'

Em looked away.

'Thank you for saving me,' whispered Rita. She didn't know what else to say. She felt for Em's hand and held it tightly. Her friend had saved her life.

The silence between them, each woman engrossed in her own thoughts, seemed interminable. Rita looked across the room to the floor where a pile of bloodied sheets and nightdresses lay close to the wall. 'How come you're here? This isn't your house. Gladys is with her man.'

'I came looking for you and Lizzie. I thought my girl might be with you. She didn't come home from the do in the Sloane Stanley.'

'The last time I saw her she was dancing with Blackie.' She remembered their closeness, the way they'd laughed . . . Rita stopped talking.

A grinding sensation in her guts made her grimace. She guessed where Lizzie was. When the pain subsided she could see by Em's face that she had had the same thought.

'Are you thinking what I'm thinking?' Em asked.

'I'm thinking, Em, that I'm starving and I'd like a proper cup of tea.'

That was only partly true. She wanted to be alone for a moment now that she was thinking clearly. She'd murdered a human being growing inside her. That was a terrible thing to do. She might have killed herself. She knew in years to come she'd have nightmares about what she'd done.

'I'll make the tea.' Em patted her hand. As she got up from the chair she said quietly, 'I'm sorry if Lizzie's gone after your man.'

Rita sighed. That had been a hard thing for Em to say. 'She's welcome to him,' she said.

Em looked at her as if she'd suddenly lost her senses.

She didn't query Rita's words. Instead she said, 'We wanted her to come out from her shell after what happened. I saw them together, dancing. She's always had an eye for him. But the timing's a bit off, love.' Em left the bedroom.

Rita felt like screaming, but the siren got in first. There was no question of running for the nearest public shelter. She could barely stand. She crawled out of bed and managed to haul herself to the top of the stairs just as Em returned, a small figure at the bottom of the steep flight, clutching a tea-towel.

'Bugger this,' Em said. 'We haven't had time to get over the last raid. How d'you feel about taking shelter?' She started up the stairs as Rita began to come down.

'We can go next door. Bob's got a Morrison,' Rita said. 'Can you turn off the electric and the gas in case of explosions?' She stopped and steadied herself, breathing deeply as she held onto the banister. She felt as weak as a newborn kitten.

'I've already thought of that,' said Em. 'I suppose their key is on the string hanging from the letterbox as well?'

Rita nodded. How she got to the bottom of the stairs she had no idea. Em helped her into the kitchen. She saw a flask on the table. 'Is that tea?'

'Yes, I'd just made a pot when the kerfuffle started. Seemed a shame to waste it.' Em's arm was firmly around Rita's waist. She'd just got the words out when an explosion close at hand made the house shake. Dust fell from the ceiling and there was a loud crack, like a window splitting.

'C'mon.' Rita grabbed the birdcage, and seed spread over the table. The bird squawked. 'Shut up, you daft canary!' she cried.

'Gimme the bloody bird,' said Em, 'you can only just about walk, you silly 'ap'orth!'

Rita could hear the planes now, the everlasting drone that she knew she would remember for the rest of her life. Em had shoved the flask into her hands but removed the birdcage. Then she slung a coat around Rita's shoulders and pushed her towards the front door, just as far-off ground fire exploded into action.

Outside, the night was almost as bright as day with searchlights criss-crossing the sky. The smell of burning filled the air.

When Pixie's front door was opened, Em shoved Rita ahead of her into the passage that led to the kitchen. She opened the front of the oblong mesh-covered shelter, its top disguised as a table, then fluffed up the pillows and blankets it contained. 'Get in there. I need to check the utilities.' She spoke loudly, trying to make herself heard above the noise outside.

'Give me the bird.'

Em glared at her but shoved the cage in anyway. What seed remained fell all over the quilt.

Another explosion, further away this time, caused the dresser to tilt and the plates on its shelves to crash to the floor.

'Stay in there,' admonished Em. Then she was gone and Rita sat back among the cushions and blankets, cursing herself that she was no use to Em. Water from the bird's dish had spilled over her nightdress – Gladys's nightdress. She was relieved to see it *was* only water. Her insides felt as though they had been wrung out like a piece of wet washing. She looked at the bird, huddled dejectedly on the floor of the cage, its feathers all ruffled.

'We're lucky, you and me,' she said, 'to have such a good friend as Em.'

There was too much noise outside for Rita to hear where Em was.

Despite the blackout curtains being in place, the kitchen was a rainbow of colours from the fires burning outside. Someone close by had taken a hit. The screaming drone of a plane caught in the gunfire told Rita it was heading towards the ground. Another huge crash shook the house.

'Move over. There must be room for a littl'un.' Em crawled in beside her. 'All the utilities were already turned off. Bob always was a safety-conscious beggar.'

From a cloth bag she produced some meat pasties. 'Get one of these down you,' she said. 'It's left over from the festivities. And you need feeding up.' She peered at Rita and shoved the pasty into her hand. 'You're as white as a bleedin' sheet.' A huge bang caused Rita to fall into Em's arms. With the loud drone of planes and ack-ack fire responding, the noise was too loud for her to hear Em's voice.

Rita was so glad she had found her and was looking after her. Why couldn't she love her own mother like she loved Em?

There was a lull in the noise, but the smell of burning still pervaded the air.

Em was trying to pour tea into the flask's cup without spilling it, although her hands were shaking. 'I see no reason why I can't stay here with you until Gladys gets back,' she said. 'We've all got the time off work tomorrow, because of the wedding. The other shift is on overtime. There's no way I can get you back to my house to take care of you. And you'll not feel too happy with my Jack moaning all the time.' She paused. 'I'll send word to Lizzie, whenever the little tart gets home,' she added angrily. 'A couple of days should see you on your feet. And it's what Gladys would want.'

'What about your Jack? Shouldn't you be at home with him?'

'He wasn't in when I was last home and I was more worried about Lizzie. I ain't worried about either of them now. If Lizzie really is with your man, he'll take good care of her. I'm not bothered where Jack is, and he can reach the cupboards where the food is kept.'

'I don't know why you don't move in with Sam.' Rita spoke between mouthfuls of meat and chopped vegetables. Bits of the rich pastry fell onto the bedding.

'Don't you? Nice example I'd be to the rest of my family. Imagine what people would say about me leaving a poor, defenceless wounded soldier to go off with me fancy man.'

'But with all this going on, you should take happiness where you can find it.'

Em handed her the tea. 'Like Lizzie?'

Rita went quiet. Then she said, 'Look, Em, there's something funny going on with Blackie.' She sipped the hot tea.

'He's a con man, a man who makes a living off the black market. What d'you expect?'

'It's more than that.' Rita took another gulp of tea. Some strength was seeping back into her bones.

'What?' There was a long silence.

She absolutely believed Blackie was capable of doing bad things. She knew he wasn't just earning money from the black market. There was something else, something sinister going on. And he was holding something back, a dark secret, as well as telling her lies. At first, going with him had been exciting, but now, deep down, she was frightened.

Rain was beating against the windowpanes. Thoughts of Pixie entered her mind. Please let her and Bob and young Sadie be all right, Rita thought. She hoped they were safe after the raid. The baby was due very soon and then their happiness would be complete.

Bob worked hard with Marlene at his side on the market stall, and she was a good friend. She recalled the tall man Marlene had been dancing with. He was a looker, all right, but a bit older than her . . .

Em was pouring more tea from the flask, careful not to spill any. She passed the cup to Rita, who declined. 'You said there's something not quite right with Blackie? What is it?'

'I don't know, Em,' she said. 'But there's more to him than meets the eye.'

The ear-splitting screech of the all-clear announced the raid was over. Rita gave a big sigh of relief. She knew exactly what Em was thinking. That they'd somehow lived through another dose of bombs sent by Hitler.

'You sure you're not running Blackie down because there's every chance he's tucked up in bed at this minute with another woman? Nothing so spiteful as a woman scorned an' all that!' Em drank from the tin cup.

Rita shook her head. 'No. I know you won't believe me, but I'm happy I'm out of it. Why else would I want rid of his child?'

'You really do mean that, don't you?'

'Yes, Em. I'm glad it's all over between us.'

Em drank the last of the tea, her eyes fixed on Rita's. 'You going to give him all his gifts back?'

Rita forced a smile. 'Not that glad, Em.'

Pixie turned over again in bed. She couldn't get comfortable.

'What's up, love?'

'I can't get to sleep. I think this little chap is playing football.' She pushed herself up on one elbow and stared at Bob.

'You're convinced it's a boy?' He ran his hand over the mound of her stomach.

In the cot in the corner Sadie threw her arm above her head and snored as only a little girl can.

It was a large bedroom, furnished well, and the landlady had waited up for them when she had been told they were on a honeymoon trip. Pixie hadn't wanted the sandwiches the woman had left on a plate covered with a damp tea-towel but she had eaten them. It had seemed churlish not to accept her kindness, even though both of them were full of good food, courtesy of Blackie.

Earlier, searchlights had filled the sky a long distance away. The dull roar of planes had passed over them, then further down the coast towards Portsmouth. No sirens had squealed so Bob and she had stayed tucked up in bed. Tomorrow they wanted to take Sadie out and show her the sights of Brighton, not that she would remember much about it when she was older.

Pixie looked at the wedding band on her finger. Bob was her saviour and her love. She stared down at him. He had his eyes closed, feigning sleep.

She thought about the wedding reception. She was sure everyone had had a good time. A smile crossed her face. Her mother had tied tin cans and old boots to the back of their van and the noise had driven Bob mad until he'd stopped in a lay-by and cut the strings.

Pixie looked around the clean, comfortable room, then over to the table where her notebook was. She had quite a pile of them now, all filled with her sloping writing. Bob teased her about her 'diaries', as he called them. He'd told her he had a present for her and would give it to her when they got home to Alma Street. She'd already guessed what it might be: she'd told him she'd like to learn to type.

His voice broke into her thoughts. 'You glad you married me?'

Pixie looked into his dark eyes. 'I thought you'd dropped off to sleep. I'm happier now than I've ever been,' she said. 'And it's all because of you.'

'I do still wonder about . . . about . . .'

She pushed her blonde hair out of her eyes. She knew the American sailor was often in Bob's thoughts. After all, Sadie was Cal's daughter, though he had known nothing about her. She had been born after he had died.

'Say his name. Cal. His name was Cal. You've got no need to be scared of a dead man.'

He sighed. 'I know, but you adored him.'

Pixie put her fingers on Bob's cheek. His stubble was

already growing through and it prickled beneath her fingers. 'But I love you.'

'I know you do. The sensible part of me tells me that. But I do sometimes wonder . . .'

'Wonder what?'

'There was no body,' he reminded her.

Pixie moved again. She'd got uncomfortable and this conversation was making her even more so. 'His destroyer, USS *Bristol*, was split in two. Very few men were rescued. Some hung from makeshift rafts for hours. Cal was not one of the lucky ones.' She bent her head to his scratchy cheek and kissed him. It had been a long while since his last shave, early that morning. He'd moaned about the shortage of razor blades and having to use a blunt one. There was still a sliver of paper on his neck where he'd cut himself. Her heart was full of love for him. 'You want this to be our first row as a married couple?'

'No, but . . .'

'But nothing.'

Sadie snorted in her sleep.

Pixie took Bob's large hand and again laid it over the child in her belly. 'There, feel your son.'

Gladys peered at herself in the bathroom mirror. 'You look like an old tart,' she told herself, rubbing away a splodge of mascara that had appeared beneath her eye. She dabbed at her neck with Evening in Paris, then stood on tiptoe and examined her figure. 'A bit on the plump side, but you'll do,' she said to herself.

The bathroom was clean, as was the bedroom, with its Utility furniture. Through the open bathroom window she could hear the sea. It would be nice walking on the shingle and sand tomorrow. She'd always had a soft spot for Littlehampton. Once, a long time ago, she'd spent a few days here with an American sailor. She remembered how smart he had looked in his white clothes and how everyone turned to stare when they walked down the promenade. Now Americans were everywhere. She wished she was younger and had it all to come. She glanced at her frilly cami-knickers thrown over the bathroom chair and smiled. She thought of them as American knickers – one Yank and they were off!

She giggled. There was life in the old girl yet!

It had been nice today, the wedding of her daughter at Fareham Register Office, then the do at Sloane Stanley Hall. Her Pixie was going to be looked after. Bob was a lovely man, and she was lucky to be able to share happiness with them and her little granddaughter Sadie, who was the apple of her eye. Bob said Sadie was the spitting image of Gladys. That sometimes happened, didn't it?

Children missed a generation and had all the attributes of their grandparents. She was lucky to have got time off from the factory for the next few days. The workers at Priddy's were doing twelve-hour shifts now. She was glad Pixie was out of it for good. She'd been in such a state when she was pregnant with Sadie, yellow skin, sores and swollen feet. Gladys picked up her lipstick and carefully outlined her lips. Better look nice for Siddy. Small crevices lined her mouth and she hated it when the lipstick bled into them.

'Gladys!' Siddy's voice cut into her thoughts. Who'd have thought she'd end up with him? He was a bit like a stick insect, with his skinny arms and bony knees, but he knew a trick or two, did Siddy. As well as the house she lived in, he owned another near Brockhurst. He had a nice little car, an Austin Seven Pearl that he'd bought secondhand and a few quid in the bank that he was willing to splash out on presents for her. She could do a lot worse. And he made her laugh. Some of the men she'd been with had made her cry.

'Just coming, Siddy. I hope you're ready for what I've got for you.'

Lizzie lay in bed at his house watching Blackie as he slept. She thought he looked like a handsome black-haired devil. But she'd got him, she thought. A thrill went through her, as she remembered their lovemaking. He was everything she'd thought he'd be and more. What was it he'd said, 'A secretary? In Priddy's? You must be pretty brainy to be in that exalted position.' At first she'd thought he was teasing her. But he'd meant it. Mind you, Rita was nothing but a common factory worker. Then she'd shown him just how clever she was, explaining about Priddy's being one of the main suppliers of ammunition, mines, rockets and shells, and that it wasn't just Priddy's but Bedenham and Frater, two other depots nearby, that were working flat out.

She felt proud explaining about the four different types of munitions factories, those producing metal casings for bombs, tanks, rifles and guns. She remembered how he'd listened to her with interest, not like some men who only pretended to pay attention. Then she explained about those factories making various types of explosives, those producing casings for bullets, which were called small-arms factories, and ones like the Gosport site, which was a filling depot and the most dangerous of all the factories, working with combustible materials.

She felt a bit guilty telling him about the new twelve-thousand-pound bombs the RAF had just begun showering Germany with. But then, they were both on the same side, weren't they? Blackie had asked if there was any truth in the rumours about the bigger engines being fitted to Spitfires. He said he had a friend who flew one.

Lizzie didn't know but she said she'd find out. She could see he was really worried about his mate.

He'd given her a bracelet. She looked at it in the darkness. It twinkled like little stars. Tiny delicate jewels in a gold setting. Lizzie wondered if it had originally been meant for Rita. Well, it was hers now, wasn't it?

She thought about Rita. She'd watched her disappear from the hall, as if she had something on her mind. When Blackie went looking for her, Lizzie said Rita had complained of a headache and wanted an early night after all the work she'd put in to make the do a success. Then she'd hung on Blackie's arm and got him to waltz with her again, pushing her body close to his so there was no mistaking what she was offering.

Lizzie had had to use all her courage to flirt with Blackie. She'd kept thinking of the smell of cigars and that brute's fumbling hands. But she told herself that if she wanted this dark-haired man and all he could offer her, she had to prove she could be better than Rita in every way. Being so like Rita in looks and build meant she was Blackie's type, so the rest was up to her. Poor man, he hadn't stood a chance.

Lizzie didn't feel bad about taking Rita's man. Why should she?

A beast of a man on a bomb site had taken her body for nothing. At least now she was getting paid for it.

Chapter Eight

Marlene hoisted the canvas top sheet over the middle bar of the stall, then pegged the sides. Bob had sawn a few inches off the main struts so that it was easier for her to handle the frame on her own. It looked like rain today, and a few of the stallholders hadn't turned up. Gosport market was a popular venue, and as she pulled the old sheets straight over the tables she expected to be busy, as long as the rain held off. Trouble was, she was keeping an eye on both stalls today as Bob had gone to a sale at Southampton. He'd said he was looking for something special. He wouldn't tell her what it was. His second stall was down near the ferry and he had Alan, a tall lanky lad, looking after it. Bob was doing well. So was she. And it was all down to him that she had beautiful Victorian jewellery on offer today.

'That's nice.' Marie from the baby stall next to Marlene's picked up a mourning brooch.

'Real hair, Marie.'

Her mate put it down hastily. 'Ugh!'

'You might not like it but it'll be gone by dinnertime.' Marlene slipped a rubber band around her fiery hair, pulling it back from her face, and laughed at the distaste on Marie's face.

'You doing all right, girl?' Marie asked, shrugging herself into another coat. She already had one on, but Marlene knew it was going to get colder before it got warmer.

'Bob lent me some money to get this little lot. I didn't have enough to bid for it at the auction. I'd already spent up on that lot.' She pointed to some antique rings. 'They were too good to miss.'

'He's over the moon about the baby, ain't he?'

Marlene nodded. Then she tied her money belt around her in time to sell a customer a saucepan from Bob's stock.

When she came back, she said to Marie, 'Remember that bloke I was with at the Sloane Stanley Hall?'

'How could I miss him? Blond and tall – where did you get him from? You never go out with blokes.'

'I'm making an exception for this one. I met him at an auction end of last year. His name's Samuel Golden. He's a bit of a toff, really. Got a finger in a lot of pies.

Well, I was with Bob at another auction at Wickham and he turns up again. Bob invites him to the wedding do and . . .' Marlene knew she was blushing '. . . he's asked me out.'

'You fill your boots, love. He's a looker, I'll give you that.'

Marie disappeared to show a heavily pregnant woman the intricacies of the hood on a Royale pram. Marlene knew she would have it. You couldn't buy a good brand-new pram – they were like gold dust – but that blue and white one was unmarked and reasonably priced.

A woman approached, wearing a black armband. She looked at the gold brooch lying on black velvet inside Marlene's showcase.

'You could remove the hair that's inside it and replace it with some of your loved one's, if you like.' Marlene opened the case, took out the brooch and handed it to the young woman.

'I have some of his first haircut,' she said.

'How old was he when he . . .' Marlene faltered.

'Five. Last week. He was caught in that bombing . . .'

Marlene said, 'You can have it for half the price on the tag.' She would still make a profit, a much smaller one, but her heart was bleeding. What if it had been her little Jeannie?

Marie came back, pocketing the money for the pram. 'You sold it, then?'

'Yes,' said Marlene, wiping the tear from her eye. 'I sold it.'

Blackie drove through the country lanes to Newbold on Stour. He frowned as he glanced at the trees and bushes with their little green buds, promising spring. A bit of dry weather and warmth would do everyone good, he thought.

Rita seemed to be avoiding him. He'd sent her a single red rose that had cost the earth, asking if her headache was better and telling her he missed her. She hadn't replied. Not a thank-you in sight.

There was no reason for her to have found out about him and that stupid Lizzie. In fact, it might be as well if he confessed, then asked for her forgiveness: women liked that. Believing they were so special that they needed to forgive wrongdoers. Lizzie was a good fuck but about as intelligent as a teaspoon. Lizzie Loudmouth! Yeah, that was a good name for her. But it was to his advantage. He smiled to himself as he tapped his fingers on the steering-wheel.

Gosport was a bloody building site. He'd crept down and had a gander at the many centres of activity at Elson shore. There was beach hardening, with nearly two thousand men working day and night to cover the stones and shingle with cement. And concrete sections, like giant bars of murky chocolate, were being laid along the shoreline. Beach Street and Stokes Bay were chock-full of armoured vehicles and lorries, and he'd been lucky not to be stopped while he was creeping about: many of the people who lived in those areas needed passes to get in and out of their own homes now. Working at night required arc lights, and only last week three men had been killed during construction of a watertight chamber when it toppled. There was obviously a great deal of underwater work going on. Funny, he thought. People could keep secrets but a bit of money, a packet of fags, or a couple of bags of groceries and a sweet voice soon loosened tongues.

The work going on in the Solent now required small boats called SLUGS – it meant Surf Landing Under Girders – and they'd been specially designed to keep concrete sections in place in the water. If only he could find out what it was all about, he'd definitely go up in his boss's estimation. But the air of secrecy that hung over Gosport was like a heavy shroud that couldn't be pierced.

Lizzie was a godsend. Working in the office, she had access to papers the girls on the workshop floor didn't. He'd keep her on a string.

He missed Rita. Never thought he'd care about the girl but he did. He bloody did.

He'd go to the secret meeting at the twelfth-century building in Ettington Park at Newbold, then get the hell out of the place. It gave him the creeps, with its huge turrets and cold stone rooms. He wouldn't mind betting that when some of the poor buggers, the prisoners of war who now inhabited the place, had got there, they were scared stiff. Good reason to be. There were supposed to be ghosts roving around.

German prisoners were increasing in numbers and it was said they ate better than some of the poor English bastards left homeless after the bombings. No wonder the English hated them. That and the fact they were trying to kill us, of course. But there was always money to be made out of war. No matter which side you were on.

Rita knew nothing of his 'other' life. And why should she? He'd been priming her for ages with gifts and holidays. He needed to know more about the work going on at the armaments factory. The more he found out, the more he was paid for the information. Maybe he'd see

Rita when he got back, find out why she was so off with him. But in the meantime Lizzie would be very useful, the silly cow.

'Get out of my room!' Pixie tried to warn Bob away from the small bedroom where she had papers all over the floor, on the bed and the top of the chest of drawers. But the heavy box in his arms couldn't help but take her attention. 'What's that?'

He tried to step over the threshold, a deep belly laugh issuing from him. 'Aha! You want my gift but you don't want me?'

She eyed him, then the box, suspiciously. 'All right, you can come in.'

His smile stretched from ear to ear. She was enormously big with child and too tired to argue. 'Don't stare at my papers,' she commanded. 'Don't you dare!'

He put the box on the small table where she'd been sitting on a chair, writing. He smelled of sweat and she adored him. The muscles rippled in his arms as he tore away the cardboard.

Pixie held her breath. Then she was jumping up and down as much as her huge belly would allow.

'Steady on, woman. It's not quite time yet for the baby, and you'll do yourself damage!'

The typewriter sat in all its glory, metal keys and black reel-threaded ribbon.

Pixie threw her arms around his neck. 'Thank you, thank you, thank you!'

Bob disentangled himself, looking as pleased as Punch. 'Can you work it?'

'Work it? You "use" a typewriter, you don't work it,' she told him.

'Can you use it?'

She looked at him, her head on one side, like an inquisitive sparrow's. 'No!'

There was silence. She laughed. 'Ask me again next week and I'll say, "Yes."'

He pulled right away from her and said, 'However did I get lucky enough to have a wonderful wife like you?'

There was another silence. 'I love you,' Pixie said. Then she pointed to all the papers littering the room. 'You knew I was writing notebooks but you didn't know what they were for, right?'

Bob nodded. 'Is it a story?'

'Not really. It's a record of the war through my eyes, just an ordinary woman and the effect on her. Me,' she added. 'To be able to type it all up will be the most wonderful thing. Will you be cross if I get on with it?'

'Cross? I'll be even more proud of you,' he said. He

ran a hand through his dark hair. 'Pixie, you never fail to amaze me.'

Rita topped up the powder in the shell case, tamped it down, then hung it on the hook and watched it move on to the next stage of its journey to completion. The wireless was playing dance music that made her feel happy. The girls around her were chatting and she was glad to be back at work. The days at home had been brightened only by Em's presence and had worn her down. Of course Blackie had called round.

He'd looked surprised when Em had answered the door, so Em had said, after she'd told him Rita wasn't at home. He'd left a single red rose that Rita had put in the dustbin. Em had sneaked it out and taken it home. Secretly Rita was pleased she'd done that, because it wasn't the rose's fault.

Her secret about the abortion, as far as she knew, hadn't leaked. The bleeding had taken a long time to stop and she'd felt ill, in pain, and close to tears. It wasn't the pain in her body, she could bear that. It was the pain in her heart and the memory of her actions.

Most people reckoned she'd had to deal with a particularly bad hangover. Too much gin at the Sloane Stanley Hall. Em had spread that gossip about, bless her.

'We've got a surprise at break-time.' Em was at her side, her clipboard in her hand. She looked all smiley. 'Did you see the new tea wagon in the yard?'

'I did wonder what that thing was.' Rita, like the other girls, was suspicious of new stuff arriving at Priddy's: it usually meant more work for them all. 'About time. I hope they make it good and strong. It'll be nice not to have to bring in a flask, as long as their prices are okay.'

'A couple called Rene and Mick are running it. Going to do the best they can with sandwiches too.' She peered at her. 'You feel all right?'

Rita nodded. '*He* came round the house again last night.'

Em turned: she'd been in the process of moving on down the benches, checking that the workers weren't slacking. 'What did he want?'

Rita was glad she didn't have to go through the palaver of explaining things to Em. Sometimes, thought Rita, Em was like a mother to her, but a mother she could pour her heart out to, unlike her real mother whom she hardly ever saw nowadays. She thought back to the previous evening. 'Gladys let him in, the daft cow. But she adores him, so it was only to be expected.'

He'd walked through to the kitchen where she was

rubbing her hair dry in front of the range. Gladys had left them alone and gone upstairs.

'I suppose you've heard I made a mistake, Rita,' he'd said. She'd stared into his dark eyes. 'I never promised to be faithful but it was a one-off. I do miss you.'

It was funny but she'd believed him.

'You and me, we've been seeing each other a while now. We understand each other, don't we?' He changed his position, moving his chair so he was closer to her than she wanted. She could smell the familiar scent of his cologne and his maleness. She stepped back and wrapped the towel tighter around her head, turban-style.

'We can still have fun. Lizzie means nothing to me.'

'You don't get it, do you?' she'd said. 'Us splitting up would have happened anyway. I feel bad now about taking gifts of food and other stuff that people can't get. It's like they're willing to put up with the shortages for the sake of saving the country and I'm laughing at them for it. It's not a good feeling any more, Blackie.'

His forehead had creased to a frown. 'Then stay with me but don't accept my gifts.'

'But you'll still be making money from other people's misfortunes.'

He stared at her. 'It's how livings are made, Rita. You'll be giving up a lifestyle.'

She nodded. 'But there's a war on and people are going without and even dying for what they believe is right. I can't shut my conscience in a box for the sake of pretty clothes. That's being shallow, and I firmly believe we're going to win this war by forgoing luxuries to help our boys fight against the Germans. Yes, you're right – I'll be giving up a lifestyle. But a lifestyle isn't a life.'

He was very quiet, then sighed. 'That was a long speech, Rita. But don't you think the German people are thinking the same thing? I don't think it matters who wins as long as individuals make money from the war.'

She couldn't believe her ears. 'Of course it matters! We don't want to be under German rule. England must be free!'

'Does it matter who rules if you have the money to do what you want?'

She was getting angry now and knew that what she was saying was *right*. 'Of course it matters. It's people like you who ignore the rules that will bring this country to its knees and I don't want any part in that.'

'If that's what you think of me, then I have no alternative but to go.'

He had been moving towards the door as Gladys came in. She'd brushed her hair and put on some lipstick, all for Blackie's benefit.

Blackie, angry, had pushed past her and walked swiftly down the passage. The door had slammed after him.

Gladys was staring at her open-mouthed, disapproving.

'Don't you start on me,' said Rita. She ran past her and up the stairs, banging the door of her room. She threw herself onto the bed and cried. She cried for the baby she'd torn away from herself, because at another time, in another place, she'd have cherished that little one. She cried because, despite all her friends, she was locked into a well of loneliness. She cried because she was being selfish, only thinking about herself. But most of all she cried for the baby she would never hold in her arms.

She'd heard Blackie's car starting up and known it was all over.

Em brought her back to the present, to Priddy's, to the music blaring in the hope it helped them all work faster. 'Are you sure it's what you want? Giving up Blackie like that?' Her friend was staring hard at her.

'Em, I'm working in this crappy factory, like the rest of us, to win a war. Blackie as good as told me that money is his god and he couldn't care less where it came from. All the feelings I ever had for that man died in that moment, Em. If your Lizzie wants him, she's welcome.'

Just then the buzzer went and Em walked away. The belt slowed and stopped but the music went on.

'Coming for tea?' Gladys slipped her arm through Rita's. 'Shall we see what the wagon's got to eat today?' Rita looked at her smiling face. Earlier she'd done nothing but talk about how kind and considerate Siddy had been on their Littlehampton trip. Rita was still amazed that so much had happened while Gladys had been away, yet she'd guessed nothing. She wanted to keep it that way.

'Yes,' said Rita, 'Let's see if the tea's strong enough to keep our spirits up.'

Chapter Nine

'Look at this, Rita.' Gladys passed the *Evening News* to her. The piece she was pointing at said, 'Guard Hangs Himself After Questioning'. 'Ain't that Ettington, the place where you said Blackie goes?'

Rita put down the blouse she was altering and began reading the article that told of a prisoner-of-war-camp guard who had been questioned by the police about the discovery of a radio set hidden in the attic of the room he slept in. One of the other guards, a Pole, had heard him using it and tried to blackmail him. The Polish guard said the man was particularly interested in the south coast munitions factories. The radio set had obviously been confiscated, but before the guard could be questioned further he'd hanged himself from a beam in his room. Further enquiries were being made.

'I don't know if it was Ettington, but it was definitely

Newbold on Stour,' said Rita. 'I wasn't aware Blackie ever went to the camp there. He told me Ettington was a huge old-fashioned house where there were supposed to be ghosts.'

'Well,' said Gladys, 'there'll be another ghost there now. He must have been a spy or something, I reckon. Why else would he hang himself over a blinkin' radio?'

Rita handed her back the paper. She thought of Blackie and his trips to 'do business', while she shopped in Stratford. But Blackie was more interested in buying nylons and watches for a quick profit. She thought back to their argument. Yes, money was definitely his god.

The rain was lashing against the windows. Rita hoped there wouldn't be a raid tonight: it would be awful to have to go out in that downpour. There was always so much to take with them for a stay in the shelters. Often they went in their nightclothes, like everyone else, with coats slung over them for warmth, and carried a flask of tea, a bag containing their identity papers and ration books, a book to read, perhaps, and their gas masks. To make their stay as comfortable as possible they had to take bedding, too, for the long nights.

Gladys put down the paper and picked up her knitting. She wasn't very good at it and the white wool was grey where she'd had to unpick.

'Haven't you finished those baby mittens yet?' She was making them for Pixie's baby. 'They'll need a wash before you give them to her.' Rita gazed at the tiny things. It brought an ache to her heart that her friend wasn't knitting them for her. Pixie had been upset when Rita had told her about the abortion: she should have been more careful in the first place. It was all right for her, Rita had thought. She had Bob and he was so different from Blackie: he was a steady man, husband material. Pixie could carry her baby knowing that when it was born she wouldn't have to worry about it being loved and cared for. Rita's baby hadn't stood a chance. She'd killed it because she cared and had almost lost her own life doing so.

The wireless was playing dance music and both women were sitting in front of the range. Gladys's legs were getting quite mottled by the heat. 'Bugger,' she said. 'I've dropped a stitch.'

'Better than droppin' your knickers,' said Rita. 'Oh, I forgot, you done that at Littlehampton!'

Gladys pretended to ignore her. Then, 'That reminds me,' she said. 'I bumped into one of your mates in Littlehampton high street. She was down there visiting her mother. Remember that nurse you got on so well with from the Queen Victoria Hospital at East Grinstead?'

'They were a lovely bunch but Edna, the little dark-haired nurse, used to come out with us when we went up the pub in the village . . .'

'That's the girl,' said Gladys. 'Well, she told me that American lad you went off with one night when you was recovering from that scarring is back. He's badly burned. She asked if you might go and see him. He's here and his family's in America. Can't be very nice for him in there, not having visitors—'

'Joe! His name was Joe. He was the first bloke I slept with after this,' Rita pulled back her hair to show the near-invisible scar. 'He made me feel like a proper woman again.' She went quiet as she remembered how she'd lost all her confidence and felt that no one could see her, only her scarred face. 'Yes, I'd like to go and see him.'

'Edna said go anytime during visiting hours. He never gets many visitors as his mates are still at the front. But you've got to see her first. She stressed that.' Gladys looked at her knitting. 'Pixie'll have had ten kids by the time I've finished these.'

Gladys was concentrating hard on her stitches, the needles clacking away, and every so often the fire would crackle in the grate. Rita thought about the red-haired young man. He was a couple of years younger than her, nice-looking, tall, and had so many freckles there was hardly room for a pinhead between them.

Their first meeting had been heated because Joe had been shy and didn't know how to talk to her. Her inflamed facial scar had taken away her usual boldness in talking to men and she'd accused him of feeling sorry for her. Later that night she realized she had been too involved with her own feelings to understand how *he* felt, being in a strange country, away from home for the first time and liable to get killed.

As the evening drew on the two of them had overcome their shyness, and later, when he'd made love to her, he'd unwittingly made her whole again. Her confidence regained, she'd written to him, answering every letter he wrote to her. But the letters had stopped and Rita had thought he must have died. Since she wasn't a relative, she wouldn't be informed of his death. But she'd missed hearing from him.

'It'll be lovely to see Joe again,' Rita said. 'And Edna. Shall I make a cuppa?'

Marlene entered the hall, bought a programme and picked up a paddle with a number on it. She scanned the rows of seats in case he had already arrived, then chose a chair near the back. Sitting at the rear of the hall enabled her to get a good look at the bidders.

She had on her new wide-legged trousers, a pink jumper and a jacket that was almost the same brown as her trousers. Marlene shook back her mane of red hair, put a newspaper on her chair, then went and looked at the goods to be auctioned.

The air smelled of tea, toasted buns and cigarette smoke. She picked up a Clarice Cliff honey pot. There were no chips. At the end of the first table there was a shoebox full of broken jewellery. Mostly rubbish. She poked around and found what she was looking for: a gold chain wrapped around some glass beads. She put down the beads and saw, at the side of the box, a marcasite brooch. It looked as if it had been burned in a fire. As did the jet and gold earring practically hidden in another tangle of beads. Lying at the bottom of the cardboard box was its twin. She reckoned the jet was Whitby, the earrings Victorian.

Marlene used her pencil and marked her programme. She'd bid on that. She didn't intend to pay much for it, though. She was only interested in the gold and the brooch; the beads she'd give to her daughter to play with.

'They're pretty.'

Marlene recognized the voice immediately, but she was studying a boxed set of matching necklace, bangle and a couple of gold dress rings. She would bid on it as well. She marked her card before turning to Samuel Golden. 'As long as nobody offers silly money,' she said. 'I've set myself a limit.'

'Haven't we all?' he said. His dull yellow hair was darkened by Brylcreem and combed back off his square-jawed face. 'I enjoyed the wedding reception the other week.' He gazed into her eyes, making her feel as though she was the only person in the room. 'Good company, too,' he added.

Marlene hadn't been out with a man since her daughter Jeannie's birth, when she herself had been barely more than a child. She worked hard and was happy to be able to provide for herself, her child and her mother, who looked after Jeannie while Marlene toiled at the market. She'd started off by working for Bob, until she'd made enough money to begin buying and selling jewellery, which had been her aim all along.

'Thank you,' she murmured. She looked up into his smiling face. His trilby was pushed to one side and his overcoat was wet. 'Has it started raining?'

'Only just,' he said. 'How did you get here?'

'Lee-on-the-Solent isn't far from where I live,' she said. She didn't want to tell him she'd come by bus. But she wasn't going to buy anything heavy so she didn't need a lift. But she'd like to be taken home by Samuel.

As though reading her thoughts, he said, 'I'll give you a lift home.'

She smiled at him as a box of antique brooches caught her eye.

'I think they'll go for a princely sum. I've seen several buyers marking their cards for those beauties,' Samuel whispered.

Marlene's heart sank. The brooches wouldn't be within her budget, especially if she was lucky enough to get the other stuff. 'What are you after?'

Samuel shook his head. 'Nothing. I came because I was certain you'd be here.'

Marlene's heart fluttered. He really was a nice man and his upper-class accent showed he had breeding. She was definitely looking forward to the lift home.

They walked back through the throng of people towards her seat and Sam took the empty chair next to her. He stood up again, excused himself to the people sitting down and presently returned with two mugs of tea, hot and steaming. 'No sugar, I'm afraid. They've run out. I wanted to buy you a cheese and onion sandwich but the man in front of me took the last three.'

Marlene accepted the tea gratefully. 'Let me pay you.'

'Don't be silly,' he said. 'It's only a cup of tea.'

The hall was full now, smelly with wet coats, warm bodies and the musty stink of old furniture. People were waiting for the auction to start.

An hour later, Marlene raised her paddle on the box of oddments and bought it for five shillings. She had two pounds left. The gold bangle, necklace and rings went to her for the remainder of her money. 'That's me done,' she said.

Furniture, bedding, bicycles and garden tools were next. This was the part Marlene hated, waiting until the end of the auction to settle up for the goods. But it was the rule: no money to change hands until the last lot had been auctioned.

The box of brooches came next. The auctioneer gave his spiel and the bidding started. Slow at first, then gaining momentum, but still a bargain lot. Sold separately, the pretty jewellery would have made her a nice profit.

'Three pounds anywhere?'

Samuel took her paddle and raised it. Marlene was shocked. She opened her mouth to protest but Sam shushed her.

'Any more bids?' The auctioneer was looking straight at her.

'I don't have the money,' Marlene hissed out of the side of her mouth at Samuel. She felt terrible – how could she explain to the auctioneer that she had no money to pay for the brooches?

'Allow me to give it to you.'

Marlene was speechless.

Just then the auctioneer banged down his gavel on the table. 'Sold to the woman with the glorious hair!'

'I'll pay you back.' She didn't know whether she was angry or pleased.

'If that's what you want. But it's a pleasure to bankroll you.'

Marlene couldn't be angry with him. He'd done it for her. 'Thank you,' she whispered.

'Will you come to the pub with me afterwards?'

'All right,' she said. She didn't need to worry about Beth and Jeannie: they'd both be in bed long before she got home. Maybe this time she and Samuel might be able to talk to each other. At Pixie's wedding there'd been too much noise to hear themselves speak.

Marlene thought back to that night. When she'd announced she had to get home because a neighbour was babysitting Jeannie, he'd walked her back and kissed her chastely on the hand before leaving her at the front door.

Maybe this man could be trusted.

*

'They've put a list of the people buried in the rubble of that cinema in Portsmouth that got bombed while *Sweet Rosie O'Grady* was showing.'

'That the picture with Betty Grable in it?' Rita turned to Em for an answer. 'And how do they know who's died?' She shivered. There was a weak sun and daffodils were pushing their heads above the soil, but the wind off the sea was cutting through her.

'I expect they've got wallets and handbags and identity cards and now they need to find relatives.' Em straightened out the *Evening News* on top of the low wall and went on scanning the names.

Rita was cold. 'I don't know why I let you talk me into coming outside. I'm frozen.'

Just then the train trundled round on the track and two men in the front called out to them. 'Get stuffed,' shouted Rita, then tossed her head and turned back to Em. 'The blokes that work here are nothing but animals.'

'Oh, God!'

Rita stared at her. 'What's up?'

'I think you'd better read this.' Em pointed at the paper.

'Oh!'

Rita went very quiet.

'Drink this.' Em pushed towards her the mug of tea she was drinking but Rita shook her head.

'Never thought my mum would end up in the rubble of the Classic,' she said. 'At least she was with the bloke she loved more than me.' She turned to Em and buried her face in her friend's overalls, sobbing bitterly.

'You cry, my love,' Em said, stroking and patting Rita's back. 'There's a phone number to ring. They need relatives to claim bodies.'

'No,' mumbled Rita, coming up for air.

'Yes,' said Em. 'I'll be with you.'

'She let that beast come into my bedroom, Em.' Rita wiped her eyes. 'I'll never forgive her for that.'

'No, love. You'll never forget what happened but you must forgive her. What goes around comes around. Your mum's paid the ultimate price. If we can, we'll give her a good send-off. It's the right thing to do. Do you have any other relatives we should tell?'

'I don't even know any of her mates as she'd lost touch with them when she took up with Malcolm.' Even saying his name made her shudder. 'Pixie knew her but I'd not ask her to a funeral, not now she's so close to giving birth.'

Em smiled. 'We don't want her having her littl'un in a graveyard!'

Rita wiped her eyes, picked up the newspaper and smoothed it out. 'I'd better phone this number, hadn't I?'

Em nodded. 'Look, I've got some other news to tell you and I don't want you getting even more upset.'

Rita folded the newspaper into a square with the phone number uppermost. She knew Em was going to talk about Blackie.

'He's taking Lizzie away for the weekend. You know how mad about dancing she is. I didn't want you to find out from someone else.'

Rita sighed. 'I suppose he came to the house loaded with goodies for you, to win you over?' She had no quarrel with Em, or Lizzie for that matter. Hadn't she turned Blackie away? All the same, she felt peeved and left out.

Em looked guilty. 'I'm not going to say I refused him. I haven't had tinned peaches in ages.'

'It's all right, love. I just feel differently about him now.' Rita put her arm around Em's shoulders. 'Don't worry about your Lizzie. I'm sure he'll treat her right.' She took Em's tea, which was still warm, and drank it gratefully. Funny how a cup of tea always makes you feel better, she thought.

The buzzer sounded, piercing the air with its shrill tone, and the girls began to drift towards the huts again. Em and Rita gathered up their belongings and Em slid her arm through Rita's. 'I'm sorry you and your mum never got a chance to sort out your differences. But I'm always here for you.'

Rita remembered how Em had pulled her through the abortion and stayed with her, saving her life. 'I know,' she said. 'And I love you for it. Em, you're the best friend anyone could ever have.'

'You're very cheerful today, Marlene.'

Bob's voice cut into her thoughts. She was singing along to Vera Lynn's 'We'll Meet Again', which was coming from a wireless through the open window of a top-floor flat.

'Samuel's taking me to a little fishing village in Cornwall for the weekend. Mum said she'd willingly look after Jeannie. She likes him.'

'More'n I do,' he grumbled quietly.

'Oh, and why's that?'

'Dunno, Marlene. There's just something about the bloke.'

'But you didn't mind him going to your wedding do?'

'An invitation to help fill a hall doesn't mean I have to like him!' He was standing on the pavement holding a mug of tea for warmth. His face was grim.

It was early morning and she'd spent a long time arranging her jewellery in the velvet-lined boxes. The gold bits and pieces had sold well. She'd already put by the money she'd borrowed from Samuel and was well on the way to making a profit, even after paying pitch fees. She shivered. She was well wrapped up against the cold but already her feet were numb.

'All I'm saying is be careful.'

She wasn't going to listen to Bob's voice of doom. Samuel had shown her a photo of the house they'd be staying in. It was near the beach, and the countryside looked lovely. Her thoughts went to the green jumper she'd spotted on Harry's stall. It would suit her to a T.

But first she was off to Southampton. Samuel was picking her up and they were going to an auction at the Polygon. He'd already told her that if she needed to buy stuff and didn't have enough ready cash, he'd lend it to her. He said he wanted her to make a success of her business.

She was fast becoming a woman of substance. And it was all because she'd met a man who was willing to give instead of take. Yes, she was definitely looking forward to going away with him for the weekend.

Chapter Ten

Marlene couldn't believe her eyes. The waves bounded up to the shore, shifting the small stones and sand, then rushed back again to join the sea, leaving curls of foamy water in their wake. 'It's like Stokes Bay but different,' she said. 'There's no sand at the bay.' Behind her there were tall cliffs with wooden stairs to the top. They'd climbed down them to walk on the perfect beach. She felt as though she was standing in an old-fashioned seascape painting.

The cold wind ruffled her hair and she pushed it back behind her ear. Looking up, she could see the sun glinting on the windows of the car that had brought them to Cornwall. She'd thought they would come by train but Samuel had told her not to worry, petrol wasn't a problem.

It seemed to Marlene that money wasn't a problem either.

'Do you like the place we're staying?' His hand brushed

against the back of her neck, making her body tingle and her heart flutter.

She turned to face him. His coat collar was turned up and he looked very smart in his dark suit and polished shoes. 'I love it. Despite you showing me pictures, I never imagined the cottage to be like it is. It's clean, comfortable, with the most gorgeous rooms, and Mrs Edwards seems a nice lady.'

She thought of the homely soul who had made them tea when they arrived, then given them a key so they could come and go as they pleased. Breakfast would be on the table at nine, she'd promised. Marlene had a feeling that Samuel had been there before because he knew his way around the area and the cottage. Marlene was too excited to ask questions and break the thrall of happiness that enclosed the two of them. 'You must let me pay something towards this holiday,' she said.

'Don't be silly. It's my treat.'

The previous evening at the auction he had made her bid on jewellery she couldn't really afford. He'd settled her bill, saying, 'You pay me back any time. I want you to make money, not worry that you didn't bid on something that would make a decent profit because you didn't have the cash.' Now she couldn't believe that he was prepared to pay for everything.

'What are you thinking?' His voice was almost whisked away with the wind.

'You told me you had a building firm. Can they manage while you're away?' It seemed he could take time off from work whenever he wanted, unlike Bob, who worked all the hours God gave.

He laughed. 'I don't *work* on the building site. I have men who do that. Same with my stalls at the markets. I'm the money behind them. I don't get my hands dirty.'

She almost said, 'Not like me,' but bit it back. After all, the more gold she bought, the more she had to sell. And things were really looking up at last. So much so that she'd persuaded her mother to give up one of the cleaning jobs that had kept them in food. Now, happily, Marlene was able to look after her mother and her child *and* put some money away.

She smiled at Samuel. Fancy him being interested in a woman like her! A good-looking bloke like him could have his pick. He had nice manners as well. He hadn't made a grab at her body, like some men would. He'd kissed her a couple of times. Kisses that had left her wanting more.

Tonight she wanted him, there was no doubt about that. And the bedroom back at the cottage had a double bed.

Samuel had whispered, 'I don't want to put any

pressure on you. I want to hold you in my arms, make you feel safe.' She knew she couldn't lie in his arms all night long without desperately wanting him to touch her, to explore her body. He wasn't going to rush her: he wanted her to know he respected her.

She wondered why Bob didn't like him. It was probably a male thing, she thought. After all they were very different. Bob was rough and ready, good-looking in a tall, dark and handsome way. But Samuel was more like Leslie Howard, who had played Ashley Wilkes in *Gone with the Wind*.

'I do sail close to the wind sometimes,' he said.

Marlene watched a fishing boat braving the angry sea. 'How do you mean?'

'I like taking chances. Mostly it comes out well. Sometimes I lose money . . .' he put out a hand and touched her cheek '. . . but usually I win.'

Marlene shivered.

'C'mon, let's get back,' Samuel said. 'I can see you're cold. Mrs Edwards said there was a stew in the oven for when we returned. Or we can go to a pub, if you'd like.'

'I'd really rather go back to the cottage,' she said. She knew she was blushing as she added, 'I think I'd like an early night.'

*

'If you want any more bacon there's just a couple of rashers left,' said Mrs Edwards.

Marlene was in heaven. It had been years since she'd been offered more bacon! Though she could have eaten more, she declined. She didn't want to appear a glutton after putting away such an appetizing breakfast.

Samuel squeezed her knee. Marlene felt herself blush, remembering their lovemaking last night. He was a man, not a bumbling youth like the one who had made her pregnant the first time she'd been touched. Now at last she knew what it was like to be truly loved. She smiled at him as though sharing a secret. He returned that smile.

His white shirt was crisp and his dark suit trousers were freshly pressed. He'd put them in the room's trouser press overnight. His jacket hung over the back of his chair, its shoulder pads precisely aligned. Marlene had on the new jumper she'd bought especially for the weekend from the market and her heather-mix wool suit with its box pleats, the colours complementing her red hair. She'd spent ages brushing it and it shone like spun gold.

'Was last night all right?' he whispered, as Mrs Edwards left the room.

'Like a dream,' she answered, blushing. She remembered how considerate he'd been and how afterwards they'd slept spooned together.

Marlene, despite initiating the lovemaking, had suddenly succumbed to shyness. But he'd taken over and when she'd woken that morning, with the sun streaming through the windows and the birds singing their hearts out, she'd felt just like Scarlett O'Hara after Rhett Butler had taken her to bed.

'I thought we'd drive to Bodmin Moor. Ever been?' he asked. His eyes were twinkling.

Marlene shook her head and set down the china teacup.

'Go and get ready and we'll be off.'

She didn't need telling twice. Back upstairs in the bedroom she put on lipstick while listening to the murmur of voices below. This weekend was turning out to be the most wonderful time of her life, apart from the birth of her little girl, of course. She hadn't even had to wash up!

It was still cold, though bright and sunny. Spring was well on its way here in Cornwall: she'd seen daffodils in bud and the air smelled fresh.

They chatted and laughed as he drove down twisting country lanes with hedges either side. Eventually, after they'd passed through many tiny villages, he came to a place called Minions.

'That takes my breath away,' she said, as Samuel stopped the car and she got out. She stretched, then stood looking at the scene spread before her.

The tall stones were set in a circle, and like nothing Marlene had ever seen before. The scene reminded her of pages in a book of fairy tales. Samuel put his hand in hers and stood close, marvelling with her.

'Is there a story behind them?' she asked.

'Oh, yes.' His voice was like dark chocolate. 'These stones are called the Hurlers. Legend has it they were men playing games on the Sabbath instead of going to church. To teach the villagers a lesson, they were turned to stone for their wickedness.'

'Really?'

'Oh, yes, and see those two over there?' He pointed across the grass. 'They were the musicians who were playing at the time.'

Marlene smiled at him. His public school accent enthralled her but she was also in awe of his knowledge. Again she wondered why he'd chosen her when he could have any woman he wanted. The moor enchanted her. 'I can see why writers and artists come here,' she said. 'All this marshland, and the sky reaching down to the crags and hills, are an inspiration to anyone.'

'No, Marlene,' he said, putting his hand beneath her chin and tipping her face towards him. '*You* are an inspiration. Look how you've built your stall up while managing to put money aside for your daughter's future. You've sacrificed all the things other women take for granted so you can keep your household going and your mother and child fed. That's inspirational.'

'No one's ever said anything like that to me before,' she said quietly. He'd made her heart swell with pride and she felt ten feet tall. She swept away the tear that had threatened to fall. What a lovely man he was. 'I'm so glad I came away with you,' she said. 'I'd forgotten there could be another life besides hard work and this never-ending war.'

He laughed and put his arms around her. 'You deserve the best I can give you. But for now, how about we find a nice little pub and have a spot of lunch, if there's any food and beer going?'

'That sounds perfect to me,' said Marlene, so happy that she would have followed him to the moon had he asked her.

She stood at the graveside. The ceremony was over. There had been only a few mourners.

'Couldn't cry, then?' Em tucked her arm through Rita's.

'Not now. Maybe it'll come later,' she answered.

Despite the cold and her pregnancy, Pixie had turned up. She'd come because of Rita, she'd said, not her mother. Rita was her best friend. Coming to the funeral was a mark of respect and the right thing to do.

'I need a sit-down and a cup of tea,' Pixie said now. Her belly was so huge that her coat buttons wouldn't fasten.

'I'll just say thank you to the minister,' Rita said, 'and leave a tip for the gravediggers. I'll meet you at the bus stop.'

As she walked over the grass Rita thought of her mother as a young woman. She had loved to go dancing, leaving Rita with her grandmother. Not to be left out they'd dance too, her nan and her, jigging around to the big wooden gramophone. Nan knew all the steps and made her laugh. Perhaps that was where Rita's love of dancing had come from.

She and her mother had been close then.

She'd lost her mother when her stepfather, Malcolm, had come on the scene. Rita remembered the noises coming from the bedroom, the giggling, the creak of the bed, the laughter, and her mother ignoring her. Nan had moved out.

Rita was eight when Malcolm had come into her bedroom and lain down beside her. He was in his pyjamas and at first Rita liked him telling her a story about a magic snake that grew when anyone touched it.

Something was wrong, she was sure it was, when he asked her to put her hand into his pyjama bottoms. But he was her new daddy, wasn't he? It must be all right to do as he asked.

Malcolm told her the snake would spit at her, but she mustn't be scared.

And so it went on. When she was eleven he put the snake inside her.

Her mother was never in the house when it happened. Her nan had got old and ill, so Rita spent a great deal of time with her new father while her mother went round to look after Nan.

She finally plucked up the courage to put a chair beneath the bedroom door handle in an effort to stop Malcolm entering her bedroom. One day Rita came home from school to find the chair missing. She felt sick when she thought about Malcolm and the way he touched her. She felt dirty and tried her hardest to keep away from him. She knew that what he'd done and was still trying to do *was* wrong. She told her mother.

There was a huge row that night. Later her mother had come to her room and said, 'You're growing up. You're lying to me because you can see how happy I am with Malcolm. He's told me how you're always looking at him. How you flaunt yourself, walking around the house in your nightdress when I'm not here. Well, it's going to stop. You're to leave the poor man alone and I want no more of your filthy lies.'

The next few years were a nightmare for Rita, with Malcolm trying hard to brush up against her or barge his way into the bathroom when she was in there. It ended when she had found the courage and the money to leave home.

Her childhood had hardened her. Rita knew men only wanted one thing. And that was how she'd ended up with Blackie.

Rita had done her duty by her mother. She'd buried her. She'd listened to the minister as he handed out unwanted advice, and smiled at the two burly men who had dug the grave and were overjoyed at the money she'd placed in their hands.

Her mother was gone. Her baby was gone. Blackie was gone.

Rita had good friends, a home with Gladys and the canary, and a good job. She was a lot luckier than some of the other munitions workers.

The blast at Priddy's had given her a scar on her face and another on her heart. Joe, the young American in the Queen Victoria Hospital at East Grinstead, was alone in England. Sussex wasn't that far away. She *would* visit him.

Chapter Eleven

'So, when are you going to visit Joe?'

Rita scratched her head beneath her turban. 'God, this thing's itchy, Em. Film stars like Rita Hayworth look so glamorous when they wear 'em – I wonder if they have to poke their fingers up the sides every five minutes.'

'I asked you a question.'

Rita looked at the smiling figure of her friend. 'This weekend. I didn't tell you because—' Tears rose and she took a deep breath. She was on the line and it didn't do to get emotional when you were dealing with the lethal powder. One tear wiped away with fingers to which grains of powder clung could cause any number of skin and eye complaints.

'You can tell me.' Em wasn't going to let the subject go.

Rita sent another filled bomb case on its way. 'He didn't want to see me.'

Em stood at Rita's side, her clipboard in her hand, and stared at her.

The wireless was playing a Sinatra song. Women were chatting and the noise of the machinery hammered inside Rita's head. Finally she said, 'After all the letters we'd written before, I thought he'd like to see a friendly face. It's fair upset me that he's said no.'

The work she was doing was mind-numbing and repetitive, but she needed a steady hand and total concentration. If any of the munitions were to leave Priddy's incorrectly assembled, the consequences could be fatal.

Em, after watching her for a few moments, said, 'Don't you remember how you first felt when you found out your face would never be the same again?'

'And don't forget I lost part of my finger!' Rita held up her hand in its glove. Nine and a half fingers seemed to work just as well as ten, though.

'See what I mean? You hardly ever mention your hand. Why? Because you've got used to it. Same as you're used to that scar. Well, he ain't got to that stage yet. All he sees is a shattered man that's no use to anyone.'

'Jesus, you know how to put the boot in, don't you, Em?'

'Am I right or am I right?' Em screwed up her face, then grinned. 'If you want to see him, and you do, go.

Just remember how long it took you to get back into the land of the living.'

Just then the buzzer announced break time and the machinery slowed, then stopped. Rita hung back to wait for Em to check the girls out. Safety rules were posted around the factory walls and anyone breaking them faced dismissal. The utmost safety measures had to be observed at all times, as Rita had experienced to her cost.

At last Em and Rita joined the queue at the tea wagon. It was nice standing in the sunshine, Rita thought. She was watching the train filled with shells trundling around the track and up the side of the shoreline bound for a designated shipping base.

She couldn't believe her eyes.

The iron chain used for holding the shells tightly packed together was trailing on the rails behind the train. Shell cases were wobbling from side to side like demented skittles. The driver, Ken Stoker, a middle-aged man who'd worked at Priddy's since its opening, seemed totally unaware of what was going on behind him. As, so it seemed, were the rest of the people waiting in the tea queue.

'Stop that train,' yelled Rita. She made to run forward but Em grabbed her and held her back.

'The train!' Rita shouted. What happened next seemed

to take place in slow motion. She saw a shell slide from the back, topple and crash to the rails. The explosion caused the driver's body to be flung high in the air from the cab before it disintegrated. A second shell followed the first.

Rita watched, horrified, as two women coming towards the tea queue from near the railway line crumpled to the ground, where they lay bloody and broken. There was a moment of utter silence.

Then all hell was let loose.

'Never thought the tea wagon would save so many lives,' said Em, as she scurried off towards what was left of the rails. They were twisted, rearing up from the track, like the ends of liquorice sticks, smoking and threatening to fall into the deep crater formed by the blast.

Rita stood as though paralysed. Her first impulse had been to run towards the train. Em had saved her life – again – by holding her back, but now Rita ran towards the far end of the yard to see if she could help.

Em appeared at her side. 'Stay!' She pulled her back. 'We'll be in the way. And another bomb could go off at any time.'

Dust was settling everywhere and the huge hole that had formed was steaming. The smell of cordite filled the air, along with the sweeter stench of sizzling flesh.

Amazingly the rest of the train was upright and the remaining shells still secure.

'I reckon the only reason the whole lot hasn't been blown to smithereens is because the train kept moving after the shells rolled,' Em said. She was gripping Rita's arm so hard it hurt.

'Bad luck the vibrations caused Ken to fall and the blast to catch him,' said Rita.

'If the train had been closer this whole yard and its buildings could have gone up,' said Em. 'It's a bloody miracle we're still in one piece.'

The noise of the blast had made Rita's ears tingle and had deafened her so she couldn't hear Em clearly. Now she rubbed at them frantically.

The tea wagon was working overtime. The fire engines had arrived, along with the ambulances. Many of the workers who had been waiting in the queue were now sitting on the wall. Some were wandering around trying to help, and a few were crying but others stood around, dumbstruck.

'Come with me.' Em dragged Rita towards the front of the tea queue.

Leaning desolately against the van a man was saying, 'I packed them in. They were secure. Secure, I tell you!'

Em said, 'It's not your fault, Gerry. You ain't never made a mistake before.'

Gerry, aware only of his own thoughts, cried, 'I packed them in. That chain *was* secure.' Another man was trying to get Gerry to drink sweet tea but he couldn't stop crying and protesting.

Em said, 'I believe you, Gerry.'

One of the firemen had come over to Gerry and put his hand on the man's shoulder. 'All right, mate?' he asked kindly.

To Rita, Em begged, 'Come with me to the offices. I got to make sure my Lizzie's okay. I reckon someone's been fiddling with the train. Gerry's the most trustworthy bloke I know.'

Rita didn't like the thought of meeting Lizzie face to face. Not now she knew that Lizzie *was* sleeping with Blackie. So far she'd managed to keep away from her, but that couldn't go on for ever.

'Mum! Mum, I'm over here.' All the office staff were standing near the main doors looking at the carnage.

Rita smiled at Lizzie, who was very pale. She knew she had to make the first move towards repairing their friendship, for Em's sake.

Em hugged her daughter. 'Thank God you're safe.'

She looked her up and down to make sure, then said, 'Where's Scrivenor?'

'He's just gone back to his office. The three people who've died have families that need to know before gossips start spreading tales.'

Em nodded. 'Coming?' She turned to Rita who meekly followed.

The office door was open and Rupert Scrivenor was standing in front of the window staring out. Em knocked, then walked in. She started talking without being acknowledged. 'I saw Jed Ward fiddling about at the back of the train earlier. I didn't pay too much attention to it then. But I think I should mention it now. If that train hadn't been so far from the buildings we'd all be in kingdom come.' As she finished, she looked at Rita. 'Rita Brown can verify all I've witnessed, except the Jed Ward bit. I should have gone and seen what the bloke was up to but I was more interested in getting my line workers started.'

Rupert Scrivenor stared at Rita, his ice-blue eyes boring into hers. 'So you can vouch that the packer is a conscientious man?'

'He has two children and works hard for them. He's well respected. I'm sure someone else had a hand in this.'

Scrivenor stopped his slow march around the office

and said to Em, 'I know you keep your eyes and ears open. Thank you for bringing this to my attention. I trust it will go no further.' His eyes moved from Em to Rita.

Both women nodded.

'This is a bad business,' he went on. 'The Fire Brigade and the Ambulance are doing their jobs but I need to get back down to them. Shall we go? Work is suspended for today and tomorrow. If I had my way, I'd close for longer, but there's a war on.'

He motioned towards the door. Rita followed him and Em outside to where rescue operations were being carried out. The air was rank and dust claimed every surface. A shroud of unhappiness hung over the yard and the workers. Em went to tell her girls they were free to go home. As she and Rita walked towards the group huddled together on the grass, Lizzie joined them.

She hung back and said to Rita, 'He still cares about you.'

'I don't want to know,' Rita said, and turned away, but not quickly enough to miss the smug look on Lizzie's face. She suddenly wanted to lash out at the girl. Not because she was sleeping with Blackie but because she needed to let off steam. She thought of the families of the three dead employees who wouldn't see their loved ones again.

*

Back at the house in Alma Street, Gladys said, 'I can't believe I missed all that action.' She tipped fresh seed into the canary's dish, then crumpled up the sand sheet from the base of the cage and threw it on to the fire in the range. 'Everything happens when I have time off. What a terrible thing.'

The kitchen was warm and they had been listening to a comedy programme on the wireless. Rita couldn't settle, her mind returning over and over to the train driver's body. 'Believe me, you wouldn't have wanted to be there,' she said. 'It brought back to me the hell of the blast I was in.' She shivered. 'We won't be forgetting them broken bodies, lying there in the yard. Not that there was much left of the driver.' She sighed. 'There'll be a few bad dreams tonight.' She put down the needle that had run out of black thread. 'We got any more cotton?' She was repairing a skirt. It was black, straight, hardly worn, but the buttonholes were too large for the buttons. She'd got it in a jumble sale at the Sloane Stanley Hall for ninepence.

'There's a new reel in the drawer,' Gladys said. 'I was lucky to get it off a bloke in the market.'

Rita got up from her chair at the table and went over to the sideboard. 'We've got tomorrow off as a mark of respect for the dead. But we're all on extra shifts afterwards to make up for lost time.' She paused. 'Coming home, I saw yet more tanks trundling down to Hardway. I wish I knew what's going on in Gosport, with all this building work on the shoreline.' As she foraged in the drawer, the front door opened and Pixie came in. The key jangled against the letterbox.

'Shut that door quickly! The heat's getting out!' yelled Gladys. Pixie had a key of her own but, like everyone else, used the one on the string. She came into the kitchen, like a galleon in full sail.

'You all right?' Rita said.

Pixie looked pale. 'No, I'm not,' she said. She shoved a letter she was holding under Rita's nose. 'I never opened any letters today until just now because I went to the auctions with Bob, just to get out for a bit. He's gone round to see Marlene, Sadie's asleep and . . .' Her voice petered out.

'Give it here!' Gladys snatched the letter and began reading it. When she finished the colour had drained from her face. 'Oh, my God. It's from Ruth, Cal's sister,' she said.

Rita took it and read aloud: '"Dear Pixie, Forgive me for not coming to see you in person but my baby is due any day. My brother Cal, your intended, has come home. It was a big shock. But a happy one. We all thought he was dead, as you know. He didn't come straight to you because he thought it would be too much of a shock. Can you telephone me? Ruth."'

'Jesus Christ!' Rita let the letter fall to the floor. 'Who'd believe it?' She went over to Pixie and took her to the big armchair near the window. 'Sit down. Don't get all hot and bothered, it won't be good for the baby.'

Gladys said, 'I'll make some tea.' She went over to Pixie and took her arm. 'Are you all right, love?' she asked.

'I don't know.' She was shaking.

Gladys let go of her and disappeared into the scullery. Presently Rita heard the kettle being filled and then the pop of the gas.

'What are you going to do?' Rita asked.

Pixie said again, 'I don't know.'

'Does Bob know?'

'No. I told you, he's out.'

'You have to tell him as soon as possible.'

Gladys stood in the doorway, a tea-towel in her hands, polishing a tin mug as though her life depended on it.

'What now? I suppose I go up to Ruth's boarding-house in Chichester and have tea with Cal.' Pixie looked at her mother, eyes full of tears, threatening to overflow.

'Don't be sarky, madam!' Gladys said, banging the mug on the table. 'But that American deserves to know you're married now. It's not his fault he didn't perish on that destroyer, like we all thought he had.' She clapped her hand over her mouth. 'Oh, Jesus, he doesn't know he has a daughter, does he?'

Rita saw Pixie put her hand to her head. 'I'll be with you tomorrow when you telephone Ruth, if you like?'

Gladys chimed in, 'That's Bob's job.'

'Make the tea, Mum. You're really not helping,' Pixie wailed.

Gladys disappeared again. Rita picked up the letter from the floor and folded it, then put it in the pocket of Pixie's cardigan.

'What am I to do?'

'Tonight you must tell Bob. He's a good man and he'll understand that you have to see Cal. You made your choice and married Bob. He's the father of your coming child.'

'Yes, but Cal is Sadie's dad.'

'One step at a time. Show this letter to Bob.'

Pixie nodded.

The canary chirped in the sudden silence as though agreeing with Rita.

Chapter Twelve

'You look like you've been selling goods at a loss.' Marlene expected at least a smile from Bob. After all, the sun was shining, there were plenty of customers about and Bob had the highest-quality bedding on his stall: it had come from a bombed hotel in Southampton. Yet here he was with a face as long as a fiddle.

He stopped counting change for his money belt. 'Can you keep a secret?'

'D'you need to ask?' she replied. His eyes were upon her and she could see a deep sadness in them.

'The American sailor, Sadie's real father, has come back from the dead.'

Marlene knew her mouth had fallen open. Her head was spinning. She tried to talk but nothing came out. She could tell he needed someone to confide in, and who better than her? She knew him and Pixie inside out, or thought she did.

He was looking at her expectantly.

'I thought the ship, the destroyer, had broken in two, with very few survivors?'

'That's what she was told. It nearly sent her round the bend.'

'I remember.' The American, Cal, had been the love of Pixie's life. Until Bob.

'His sister wants Pixie to meet him. There's stuff needs to be sorted out. Apparently he was out of it all for a long time after the rescue, with memory loss, injuries to his head.'

Marlene nodded. 'How's Pixie coping?'

'The baby's close. She's walking around like she's the one banged on the head. Even stopped clacking on the typewriter I got for her.' He shook his head. 'That's not good. Apparently, Ruth, Cal's sister, hasn't told him about Sadie. She reckons it's not her place.'

Marlene nodded. 'How do *you* feel?' Though she could see how he was taking it: badly.

'Like I'm going to lose her. Like I'm going to lose my Sadie.' He turned away but not before she'd caught the glisten in his eyes. Bob was a strong man and this wasn't like him at all. There had to be something she could say to cheer him.

'But she's pregnant with your baby.'

'I loved her enough to take on another man's kiddie. He'd probably take on mine. Not that I'd let him,' Bob said. His voice had risen.

Marlene stepped away to serve a woman then came back, putting the money in her belt. Bob looked dreadful, worse now than before.

There was a brief flurry of selling on both stalls, before they could carry on talking.

'You have to take Pixie to see him.'

'No!' His voice was so loud that a passer-by looked worriedly at them.

'Don't be silly. She can't go by herself and that way you'll be there for her if things don't turn out well . . .'

'I don't like the idea of taking my wife to Chichester to deliver her into some other bloke's arms!'

Marlene had never seen him so angry. She put her hand on his arm. 'Trust me, it's all you can do.'

He looked at her for a long time, then walked away, his shoulders hunched, like an old man's.

The line was unusually silent. Even the wireless and the cheerful music from *Music While You Work* did nothing to lighten the atmosphere.

'This is a dead an' alive hole today,' Gladys said. She blew a few grains of powder away.

'What do you expect? First day back after the blast.'

Rita moved to one side as Em came up to oversee what was going on. Rita could smell baking on her: Em loved making cakes when she could get hold of the ingredients, which was more often now that Blackie was cosying up to Lizzie.

'Did you hear about Jed Ward?'

Rita frowned. 'What's he done now?'

'Disappeared.'

'He was here the day before yesterday.' Then Rita remembered Em saying she'd spotted him fiddling with the chain at the back of the train.

'His missus took his dinner up to the Crown to throw at him because he didn't go home and found he hadn't been in since before the blast.' Em tapped the pencil on her clipboard. 'It's a funny business.'

She looked at Rita and shook her head, as though warning her not to breathe a word to Gladys about Jed Ward. Rita knew she wanted Gladys to believe Em was simply enquiring about one of the workers who hadn't turned up for work.

'I bet he's found himself a bit of rough,' said Gladys.

'Never liked him. He was only Blackie's lackey for what he could get out of him.'

Em snorted. 'So you won't be wanting a big slice of my Victoria sponge because I got the ingredients being a lackey to my daughter's boyfriend?' She glared at Gladys, then stalked away.

'Well!' said Gladys.

'That told you, didn't it?' Rita said.

When the buzzer went for break time, Rita was glad to get out in the open air, even if it was a palaver changing clothes and shoes.

The yard had been cleared, the crater filled and, miraculously, the train lines renewed. She was aware, as she queued at the tea wagon, that her work, filling the bombs and shells, probably had something to do with Gosport being like a building site and the shorelines blocked off from ordinary people. Troops seemed to be working at top speed day and night.

Women and men were chattering nineteen to the dozen as though they'd lost all memory that this yard had recently been the scene of such carnage. Was it the war that made people forget so quickly and get on with their lives?

Rita was looking forward to her day off, which she'd changed to a Tuesday to make it easier catching buses and trains. Joe didn't want her to visit him. Yesterday she could have gone to East Grinstead, but had decided to think things over. Now she was determined she'd take no notice of him and would visit him anyway. She'd discovered a box of chocolates Blackie had given her. They would make a nice gift for Joe.

She'd managed to keep out of Blackie's way since the break-up. And although she spent a great deal of time at Em's house, when Em wasn't down the Fox with the girls, she rarely bumped into Lizzie. But she'd noticed the smart clothes Lizzie now wore when she glimpsed her at Priddy's. Presents, no doubt, from Blackie. She thought hard, but no, she didn't miss Blackie.

She also thought about Pixie. Would she fall in love with Cal again and leave Bob? Bob loved the bones of her.

Rita sighed deeply, wishing more than anything that she had someone to love who would love her in return. Proper love, like Bob and Pixie had.

The queue was moving now and she was getting closer and closer to her much-wanted cuppa. She looked down the line to see who was ahead of her just as a dark-haired man caught her eye. He'd been chatting to a woman behind him and she guessed the woman had asked his name, for she heard him say, 'David Wayne.'

The big blowsy woman was now laughing uproariously. For a moment their eyes locked, and something flashed between David Wayne and herself. Rita wondered who he was. A new worker?

'You could have waited for me!' Gladys squeezed herself in beside Rita.

'Don't push in, we're all thirsty!' a voice shouted from the back of the queue.

'Me mate's savin' me place,' snapped Gladys. She nudged Rita's arm and grinned at her.

Rita looked along the line for the man she'd been staring at, but he was gone. Her eyes roved up and down the queue. He couldn't possibly have got served yet. How strange, she thought. You don't queue for a cup of tea for ages then suddenly decide you don't want one. A cold feeling ran down her spine. Why had David Wayne disappeared?

Back on the line Rita couldn't wait for Em to approach her, but that afternoon her friend was in and out of the workshop all the time. At last she appeared by Rita's side. 'I'm glad to see you,' Rita said. 'Something strange happened at break. Well, normally I wouldn't think anything of it but, what with all the funny things going on here at the moment, I thought I'd mention it.'

'Get to the point, Rita. I'm just off to the office.'

Rita said, 'There was a bloke in the queue I'd never

seen around here before. He was chatting to that Ida Franks – you know, big woman, loud mouth?'

Em nodded, looking around at the workers.

'He told her his name was David Wayne. But one minute he was there and the next he was gone, like he'd disappeared in a puff of smoke.'

'There's no David Wayne works here!' Rita had Em's full attention now.

She stepped back in surprise at the sharpness of Em's tone. 'But—'

'But nothing. If you stop me to talk rubbish like this, Rita, we'll never win this bloody war. You've made a mistake. Forget it.' And before she could say anything else, Em had gone on her way.

Gladys had been listening, eyes wide.

'Did you see that bloke in the queue talking to Ida?' Rita asked.

Gladys shook her head. 'I never noticed nothing,' she said, frowning. 'Ask Ida.'

'Yes, that's the thing to do,' Rita said. But why had Em bitten her head off? Rita wasn't going out of her mind. There had been a bloke.

When she asked Ida Franks in the changing room, Ida said, 'Was I talking to someone? I don't remember.' She puffed as she pulled on her fur-lined boots. 'More interested in getting something to eat before it all went. Anyway, there's new blokes and girls working here all the time.'

Marlene stood in the hallway of Samuel Golden's flat. 'Gosh,' she said. 'This is a bit of all right.'

'I was lucky to get this place. They're sought after. Apparently George the Fourth, when he was on the throne, visited the Anglesey Hotel on the corner. We'll pop in for a drink one of these days, Marlene. Did you know this semi-circle of white Regency houses was built in 1830 or thereabouts? Because of their provenance – Jacob Owen was the likely architect – these places rarely come on the market. I snapped this one up as soon as it became vacant. Mind you, I paid the earth for it.'

Marlene was amazed at Samuel's local knowledge. But he was so knowledgeable about everything. 'I daren't think about how much it cost you,' she said.

Samuel helped her off with her coat. He smiled. 'Would you like a drink?'

'That would be nice,' she said.

Her mother was looking after Jeannie so there was no need to get home early. She was hoping he was going to suggest she stay the night. They'd been to a big auction in Southsea and she'd overspent, as usual. Samuel had been pressing her to take his money. She loved it that he wanted to help her make a good profit. 'Speculate to accumulate' was his favourite saying.

She gazed around the tastefully furnished living room. The chandelier must have cost a fortune, she surmised. And, typically, the antiques were in keeping with the Georgian house. 'I'll pay you back tomorrow,' she said. 'I'll take some money out of the post office.' She had a savings book and rarely touched it, except to put money in. But this time she'd really overspent.

'There's no hurry,' he said. 'I'm not worried.'

Neither was Marlene. The goods she'd bought were excellent value and she'd certainly make a nice profit. They were boxed up in the boot of Samuel's car.

He'd poured her a drink.

'What's that?'

'Sherry, my dear. It's amontillado, I hope you like it.'

Marlene tasted it. 'Oh, it's nice. It tastes warm and sticky, like toffee.'

He laughed. He must think her very naive. She took a larger sip and realized she'd finished her drink. He didn't say anything, merely refilled her glass from the cut-glass decanter. She saw he had sipped his slowly. Perhaps she should do the same instead of drinking it straight back. Already her head felt fuzzy.

They'd gone to a pub on the seafront at Portsmouth. The place had been quiet and there'd been alcoves for dining. He'd asked her if she'd like a meal and she agreed. She was already tired from working at Gosport market and being on her feet all day. Good food had seemed just the answer. The pub had magically rustled up chops. Marlene thought she'd died and gone to Heaven.

'I'd like you to stay with me tonight, if you can?'

He had made his request shyly. Marlene laughed. It was what she wanted, too, so that she could lie in this lovely man's arms.

'Show me the bedroom,' she replied. She looked amazed at her empty glass. 'After I've had another sherry.'

Rita got off the bus outside the Queen Victoria Hospital.

It seemed funny being back at the place where she'd spent so much of her time after the factory blast. The Plastic Surgery and Burns Unit at East Grinstead in Sussex had twelve male and twelve female wards. In the distance she could see people in dressing-gowns walking and sitting on benches around a large lawn. It was towards the male wards that she went.

There were fields all around the hospital, and now that spring had arrived, a few wild flowers and a great many daffodils lined the narrow driveway that led to the main entrance. She took a deep breath. Birds were singing in the hedgerows, their voices a cheery prelude to the fine weather ahead. Why did the air smell different in the country? It was all fresh and new.

Would Joe be pleased to see her after all?

Rita had telephoned the hospital and asked to speak to Edna. She'd requested permission to visit and been told Joe had had no visitors since he'd arrived. His family lived in the US and it wasn't the easiest thing in wartime to jump on a ship and travel to England. He had turned away anyone trying to visit from his unit. Joe was a difficult patient. Edna had told her he might even shut the door in *her* face. That made Rita all the more determined to visit him.

She hoped to be reunited with some of the people she'd known during her stay at the hospital, but the war caused people to move on quickly. Fellow patients had been discharged and the staff that had befriended her had mostly taken jobs in other hospitals. Except for Edna, who seemed content in her work. She was small, chirpy and full of life, just like a friendly sparrow. She clasped Rita tightly when they met.

'I feel as though I'm visiting the hospital for the first time,' Rita said. 'I thought it would seem familiar.'

'New buildings, new patients,' came the cheery reply.

'You look terrific. We did a good job on you.' Edna lifted Rita's long hair away from her face and smiled. 'A very good job.' Then her smile faded. 'He's in the garden. Come with me, but don't expect miracles.'

The pretty nurse smoothed her stiff apron and walked back out of the main doors onto the gravelled path towards what would be, when June arrived, a beautiful rose garden. Now the bushes were stumpy and sharply angled.

'I won't come any further,' Edna said, giving her a friendly push forward.

Rita could see a lone figure sitting on a wooden bench. The nurse left her to walk on. She felt nervous. 'Hello, Joe,' she said.

It was as if he'd been deep in thought, for he'd not looked up as she'd approached. But now, at her voice, he raised his head.

Rita stared, willing herself not to turn away or to cry.

He'd been a boy before, and now he was a shadow of a man.

Chapter Thirteen

'I never asked you to come and I don't want you here.' She'd forgotten his drawling American accent.

Part of his head was covered with bandages that also obscured his left eye. Tufts of his hair, not as red as Rita remembered, poked through the gauze. The crutch stood against the bench, and his trouser leg was fastened with a large pin below the knee. He wore a dressing-gown of striped cotton over a thick jumper.

'That's a nice welcome, Joe.' She hoped he couldn't hear the thudding of her heart.

'I told you to go. What did you come for? To have a laugh at a kid full of hope who fucked you on the sofa and now can't even raise a smile?'

He turned away from her. At least, she thought, he remembered them making love the night before he left England. He was now fiddling with the belt of his dressing-gown. His mouth was a thin, straight line and there were frown lines on what she could see of his forehead.

She had been told to expect his surliness. What she hadn't expected was for it to hurt her so much. She put out her hand and touched his cold fingers. He didn't pull away.

With a sudden roar, many planes practically blacked out the sky overhead. Rita ducked automatically and was grateful to see the eight Spitfires flying low, no doubt on their way home.

She wasn't prepared for Joe's scream as he curled himself into a sort of shivering ball, his arms over his head.

Don't panic, she told herself. He would be even more disturbed if she showed fear. Shell-shock, that was the term, she thought. When she'd been in this hospital she'd met several men suffering from the war terrors of the past.

She knelt down on the earth beside him. Joe's whole body was still shaking, and he was making a keening sound. Rita wasn't sure what to do. Should she run and get someone, a nurse perhaps? Or should she stay quietly by his side waiting for him to calm down? She decided to wait it out. After a while he became still.

'The planes have gone,' she said softly. 'Have the

doctors told you what this is?' She wanted to put both her arms around him.

'Combat stress reaction,' he said. He was looking at her with hollow eyes. His voice was cracked. 'That's the darned name for the way a noise can reduce a man to a snivelling wreck or leave him staring into nowhere, remembering how his buddies died around him.' He stared at her. 'I really don't want you here,' he said. 'You're nothing but a damn do-gooder.'

He held on to the arm of the wooden seat while he hauled himself upright, before grabbing the crutch and shoving it beneath his arm. He proceeded to walk away from her.

Rita watched him hobble over the grass to the entrance door of the building. She rose and wiped soil from her hands and clothing. Her heart was beating fast as she used her thumb to wipe away a couple of tears. She sighed heavily. So, she thought, what had she gathered from her visit?

Joe was emotionally shocked. He'd lost half his leg. There was some kind of injury to his head and it was possible, from the patch she'd spotted beneath the bandage, that he'd lost an eye. This, no doubt, meant facial scarring. He was also a long way from his home in America, and his parents.

She rose from the seat and, with a glance towards the rose garden and the clipped bushes, began to walk towards the exit. In another month or so those roses would be well on the way to their true beauty. By June they'd be heavy with blooms. But how would Joe fare in another month?

She reached the drive and walked on towards the bus stop, still thinking about the roses, the hospital, Joe and herself.

How had she coped with her own scars? She hadn't. Not on her own. At first she'd been like a pruned rose bush, then, as time passed and she allowed people to befriend her, she'd begun, like the roses, to grow, to open her petals, to bloom.

She'd been like Joe, his maimed body and mind consuming him.

All she'd wanted to do was to hide away, but the staff here and her friend Pixie hadn't let her. She thought suddenly of the local pub that was used to limbless and bandaged customers. Edna had hauled her along with the other patients. She'd discovered, to her amazement, that she had enjoyed the outing.

But what if those friends hadn't bothered with her? She certainly wouldn't be in the frame of mind she was today, which she had to admit was pretty good, considering all that life had thrown at her.

Rita turned and walked back towards the hospital.

Joe and she had shared so much, by letter, after their initial casual coupling. She was going to help him, whether he liked it or bloody well not. She ran her hands down her grey skirt, above which her grey jacket, with the peplum, emphasized her slim waist. Her grey hat with the red feather was set jauntily on her long dark hair and the pussycat bow on her white blouse gave just the right touch of sophistication. Her black high heels clacked noisily on the steps up to the front door.

She wanted the old Joe back. And she was bloody well going to have him.

It was three in the morning when Marlene crept out of the bathroom. Fully dressed, she hadn't wanted to wake Samuel but she needed to get home. It was market day. She sat on the edge of the four-poster bed remembering his tenderness the previous night.

He opened his eyes, and immediately smiled at her. 'How can you look so beautiful so early after so little sleep?'

She knew she was blushing.

'I'll have to think about keeping you so you won't have to work any more,' he said, as he rolled away from her and grabbed at his clothes left on the chair overnight.

She didn't reply. The words seemed to be asking her to marry him, didn't they? She sighed with happiness. She wouldn't press him, though: it wouldn't be right.

He sipped at the tea she'd made for him. It was funny being in a man's kitchen. Especially one that was fitted out with gadgets she couldn't afford – she didn't know what some were for. She'd opened the door of the huge fridge and found it full of foodstuffs she was unable to buy. But, then, money talks, Marlene knew.

What would it be like to live in a flat that had a bathroom?

She didn't hurry him. He was aware of her early-morning start at the market, and within half an hour he had dropped her off outside her house and she was back in her usual routine of making a flask of tea and a sandwich.

'Oh! You made me jump!' Her mother, small, dark and nicely rounded, came down the stairs and stood by the range. Marlene had already riddled it through, got a glow going with the coals and filled the scuttle.

'Did you have a nice time?' Her mother began folding Jeannie's clothes, which had been left over the fireguard to dry.

'Oh, Mum. I don't know what he sees in me, but he makes me so happy.' She put her arms around her mother and kissed the top of her head, then went back into the scullery and put on her layers of work clothes to keep out the cold. Spring it might be, but that didn't mean she could keep warm.

'You deserve it, love,' came her mother's reply. 'Get out and enjoy yourself. Jeannie's all right with me.'

Marlene smiled gratefully at her mother, then thought about the jewellery in the box in the hall. It would look good on the stall today. Without Samuel lending her the money to buy it, she wouldn't be doing half as well as she was.

She went upstairs to kiss her sleeping child, who was sprawled across the bed, her small body warm and smelling of talcum powder from her bath the previous evening. She stood looking at the little girl, thinking how fortunate she was to have her. Then, downstairs again after bidding her mother goodbye, Marlene picked up the van keys along with her flask and the packet of sandwiches. 'Samuel's far too good for me, Mum.'

'Who the hell do you think you are that you can order me about?' Rita sat down on the edge of the bed with such force that its heavy mattress practically groaned.

As she'd spent time in the hospital she was familiar

with its layout, and a brief word with a nurse had put her on the right trail to Joe's ward and his single room.

He was lying on top of the bed-covers, the wireless playing soothing classical music. The sash window was open at the bottom, letting in crisp air.

'Who do *you* think *you* are coming here uninvited?' He threw down the book he was reading, which clattered onto the floor.

'I *am* invited. A long while ago you told me in a letter that you couldn't wait for leave so we could meet up because I was someone special in your life. So, I'm here!'

His mouth pursed and his frown deepened. 'That was another Joe and another time,' he finally said. He let out a deep breath.

'Rubbish! I'm Rita. You can't bullshit me. Underneath those bandages is the bloke who made love to me and changed my life!'

Joe's mouth fell open. Rita could see he didn't know how to handle the situation.

After a long while he said quietly, 'Well, I won't be doing that again.' He turned his angry face to the window.

The rattle of the medicine trolley's wheels stopped outside the open door. In came a nurse carrying a glass. She looked apologetically towards Rita, then grinned at Joe. 'Time for your tablets,' she said. She turned to Rita, her brown hair shining in the light, despite the perky white cap that was designed to hide it. 'Hello – nice to see he has a visitor.' She nodded at Joe.

'I am here, you know,' Joe snarled. 'You can talk *to* me, instead of *about* me.'

'Not when you bite my head off like you usually do.' The nurse handed him the two tablets in the small cup. 'Swallow.'

Joe placed them in his mouth.

The young nurse swung away.

Rita rose and followed, waiting until she'd moved the trolley in front of the next doorway. She asked, 'Can you tell me anything about his condition?'

The nurse paused. 'You can ask to see the specialist. He'll give you the proper details. Are you a relative?'

Rita thought quickly. 'Once we were practically engaged.' God forgive me for stretching the truth, she thought. But she was aware that information about a patient's health was given out only to relatives.

The nurse's eyes softened. 'All I can tell you, apart from the obvious – the loss of his leg and an eye – is that the nervous condition causes terrible nightmares. He has a single room because in a ward he disturbs the other patients. Joe is unable to withstand noise, and is depressed. His pain we can alleviate with drugs. His injuries will eventually heal and he's due another operation on his eye next week. He'll never see again from that side, but with a glass eye, he'll cope and eventually his sight will settle. He's due more plastic surgery and the scars will eventually fade . . .'

'I know all about scars,' said Rita. She swung her dark hair back from her face.

The nurse ran a finger along the silvery line. Her face betrayed no emotion. 'Is that one of ours?'

Rita nodded.

The young woman looked pleased, almost as though she'd performed the operation herself.

'I do know some of what he's going through. I want to help,' Rita added.

'He's so far down he can't believe he'll come out of this.' The nurse looked sad.

Rita asked, 'What's your name?'

'Patsy.'

'If I give you a telephone number, would you keep in touch if anything serious happens?' Rita was going to give her the number of the office at Priddy's. It wasn't something that people did, but she knew the office girls would come and find her in an emergency.

Patsy smiled. 'Come to the office before you leave,' she said. 'It's good that someone is taking an interest in him. He's scared everyone else away! Look, I must go now.' She was looking at the watch pinned on her apron.

Rita touched her arm lightly. 'Thank you,' she said.

Going back into Joe's room, she was surprised to see him settling himself back on the covers. There was a strange look on his face. She realized he'd got up, wandered about, then sneaked back to bed when he'd heard her returning. The window was now closed. Perhaps it had caused a draught. Something wasn't right. She peered at Joe and saw consternation in his face.

She looked again at the window. A piece of white ribbon was tucked into the corner of the frame.

'You've been spying on me!' Joe spat the words at her.

Taken aback, Rita said, 'Not really. I asked Patsy about you. She told me nothing I didn't already know. She explained I'd have to talk to your specialist if I wanted more.' She was anxious to put his mind at rest: she'd suddenly remembered how paranoid she'd been about what people were saying behind her back, when she'd been here. 'And I'm not your relative so he won't tell me anything, will he? Careless talk costs lives inside a hospital, the same as inside our factory.'

'Bit late to worry about that when I've got a face to frighten the Hun away.'

Rita ignored his self-pity. She opened her bag and took

out the small box of chocolates. 'I'm going now. But you're not getting rid of me as easily as you think. I'll come back. In the meantime, you can feed your miserable face with these.' She put the chocolates on the bed where he could easily reach them and walked out.

Rita sat in Em's living room wading through a large lump of bread pudding, still hot from the oven. The sultanas and currants were plump and delicious. Maybe Blackie had provided them. The wireless was on in the kitchen and she heard the clink of spoon against china that meant Em's old man was eating as well. He was still being polite to Em and that was all Rita cared about.

'This is lovely.'

Em smiled with pleasure, and Lizzie, who was sewing the hem of a jumble-sale skirt, agreed, her empty dish on the floor.

'Of course, the fruit came from Blackie,' Lizzie said.

Em sighed.

'I thought as much,' Rita said. 'Don't try to annoy me when I've been provoked already today by a bloke who's worth ten of a man who makes money off the misfortunes of others!'

Lizzie's face fell.

'Sorry, Lizzie, I didn't mean to snap. Don't forget, I

know Blackie and the way he works. I only wish I knew what's making this other bloke tick.'

Lizzie stared at her. 'He still talks about you, Blackie does.'

'How d'you cope with that?' Actually, Rita didn't really care.

'Same way as I cope when we get into bed.' She glanced at Em as if she might have offended her, but Em was engrossed in the magazine she was thumbing through.

Rita looked up from the dish she was scraping out. 'Must have been hard after them two men . . .'

Lizzie closed her eyes as though to blot out the memory. 'I cringed whenever a man was near me. Panicked at work whenever I was alone with a bloke in the office because I thought he might pounce on me. That night all I could smell was cigars . . . I think one of them had been smoking a cigar before . . .'

'You don't have to talk about it, Lizzie.' Em rattled a page crossly.

'I do, Mum. Otherwise it festers inside me. I've had my eye on Blackie for ages. I had to get over what happened else he'd have walked away from me. No bloke wants a woman who can't show him affection. I thought it was my fault, you see, the rape, that I'd no business walking out alone at night. No business wearing high heels that made my legs look nice. That I'd encouraged it to happen simply by walking in a deserted place. Then, when Blackie actually took some notice of me, I had to stop myself being scared or lose him before it started. I'd do anything to keep him, anything. And . . . and I'm actually jealous of you . . . You could break my heart by telling Blackie you still fancy him.'

Rita put the basin and spoon on the floor, then got up and went over to the sofa. She bent down and put her arms around Lizzie. 'I don't want him back, love. You've nothing to fear from me.'

Lizzie was crying softly. The fire spat out a splinter of wood that began to smoulder on the rag rug, until Rita got up and stepped on it. 'We don't want to be burned alive,' she said. She pulled the fireguard into place. 'I don't want you lot dying in your beds.' Then she looked deep into the flames. 'Dying . . . bed . . . Oh, no!' She stood for a moment, staring at Lizzie without actually seeing her. Then she snapped back to life. Suddenly it all seemed so clear to her. 'Lizzie, will you come to the phone box with me?' She left the room and shrugged on her coat in the hall.

'Wait for me.' Lizzie uncurled herself from the sofa and made a grab for her coat, which Rita was thrusting towards her.

Em's voice came from the living room: 'I suppose you know it's raining?'

'Can't be helped. We won't be long,' Rita called.

Lizzie was tying the belt of her coat around her and had already put on her headscarf. The door slammed behind them and, arm in arm, Rita hurried them towards the red phone box on the corner of Queen's Road. 'Come in with me.' She opened the heavy door. 'I just hope she's still on duty.'

She put the pennies into the slot and breathed a sigh of relief when Patsy was called to the phone. Lizzie was watching Rita as though she was out of her mind.

'Patsy, I'm not telling you how to do your job, certainly not, but something's occurred to me. Could you please watch while Joe takes his tablets? I noticed this afternoon you gave him his medication and expected he'd swallow it. I've got an idea he's not taking it. Look, I have to go, my money will run out any minute but I'll talk to you tomorrow.'

Rita was standing holding the receiver but the phone was now dead.

'You've got to go into work tomorrow.' Lizzie was indignant. 'You can't just swan about visiting old boy-friends when Priddy's has asked us to work double time.'

Rita pushed open the heavy door and they walked out

into the rain, which was much heavier now. 'I've an idea this bloke is going to do something silly. I'm taking the day off whether old Scrivenor likes it or not.'

'Damn!' Lizzie gasped, putting her hand to her head. 'Mum told me she had something to tell you about Scrivenor. I think she's forgotten.'

Chapter Fourteen

'I thought I told you I didn't want you coming here?'

'What you want and what I want are two different things. Enjoy the chocolates?' Rita looked at the half-empty box on Joe's bedside table.

He blushed. His room smelled as though it had been newly disinfected. She sat down on the edge of the bed with its pristine white sheets and blue coverlet. She'd dressed carefully, hoping to arouse some sort of reaction in him. Several men had smiled at her on her train journey to the hospital so she knew she looked good. In the carriage an airman had given her his seat. But Joe showed no interest in her at all.

He didn't answer her question. The heavy silence hung in the room like a dark shroud.

Rita got up and went to the sash window. It was closed. She pushed up the bottom half. Then she turned towards him. The look in his eyes was enough to tell her she was right. She pulled at the piece of ribbon and drew onto the sill a large package rolled in greaseproof paper. She stood there with it in her hand.

'You damned nosy bitch!'

Ignoring him, she carefully opened the package to reveal several tablets kept dry and safe by the grease-proof paper. Instead of taking his medication he'd saved it.

'When were you going to kill yourself?'

'When I had enough to make a good job of it,' he said, so defiantly that Rita wanted to hit him.

Suddenly it was as if all the fight had been knocked out of him. He began to cry. She went to him and sat on the bed. She wanted so much to put her arms around him but didn't dare. He was crying in front of her. Joe had at last let a little of his armour fall away.

Gradually his shoulders stopped shaking. She took a chance and covered one of his hands with her own.

'How did you know?' he asked, as soon as their skin touched.

'I told you. I've been where you are now.'

'I feel so guilty.' He looked up at her. His one eye was full of pain.

'Guilt doesn't help anyone,' Rita said. 'Now, if you

promise to let me visit you, I'll simply get rid of these . . .' she opened her hand to reveal the tablets '. . . and not tell anyone. If not, I'll give them to the hospital authorities and they'll put you somewhere a hell of a lot nastier than this place. A hospital where you'll be in the company of real loonies.' She could see her threat had upset him. But there was still no answer. 'Well?' Her question hung in the air.

'Why do you care?' His voice was soft, his good eye bloodshot, yet trained on her. Rita knew the importance of giving him the right answer. One that would give him hope, but not a false promise.

'Because, Joe, if it wasn't for people who cared about me, I'd have tried to do the same.'

He was still staring at her intently. 'Will you visit me again?'

Rita's heart leaped. 'I'll come whenever I can,' she said, trying not to sound overjoyed, although she was. Her heart was beating so fast she was sure he'd comment on it. 'But the armaments factory won't be happy with me taking time off. I should be working today . . .'

'You're a good person, Rita Brown,' he said.

'Well, long ago you made love to me. You made me feel like a woman again.' She gave a sudden smile. 'Remember that sofa, how lumpy it was? I wonder if it's still there.' Her voice was wistful. For a moment she was back in the past with the eager young man Joe had been before he'd gone to war . . .

'That part of my life's gone.'

She hated the bitterness in his voice. 'It's not gone, it's asleep. And there are other ways of loving people. I thought no one would ever make love to me with my face looking like it had been scraped by a cheese grater. But you did, and I'd like to believe it was because you cared.'

'I did . . .'

'The next day when you'd been sent abroad I felt as though there was more to life than I'd ever thought there would be during my stay here. *You* did that for me.'

Rita saw Joe was tired. He'd put his head back on the heaped pillows. She was weary too. She'd been awake all night, terrified he'd harm himself before she could get to him, but she couldn't inform the hospital of what he intended in case it did more harm than good.

Rita stood up, letting his hand drop. She bent forward and kissed his bandaged forehead. 'I'll come back in about a week's time . . .'

'You promise?'

'Yes.'

Then she walked out of his room, her heart much lighter than it had been when she'd arrived.

*

'So you've decided to come in today, have you?'

Rita smiled. 'I'm sorry, Em. I won't be taking any more time off, and I'm ready for all the overtime you can put my way. I'm going to see Joe a week on Saturday. That's where I was yesterday.'

Em frowned. 'Lizzie told me all about the phone call. Were you in time to stop him hurting himself?'

'This time, yes, but who knows what he's planning for the future? He's in a bad way, Em. When I left him he seemed happier, but I know from my own experience that it doesn't last. Bad thoughts gnaw at you like a dog with a bone.'

Em made notes with a pencil on her clipboard. 'I want to thank you for being so kind to Lizzie, what with Blackie an' all. Taking her into your confidence, like you did. You're a very generous woman, Rita.'

Rita blushed and went on measuring the powder into the bomb cases. She realized she was hungry. 'You didn't bring any of that bread pudding in, did you, Em?'

'As a matter of fact I did.' Em glanced about furtively, then whispered, 'But there's only enough for the three of us, me, you and our Lizzie, so don't broadcast it about.' She put her hand to her forehead and sighed. 'Look, yesterday I was supposed to send you to Mr Scrivenor's office, but you weren't in. I didn't want to tell him you'd had a day off, not with all of us working double shifts like we are, so go to him now, and you can tell him I forgot. That'll sound better than you not being here.'

Rita thought how kind Em was to take the blame. 'What does he want?' He wasn't about to sack her, was he?

'How would I know?' Em tutted and set down her notes on the worktop. 'Give me your gloves. I'll take over for you on the line.'

Two minutes later Rita was walking through the corridors until she reached Scrivenor's office. She knocked on the door. After a while he opened it. He frowned, as though it was a surprise to him that she was there. He soon recovered himself. 'Come in and sit down, Miss Brown.'

Rita did as she was told, after moving some papers off the only chair available. 'You wanted to see me?'

He looked her up and down as though she was a garment he was thinking about buying. 'You've been here some time.'

Rita felt uncomfortable beneath his scrutiny, but it wasn't as though he seemed cross with her, more that he wanted to ask her something. When it came, Rita was shocked. 'I want to ask you out for a meal, tomorrow evening, if that's convenient for you?' His forehead creased. 'Actually, tonight would be better. Do you have any previous engagements?'

The back of her neck went sweaty. How many of the factory girls would give their right arm to have the handsome boss ask them this question!

She thought carefully. Was she attracted to him? Not really. He was her boss, for Christ's sake. He brushed a fleck of something from his cuff and stared at her, waiting for her reply. She thought about a free meal in a restaurant against a meal made by Gladys. If she saw another tin of Spam . . . Her mouth began to water at the thought of fresh vegetables, maybe a nice gooey pudding. Some decent coffee would be lovely – the ersatz stuff was like mud. She missed Blackie's luxuries.

'No,' she said.

'Right.' He looked relieved and fiddled with some notes on his desk. 'I have your address and I'll pick you up at seven. Is that convenient?'

'Yes,' she said.

She turned away, and as she reached the door, he said, 'I trust you'll keep this between us?'

'Yes,' Rita said again, and left the office, closing the door behind her, stunned.

*

Gladys pushed open the front door and she and Rita tumbled inside.

'My head aches,' Gladys said. 'Hello, my pretty boy!' The canary jumped from swing to bar, his singing soothing after the constant chatter at the factory. She said as much to Rita. 'I love the music on the wireless but sometimes it gets on me nerves.'

'I'll sort out his cage while you make the tea,' Rita said, as Gladys dumped her flask and bag on the table, then went through to the scullery. Gladys drank tea until it was coming out of her ears so she took a flask to work as well as waiting in line at the tea wagon. Rita heard the tap turn and water swirl into the kettle. She took a packet of sand sheets and the box of seed from the sideboard and set about cleaning the canary's cage.

'What d'you fancy tonight for tea?' shouted Gladys.

'I'm going out.'

Gladys came and stood in the doorway. She was taking off her coat. 'That's good because my Pixie asked me round for a bite. She's worried about going to Chichester. Where you off – somewhere special?'

Rita shook her head. 'Not really, just with a mate.'

'Wish it was Blackie you was going out with.' Gladys sighed. She dropped her coat onto a kitchen chair and went back into the scullery.

'You might as well get it into your head that I'm through with him. I've even told Lizzie she's got my blessing.' Rita was peeved that Gladys never listened to her.

From the scullery came a derisive sniff. 'Anyway, there's someone else,' Rita said.

Gladys was back in the kitchen like a shot. 'Who? Who?'

'You sound like a demented owl.' Ignoring Gladys, Rita spoke to the canary. 'There! Now you've got a nice clean cage.'

'Bugger that canary! Who's taken your fancy now?'

Gladys disappeared without waiting for an answer and came back into the kitchen with the teapot and two cups on a tray. 'Is that milk on the table all right?'

Rita picked up the bottle and sniffed it. Salt and pepper, milk and the sugar bowl were usually left in the middle of the kitchen table. 'It'll do,' she said. 'Look, I had time off to visit Joe – you remember Joe, the American I wrote to for a while?'

Gladys poured out the opaque brown tea. 'Didn't you think he was dead?'

'Yes . . . but he's not. He's got combat stress reaction . . .'

'You don't want to get mixed up with a loony!'

Rita was angry. 'That boy got ill fighting for us. Us,' she repeated. 'He's most certainly not a loony.'

'Well, whatever way you dress it up, it's shell-shock. Em's ol' man has it and he's a loony.' She put her forefinger to the side of her head and twisted it as though to show a screw was missing. Then she poured milk into the cups and peered at the tea with distaste. Lumps of fat were floating on the top.

'Don't worry, I ain't fussy,' said Rita.

'No, you certainly ain't fussy to go out with *him*.'

Gladys thought she was going out with Joe tonight. Rita didn't correct her and Gladys continued, 'Look, love, I don't mean to be nasty to you – why, you're like me own daughter. I just wish you could find a decent boy to settle down with. Blackie was lovely.'

Rita got up from the table and went to where Gladys was now perched on the arm of the chair. She took her teacup out of her hands and put it on the table, then gave her a big cuddle. 'I know you do, and I know you liked Blackie, but it got so I couldn't think of him doling out stuff that ordinary people couldn't get hold of. It isn't right. We've all got to pull together. Otherwise bloody Hitler might just as well come over and be our new prime minister.'

She pulled away from Gladys and went upstairs to look through her wardrobe to see what she could wear that would be suitable for Mr Scrivenor. He'd be used to women with expensive tastes. Rita had some nice clothes, thanks to Blackie, and it had seemed a shame to cut off her nose to spite her face by getting rid of all his gifts. To her it was enough that their affair was over. She'd made her point and given Lizzie her blessing.

The back bedroom smelled of damp mixed with Evening in Paris perfume. In the built-in cupboard she riffled through garments, deciding on a plain black knee-length dress, black high heels and a string of pearl beads. She would pile her hair up and paint her nails red. Leaving the clothes on the bed, she went downstairs again.

The canary looked even happier now that Gladys had stuck a piece of cuttlebone through the bars of its cage. She'd left the back door ajar and was in the garden unpegging the washing that had been out since early morning, but was now even wetter.

Rita was using the rest of the water from the big kettle to have a strip wash at the sink when Gladys came in, moaning, 'I'll have to rinse it through again. The smuts in the air have left dirty marks on it all.'

'When you going round Pixie's? Don't worry about the washing. I'll rinse it all through and wring it out ready for the mangle.' The huge iron monstrosity lived in the backyard and Rita thought she'd get up early and put the washing through ready for the line, as long as it wasn't raining.

Rita knew Pixie was at home because she had heard Sadie yelling.

'You trying to get rid of me?'

'No, but I wish you'd shut that bloody door while I'm standing here in the nuddy!'

Gladys laughed and went off, closing the door behind her, having left the pile of wet washing on top of the copper in a pail.

Rita was alone in the house when the car drew up outside. She was ready and waiting for Rupert Scrivenor.

Chapter Fifteen

He led the way to a table in an alcove at the Osborne View. It was light enough to see the sea and the ships through the large windows, even though they were criss-crossed with tape and any moment the blackout curtains would be drawn. The whole length of the Solent was set with barbed wire above the pebble beach to encourage people to stay away from the shore. Even here, almost in the countryside, trucks and mechanical diggers were in evidence.

He took her black coat and put it, along with his own, on the coat-stand near the door, then pulled out her chair so she could sit down.

'You look delicious,' he said.

It seemed a funny word to describe her, she thought, but she didn't mind. 'You look very smart,' she replied. He was wearing a black suit and had a pocket handkerchief in pale yellow in his top pocket. He smelled nice and musky, with just a touch of Brylcreem on his blond hair to stop the front falling onto his forehead. Rita noticed his long fingers and polished nails. He was certainly not a man who got his hands dirty. She thought of Blackie, his chunky gold sovereign ring and his hands, which were clean but hard. Rupert's looked soft.

She glanced around the restaurant. There were bottles of strange liqueurs on the shelves. Their colours glittered, reflected in the mirror at the back. A waiter came over with two menus and Rita took hers and began to read.

Scrivenor ordered a bottle of white wine. 'God knows what it'll be like,' he said to Rita.

'That one's quite pleasant,' confided the waiter. He looked at Rita, then at Scrivenor, who nodded.

She wasn't astounded by the high prices. After all, Blackie had taken her to some quite exotic places to eat.

'The steak is off,' whispered the waiter. That meant the restaurant couldn't get any.

'The war again,' said Rupert. He pursed his lips and gazed at her. She noticed his eyes were almost violet. 'I don't want anything to start and I'm settling for the fish. You choose anything you like.' His voice was soft.

'I'd love a pork chop, a nice big fat juicy one,' Rita

said. She glanced about her. Only a few tables were occupied. The restaurant was all dark oak and highly polished furniture.

The waiter reappeared with their wine and poured it for Scrivenor to taste, waited for his approval, then filled their glasses. After he had taken their order, Rita settled and looked around again. She thought she might enjoy herself tonight, if only she knew the reason for this unexpected meal.

'I expect you're wondering why I asked you to dinner,' he said, almost as though he'd read her mind. He reached across and took her hand. 'First, I must tell you you're a damned good worker and Em, the overseer, thinks very highly of you.' He paused. 'Before we go any further I must tell you that I didn't ask you out to lure you into bed. For a start my friend wouldn't like it. He's very jealous.'

Rita frowned. Was he telling her he was homosexual? She sat back on her chair, amazed that he trusted her not to impart this information to anyone else. She stumbled over her words. 'All the women at work fancy the pants off you.'

He laughed. For a moment she thought he was teasing her. He was the boss, wasn't he? And so good-looking . . . And for men to be together *like that* was a crime. She thought of the homosexuals Blackie had introduced her to, flamboyant men.

'I know,' he said, then gave her a gorgeous smile, like a little boy who'd been caught stealing biscuits from the tin. 'I want us to be friends. I trust you'll keep my secret?'

She'd met quite a few homosexuals, but never one who was so masculine. Some of Blackie's friends even wore make-up. Obviously not in public: many people hated homosexuals, and they were often beaten up. 'Of course. I'm glad that's out of the way,' she said, taking a large mouthful of wine. 'So, why am I here?'

'I must ask that, if you refuse to do what I'm going to ask of you, you will keep our meeting and what we talk about secret too?'

Rita nodded. 'Yes.' What on earth was going on?

He drank some wine, set down the glass and gave her his full attention. 'A few days ago you mentioned to Em that you'd spotted a man in the tea queue you hadn't seen before. You even had his name. Am I right?'

Rita nodded. 'Em told me I'd made a mistake but I heard him say his name was David Wayne. She assured me no one of that name was on the payroll.'

'You were very astute to recognize his presence. Even more so to ask about him.' He kept his solid gaze on her. 'David Wayne does exist.'

'So I was right?' Rita sat back in her chair.

'Yes, you were. He didn't blend in exactly as I'd hoped.'

'What d'you mean?'

The waiter appeared with their food. Immediately Rita stopped talking and waited until their plates were in front of them and the man had left them to it. 'This looks nice,' she said. She was disappointed the chop was only half the size she'd had in mind when she'd ordered it but it looked delicious.

'They do a really nice spotted dick here,' Rupert Scrivenor said. 'I intend to order it – that's why I denied myself an hors d'oeuvre.' He winked at her.

She laughed, and suddenly felt completely at ease with him. It was as if he'd turned from being her boss into a mate, all because he liked a stodgy pudding! 'So . . .' Rita ate some creamy mashed potato '. . . why did you invite me here? And, if I may ask, why did Em deny that man's existence?'

'One thing at a time. Em is sworn to secrecy. We're working in peculiar and dangerous times. No doubt you've noticed the south coast is awash with troops. Most of them are living in makeshift quarters, some even sleeping in their vehicles. The good people of Elson have been inviting them in for meals, allowing them to take advantage of a bath and friendship.'

Rita watched as he delicately separated bones from the fish and almost wished she'd ordered the same.

'I can't tell you everything I know – but it's important we keep up a high standard of workmanship, filling shells, mines and bombs. But, most of all, it's vital that no information is leaked from Priddy's about what we're doing and the huge level of munitions we're producing. The general public *has* to be kept in the dark. Secrecy is of the utmost importance. Spies are everywhere, Rita.' He put his fork down, picked up his wine glass and sipped. Rita didn't say a word. She knew whatever it was he was going to ask of her she mustn't miss any of it. He put his glass back on the pristine white tablecloth and stared at her.

'I firmly believe the two bombs that slipped from their secure moorings on the train was treachery. Someone, I'm naming no names, meant it to happen but, alas for them, the bombs fell short of the buildings they were meant to destroy. I think they wanted to blow up the machinery rooms.' He put his hand to his mouth and coughed. 'The fact the train rolled forward was an absolute blessing. Had all those shells exploded, we wouldn't be here now.'

Rita's fork stopped halfway to her mouth. 'Is that really what you think? That it was sabotage?' Suddenly the chop and mashed potato didn't taste so good after all.

He nodded. 'I don't know if you read the recent newspaper article about the guard who hanged himself at the prisoner-of-war camp?'

'Near Stratford-upon-Avon?'

He looked surprised that she remembered the incident. 'Yes,' he said. 'Well, it's come to our attention, I daren't tell you how, that information is being leaked from Priddy's.' He tapped his knife on his plate and gave a deep sigh. 'A couple of days ago another guard at the same camp was discovered using a long-wave radio receiver. Names were bandied about. Nothing was proven but the whole situation smacks of loose security at *our* factory. The information discovered could only have come from someone *here*.'

He shook his head. 'I'd installed David Wayne to keep his ear to the ground. You, unfortunately, spotted him.' He cut a piece of fish and put it into his mouth. When he'd swallowed it, he said, 'I need to replace him.'

There was a long silence before he continued. 'My mistake was putting someone into the workforce who was an outsider. You recognized him as a new worker. Thus he attracted attention. Not what I wanted at all.'

He sat staring at her, until she felt compelled to say, 'You want a spy?'

'If you wish to put it like that, yes.'

'You're asking me?' It was suddenly very clear why he had invited her to dinner.

He nodded.

'I'm not sure I could do that to my friends.' Rita hated the thought of watching the women whom she'd known for so long. After all, there was trust and loyalty to think about, surely.

'But what if those so-called friends were selling secrets that could lose us this war?'

'That's a different kettle of fish.'

'I'm afraid, Rita, in times of war, our friends are often the ones to betray us. I can't tell you more than this but information about a possible invasion . . .' Rita opened her mouth to speak but he put out a hand to halt her '. . . a possible invasion has filtered back to us. The recent bomb blast is proof that there's a traitor among us. That, coupled with the artillery lining our streets, is evidence that may warn Germany and Hitler to be ready.'

Scrivenor was trusting her with news that was surely a great secret.

'The government have changed the locations of the large-scale military exercises taking place in southern

England, using fake concentrations of troops and dummy ships in different harbours to keep the enemy guessing. All visitors have been banned from coastal areas, all overseas travel restricted and even diplomats forbidden to go abroad. All dispatches are scrutinized. You've already witnessed the amphibious operations here in the Channel, and the air force is attacking Germany in an effort to soften up their railway marshalling yards, airfields and military positions.' He paused. 'It's of the utmost importance you don't breathe a word of this. But the fact you came back to work after the explosion that put you in hospital shows me you have great strength of character and mind. I know I can trust you. Emily has vouched for your ability to keep calm under pressure and your determination to see things through to the bitter end, while keeping your mouth tightly shut. Will you help?'

He must have made a deliberate study of her, Rita thought. How long had he been watching her? She wasn't thrown by his request. Could she, Rita, unobtrusively listen, watch? Could she do this to her friends? Em had evidently been doing it for some time and she hadn't guessed. Could Rita spy on her workmates for the good of her country?

For a while there was silence. 'All right, I'll do it,' she

said. 'Em is a dear friend of mine. Would it be possible for you to keep this a secret from her?'

'If that's what you want. And why didn't I think of it? Walls have ears. She's a stalwart worker, but I can see the temptation to talk might be hard, as you're friends.'

Rita nodded. Her head was whirling.

'You'll answer to me,' he said. 'Will that do?'

Again Rita nodded. She looked down at her plate and saw that she'd eaten her chop without savouring it. As though guessing her predicament, Scrivenor laughed. 'Don't worry,' he said. 'I can assure you the spotted dick will be memorable, although I think you'd do better to come and have a meal at my home. My friend is a marvellous chef.'

'That would be nice,' Rita said. 'But tell me, you explained what our troops are doing around Hardway, plus the reason that Priddy's is working full out to provide mines, bombs and ammunition. What would have happened if I'd said I wanted no part of this?'

He reached across the table and, again, held one of her hands. 'I knew you wouldn't give up a chance to help our country win this war. I didn't call on you on a whim, you know. I *have* researched you well. I know you are the sort of woman I can rely on.'

Rita knew she was blushing.

'Of course, there'll be an increase in your wages.'

'Oh, I never expected . . .'

'Of course you didn't, but recompense will be made.'

Rita was beginning to feel better about the whole thing. In fact, it was really quite exciting.

Suddenly she thought about Joe. She couldn't let him down. Since her last visit to the hospital she'd done nothing but worry about him. She wanted his cheeky smile back. It seemed he'd forgotten what happiness was. She'd taken away from him his means to do away with himself. But that didn't mean he wouldn't find another way to do it. He couldn't see he had a life ahead of him, or if he did, he couldn't see himself coping with his injuries. The biggest hurdle, though, was his shell-shock. But the wonderful East Grinstead hospital doctors would do their utmost to heal it, as well as his physical injuries.

Her own scars had contributed to her lack of self-confidence, so she was well aware that Joe needed to be treated normally by his fellows, yet with compassion and a greater understanding. Suddenly she realized she was thinking a great deal about a man who now cared little about her. Well, he'd cared once. She would make him care again. She wouldn't give up.

She came back to earth as the waiter, clattering the

china, took away their plates. When he came back, he said, 'Would you like the sweet menu?'

'Two large portions of your spotted dick with custard,' Scrivenor said. Rita opened her mouth to speak but he went on, 'I promise you, it's delicious.'

Rita laughed. Tonight she seemed to have made a great many decisions. This last one, about the dessert, had been made for her. 'I'll take your word for it,' she said happily.

Chapter Sixteen

Marlene set down the mug of tea and the bacon sandwich on the corner of the table and touched Bob on the shoulder. He had his back to her. 'That's supposed to be meat but it's more like welded-together sawdust. Still, it's filling and hot,' she said. When he turned she saw that his face was streaked with tears, his eyes red. 'Oh, Bob, whatever's the matter?' She'd never seen him so distressed before. When they'd been unpacking the stalls early that morning it had been dark and Bob wasn't chatty at the best of times. She'd not realized anything was amiss.

He swallowed. 'I'm not going to be here tomorrow. I'll be running Pixie to Chichester. Ruth, Cal's sister, has made arrangements for him to be at her guest-house.'

'Oh, Bob.' She thought of Pixie, huge with her baby. He wiped away another tear with the back of his hand. Marlene wasn't used to seeing grown men cry. Especially not strong men like Bob. 'You don't have to worry about the market,' she said. 'I can manage.'

Around them the market was waking up. Vans were leaving the centre of the street so people could walk through the gaily coloured stalls set up for the day in Gosport. Music was playing somewhere close by and the smell of greasy food from the tea stand filled the air. Marlene heard a raucous laugh. It was business as usual.

'I'll be here to set up,' he said, wiping his face again.

'I told you not to worry,' she said, taking a slurp of her tea. 'Drink up,' she said. 'A bit of warmth will do you good.'

'I haven't been eating properly since we found out that Cal's alive,' he confessed. Marlene was happy to see him drink the tea. 'I just know as soon as she sees Cal she'll want him back. I'll lose her. I'll lose Sadie. Pixie and that little girl are my world.' He put down the mug and turned away. Marlene could see that he was crying in earnest, yet trying hard not to let her see his distress.

A woman in a headscarf picked up a saucepan. 'How much?'

Marlene told her and the woman fumbled in her handbag, producing the correct money. She slipped the cash into Bob's money belt and left, giving Bob a funny look but clutching the saucepan to her chest.

'D'you want to go home?'

Bob shook his head. 'I can't function properly there. I keep looking at her and thinking, she'll be gone soon.'

'Well, you're getting some funny looks here.'

'People don't understand, Marlene. I've loved that woman for ages, and when we got married it was the happiest day of my life. But before that she was head over heels in love with Cal. They were going to get married, you know.'

'I remember,' Marlene said. 'When he was declared missing, believed dead, it was only the baby that kept her sane.'

He took a grubby handkerchief from his coat pocket and blew his nose hard. 'After all this time, finding out he isn't dead is pulling us apart. God forgive me but I wish he *had* died!'

'That's a wicked thing to say. The Americans are helping us win the war, Bob.'

A dark-haired woman was looking at the jewellery in the largest of Marlene's glass-topped boxes. She seemed interested in the gold pieces. 'Want me to take it out for you?' Marlene asked.

The young woman nodded. She had her eye on the antique Celtic brooch. It was one of a number of brooches that Samuel had loaned Marlene the money to buy. And now Marlene could tell the woman wanted it by the way she turned it over and over in her hands.

'Is it gold?'

'Nine carat,' said Marlene. She showed her the markings on the back.

'How much?'

Marlene told her and could see she was interested.

'It's a special gift for my mum,' she said. 'We've an Irish background and I just know she'll love it.'

'Birthday?'

The woman nodded. 'I'll take it.'

Marlene put the money into her belt and handed her the brooch, wrapped in tissue and a pretty hand-made bag, tiny enough for the gift and fashioned from wallpaper. She believed in making her jewellery look special. It cost practically nothing to make the small bags, using flour-and-water paste to stick the corners together and colourful wool for tiny handles.

The sale of that brooch had secured her pitch fee for the day and her overheads. Anything else she sold was pure profit. She marvelled that with Samuel bankrolling her, sometimes with quite enormous sums of money, she really *was* doing well. She always paid him back promptly because the gold sold, and her large stock of jewellery meant she could provide gifts for all occasions. She knew her mother was proud of her. And she was proud of herself. Having money put aside meant she didn't need to worry about the future. And it was all due to her own hard work.

A few moments later she sold a gold necklace to a lad for his girlfriend, then a wedding ring to a woman who had been bombed out and had lost her own. 'I don't feel properly married without me ring,' the woman said.

'Well, that one will make you feel closer to your husband again,' Marlene said.

'I don't want to be closer. Bert died when the bomb fell on the house. It's to stop the blokes pestering me now I'm single again!' The peroxide blonde gave a lusty laugh as she handed over the cash.

Marlene drank the last of her mug of tea, which was now stone cold. She glanced at Bob, who had quite a queue waiting. He looked as though he had his customers under control, giving them the old market-stall patter. His jokes didn't mean he'd forgotten about the pain that tomorrow's visit to Chichester might cause. He was a professional and could hide behind his façade of chatter.

She thought about the weekend she and Samuel had spent in Kent. They'd stopped at a small B-and-B in a place called Ashford and made love all night long. Marlene felt sure that he was going to ask her to marry him.

On the way back they'd discussed their finances. She was surprised at how much property Samuel owned. He'd bought bombed houses, managed to employ some men and magically get hold of materials to rebuild. People were crying out for homes of their own. He told her he took chances because he knew the homes would resell quickly. Which was one of the reasons he urged her to take chances and buy as much gold as she could to sell. Again he'd said the magic words, 'Speculate to accumulate.' Marlene had to admit he knew what he was talking about.

After her little flurry of sales, she looked at Bob again: he was standing dejectedly, staring into the distance. 'You're gonna put the customers off if you don't cheer up.' Marlene didn't mean to be inconsiderate, but a market trader with a frown and no patter was on a losing streak. 'She won't leave you. She's having your baby.' He looked at her and she felt so sorry for him. She went over and put her arms around him. 'Pixie loves you,' she said. 'Is there anything I can do, apart from looking after your stuff tomorrow?'

'No,' he said. 'I'm sorry for being such a wet blanket. I'm glad I can talk to you. You're a really good mate, Marlene.'

'Have you talked to Pixie about how you feel?'

He sniffed. 'She knows I'm scared. How can she not? I think she's nervous of seeing Cal as well.'

'When she talks to him, I hope you'll stay in the room with her. If you don't, if you simply drop her at the guest-house and drive away, you'll be wondering forever what was said. But somehow I think Pixie's already thought about all this.'

Marlene pulled away from him, willing him to look into her eyes. Bob had given her a start on the markets. He'd provided her with a job when everyone else had pushed her from pillar to post because she was unmarried and had a kiddie. He'd taken a chance on a skinny, red-haired girl and been made the subject of gossip into the bargain. She had such a lot to thank Bob for.

'I can't influence your Pixie. But I know she loves you. And if you need me, I'm here for you.' She meant it.

The Fox was full of troops and American airmen. Em watched as Gladys finished the gin and orange she'd not long served her. Em was helping Sam behind the bar. There were so many men in Gosport now and no one knew what they were doing there, certainly not themselves. At night the pubs were overflowing.

'I just want to know why all leave is cancelled,' said a sailor, and smoothed flat his square collar. 'I'd like to see my missus and the kids up in Warwickshire.' He drank some Brickwood's Ale and set the pint pot back on the counter. Gladys appeared at the side of him. Em looked at her neat figure in the navy two-piece. That woman certainly held her age well, she thought.

'Where d'you come from?' Gladys asked the man, though he'd directed his words at Em.

'A little village called Moreton,' he said.

'Oh, I know where that is. Pretty place,' said Gladys.

Em knew for a fact that Gladys had never set foot in Warwickshire.

'Do you? Would you like a drink?'

'I don't mind if I do,' said Gladys, treating him to a smile. Em went to the back of the counter, poured Gladys a gin, then dripped in the orange squash. She put it on the counter and glared at Gladys. That was her all over, she thought. A leopard never changes its spots. Siddy, her landlord and fancy man, had gone to London on business, so Gladys was out gallivanting. Siddy was a nice bloke, and Em hoped Gladys wouldn't hurt him. She took the money the sailor offered and went off to serve an airman.

Em liked being behind the bar. It was worth the rows that her old man initiated as soon as she went through the front door. He'd started his games again, hurting her at every opportunity. Her left arm was covered with bruises from where he'd slammed the cupboard door on it while she was searching for a tin of cocoa. All she was doing was helping out in the bar. She'd told Sam she wouldn't mess her husband about by carrying on with him.

Trouble was, Em knew her husband had been behind Lizzie's rape. The attack had been meant for Rita because Rita was a damned good friend to her and he couldn't handle Em having friends. Blackie had had a word with him. She never did find out what form those words had taken, but for a while Jack had been nice to her. Now her husband's aggression was building again. Em was scared stiff that Jack would harm her permanently. That was why it was such a pleasure to work a couple of hours in the bar where the noise and music cheered her.

And Sam? He said he'd waited so long for her that he could go on waiting. Of course he knew nothing of Jack's antics.

Lizzie was sitting in the corner with some of the Priddy's girls. There was a lot of laughing going on. She'd seemed to be coping well since the attack, though you never knew what went on in anyone's head, not even your own daughter's. Em was glad Lizzie and Rita were proper friends again. Lizzie was only in there tonight because Blackie had gone off on a bit of business, so he'd told Lizzie. But he was taking her to that hotel she liked so much in Stratford at the weekend.

Lizzie had done a daft thing telling Blackie that Rita was seeing the young American. He'd been angry, like it was Lizzie's fault Rita had gone to the hospital. He'd wanted to know all about it. But that was Blackie, wanting to know the ins and outs of everything.

Cigarette smoke swirled around the bar and the smell of stale beer hung in the air. Music trilled from the wireless, big-band music that the Americans especially liked. There wasn't room to dance, but a few couples were smooching to the tunes.

Gladys's sailor was waiting at the bar to buy her another drink. Em saw she looked quite tiddly. She hoped Gladys wasn't going to leave with him.

A wave of laughter came up from the end of the bar. Em glanced at Sam, who was telling some American lads a dirty joke. He must have felt her eyes on him for he turned and winked at her.

Em winked back, and for a moment they were cocooned in their own special world.

Chapter Seventeen

Pixie was glad that she and Bob had arrived at Ruth's Chichester guest-house before Cal and his nurse. On the drive up they'd hardly spoken, both locked in their own thoughts. Every so often Bob took a hand from the steering-wheel and squeezed her knee. She knew he was thinking about her and wished she could alleviate his fears. Before the news about Cal had reached her, Pixie could hardly believe her life had become so perfect. She had a wonderful husband, a little girl who was the apple of her stepfather's eye and a home she was content with. An added factor was the new baby to look forward to.

Ruth, dressed in a smock and a wrap-around green skirt, was carrying her baby high. She, too, was due to give birth any day.

'Come on in,' Ruth said, ushering them into the warm

sitting room. There were several rag rugs strewn across the carpet. Pixie had made them when she'd lodged with Ruth and it was comforting to see her friend still cherished them. Cups and saucers and covered plates of food sat on a tray on the small table and the air smelled highly of polish.

'How's business? And your other half?' Bob asked, after Ruth had made them comfortable and presented them with tea. Pixie saw he was trying to cope with a tiny china cup and saucer that seemed too small for his hands. He liked Ruth's husband, who was stationed locally, in the Air Force.

'Slow at this time of the year, Bob. It'll pick up about Easter time. My husband would have liked to see you, said you and he don't get together often enough, but he's not been granted leave with all this building work going on in the Channel and on the beaches. They've put barbed wire along the seafronts, and Chichester harbour is awash with forces personnel. There's meeting after meeting going on at the airfield. Though I'm told little enough about anything. I read more in the newspapers.'

Her American accent had softened so that she sounded almost English. Pixie thought how well she looked.

'Who's got Sadie?' Ruth asked.

'She's with Marlene's mum.' Pixie could have kissed the woman for offering to look after the little girl. 'Have you said anything . . . ?'

'God, no!' Ruth shook her head. 'Cal doesn't know he has a child.' It was almost as though Ruth had tuned in to what Pixie was thinking. 'When he arrives you'll see why I didn't want to complicate his memory of you. Anyway, it's really up to you to explain about Sadie and the past, isn't it?'

Bob looked at Pixie. She knew he was thinking Ruth had made the right decision. She nodded thoughtfully.

There was a heavy silence in the room. Pixie heard a car draw up on the gravelled hard-standing outside the house. Then a woman's voice, and a knock on the front door. Her heart was thudding. She wanted the deep chair she was sitting in to swallow her. She glanced at Bob and saw worry etched across his face.

Ruth rose to answer the door, and a blast of cold air came in, along with a woman who seemed very young, Pixie thought, to be a nurse. Her dark hair cascaded down her back from a ponytail and her blue gabardine coat showed her neat figure.

Behind her was Cal.

It was like looking at a male version of Ruth, with his blond hair and pale good looks. His eyes travelled around the room, then settled on her. Pixie thought everyone in the room must be able to hear her heart hammering.

He came across the floor in a couple of ungainly strides, bent down, and put his arms around her. Then, with difficulty, he knelt in front of her on the swirly-patterned wool carpet. 'Oh, Pixie,' he said.

Pixie's eyes took him in, along with the remembered smell of the man she'd loved. She was immobile. Then, slowly, her hand reached across and ruffled his hair. Cal was the man she'd loved. Yet he was *not the same man*. He looked at her and his eyes reflected the suffering he'd endured. Pixie found she couldn't say a word, only stare at him.

'Tea,' said Ruth, briskly, wiping the corner of her eye with a handkerchief. 'I'll make more tea.' Pixie knew Ruth wanted to escape the scene unfolding in front of her. The nurse, her face immobile, perched herself on a high-backed chair, her long legs elegantly crossed at the ankles.

'Do you want me to help, Ruth?' Bob rose.

'Please don't go,' Pixie said, looking at him. Then she turned back, gazed into Cal's eyes once more and said, 'This is my husband, Bob. Remember, he lived next door to me?' Pixie felt as though she was apologizing for marrying him.

Cal used his hands and the arms of her chair to heave

himself up and went to stand in front of the fire. 'Yes,' he said, 'I remember.'

Pixie expected the two men to shake hands but they didn't. Instead Cal turned towards the nurse. 'Jennie, this is Pixie.' Pixie thought it was a strange thing to say. Surely everyone, including the nurse, couldn't fail to see or know who she was. She smiled at the glamorous young woman, feeling dowdy beside her.

Jennie was taking off her coat, revealing a slim body in a grey wool skirt and matching jumper. 'I know all about you, Pixie. It's good to meet you at last.' She didn't move across the room, but she treated Pixie to a dazzling smile as she handed Cal her coat.

Pixie saw that Jennie was watching Cal's every move. Even as he left the room to take her coat into the hall, Jennie waited, watching the door. They shared a smile as soon as he stepped back again. Why, she thought, the girl was jealous and trying hard not to show it. That could only mean one thing. Jennie was in love with him.

Her eyes lit on Bob. The pain in him was terrible to see. Then it was as if she was looking at him through different eyes, his eyes. He knew he was a working man, with dirt beneath his fingernails from the market gear and calluses on his hands from erecting heavy stalls. His face was weather-beaten and, though he was neatly dressed in his Sunday clothes, he was no visual match for the handsome, uniformed American. Bob knew he was rough and ready, that he could never be like the young man who had been her lover before him. For a moment Pixie wanted to cry out that outward appearances didn't matter, that it was what was in a person's heart that counted. But she didn't.

She couldn't help but notice the stiffness of Cal's lower limbs. He moved with measured steps, holding on to the backs of chairs, the edges of tables. She doubted that the others would remember his easy walk, but she had known every inch of him. She remembered his body almost as well as she knew her own. Whatever had happened had left scars, maybe mental ones as well. Perhaps he would tell them later.

Ruth returned with washed crockery and a larger teapot. She'd put plain biscuits on a plate, arranged with their ends touching in the centre of the dish. Pixie wondered why, as no one had so far helped themselves to a dainty sandwich or, indeed, any of the other biscuits. Perhaps Ruth, too, was nervous. Bob took the tray from her and put it on the table.

'D'you want me to be mother?' Pixie blessed Bob for trying to lighten the heavy atmosphere. She also knew that pouring tea might give him the excuse he needed not to watch her and Cal's every move. Pixie knew it wasn't jealousy Bob suffered from – there wasn't a mean bone in his body – but he *was* in pain. The fear of losing her and the life they'd built together was as painful to him as a broken bone. But still Pixie was silent. Ruth smiled. 'I'll do it,' she said. 'I get enough practice in this place. Cal, why don't you fill us in on what happened?'

She was trying hard to keep things going, thought Pixie, to put a halt to the unnatural silences.

Cal sat down on a hard chair next to Jennie. Pixie could tell Jennie had to hold herself back from touching him. She made do instead with stealing another shy glance.

'I did write you, Pixie, every day. Even though I knew you'd get the letters in dribs and drabs. I wrote mostly in the evenings, lying on my bunk . . .' He stopped talking about the letters as though he'd grasped it wasn't what his audience wanted to hear.

'USS *Bristol* was torpedoed and the ship was practically broken in two. I almost stepped into the gap, but was saved by my buddy. I was hit by part of the collapsed ceiling when it fell. Of course, I didn't know what was going on at that time. The details came later when I was in hospital.

'Apparently the blow to my head knocked me silly but I was dragged to a life-raft and somehow managed to hang on – or, rather, my buddies helped me stay awake enough to hold on for about twelve hours until we were rescued. I found out later that there were others in that dinghy who were in a far worse state than me.

'They gave me a Purple Heart, just for staying alive.' He sighed. 'That's it in a nutshell, but when eventually I woke in the nice, clean hospital bed, I didn't know who I was. I'd left my memory on that broken destroyer along with my foot.'

He lifted a trouser leg. A steel and wood contraption joined his leg to his shoe.

Ruth gasped. Pixie realized that Cal might have told his sister what had happened but she was now seeing the evidence for the first time. She went over to her brother and clasped him to her huge stomach. Ruth's swollen eyes showed she had been crying afresh, probably when she'd made excuses to go to the kitchen. No one else in the room spoke.

Pixie filled the silence. 'I never knew,' she said. Jennie was gazing at Cal with adoration. Her face went bright red when Cal, disentangling himself from his sister's grasp, and ignoring Pixie's remark, added, 'Jennie urged me to get on with the business of walking, of living again. I had no idea who I was. My dog-tag', he motioned to the chain worn at his neck, hidden beneath his suit, 'told me my name. But, as far as I was concerned, that person could have been anyone.' He sniffed and shook his head. 'It was like starting life all over again, but instead of being a baby and learning to walk and talk, I was supposed to *know* if I liked music, if I had parents, a girlfriend . . .' He paused. 'I knew nothing. It was as though my life had begun in the hospital.'

He looked across the room at Pixie. She was listening intently, trying to understand how it must have been for him. Suddenly she was eternally grateful to Jennie for helping Cal back on the road to recovery. His gratitude to her showed in the way he kept glancing at her, as though for approval.

No one was speaking, all of them intent on his next words.

'One day Jennie and I were out walking, if you can call my early efforts walking, and we passed a hall advertising a dance on the following Friday. It began to rain, a terrific downpour. Of course I had no way I could quickly remove myself to shelter so the rain fell on the two of us as we held hands trying to run. I had the strangest sensation that I could dance, had been dancing, and that I had been laughing in the rain, holding hands before.'

Pixie felt the tears rise. Her eyes flew to Bob's face.

She could see he was hurting more and more with every memory of Cal's that unfolded.

Cal and she had been dancing when she'd run from him and Rita, leaving them in the Connaught Hall. There'd been a thunderstorm, and Cal had come after her. Wet through, they'd booked into the Black Bear for the night. It had been the first time Pixie had ever made love to a man. Sadie was conceived that night and Pixie never saw Cal again.

'After a while, snatches of conversation came back to me. I didn't know who I was talking to, but I knew it was real.' He looked at Jennie. 'This woman was so incredibly patient with me. Never laughing when I told her of peculiar things like smells reminding me of different places, or of people. One day Jennie wore a perfume I'd not previously noticed. I remember wondering why she had dark hair instead of blonde. Silly, isn't it? She told me her father had got hold of a bottle of Evening in Paris and made a present of it to her. And I remembered someone else wearing it.'

Pixie raised a hand to her forehead. Evening in Paris had always been her favourite perfume and she'd been wearing it the night Sadie had been conceived . . .

'A couple of weeks ago I read in the newspaper of an explosion at Priddy's Hard. It was like I'd been hit on the head all over again. I suddenly felt afraid for the workers at the armaments factory. Though, of course, I knew no one who worked there.' He looked across the room at Pixie again. 'That was the beginning of remembering *you*, Pixie.'

So far, Pixie hadn't moved from her position in the deep armchair. The baby was now pressing on a nerve and she crossed her legs to ease the strain. Cal had been told of her marriage to Bob, and that she was heavily pregnant with Bob's child.

Pixie thought it was ridiculous that she and Cal had to decide what to do with the rest of their lives when they'd been apart for so long that both had taken different directions.

Cal's references to Jennie showed he cared a great deal for her. And it wasn't just because he was grateful that, as a nurse, she'd looked after him. Jennie might be young but it was obvious she was captivated by the American. Bob was staring at Pixie. She looked away but not before he'd seen her tears.

She couldn't ignore the look of pain on his face. His dear, dear, face. Bob was worn by work, but that work had given her food, a roof over her head, and he'd done all that for her. Loving memories didn't put food in bellies. Memories had to be put behind her. It was the here and now that counted.

And suddenly she knew what she had to do. It was vibrantly clear and her heart and head told her it was the right thing.

'I'll always love you, Cal. You were my first . . .' She faltered. 'But our love was very passionate and very new. Now our lives are entirely different. I'm glad we've met again and I'm glad you're alive. Thank you for the good memories. I shall cherish them my whole life.'

Pixie saw Jennie's shoulders relax as though a huge weight had been lifted from them. Bob put his hand to his forehead and sighed.

The fire was still crackling and Pixie watched a bright spark jump from a log and fall on the tiles where it glittered then died. Cal got up and walked unsteadily to Ruth, putting his arms around her shoulders. He didn't look at Pixie. It was almost as if the afternoon had been too much for him and he was glad it was finally over. Yet he had no idea what to say or how to behave towards the woman who had once been the love of his life and had now made it abundantly clear that she wanted him no more.

'We're going for a drink at the canal-side pub near the bridge. A slow walk will help me clear my head. I need to think. We'll take you up on the offer to stay here tonight.' He looked to his sister for confirmation.

Pixie heard Ruth say something she didn't quite catch

but there was a smile shared between them before Ruth kissed him on the cheek. Cal left Ruth and again knelt in front of Pixie.

'Bob's a lucky man.' He gave a big sigh. 'This bloody war has a lot to answer for.'

He rose, and now shook Bob's hand. Then Bob got up to walk with Cal, Jennie close on his heels, to the front door. Ruth disappeared into the kitchen, taking a tray full of crockery and uneaten food with her.

Pixie pulled out her handkerchief and blew her nose. No goodbyes had come from her. After her speech she'd been a spectator. She knew when she and Bob had left the guest-house Ruth would meet up with her brother and they would discuss the situation. She also knew Ruth would keep the secret of Sadie's birth, leaving Pixie to do as she thought fit.

When she heard the front door close behind Cal and Jennie, she hauled herself from the deep chair and went out to the kitchen. 'Do you think, Ruth, I did and said the right things?'

Ruth turned the tap on and watched the water run into the enamelled washing-up bowl. 'I know my brother better than anyone. You've broken his heart.'

Pixie grabbed at her arm. 'It was the best thing for everyone, including him.'

Ruth turned to face her. 'What do you mean?'

'You must be blind if you couldn't see that girl, Jennie, trying one moment to act sophisticated and professional as though she really was *only* his nurse then the next minute looking scared stiff and smiling at him constantly to show him she cares. She might have started out as his nurse but she's by his side now because she loves him.'

Ruth sighed. She was digesting Pixie's words. 'What about his child, Sadie? He's got a right to know he has a kiddie.'

'He won't have such a good life hampered by his daughter and me. At least this way, not knowing, he's free to live unencumbered by the past. He might even want to go home to America. He and Jennie can have a good future together. Maybe marry and have children of their own.'

'But you'd do that, deny him Sadie?'

'Only because I care about *his* future and my Bob's. Sadie knows Bob as her daddy. Let it stay like that.'

Ruth was quiet. Only the ticking of the clock disturbed the silence.

'What about Sadie? She should be aware Bob's not her true father.' Ruth stood in front of Pixie, a tea-towel in her hands. She was twisting it nervously.

'I agree.' Pixie would never lie to her daughter. 'When

she's old enough to understand, I won't keep the truth from her. Like your brother said, this bloody war has caused so many heartaches. But after all Cal's been through, he deserves a chance of happiness.'

'He could be happy with you. I just want what I think's best for Cal. It's obvious he still cares for you.'

'*Still* cares is not enough. We're two very different people now. And, Ruth, what you think is best for Cal may not be what *we* want. I'm married and I wouldn't want to hurt so many people. My children, Bob, my family, even Jennie. I believe now that you can love two men at the same time. But Cal belongs to my past. Bob is my soulmate.'

A cough startled her. Pixie looked towards the doorway. Bob was standing there, his bulk almost blocking the opening. Pixie realized he had heard everything. She felt the blush rise over her neck, her face.

'What d'you think, Ruth?' Bob aimed his question at her. 'Has she done the right thing? Or will you tell your brother about Sadie?' He paused. 'If I was in his position I know what I'd want, and that's a new start. If he still loves Pixie it will break his heart to see Sadie and her in a loving environment with another man. I couldn't do it. Could *he* cope mentally? Or would he prefer to begin a relationship with a girl like Jennie who obviously loves him?'

Pixie sat down on one of the kitchen chairs. Bob walked over to her and stood behind her, his big hand on her shoulder. 'I promise you, Ruth, that little Sadie will want for nothing. You're welcome any time at my house to see her. I know we'll stay friends. Sadie will be my girl. I already love her to distraction and she'll have whatever her heart desires. And when the right time comes we'll *all* be together to explain about her conception and the decision made this afternoon.'

Ruth turned on the tap, letting the cold water run into the washing-up bowl, cooling the scalding water from the kettle. She watched it drizzle over the crockery. Then she turned the tap off, wiped her hands on the tea-towel, threw it onto the work surface and pulled Pixie to her feet, putting her arms around her. 'You and I have, in the past, been through a lot together. My own baby,' she leaned back and patted her stomach, 'is growing safely inside me because you came to this house, helped with my lodgers, and I was able to relax enough to conceive. I owe you everything, Pixie. Now you're doing the same for Cal, giving my brother a chance of happiness. I'm still not sure you're doing the right thing, though.'

Pixie thought about her mother. Gladys had done terrible things in her life but she'd never lied. She'd brought Pixie up to believe in the truth. Could Pixie live a life built on an untruth about Sadie's real father? Could they be happy knowing Cal had been denied the truth about Sadie?

'Bob, get Cal back!' She knew he couldn't have got far. Walking was difficult for him despite the nearness of the pub.

Bob was clearly surprised but he didn't argue. A look of complete understanding passed between them. The front door banged. She heard the van start up.

'Whatever happens, Cal deserves to know.'

'Thank you,' said Ruth. Her relief was visible. Just then Pixie's baby gave an almighty kick that Ruth, so close to her, felt. She looked into Pixie's eyes. 'He's going to be a footballer!'

Once more Cal sat on a chair and Pixie faced him. Jennie stood behind him and Bob and Ruth sat side by side on the sofa.

'I should have told you something, Cal,' Pixie said. 'You have a child, a little girl.'

Cal gasped. Jennie's fingers on the back of the upright chair went white.

Bob searched in his inside pocket. He handed the picture to Ruth so she could pass it to Cal. The room was silent but there was an air of expectancy. Cal took the photo, which was dog-eared from being in Bob's wallet. His hands were shaking. 'But we only made love once . . .'

That wasn't what Pixie had expected him to say. Quickly she replied, 'That's all it takes.'

He was still looking at the photograph.

'Why didn't you tell me about her earlier?' Cal passed the photograph back to Bob.

Pixie sighed. Her reasons sounded feeble now. 'She believes Bob to be her daddy and I didn't want her life turned upside down. I also think you'll have a greater chance of happiness without a little girl to look after part of the time.'

'Part of the time? What do you mean?'

'I thought once you found out about your daughter you'd want a share in her life—'

'But I don't know the first thing about children.' He looked up at Jennie. 'Though I had hoped one day . . .' He coughed and put his hand to his mouth. 'Pixie, I needed to see what your reaction to me would be and whether the feelings we had for each other were still there. Now I know they aren't.'

Pixie stared at him. It was as if she was talking to a stranger. 'No, but you *are* her father.'

'Do you need money? I hope to return to America

but I'm not disputing the girl's mine and I can make arrangements so she'll never go short.'

Pixie saw the redness creeping up Cal's neck. She was about to say something when Bob said, 'We don't need money, mate! I can provide for my family—'

'Don't argue! This is my daughter . . .' Pixie said, close to tears. She could see Bob was angry.

Ruth had struggled to her feet. 'I think we need some more tea and to decide calmly what to do for the best.'

Pixie blessed her for defusing the heat that filled the room.

'This is a great shock,' Cal said.

At this Jennie, who so far had listened but said nothing, bent forward and whispered in his ear. Cal suddenly looked at Pixie, then said, 'It would have been so different if I'd known. You must have found it difficult carrying a child and being alone.'

This was what the whispering had been about, Pixie thought. Jennie was reminding him that being pregnant and unmarried was a difficult situation for a young girl.

'She was worth every tear of unhappiness,' said Pixie, 'and I was lucky to have good friends.' She could hear Ruth rattling about in the kitchen and hauled herself out of her chair to help.

*

The air inside the living room seemed clearer when the tea had been drunk and tempers restored, though Bob was no longer cheerful. He sat grim-faced, staring at Cal. Then he said, 'Will you be happy if I bring your daughter up as my own child? You can see her any time you want,' a hint of sarcasm dropped into his tone, 'or when you visit England. And I promise I'll never keep it from her that she has another father.'

'I think that's an excellent idea.' Jennie's voice was sharp and clear. Cal nodded but didn't speak.

Pixie sighed with relief that everything seemed settled. She'd had enough of sitting in soft chairs that made her back ache.

'Yes, that's best. No lives are disrupted,' said Cal.

Pixie gazed at the stranger she had once loved. Now she didn't care if she never saw him again. 'I want to go home,' she said. She rubbed her hand across her large bump. 'He's been lying on a nerve all afternoon.' She was so glad the tension of the day had ended. 'I think I need to lie down,' she said. 'And thanks, Ruth.'

Ruth turned to Bob who was now close to Pixie. 'You're a man in a million.'

Bob's arm snaked around Pixie. 'Let's get off, love,' he said.

Chapter Eighteen

The bombing started as they neared Portsmouth, the siren wailing, like a demented calf searching for its mother.

'We'd better pull over and get in a shelter somewhere,' said Bob. He hadn't spoken since leaving the guest-house. Pixie knew there was no need for words. They loved each other and she was satisfied she'd been able to speak her mind in front of him. So many women had no say in what went on in their marriages or, indeed, in their lives.

'He never even asked her name,' Pixie said. 'If only we could see into the future, how different things would be.' Bob put his hand on her thigh. She now had to tell him some more news. 'My waters have broken.'

Mindful of the road, he turned briefly and squeezed her leg. 'Messed up my van, have you?'

He was making a joke to keep her calm but Pixie knew he was both worried and excited.

He added, 'That's a good reason to find a safe haven.'

'And have strangers gawping at me?'

'It will take us about half an hour to reach Alma Street. That's without the problems of this raid. If we meet obstructions it'll take much longer. Even I know second babies come quickly. How d'you feel?'

Pixie knew he was willing to do whatever she wanted.

'The pains are gaining on me. I had a backache when I woke up this morning but I didn't tell you because I know how you worry. You'd have cancelled today and I wanted to get it over with. The ache was one of the reasons I sat in the chair and didn't move much at Ruth's.'

'And there was me thinking you didn't want anyone to see you so big when that Jennie was such a skinny little thing.'

'I'll ignore that. Oooh!'

'I really think we should pull over.'

'No!' Just then the sky was lit up as a bomb hit a tower near the shoreline at Portchester. Orange flashes were bouncing on the roads and houses. Searchlights lit up the sky.

The van was crawling along in the near-dark with

barely a glimmer coming from its lights but now Bob turned them off altogether. The slightest gleam on a darkened road might be seen by an enemy plane and they'd be wiped out as easily as a fly, squashed on a wall.

Bob had driven on the hill road. Below them the colours in the sky and the burning buildings showed up the roads and shoreline that surrounded Portsmouth and Gosport. The panorama was terrifying.

'Hold on, girl!' Bob had to swerve round a pothole that had appeared in the road near the old fort. All this land was War Department property and the enemy planes' navigators would be hoping for direct hits. 'I really think we should pull over!'

'We'd be sitting ducks! I can hold on,' Pixie shouted, as a pain gripped her. What a ridiculous thing to say, she thought. The baby was coming, being born at its own pace and there was nothing she could do to slow it down. 'I want to be indoors, not out here among the grass and hedges and falling bombs. What if something goes wrong?'

Bob muttered, 'What else could go wrong?'

Pixie began to laugh. Whether it was nerves, or the predicament they were in, it suddenly seemed very funny. Bob put his foot down on the accelerator. Pixie gritted her teeth, determined not to cry out. The more she allowed the pain to show, the more likely Bob was to stop the van and make her comfortable among the detritus of his stall and its goods piled in the rear of the van so she could give birth.

The whining planes and pounding ack-ack guns were like fireworks, she thought. Bombs were falling to earth and blowing up the shops, houses and factories along the south coast. Oh, how she wished they were off this hill above the city of Portsmouth.

Pixie put her hands across the tightness of her stomach and said, 'Don't worry, my son. I'll look after you.' She knew it was a promise that she might find impossible to keep.

Even with the windows tightly shut, the smell of burning crept into the cab, making Pixie want to heave. Bob foraged down by the side of his seat and handed her a brown-paper bag. 'I usually give these to customers when they buy something,' he said.

Pixie couldn't smile: she was busy throwing up.

And then they were on the descent of the hill and driving into Fareham. Here the lower road was awash with ambulances, mostly going in the direction of Portsmouth.

'Something big's been hit,' said Bob. Pixie looked at his face. It was grim. 'I hope my girl's safe,' he said.

Pixie felt suddenly ashamed that she hadn't given Sadie

a thought. She'd automatically trusted Marlene and her mother to care for her as they would their own little girl . . . 'She will be.' Pixie gasped as another pain gripped her. Bob had said 'my girl'. *Sadie was his girl.* If anything, Sadie loved her daddy more than she loved Pixie, but that was the way with fathers and daughters, wasn't it?

The Fareham to Gosport road was almost impossible for Bob to navigate. Houses had been hit and people were sitting around on kitchen chairs and boxes with blankets over their shoulders. Grey smoke was pouring into the sky and a WVS tent had been set up with women serving steaming cups of tea. Pixie couldn't believe they were helping people before the all-clear had sounded.

Rubble was strewn across the roadway and Bob carefully manoeuvred round the worst of it, apologetic to Pixie when the van rocked as he negotiated fallen bricks. 'Let me pull over, Pixie. There are women here who can make you comfortable.'

'They've got enough to do with the injured. I want to go home.' And it *was* all she wanted, to be in the warmth of her own kitchen, to smell its familiar smells and for everything to be all right. But what if something went wrong? Would Gladys be next door when they got to Alma Street?

Another pain had started. She cried out and shut her eyes in an effort to will it away. When she opened them, she saw the Alma pub on the corner of her street. On the opposite corner, where the Haytors lived, there was a huge gap. Furniture was lying in the street. Amazingly, a small table and a kitchen chair were upright, almost as though someone was coming to sit outside and watch what was going on. Another ambulance was parked to the side of the road, and sitting at the back facing the road was Georgie, the Haytors' sixteen-year-old son. He had their orange cat under his arm but he was as immobile as the cat allowed, his face as white as bed linen. A trolley with a sheet completely covering it was standing near the open back doors of the ambulance. And still the sky was filled with noise and smoke and colour.

'Stop, we must help,' began Pixie. She could hear someone screaming.

'Are you crazy? You'll just add to their distress!'

A fireman moved the covered trolley so Bob could drive through the rubble and he parked practically outside their front door. 'This whole row of houses could be demolished at any moment,' shouted the fireman.

Pixie was doubled over. It was impossible for her to straighten up.

Bob slipped his key into the front-door lock, glad his

house was on the opposite side of the road to the fires, then opened the van door and lifted Pixie out as though she was a doll. He carried her into the kitchen, moved the table to one side and laid her on the rag rug in front of the range. Immediately Pixie relaxed in the familiarity of her own home.

The room shook as another bomb fell not too far away.

'Let's get you undressed.'

She felt her lower clothes being yanked off and then she was unceremoniously pushed into the Morrison shelter.

In between crying and yelling, she was aware of Bob running about the kitchen and scullery. He was collecting towels, which he dumped by the side of the open shelter. 'Drink this.' He put a cup of cold water to her lips. 'I'll make tea later, when it's safe to switch on the gas.' After a few sips had gone down, he said, 'I'm going next door for your mother.' Not giving her time to argue, he disappeared. The pain subsided but she was aware that the baby had shifted low inside her. She gripped the bars of the shelter as another wave of excruciating pain suddenly swept over her. Sweat was pouring off her as Bob returned, grumbling about the house being empty and the possibility of Gladys being in the public shelter. She heard the tap running, and then he squeezed into the shelter at her feet.

'I've never been a midwife before,' he said. 'You'll have to tell me what to do.' He tried to wipe her forehead with a damp cloth but suddenly Pixie hated him and wanted him out of the way.

This time the pain tore into her, almost splitting her in two. The overwhelming urge to push produced sounds Pixie never knew she could utter. Then a brief easing of the torture before the final bearing down and the utter relief as the child slithered from her body to be swept up by Bob and laid on her near-naked breast.

'It's a baby!' he cried. 'A boy.' His smile was wide. 'I got the scissors. Where do I cut the cord?'

Bob was laughing and crying, and Pixie was filled with joy as she looked into the wide-open eyes of the waxy scrap of humanity, waving its tiny fists and lying warm and safe on her flesh.

'Leave enough room to tie the cord,' Pixie said, so calmly she almost couldn't believe it was her own voice.

Bob began daintily fiddling with the scissors. The yelling began as Pixie heard the siren scream for the all clear, paling in contrast to the noise from her child.

It was then she seemed unable to keep her eyes open.

All she could think of was that the child was alive and safe. At last she relaxed and drifted into sleep.

Bob was gently shaking her shoulder.

Pixie was still in the Morrison, but the bedding about her was clean and smelled washday fresh. She was wearing her flannelette nightdress and she could smell freshly brewed tea. At the side of the shelter was the Moses basket she'd prepared and inside it was a little lump.

'Washed, clothed and you're the same.' Bob looked tired. His stubble was growing, leaving a dark shadow. He looked enormously proud, and Pixie could see he'd shed tears.

'How could I have slept?' She was aware of how tired she still felt.

He took her hand. 'You've been a busy girl,' he said. He picked up a cup off its saucer and held it out. She got up on one elbow to take a sip. 'How do you feel?'

'Happy,' she said. And she was. Her heart was pounding but it was bursting with happiness. 'Can I hold my baby?'

'Of course,' he said, setting the cup down, then lifting the tiny bundle. As Pixie sat up, Bob pressed the child into her arms.

She pulled the shawl away to find the baby sweet-smelling, clean and wearing a nappy. The cord had been neatly tied and covered with gauze. Pixie smiled.

'What's this?' she said. He had stuck two plasters crossways in the shape of a large X to keep the gauze in place.

'I told you I'm not a midwife,' Bob said. 'But your mother's back now and I've sent her to telephone for the doctor, if he's available. The street was hit pretty hard.' He sighed. 'Don't worry about Sadie. She's staying the night with Marlene.'

Pixie wrapped up the sleeping scrap, its dark hair and incredibly long dark eyelashes fanning pink cheeks. She'd already made a note of the correct number of fingers and toes before she tucked the shawl around the baby and cuddled it to her.

'I love you,' she said to Bob.

'And I love you,' Bob replied.

Then Pixie remembered the fear she'd felt before her baby's birth, that perhaps she couldn't love another child as much as she loved Sadie. Her child's eyes flickered and latched to her own. Here he was, her second child. And here *it* was.

That great love.

Chapter Nineteen

'So, you got two fellers on the go now?'

Rita stopped pouring the lead azide into the small copper container. It looked like caster sugar but this particular powder was so powerful it could injure her skin if not poured correctly. She stared at Gladys, whose lipstick had settled into the lines around her mouth, as usual. Rita wished she'd wear a less deep red shade so it wouldn't be so obvious. Still, you wore whatever make-up you could get hold of these days. Rita had given Gladys the remainder of her old lipstick when Blackie had presented her with the new one, but Gladys continued wearing the dark colour that did her no favours.

'I beg your pardon?' said Rita.

'Don't get all hoity-toity with me. You're seeing the lad in hospital, that American, and now you got old dreamboat on a string.'

Rita finished tamping down the powder and moved it on so she could start on the next container. The air stank of gunpowder and for once the workroom was warm, so warm, in fact, that the women's combined sweaty smells were making her feel lightheaded. Perhaps Gladys was losing her marbles, Rita thought.

'You were seen in the boss's car, just the two of you. Apparently you were dolled up to the nines.'

The penny dropped.

'We only went out for a meal.' Rita tried to make it sound as though it was a normal occurrence.

Gladys grinned at her, like a demented Cheshire cat. 'What's he like?'

If only I could tell you, thought Rita, thinking about him not fancying women. 'All right,' she said nonchalantly. There was no way she could explain anything to Gladys about Rupert Scrivenor and the task he'd given her. So, if the girls thought she'd been on a date with him, perhaps the easiest thing to do was to let them believe it.

'You going out with him again? Did he kiss you?' Gladys's eyes were sparkling. No doubt she was thinking of the gossip she could spread, thought Rita wickedly.

'One question at a time. No, he didn't kiss me. Yes, we went out for a meal and the best part of it was the food. No, we're not going out again. It was a one-off.'

Gladys looked disappointed. 'Why not?'

'I reckon he was at a loose end. He doesn't come from round here, so he doesn't know many people. We didn't have anything in common.' At least that was partly true, thought Rita. And it should shut up the gossips.

Gladys was now using all her concentration to fill the copper shells. It was the end of the conversation. Until Gladys quietly said, 'You should have stayed with Blackie.'

'And you shouldn't be in the Fox flaunting it when you got your landlord on a string.'

'How d'you know that?' Gladys looked flustered.

Rita didn't want to tell her Em had spilled the beans about Gladys chatting up the men in the bar. So she merely shrugged and said, 'Pot calling the kettle black?'

'I wasn't born on this earth to be with one man,' said Gladys, with a far-away look in her eyes.

'Perhaps not, but that long streak of a bloke loves you to bits. Don't go off the rails, not when Pixie needs you.'

For a while there was silence between the two friends, but Gladys couldn't keep quiet for long and pretty soon they were talking animatedly about Pixie, the baby and her meeting with Cal.

Until lunch break they oohed and aahed about the new baby and praised Bob's prowess as a midwife. Rita knew that the doctor, who'd called in the next morning – he had been busy with people hurt during the bombing – had praised him for his cool head in dealing with the birth.

'She's got it all, now, hasn't she?' Gladys said wistfully. 'But I knew she'd never leave Bob for that Cal.'

Rita ignored her. Even Pixie hadn't known how she would react at seeing her first real love.

Em came up to them. She tapped her clipboard with a sharpened pencil. Rita noticed a large bruise on her wrist that disappeared into the long sleeve of her boiler suit. It looked nasty. 'It might help this country if you two got a move on instead of gossiping,' Em said.

'Sorry,' Rita said, as Em moved away, leaving them to it.

'So he's up to his nasty tricks again?' Gladys meant Jack.

Rita watched as Em made her way towards the exit. Such a lovely person, she thought. Yet the only happiness she had was snatched moments in a busy pub. Rita thought she deserved any love she could grab with Sam.

Her eyes roved around the long room. She hated spying on her friends. It seemed disloyal, as she'd known most of the women for years. Rumours about the war's progress were rife. She'd heard that Southwick House in the countryside just outside Fareham was the headquarters for something big. Yesterday she'd overheard several blokes in the tea-wagon queue say there was a maze of tunnels connecting the forts on Portsdown Hill, but no one seemed to know why that mattered. Despite the huge posters saying 'Careless Talk Costs Lives', people still gossiped and much of what they said was common knowledge anyway. Rita watched, listened, remembered, and waited to be called to Scrivenor's office. For the sake of her country, she would be ready for anything out of the ordinary that came to her notice. She wondered how much Em knew of what was going on between her and Scrivenor.

When the buzzer went and everyone downed tools, Rita waited for Gladys and walked with her towards the tea-wagon queue.

'Think he'll give you a rise, Rita?' Fat Mary yelled. Some of the girls giggled. 'He will if you give him something back!'

'Take no notice,' Gladys said. 'They'll only do it all the more if they see you're rattled.'

So Rita ignored the taunts. The girls would soon find someone else to tease.

Gaetano de Angelo, the Italian packer, was in front of her.

'With all this going on, why no more jobs?' He ran his fingers through his shiny dark hair. He was a good-looking man, with soulful brown eyes. 'I no understand why sailors of Canada and America live in tents on Grove Road field. Why so much work for them, but ordinary people no work if not possible for to be in forces?'

Rita strained to see who he was talking to, but it looked as though he was just letting off steam.

'Can't stand bloody Italians,' Gladys whispered. 'His parents came over here to open a café before the war, and Gaetano should have joined up to fight for us, but his hearing's bad so he won't be called up.'

Nobody answered the Italian because no one could: there was no answer to give him. Rita was waiting to hear his usual plea when his cuppa had been poured: 'I no have all the money.'

'Here, mate,' said a big bloke, another packer, who looked like he wanted serving quickly. He tossed a coin towards Gaetano, who smiled his thanks, paid, and went to sit on the wall with his tea. Later he was joined by the big bloke, who spoke a few words to him, then moved away to sit with some other men.

'The Italians aren't liked. There's some in that prisoner-of-war camp near where Blackie used to take you dancing. First they fought against us with the Germans at the beginning of the war, then changed sides to fight *with* us. Can't trust the buggers.'

Rita wasn't going to get into an argument with Gladys about how *she* saw the war and the Italians. Gaetano did a good job, earned good money, but never seemed to have enough to pay for his needs. She began to wonder why.

By the time she and Gladys were served, she'd had plenty of time to watch the Italian. He was shunned by the rest of the workforce. Yes, they actually ignored him. Everyone bought their tea and chatted in groups while they drank it. Gaetano sat alone. She decided he was worth keeping an eye on.

'Who's the boss's pet, then?' Bertha Pratt jeered. She was so close Rita could smell the cheese and onion sandwich the woman had just eaten.

'While they're talking about you, they're leaving someone else alone,' said Gladys, cheerfully.

As Em turned the key in her front door, the smell hit her. The place reeked of shit.

She let out a huge sigh. A long shift had taken it out of her and all she wanted was to get something to eat and go to bed. It was eleven o'clock at night, she'd been at the factory since five that morning and Lizzie, who normally worked an eight-hour day but was also on extra shifts, had gone to Blackie's house as they were leaving early in the morning for a dance. She thanked God her daughter wasn't coming in to this lot.

'That you, Em?'

The voice was contrite and came from the kitchen.

Trying hard not to breathe through her nose, she picked her way along the floor, trying to keep her feet out of the stinking mess criss-crossed by wheelchair marks.

'I'm not well, Em.'

He was sitting in it.

'Why didn't you get onto the lavatory, Jack?'

He could manage to wheel himself to the outside lavatory and hoist himself onto the seat. There were wooden ramps instead of steps at the door and although his legs were useless, his arms had the strength of ten men. There was also a hospital bedpan in the front-room cupboard.

'It all came on too quick,' he said. 'Shall I put the kettle on for tea?'

'You think I want a cuppa with this all around me?'

He cast his eyes downwards. She felt almost sorry for him. Once he'd been the tall, handsome man who'd swept her off her feet, sat her on the pillion seat of his Norton motorbike and roared off into the sunset. Well, to Lee Tower Ballroom, at any rate, where they'd danced the night away

And look at him now.

All for the sake of his country.

She went over to the sink, pulled back the curtain beneath it and took out the metal pail. She filled it with water and put it on the gas. Then she did the same with as many large saucepans as she could lay her hands on. She needed hot water, and plenty of it.

With her sleeves rolled up high, Em hauled her husband out of the wheelchair and stripped off his trousers and underwear. With the first bucket of water and some carbolic soap, she washed him. Then she sat him on a tall stool.

'Stay there,' she said, puffing hard. Her lips turned up in a small smile. There was no way he could go anywhere without his wheels.

Em pushed the wheelchair into the garden and set about sluicing it thoroughly, her eyes stinging with the disinfectant fumes. She didn't think about the stench, just scrubbed and wiped, marvelling that he was content to let her get on with it. Eventually she helped him back into the clean damp chair with fresh pyjamas on his wasted body.

It took three hours to clean the house. While she was doing it, she couldn't bring herself to speak to him.

She knew this was her punishment for going to the Fox.

When, finally, she was satisfied, she turned to him. He was reading his library book, *The High Window* by Raymond Chandler. She pulled down the top of the book and kept her fingers on it. 'Do that again and you can stay in it,' she said.

'I was ill, Em.' His voice grated on nerves already stretched to breaking point. She let her hand fall from the book. He turned a page and went on reading. 'I'd really like a cup of tea.'

Em didn't answer, but instead walked down the scrubbed passageway to the middle room that was now his bedroom. She'd long since stopped dragging him up and down the stairs.

His bedding needed changing. He must have hauled himself on to his bed. Probably to make the mess spread further. Soon the soiled sheets were soaking, ready to be washed tomorrow. The strong smell of disinfectant had taken over and she was happier.

Em decided to put out his clean clothes for tomorrow. She looked at the clock: she had four hours before she had to get up for work. She opened the wardrobe door.

She found a small cardboard box tucked between his jumpers.

Was she meant to discover it?

Was it the cause of his 'accident'?

The laxative was almost all gone. 'Easy to swallow' said the label on the box.

Chapter Twenty

Marlene thrust out her hand and wiggled her fingers. The ring glittered, almost outshining the early-morning sun.

Bob grabbed her hand and stared. 'He's got good taste.'

'I've got good taste, you mean!'

He was confused. Marlene sold jewellery, but she didn't wear showy pieces. He let her hand drop.

'I'm engaged!' She laughed at his bewildered face.

He shook his head. She tossed back her magnificent hair and laughed all the more.

'Samuel asked me to marry him and I said yes!' She wiggled her fingers once again. 'He's putting together a deal on a couple of houses down Queen's Road and I said, sooner than waste money he needs now, why didn't I choose a ring from my stock? He can splash out later when the deal's done.'

'Oh, I see,' said Bob. 'Then congratulations, if that's what you want.' He bent towards her and gave her a hug. She smelled of lily-of-the-valley perfume.

She pulled away. 'I know you don't like him, but that's because you're as different as chalk and cheese.'

'Is that so?'

'Well, you don't like him, do you?'

'No.' A customer was sorting his money, setting coins on the stall, with a pair of white sheets tucked beneath his arm. Bob took the money, put the sheets into a brown paper bag and handed them back with a grin. 'Ta, mate.'

'You gonna tell me why you don't like him?' Marlene asked, dancing about him.

'There's something fishy about the bloke,' Bob said. 'For a start he reckons he's got blokes managing market stalls for him, but I ain't never heard you say what he's bought at those auctions.' He paused for a moment. 'I know most of the stallholders and they're like me, working on their own stalls, not someone else's.'

She opened her mouth to speak but he put up a hand to silence her. 'Oh, I know he's ready and willing to help you build your business, but what about his own? Who buys stuff for his so-called stalls?'

Marlene frowned. 'Perhaps his stallholders buy it but with his money . . . After all, nobody but the person running the stall knows the actual needs of the customers, right?'

He couldn't argue with that, and now he felt mean for spoiling what had been, until now, a happy day for her. 'I'm sorry. He's your bloke. You know him better than anyone else.'

He watched as she turned away to take out a gold bangle from her locked jewellery case and hand it to a man to examine.

Samuel might be the best thing that had ever happened to Marlene. She'd not had a good start and by sheer hard work had turned her life around. Now she had a few bob behind her and she'd got her mum to give up charring.

Bob knew how profitable a stall could be. He and Pixie didn't go short and neither would their two kiddies.

'That's the third bangle I've sold this morning,' she said happily.

He smiled at her.

'Get much sleep?' She was tying back her mane of hair with a ribbon.

'What d'you think?' He was having a moan, but the truth was he adored the kiddies. He didn't mind getting up in the night to feed and change the baby because he could cuddle his little boy until his eyelids drooped and he fell asleep again.

'Your baby is lovely. But I remember the sleepless nights I had with my own. Chosen a name yet?'

'Don't you start! I've had Gladys chewing my ear off about naming him.'

'I bet she wants you to give the little one some high-falutin name?'

'Raymond! Raymond, I ask you!' He wrinkled his nose.

'What does Pixie think?'

'George.' He smiled. 'It's the King's name and I like it.'

'Good strong name,' Marlene said, after a while. Then: 'You and her all right after meeting Cal?'

Bob nodded. 'He's a good-looking beggar.'

'Looks don't matter. It's what's in a person's heart what counts.' Marlene turned away to help an old woman with an antique brooch that was pinned to the black velvet cushion.

Marlene was right about that. Bob was glad that Pixie seemed content to be with him. Why, she'd even said she'd like another child when George was about two years old – if another didn't make an appearance before that.

Pixie was happily tapping away on her typewriter whenever the baby would give her five minutes' peace. He loved her because she made her own happiness with the children and her home. Pixie was his life. They'd have to think about getting the little one christened soon. He and Pixie ought to have a chat with Reverend Michael at St John's. He wondered if Rita would agree to be godmother? Pixie would like that. Maybe they could have a small do afterwards – hire the Sloane Stanley Hall again and have a bit of a dance. This time he'd fork out. It wouldn't be as lavish as their wedding, but that didn't matter: like Marlene had said, 'It's what's in a person's heart what counts.'

Rita eyed the Italian, then sipped the tea she'd just purchased from Rene at the wagon. The same big bloke forked out for Gaetano's again. Yesterday, everyone had been paid. What was going on? What hold did the Italian have over the man that he would pay for his tea? Was he being blackmailed? Perhaps for more than just tea . . . Admittedly, the small Italian didn't look the sort to throw his weight about, but you never knew what these people were capable of . . . Look at the so-called Mafia, and their involvement in the war, not that she knew much about it. And that gangster, Lucky Luciano, running the waterfronts in America. Weren't they all Italians?

'When you seein' that American?'

Gladys's voice brought Rita out of her trance. 'Tomorrow,' she said.

'I think you're falling for him all over again.'

'Oh, shut up! I just want to help him.' Rita glared at Gladys, who was eating a rather stale-looking sandwich. 'Why are you so nosy?'

'Because I care about you.' Gladys brushed crumbs off her skirt. The two of them were sitting on the wall in their usual spot.

It was true. Gladys had taken her in when she'd been discharged from the Queen Victoria Hospital and had helped her get her life back on track. Rita closed her eyes and lifted her face to the sun, which was getting warmer by the day. The other women on her shift seemed to have given up teasing her about going out with the boss and she was glad, especially now that he'd invited her for a meal at his home in Lee-on-the-Solent.

'Hello, you two.'

Lizzie stood before them. Her hair hung down her back, shiny and dark. The office people wore different clothing from the factory women and the dreaded turbans didn't feature. Lizzie had on a dark wool dress with padded shoulders, nylons and black shoes.

'Stockings, eh?' Eagle-eyed Gladys never missed a trick.

'Blackie—'

'We know! He got them for you!' Rita laughed as Lizzie turned bright red.

'He gave me a boxful because he felt bad about leaving me on my own in Stratford while he went to some place in the country.' Lizzie patted her hair back into place after a gust of wind had ruffled it, sending rubbish blowing around on the grass.

'Nice dance?' Rita missed the dancing. She and Blackie used to have such a laugh . . .

'Yes,' Lizzie said. 'I don't suppose you do much dancing with that American.' That was unkind, Rita thought: Lizzie knew Joe had lost part of his leg and it would be a long time before he thought about dancing again. Still, she couldn't be really angry with her – the rape had left her scared of the dark and of men, Em said. It would be a long time before she got over it, just as Rita would never get over the abortion. Sometimes she lay awake at night crying about the awful thing she'd done. Ending a life before it had begun was a crime.

Rita felt a hand on her shoulder and turned to see Em. Rita had heard about Jack's latest escapade. The man had finally flipped, she was sure of it, so she'd taken to going round to Em's at night again. Jack couldn't be trusted not to harm his wife and Rita hoped her presence would make him think twice. The effect of Blackie's warning seemed to have faded, but Jack didn't lash out at Em when someone else was around.

Unfortunately Lizzie wasn't at home enough to limit her father's attacks on her mother, always out with Blackie.

'There's a decoy invasion plan going on,' said Lizzie, trying to gain her friends' attention. 'We've convinced the Germans there's a quarter of a million troops in Scotland ready to invade Norway.'

Rita stared at her. 'How d'you know that?' This information hadn't been in the *Evening News* or on the wireless. If it had, the rest of Priddy's would have been gossiping about it.

'I've been typing up government letters this morning. Yesterday we got important information from them asking us to co-operate by upping the amount of bombs and weapons we're producing. We need to fool the Hun that loads of troops are going to invade Norway from Scotland. They'll end up fighting nobody!'

'But why?' Rita asked, then realized that the enemy would concentrate their men and arms in the wrong place.

'Well, I don't know that, do I? I just do as I'm told!' Lizzie pouted.

'You ever thought it's wrong to tell us anything about what you do in that office?' Rita was annoyed with Lizzie. Sometimes, she thought the woman had fresh air inside her head instead of brains.

'Don't see why. We're friends. Anyway, we're all on the same side.' Lizzie flipped her hair aside and it rippled in the sunlight. Rita could see she didn't like being ticked off, especially by her. 'It's not like we're really going to have a quarter of a million of our men there, is it?' Lizzie was trying to make everyone think she had done nothing wrong.

'Shut up, Lizzie,' said her mother.

'Well, it's not!' she persisted.

Em shrugged.

'Blackie thought it was a hoot!'

'How does he know?' Rita remembered how he'd quizzed her endlessly about what went on at Priddy's.

'The original letter came last Friday, before we went off to Stratford. These letters are follow-ups. Anyway, Hitler's only ordered the U-boat commander to send ten submarines to Norway to guard against the invasion! So it worked, didn't it?' She went off into fits of laughter.

Em was staring at her daughter as though she could lean forward at any moment and strangle the life out of her. Then she caught Rita's eye. Something strange passed between the two women, a sort of understanding, yet Rita knew neither of them would ever speak of it. She took her newspaper out of the carrier bag that held her lunch tin and opened it just as the buzzer went, warning them all to get back to their posts. 'It says here the Luftwaffe are bombing hell out of London in what they call the Little Blitz. Already about a thousand people have been killed and more than seventeen hundred injured. Where will it all end, Em?' She refolded the paper and put it back into the bag.

'No one knows,' said Em, tucking her arm through Rita's. Then she smiled. 'Come round my house tonight for your tea, love. I got a nice bit of fresh haddock.'

Chapter Twenty-one

Joe was sitting in a patch of sun, his face turned towards its warmth. Rita had to make sure it was really him on the wooden bench near the rose garden. 'You look different,' she told him.

'My face is cold,' he said, blinking hard.

'I should think so. It's been swaddled in bandages and now you have two eyes and no bandages.'

'Does it look all right?' He stared straight at her.

Rita put her fingers beneath his chin and turned his face towards her. The glass eye was a remarkable match to the real one.

'I can see you better now,' he said. He gave a tentative smile.

Rita could smell toothpaste and he had smoothed his hair with Brylcreem. He must be feeling better to have started taking an interest in his looks, she thought happily. 'That eye's not capable of making your sight better, though.'

'Well, during the three days since I've had it, my senses seem to have forgotten I only have the one working eye. The first day I was very unsteady on my feet and kept bumping into things, unable to judge distances. Now I've got the hang of it and I feel much more of a man.'

Around the glass eye, red scar tissue reached into his eyebrow. Rita knew that it would fade to a silvery line and then, with the sun tanning his skin, would become unnoticeable.

His red hair had grown beneath the bandages, while his aquiline nose and well-shaped lips were unmarked. 'You're a bit of all right.' She giggled.

He frowned. 'I still can't . . .'

She knew what he meant. 'You've got plenty of time for that to put itself right,' she said. She didn't know if it was the truth, but it seemed to be what he wanted to hear because his face lightened and he smiled at her again.

She sat on the seat beside him. 'I've got something to ask you. Pixie's had her baby, a little boy. She and her husband are planning a bit of a get-together and I'd like you to come with me to Gosport to celebrate with them. Please say yes?'

'I don't think I can leave here on my own.'

She guessed he hadn't even thought about it, just said the first thing that came into his mind. Now he looked uncomfortable. 'D'you mean they won't allow it, or you've lost your nerve?'

Joe gave a big sigh. 'Both, Rita. Don't forget, my wounds are dressed daily and . . .'

'I can ask the doctors about that.' She was sure that if the doctors let him leave the hospital they would show her how to clean his leg wounds. After all, when she'd been there the staff had encouraged long-stay patients to get away from the hospital and mix with the outside world. It was all to do with gaining confidence.

'But the noise . . .'

In the hospital the relative peace and quiet had helped dispel the memories of the gunfire and bombing that had been embedded in his mind and turned him into a shambling mess of a man.

'My friends are kind people.' Immediately the words had left her mouth she cursed herself. She was assuring him that if he had a fit or a panic attack her friends would think nothing of it. And it was Joe who wouldn't be able to cope. He wouldn't be able to take their pity. He was a brave man but he wasn't brave enough to let people see him at his lowest ebb.

'I didn't mean . . .' Oh, why couldn't she keep her

big mouth shut? All she was doing was making things worse.

He took her hand and held it. 'Would it mean a lot to you if I came?' He was looking into her eyes and she was gazing back at him. Something like an electric shock seemed to pass through her.

'I want to show you off. I want *you* to see baby George.'

Damn! Show him off? He wasn't a prize bull at an auction. He wasn't even her boyfriend. Whatever had happened between them before he'd gone to war was all in the past. 'It's the baby.' Her words were unsteady. 'He's such a little love.'

Pixie's baby had filled a void in Rita. He wasn't a replacement for her own child, but she couldn't help lavishing love on the tiny boy. She'd peer at his little fingernails and hold his chubby hands, which gripped her thumbs as though he didn't want her to leave him.

Pixie had asked Rita to take her children and bring them up as her own, if anything happened to her and Bob. Rita felt honoured to have been asked. Of course, Gladys would always be their nanny, but Pixie had said her children needed someone who would bring them up in the way she and Bob might have done. Gladys was loving towards her grandchildren but, as Pixie remembered from her own childhood, likely to vanish off the face of the earth if she took a fancy to a man. It was in her nature to want a man to show her a good time and shower her with love. Bringing up grandchildren would be a hindrance.

'Look, you could stay with me and Gladys,' she added now. She could turn the downstairs front room into a bedroom where he could have complete privacy. Gladys would be thrilled to have an American staying in the house, even if it was only for one night. 'I don't think you could get back the same night.'

'I couldn't manage public transport . . .'

Rita was overjoyed. Instead of making excuses, Joe was now asking sensible questions about travel. She hadn't thought about how she would get him to Gosport. It was too soon for him to use a coach or train – much too tiring for him. She wondered if she might be able to persuade Bob to pick him up in the van. And if Bob was going to be too busy making last-minute arrangements for the christening party, would he let Marlene use his van? Since she'd learned to drive she'd become even more invaluable to him . . .

'All right. I'm willing to take the chance if you are.' Joe squeezed her hand.

Rita nearly knocked him off the seat, lunging at him. Too late, she realized she was kissing those kissable lips.

She broke away, putting both hands over her mouth. 'I'm sorry. I never meant . . . Whatever must you think of me?'

And then he was laughing at her. Her heart was beating so fast she was sure he could hear it. Oh, what a fool she was, throwing herself at him like that. A tear had risen and she blinked it back. He let go of her hand and put his fingers to her chin, twisting her head towards him. 'I think you're a kind, wonderful girl,' he said. And kissed her lips, moving his tongue inside her mouth until Rita thought she might die with the sweetness. Eventually he pulled back. 'I wish . . .'

Rita saw the sadness roll across his face, like clouds gathering when a storm is imminent.

He sat back on the seat, then murmured, 'Let's go and see if we can cadge a cuppa and some cake.'

Without waiting for her reply, he used his crutch to hoist himself upright and looked down at her still sitting there.

Rita rose, picked up her handbag and put her arm through his. Together they walked across the grass to the hospital's café. She knew he wanted to be with her but didn't know how to be *alone* with her.

The rest of the afternoon passed quickly, the two of them chatting, drinking tea and sitting in the warmth of the canteen with the other patients and their visitors.

Rita was sad when she had to leave, her life regulated by coach and train times. He didn't mention the kiss, but she knew they had reached a new stage in their relationship. 'Love' was a big word for him to use, despite his protestations of love in the letters they had exchanged before he had been wounded. And, as yet, he hadn't talked about how his injuries had come about. There was such a lot they didn't know about each other. It was as though their love affair had been halted, life had gone on, and now . . . Was it possible that the passion could be rekindled? Rita thought it could. She had felt the reincarnation of love in that kiss.

There was plenty of time ahead for them to share secrets. She believed that if you truly loved someone there must be no secrets between you.

She shuddered. That meant she must tell Joe about the abortion. Not now. Now was the time to plan his visit to Gosport.

On the way home on the train, looking at her reflection in the carriage window, she knew she'd fallen back in love with him. Not the young man he'd been, but the one the war had changed.

*

'Ruth's had a little girl.'

Pixie brandished the letter, one of two delivered not five minutes ago that morning by the postman. Gladys held an almost asleep George.

Sadie was drawing a picture, sitting at the kitchen table, using crayons her Auntie Rita had got for her from the market.

'I bet Ruth's delighted,' Gladys said. George had dribbled, so she wiped his mouth and chin with the bottom of the bib.

'Nine pounds one ounce, Mum.'

'Jesus! That's a big 'un! She all right? Does she say anything about, you know, what's-his-name?' She glanced at Sadie, her head bent over the colouring book.

'You can say his name, Mum. It's Cal, short for Callard,' Pixie said.

'All right! I only asked.' George was asleep.

'Cal and that nurse have gone to Scotland.' Pixie waved the letter at her mother.

'She couldn't wait to get him away from you, then.' Gladys laughed.

Pixie glared at her. 'It's over and done with.' She'd made her choice. 'I'm surprised we still get the post as regularly as we do, what with all the bombings,' she said. Now she opened a thick white oblong envelope and pulled out the letter. Her eyes scanned the print. Then she reread the single page. And gasped.

'What's the matter with you?' Gladys was staring at her. 'It's not from Cal, is it?'

'No, Mum. I told you, that's done and dusted.' The hand holding the letter was shaking. 'I can't tell you what this is about. Bob has to know first.' She put it down on the table. A smile crept over her face. Excitement coursed through her like molten lava pouring down a mountainside.

'What's the matter, love?' Pixie looked at them both, Gladys and George, her heart full of love.

A squeak of crayon, and Sadie said, 'This is a picture for you, Mummy.'

'Thank you, my love,' Pixie said. The yellow sun her daughter was colouring was a big round circle with spider legs spreading from it. 'I thought I couldn't be happier, Mum,' she said, 'but this letter is the icing on the cake.'

Rita rounded the gate and said goodbye to the gatekeeper. Suddenly Blackie was standing in front of her.

'Make a girl jump, why don't you?' she said.

'Sorry.' He handed her a bunch of flowers. 'Got these for you.'

She could smell his familiar cologne. His eyes sought hers.

Rita took the flowers and buried her face in the blooms. 'You be careful Lizzie doesn't catch you giving me flowers.'

'I didn't come here to talk about Lizzie. I want you to come out with me.' He pulled his coat collar up. It was more a nervous gesture.

'I can't.'

'Why not?'

She sighed. She knew he had a hard time believing she didn't care for him, especially when she'd loved him before and hadn't hesitated to tell him so. 'There's someone else.'

'That American?'

'Lizzie's got a mouth like a barn door, hasn't she?' She began to walk away.

'You're only going with him out of pity.'

'I don't think you should tell me how I feel about people.' Rita was angry now.

'Let me take you dancing. You know you love to dance.'

He leaned in to kiss her. She stepped back. 'I'm going home to get some stuff, then to Em's to stay the night. She left an hour before me and she's getting my tea ready. Lizzie's already told me you've asked her to go out with you tonight. I don't want to hurt Em or her daughter. What we had is gone, Blackie.'

'Look, I made a mistake.' He was begging her now. 'We can start again.'

'No! Now I'm not taking gifts off you I don't feel like a kept woman. I'm like any other woman who scrimps and saves because of the war.' Rita thrust the flowers back at him. 'Go away and leave me alone.'

A couple of women passed by and began giggling at Rita's raised voice. One of them turned and stared at Blackie.

Rita walked away from him. It wasn't easy to sever all ties when you'd cared for a person, but he and Lizzie were meant for each other.

She began running down Weevil Lane, the tears coursing down her cheeks. She wanted very much to be indoors with a cuppa while she packed her nightie and curling tongs into a bag. She didn't look back, but she knew he was still standing in the road watching her.

Em sat at the kitchen table, her head in her hands. Both arms were a mass of bruises. The skin was torn on the left one and blood had crawled down to the elbow before it had clotted. Her left eye was swelling. She could feel the skin stretching.

The wireless was on and Jimmy Dorsey's 'Tangerine' was softly playing.

It was the calm after the storm.

Jack had been waiting for her as soon as she'd opened the door. The chair was filling the hallway so she'd had to squeeze by it to get in. His face was full of hate.

'Bitch!' he'd said, and grabbed her hand. She'd fallen against him and he'd taken advantage of that to punch her. The strength in his hand was like a steel clamp holding her wrist, while he hit her with his free fist.

She'd screamed, but no one had come. They never did.

She'd fallen to her knees, his hand still manacled to her wrist. He said nothing beyond a series of satisfied grunts until gradually his grip loosened and she was able to pull herself free of him. That was when he'd hit her in the eye. She'd screamed, stumbled against the wall and managed somehow to make a successful bid for freedom, staggering to the relative safety of the kitchen.

He hadn't come after her. He'd wheeled himself into the front room.

Hanging over the sink she'd vomited, then drunk a glass of water, wondering what had set him off this time. He'd called her a bitch. Why? She hadn't been out all week, except to go to work. Rita could verify that. She had been with her most nights as well, because Jack didn't swear at her so much when someone else was in the house. Lizzie was so embroiled with Blackie that she hardly ever came home now.

After Em had taken off her coat, and crept painfully past the closed living-room door to hang it up in the hall, she'd remembered that she'd offered to cook for Rita.

Back in the kitchen she had been peeling potatoes when the plaintive cries had started.

'Em? Em, I'm sorry. Em, come and talk to me?'

She was frightened and stayed in the kitchen, not wanting to be hurt again. She wanted Rita to get to the house, because with someone else around Jack wouldn't hit her.

She'd peeled enough potatoes for the three of them. Washed them, then cut them and put them into the large saucepan.

'Em? I don't want to come and get you.' His voice was louder. Had he wheeled himself into the hall? She was too frightened to look.

'Em?' Oh, how she hated his wheedling voice.

The crash came next. Jack didn't cry out. Em knew what he'd done. He'd tipped the chair so she'd have to go and pick him up. It was an old trick. He knew she wouldn't leave him lying on the floor. But she was rooted to the spot near the sink.

She listened carefully. There were no sounds coming

from the front room. Em lit the gas and watched the blue flames curl up the side of the pan. She got out a tin of peas from the cupboard, opened it and poured them into the smallest saucepan. The fish was on a gauze-covered dish. Haddock.

The silence was soothing, but deep down she knew something was wrong. Why wasn't he yelling at her to come and pick him up? She was supposed to go and lift him back into the chair. As she pulled him up, he would start on her again. Em shuddered.

It was nice, this silence, with only the hissing of the gas beneath the potatoes. After a while she went down the passage. What kind of wife was she to leave her husband on the floor, even if he had tipped over the wheelchair on purpose?

As she pushed open the door, she marvelled at the silence from within the room.

He was lying on the floor, his head on the stone hearth. Blood had pooled into the fireplace. The brush and tongs were shining wet and turned on their side.

'All right, I'm here.'

He didn't move. She looked down at him. His eyes were open.

'I'm here,' she repeated.

Em knelt, steeling herself, expecting him at any

moment to move quickly, to hit her around the head or, indeed, any place he could reach.

But he hadn't even blinked.

Then: 'You're dead!' She shook him, heart pounding, still expecting him to attack her. But he rolled a little then settled back in the same position.

He *was* dead.

Em rose and left the front room, shutting the door behind her. She went back into the kitchen, pulled out a chair and sat with her head in her hands. Unmoving, even when the water ran dry in the saucepan and the potatoes began to burn.

Rita let herself into Em's house, dropped her bags on the polished lino and went through to the kitchen as fast as she could. 'Em, what's burning?'

She'd run into a cloud of black smoke and found Em sitting stock still at the table. Rita took one look at the blackened saucepan and the flames shooting up its sides, turned off the gas, opened the back door, grabbed the pan and threw it into the yard where it crashed onto the cement path. She turned back and fanned the back door, forcing the smoke to billow out of the kitchen. Then she stared at Em, who still hadn't moved. 'Em, snap out of it. It's only a burned pan.' She sat on the chair next to her and tried to prise Em's hands away from her chin. Her friend's eyes were glassy. 'The smoke'll soon go,' she added, her eyes watering with it.

'He's dead,' Em said.

'Who's dead, love?'

Em rested her chin on the tips of her fingers, her elbows on the table. 'I didn't kill him.' She said it very softly and clearly, then let her hands fall away as she shook her head. 'I didn't kill him. He did it himself.'

Rita's heart dropped like a stone. 'Where is he, Em?'

'In the front room.'

Rita slid her chair away, grasped one of Em's hands and pulled until Em was on her feet. 'Show me,' Rita said.

It was then she noticed the bruises on Em's arms and the line of blood, dried and dark, on her skin. Her eye was swollen. Why hadn't she noticed the state her friend was in when she'd come into the kitchen? The burning saucepan had eclipsed all other thoughts.

Rita led Em down the passage and opened the door to the front room. 'Show me,' she said.

The chair was as Rita had seen it many times. She could tell immediately what had happened to the man lying in front of the hearth, his head covered with blood. It was so dark it was almost black.

Em gave a little whimper, like a small animal in pain.

'We have to phone for an ambulance, a doctor.' Rita put her arm around Em's shoulders.

'He's dead, I tell you, dead!' It all came out then, the words tumbling over themselves, until at last Em repeated, 'I didn't do it.'

'I know, but we have to tell someone, Em.'

Em looked at Rita as if she had suddenly woken up. 'Of course,' she whispered. 'Shall we go to the phone box together? Perhaps the police? I don't want to be left with him.'

Rita went out into the hall, fetched their coats and picked up her handbag – she'd need coppers for the telephone.

Em was about to close the door behind them.

'Leave it. The draught will blow away the stink of the burned pot.' Rita linked her arm through Em's and they walked together on the wet pavement towards the red telephone box.

Chapter Twenty-two

Marlene gazed at the snoring man beside her. And why not? she thought. She and Samuel had made love in the small chintzy room, and in another hour she would be wined and dined at a country inn, wearing a new blue dress that enhanced the colour of her hair and emphasized her slim figure. At that moment she had no worries. Her mother was looking after her daughter, and Marlene was taking a couple of days away from the stall because she could afford to.

Samuel's lovemaking had been slow and easy. He was only the second man she'd ever slept with. Though you couldn't really call Jeannie's father a man as he'd been fifteen at the time and their coupling more of a lusty experiment. Samuel knew how to touch a woman in all the right places to give pleasure so intense that she hadn't been able to stop herself crying out.

Almost as if he knew she was staring at him, he opened his eyes.

He was hard and full against her soft body. He drew her against him so he could kiss her lips, softly at first, then with a hunger that grew until he was moving her errant hair away from her cheek and brushing kisses along her neck, her chin, her nose, her forehead.

Samuel stopped, looked into her eyes and positioned his body perfectly inside the curved hollow of her hips. She ran her fingers around the satiny hardness of him and guided him inside her.

He pressed gently into her willing body, then endlessly deeper, and she clung to him as he moved on top of her, drawing him in and letting him go.

Marlene knew he was for her, that they would always be together. They were as committed in their bodies as in their minds.

The sweet smell of their passion rose from the white sheets and engulfed her. Her heart felt such compassion, such love for him. Until her body, along with his, gave way in a final exultant wave of ecstasy that left her breathless.

Afterwards he curled himself around her. His face was buried in her neck, and in her red hair. She felt one breath between them, one beating heart, and she was so full of Samuel that she thought she might explode, so great was her love for him.

Moments later, when Marlene awoke, Samuel was sitting on the edge of the bed watching her. 'Time to get up,' he said. His fingers traced her face. 'That was the best sleep I've had for a few days,' he added.

Marlene yawned as she pushed her legs out of the bed and sat on the edge with him. 'Why haven't you been able to sleep?'

'I don't want to worry you with my problems.' He pulled her to a standing position, then lifted her hand and kissed her engagement ring. 'Come on, get in the bath and we'll go out for some dinner.'

He was freshly shaved and dressed, except for his suit jacket. He went over to the window, staring out at the nothingness the dark had created. It worried her that he was unusually quiet.

Later, when they were sitting in the small restaurant in the village at the back of the Carter's Arms, waiting for their food to be brought to them, Marlene remembered what he'd said about sleep.

'I would have thought this place would sooth anyone's nerves so they could sleep.' She thought about the small sandy beach, the narrow passages where smugglers once roved and the boats in the harbour that reeked of fish. 'I love it here,' she said. 'But what's troubling you?'

'Don't let's spoil this lovely weekend,' he said. Marlene saw his eyes cloud as the waiter approached their table.

She absolutely loved the fresh fish and was savouring each succulent mouthful. She noticed Samuel had left most of his and was idly pushing food around his plate. Around them the inn was busy. Cigarette smoke curled up to the ceiling and the smell of beer was comforting. Samuel was lost in a world of his own.

'Come on,' Marlene said. 'If we're to be married I don't want any secrets between us.'

He shook his head. 'I'll work it out somehow,' he said.

She placed her cutlery on her plate. 'Samuel, I've not been married before and I want to stay married after I've walked up that aisle, so you've got to be honest with me. What concerns you now concerns me.'

He gave a huge sigh, reached across the table and held her hand. 'All right then, I'll tell you.' Their eyes locked. 'I always live my life by taking chances. Not haphazard chances, but I like to aim high, and make a gamble that leaves me well off. But I've made a mistake. Or, rather, it's been made for me.' He turned his head away.

She frowned, expecting him to carry on talking. There

was silence until he said, 'No, it's really no concern of yours.' Again, silence.

'What's happened?' She had never seen him so down, so desolate.

'My building business . . .' he took a deep breath '. . . is in trouble. I have a creditor who wants his money straight away. He won't give me any more credit for building materials until I've paid off what I owe him. Normally he and I work in tandem but his wife's ill and there've been medical bills. He needs his money now. I need his materials. I have market stalls, but I can't take the money from the stallholders. They need to buy more stock. They've families to support. I don't want to put their jobs on the line. You're in the business so you know that new stock has to be purchased regularly.'

Marlene, now sipping her coffee, waved away the waiter. Samuel went on, 'The man can't even wait for a month when the sale of the two houses down Queen's Road in Gosport will be finalized. The for-sale notices have already been changed to "Sold".' Marlene remembered the houses near the corner: they'd been bombed but sold as near-derelict and had now been refurbished. She'd seen the noticeboards.

Samuel paused. 'If I pull out I lose everything for the sake of two thousand pounds.'

Marlene gasped. Two thousand pounds was a fortune! She put her hand across the table and grabbed at his fingers, holding on tightly. She could lay her hands on thirteen hundred. She'd worked her guts out to save that money and it lay in the post-office savings book in her bedroom drawer. It had been saved to ensure a good future for her child. That left seven hundred pounds wanting. What if she asked Bob to lend her the rest of the money and put up her house as security? It had to be worth nearly that much. A nearby house had sold for eight hundred pounds only last week.

There was no risk. Samuel had explained his predicament. She knew he managed his affairs well. He couldn't help being put in this position, could he? And hadn't he offered her money time and time again at the auction houses? She was going to marry the man, for Christ's sake. Surely he wouldn't refuse her help after all the help he'd given her?

'I can get the money,' she said. 'I'll need a few days. Will that do?'

'For God's sake!' he exploded, pushing back his chair so that it scraped on the tiled floor. 'Do you really think I'd take *your* money?' His voice was so loud that the other diners had stopped eating to stare at them.

'Let me, please?' She was begging him now. He was standing at the table glaring down at her.

He turned his head away. She swore there were tears in his eyes. She saw him look around apologetically, then sit down again. Conversation between the other customers and diners started up again.

'What risk am I taking when you'll pay me back as soon as the sale of the houses goes through? You can't complete on their sale if they're unfinished, can you?'

'I can, but I'll be lucky if I can raise a few hundred on each property. Finished, those houses will provide a decent profit and I was hoping to splash out on a decent wedding with what's left over.'

She said firmly, 'Then it's settled. I'll get the money. Stop worrying.'

He was now looking into her eyes. 'I'm so lucky to have found you, Marlene,' he whispered. He picked up her hand, running his fingers over the antique jewels in her ring. 'We'd better get you a proper engagement ring as well.'

'So you see, Bob, I need to ask for your help.'

Marlene looked forlorn, standing behind her stall with a steaming mug of tea in her hand. It was barely light, although the mornings were warming up nicely now.

There were very few punters about but, then, it was well before the early-morning workers would walk down the high street to the ferry for Portsmouth.

Marlene set down her tea, pushed back her long hair and secured it with a rubber band.

He didn't want to give her the money, but he'd listened carefully and decided that her plea made good sense. It wouldn't hurt him to own her house, if everything went wrong for her. The good thing about owning property was that it had a habit of rising in value unless, as had happened already to some of the houses in Gosport, it was bombed.

Marlene believed in the bloke. She loved Samuel Golden. So much so that she was willing to hand over her entire savings and put her house up as surety.

Of course Bob would give her the money. Instinctively he knew it was what Pixie would advise. They'd discuss it tonight after tea when the kiddies were in bed. After all, he was a married man now and his wife deserved an equal say in big decisions.

He still didn't trust Samuel, but he wasn't digging into his pocket for *him*: it was for the skinny girl who'd worked her arse off for him, out in all weathers, uncomplaining and always with a cheeky grin on her face.

'You got the house deeds? They're not with a solicitor?'

'Why should I pay a lot of money to have the deeds left in a solicitor's safe when I can hide them in the house for free? Anyway, an office is just as likely to get bombed as my house.'

He nodded. 'Come round tonight and I'll give you seven hundred and fifty pounds. If you don't return the money to me within a month I'll send off the deeds to the Land Registry office and you must sign the house over to me. That being so I'll expect you to pay rent and, in effect, I'll be your landlord. Give me back the money in full, and I'll hand back the deeds to you.'

Marlene threw her arms around his neck. A man's voice interrupted: 'When you two lovebirds have finished, how much d'you want for this pair of sheets?'

Em dropped the handful of earth onto the coffin and stood aside so Lizzie could do the same. The sun was already warm and the last of the bluebells were nestling together beneath the bushes and in grassy corners at Ann's Hill Cemetery. It was nine in the morning.

Lizzie was crying. The earth made a dull thud on the wood. Rita could see Em wanted to cuddle Lizzie, but she didn't have the heart to show emotion when she still hadn't been able to cry for her husband. Lizzie stepped back from the gaping hole and Blackie enveloped her in his arms. She was remembering her father as he had been before the war, when he'd loved her and Em, Rita thought. He would always be that man to Lizzie, not the monster he'd become.

Blackie wore a black armband out of respect, and several of the deceased's friends were similarly attired. Blackie moved towards them and began talking about the war. His voice carried across the still of the morning. 'I see Hitler doesn't believe we can produce an invasion on Normandy. He called it, "a bare-faced piece of play-acting". Apparently he's still got the bulk of his armour in the east.'

'Well, something's going on, and it's going to happen soon. My son Alf has been told that all leave is suspended until further notice.' The man took off his flat cap, folded it and put it into his raincoat pocket.

'Invading Hungary,' said Blackie, 'his former ally, to make sure the oil from her oilfields is handy, shows the Soviets are closing in. I also read he's taking troops from France.'

Rita glared at Blackie. Always the war with him, his one topic of conversation, she thought. When he wasn't asking questions, he was telling people what he thought, just to get them talking. But a funeral was neither the time nor the place.

'Enough, Blackie.' Her voice carried towards him and he stared at her. 'Shut up about bloody Hitler. Em don't want you spouting off. Look what the fighting did to her husband.'

Rita walked towards her friend and squeezed Em's arm. The clergyman moved away, to stand expectantly, waiting to shake the mourners' hands as they left the hallowed ground.

'Glad you told him to shut up,' whispered Em. 'He talks sense but he don't know who's listening. "Even walls have ears."' She had quoted the poster advising people to be careful when talking about the war. 'I had a go at our Lizzie for speaking so openly about what goes on in the factory.' She sniffed. 'Most of the workers haven't a clue and it's better that way. I hate to admit it but my girl's got a big mouth.'

Rita nodded. The funeral was over. All that remained was the filling-in of the rectangular hole. The small gathering was dispersing.

'There's no get-together to celebrate his life,' Lizzie said, between sniffs, wiping her nose with a large white handkerchief. She left Blackie's side and wandered over to link arms with her mother.

'There's no money for that hypocrisy.' Em's voice cut through the silence that birdsong was trying to fill.

'C'mon, Lizzie, I said I'd treat everyone to a drink.' Blackie ran his hand through his glossy hair.

'But I didn't *want* a show.' Em drew her shoulders high as she took a deep breath. 'He went in a bad way. Alone. I don't want to speak ill of the dead, but he wasn't a nice man at the end of his life. I've still got the bruises to show for that.' Her voice was bitter.

'Time will help you see things differently,' said Blackie.

'Maybe, but you weren't on the receiving end of it.'

She turned to go, her heels sticking into the damp earth and making small sucking noises as she walked. Rita could see that she had had enough.

Perhaps twenty or so people had turned up to say goodbye to the man in the coffin. Near a yew tree two gravediggers stood smoking.

'I'm thankful it wasn't a drawn-out affair,' said Em. She looked tired and there were two dark crescents beneath her eyes. Rita knew that since her husband's death she'd hardly eaten and her face was gaunt, her soft roundness hardened into sharp angles.

Rita squeezed her arm. 'Accidental death. Though even I was surprised the coroner's verdict came so quick,' she added. 'But with the bombing still going on and deaths happening all the time, the authorities don't want bodies hanging about . . .' She stopped. 'I'm sorry, Em. I didn't mean . . .'

'Forget it.' Em moved sideways to avoid treading on a grave. 'I feel like I've been given a new lease of life. Does that sound awful?'

Rita shook her head. 'I couldn't have done what you've done, standing by him.'

'You don't have to. Your Joe sounds a different kettle of fish altogether.'

Rita thought about him. A warm feeling spread through her. She turned and looked back to the grave. The diggers were shovelling in earth.

Lizzie and Blackie were walking slowly along the gravel path towards Blackie's car. She'll be all right with him, thought Rita. Lizzie might break down later today and cry, but Blackie would take care of her.

'We could go down to the Dive, have a bun and a cuppa,' she suggested.

Em stopped, twisted round and faced her. 'Would you think I was a selfish bitch if I went to the Fox?'

Rita began to laugh. 'I reckon that's a bloody good idea,' she said. 'You deserve a bit of happiness. If I was you,' she said, 'I wouldn't bother going home tonight.'

Em stared. 'Really?'

'Really,' said Rita. She put her arms around her friend.

'You got the rest of the day off, as have I. Go to the Fox, let Sam take care of you.'

A smile lit Em's eyes. 'What about you?'

Rita smiled back at her. 'I think I'll go to East Grinstead and give Joe a surprise.'

Chapter Twenty-three

Sitting on the train, Rita watched the fields rolling by. Out in the country you'd hardly believe there was a war on, she thought. The trains told a different story. Young men with kitbags sitting on the floor or anywhere else they could perch, resting before getting to their bases to go Heaven knew where. The air was full of swirling cigarette smoke, chatter and laughter as though being cheerful was some kind of talisman that would protect them from whatever horrors they were travelling towards. In her compartment two young girls clung to two airmen as though loath to let them go, and an older woman, alone, was reading a letter. Tears fell on to it. The paper was black-edged. Her husband or her son? Rita might have spoken to her, commiserated perhaps. But the funeral early this morning had been depressing enough. She had used up her strength in helping Lizzie to stop crying and couldn't go through that performance again with a total stranger.

All she wanted to do was see Joe.

After the swiftness of the train, the bus journey was long, twisting through country lanes with the roadside a mass of wild flowers. At last, through the trees she saw the hospital and her spirits rose. The conductress stood to one side as Rita stepped out. So many women doing men's jobs, she thought. Filling in, keeping the country going while the men fought. The driver was a woman, too, she noted, as the vehicle trundled off down the lane.

She began walking up the gravel driveway, smoothing her black costume over her hips. All the sitting around had made the skirt ride up and she wanted to look good when she saw Joe. She could still smell the faint scent of Evening in Paris from where she'd dabbed it on her pulse points earlier in the day. She wondered if she'd ever go to Paris.

The sun, warm on her face, made her think of Em. Rita hoped she'd get the welcome she deserved from Sam at the Fox. *Of course she would.*

Sam and Em had fallen into a heartfelt, though unconsummated affair when Jack was away fighting.

He'd been a shoulder to cry on when Jack wrote that

he was the father of an Italian girl's baby. Em had been devastated at that news and Rita had begged her to come out with the girls if only to stop her moping indoors on her own. Until then, Em had had only one thought in her head and that was to do her job at Priddy's to the best of her ability. She never went out, believing she owed it to Jack to be as chaste and honest as possible. He was, after all, fighting for his country. Her marriage vows meant everything to her. Sam had fallen for Em in a big way. So much so, she'd told Rita, that he would abide by whatever decision she came to regarding her marriage.

When Jack had come home on leave, she had believed him when he told her the affair was over. The platoon had been moved from Italy to Africa. He said he realized what a fool he'd been. Em couldn't forget, but she had forgiven him.

Sam had decided to wait in the background. Em went out for nights with the girls when Jack went back to barracks but she went home alone, always.

When Jack was sent home after the blast, Em realized he'd be in a wheelchair for the rest of his life and that shell-shock had unhinged him, but she knew it was her duty to look after him. His cruelty shocked her, but she wouldn't leave him: it was her mother's house they lived in – and she wouldn't turn him out, because sometimes she glimpsed the man she'd married and loved.

Em had stayed away from the Fox, never giving in to temptation with Sam. Sam heard on the grapevine of Jack's cruelty, but Em had long ago persuaded him not to interfere in what went on behind closed doors.

Em deserved some happiness now.

She had been more like a mother to Rita than her own. Em talked to her in a way she couldn't talk to Lizzie, and when Lizzie had left home to live with the man she hoped to marry, Em was glad her daughter couldn't see her unhappiness.

Rita thought back to that morning and the way Em had held Lizzie as she'd cried. Of course she was devastated by his death: he was her father.

Out of habit Rita looked across the field to where Joe liked to sit, on the wooden seat near the rose gardens.

He wasn't alone.

A very young blonde woman, wearing navy and white, was sitting facing him on the seat. She was extremely pretty. A bit like Pixie, skinny, and her eyes were on Joe's face. Rita stopped, then moved behind the trunk of one of the large trees lining the long driveway. Joe's walking stick was propped against the seat. She couldn't hear what he was saying, but it was obvious something important was taking place. At her feet, fading bluebells threw up their heavy scent.

He put his hand into his pocket and pulled out a small box. The girl's mouth opened in amazement as she took it and lifted out a ring. She slipped it on her finger, admiring it, all the while talking animatedly.

Joe took up her hand and twisted the ring around. He was talking to the girl, his eyes on her face. She leaned towards him and he put his arms around her to hug her tightly, his lips brushing against the white headwear that denoted her job as nurse.

Rita had seen enough. Not caring about the noise she made, she bolted from her hiding place and ran back down the driveway towards the lane. Twice she stumbled because her eyes were full of tears so she didn't see the potholes.

How could Joe be in love with that girl, yet pretend there was something between himself and Rita? Why, she'd even got him to agree to come to Gosport for George's christening. How could he do that when it was obvious he was in love with that blonde?

Rita had felt in Joe's kisses that she meant something to him. There was no mistaking that the love they'd shared before had been rekindled. How could he raise her hopes like that when all the while there was someone else? After all, you had to have known someone a while to give them a ring, didn't you? Why had he led her on?

The sweat was running down to the small of her back, making her clothes stick to her. At the bus stop she paused. Would she be able to catch the bus on its return journey? Joe's face was tormenting her. The girl had looked like a nurse, yet apart from the two nurses Rita now counted as her friends at the hospital, he'd never mentioned anyone else.

Rita scrubbed at her eyes with her handkerchief. Every time she'd visited before, he'd known to expect her. This time she'd come as a surprise, and what a surprise! Why, she'd even been taken in by the nurses who had told her Joe had no one to visit him. He didn't need visitors from outside if he'd fallen for one of the staff, did he? But what if she'd made a mistake? What if there was some other explanation for him giving that girl a ring? No!

Joe had seemed honest and sincere. She thought of the bad things people said about the Americans. Over-sexed, overpaid, over here. Well, she'd certainly picked a bad one. And Blackie wasn't honest either.

She wiped her eyes again, not caring that her mascara must have run.

The birds were whistling for all they were worth and the rustling in the undergrowth brought her to her senses.

Why was she waiting at the bus stop for a bus that wasn't due to appear for at least another hour and a half?

Rita began to walk. To stop herself thinking of Joe in that young woman's arms she made herself think of other things.

But Joe's face kept inserting itself into her thoughts. Had either Joe or the girl known she was watching them? Rita didn't think so. She'd never forget the look of pleasure on the girl's face as she'd put the ring on her finger. And what did that mean? Were they engaged? Again she stumbled, tears blinding her. This time she fell to the ground. When she got up, she saw she'd grazed her knee. Rita cried even more.

The journey home was an absolute nightmare. When she got off the train at Portsmouth Harbour station she knew she didn't want to be alone. Em would no doubt be at the Fox, but to go home to Gladys meant explaining what had happened and she wasn't ready for that yet. Inevitably Gladys would say, 'You should have stayed with Blackie.'

After getting off the ferry it seemed the salty air of the expanse of water between Gosport and Portsmouth had comforted her. She went into the public lavatory in the Ferry Gardens and in the fly-specked mirror began patching up her make-up.

She'd cried so much her face was blotchy. She took out her mascara block, spat on the brush and began to coat her lashes. A bit of powder, concentrated under her eyes, and a firm outline of red lipstick made her feel better. She took out her small hairbrush and brushed her hair until it gleamed. Then she took a few sheets of hard shiny toilet paper, wetted them and scrubbed away at the graze on her knee. If she'd been wearing stockings they would have been ruined.

She waited at the terminus for the Forton Road bus, and when it came in, she sat just inside the open doorway. The smell of cigarettes was strong, complemented by the spent butts on the floor.

It hurt so much to think about Joe.

She decided not to tell Pixie what had happened. She was looking forward to a cuddle with George. Even the milky smell of him would make her feel better. As the driver jumped into the cab and the conductress took her fare, Rita was already looking forward to the cup of tea she'd get at Pixie's.

'We're off to London tomorrow.' Pixie was so excited that her voice was shrill. She put down the white bonnet she was knitting for George.

'Lucky I'm not working,' Bob said, his voice carrying in

from the scullery where he was clattering about, making tea while having a shave and a wash. 'Though I don't fancy going on the train with the baby.'

'I could look after George,' said Rita, quickly.

'No work?' Pixie stared at her.

Rita looked away. Of course she had to work.

'I can't leave George behind. I'm breast-feeding, remember?' Rita nodded. She'd forgotten that. 'And Mum's already promised to have Sadie,' continued Pixie.

'So there's nothing I can do?' The kettle in the scullery started whistling.

Bob poked his head through the doorway. He had shaving soap on his face, his hair was wet and he was naked from the waist up.

'Get dressed!' said Pixie, with a laugh.

'I just wanted to say thank you for the kind thought, Rita.' He used a towel to scrub the water from his chest, then disappeared again. The kettle wound down.

'Well, are you going to tell me why you're off to London?'

Rita saw Pixie blush. She went and curled up in the big old armchair, leaving her knitting on the table.

Bob came in from the scullery, carrying a tray. He'd put his pyjama top on.

Pixie said, 'Bob, what will Rita think of you dressed like that?'

'Better than if I'd left me top off,' he said. 'Anyway, Rita's like family. She don't care what I'm dressed in.'

Rita smiled. It was nice to think that these people loved her like she was family. This afternoon's shock of finding Joe with another woman still hurt but Pixie and Bob were making her see there was another kind of love. A love that was stronger, the love of good friends. She saw Pixie had put a hanger on the back of the kitchen door and Bob's best suit, the one he'd got married in, was pressed and hanging over it neatly. Pixie's pale grey costume, the one that made her hair look even blonder, was draped over the back of a kitchen chair. And her black shoes were standing to attention beneath the sideboard.

Bob said, 'Tea?' Without waiting for an answer, he began pouring from the brown teapot.

Just then a scream pierced the air. Pixie sighed and made to uncurl her legs and rise from the chair.

Rita said, 'Stay there, I'll go.'

Bob put down the teapot. 'He can't want feeding, not yet.'

Rita climbed the stairs and went into the back bedroom, which was warm because the range below in the kitchen sent the hot air upwards. Sadie was fast asleep. Her thumb was in her mouth and the eyelashes fanning her cheeks were long and feathery. Rita bent over the cot and gently planted a kiss on her forehead.

'You smell of lovely little-girl things,' she said quietly, and pulled up the quilt so it covered her shoulders.

She turned to the crying baby in the small cot in the corner and looked down at him. Immediately he sensed her there and quietened, opening his eyes to stare at her.

Rita picked him up. 'All that crying and no tears,' she said. His tiny mouth was making little sucking noises but his eyes still held hers. It was like he was looking into her soul, she thought. She held him close to her, feeling his heart beating fast. Such a feeling of contentment overcame her that she didn't want to put him down ever. But his nappy was soggy.

She felt the cot sheet. It was dry. So, magically, was his long white nightie. She looked about the bedroom and on the top of the chest of drawers saw a pile of fresh terry-towelling nappies and a smaller pile of muslin squares. Rita picked up what she needed, with one hand, and added a jar of cream. Then she sat down on the old chair that stood in the corner of the room. George was still making snuffling noises. As she laid him across her lap his tiny hands clutched at the air.

Slowly she unravelled his clothes and took out the curved pin, then put the wet nappy on the floor. 'You're only little but that's a lot of pee,' she said. His eyes found hers again.

She rubbed cream into his crevices and put on the nappy. She held him close, just for a moment, then put him down in the cot.

George didn't move. He just stared at her. Then his eyelids drooped. She was holding his hand, and as soon as she thought it was safe to move, Rita extricated herself from his firm grasp and laid a cover over him.

She stopped in the doorway and gave a last look at the sleeping angels. 'God bless,' she whispered, and pulled the door to.

Pixie was drinking tea, still curled on the chair, and gave her a grateful smile as Rita took the soiled nappy into the scullery and rinsed it under the tap before putting it to soak with some others in a bucket beneath the sink.

On the table was her mug of tea, strong, just as she liked it. She took a gulp. 'Look what your son's done to my costume!' There was a large wet patch on the front of the skirt. 'Oh, well, it'll come out in the wash,' she said.

'For God's sake, tell her, Pixie.' Bob was laughing.

Pixie let out a huge sigh. 'Remember that letter I had about my notebooks?'

Rita nodded. 'The notebooks you typed up?'

'Yes. Well, a publisher in London, Simon Schultor, has asked me to go to see him. They're big publishers,' she added. 'They're interested in my book.'

Rita put down her mug, went over to her and knelt in front of the chair Pixie was sitting in. 'I'm so happy for you. How exciting! I wonder what'll happen next,' she said. 'Look, if you need anything, any help with George or Sadie, just let me know. This Simon wouldn't get in touch with you if he didn't already like what you've written.'

'Thanks,' said Pixie.

Rita saw suddenly how tired her friend was. But it wasn't easy looking after a couple of kiddies, was it? And George was tiny: he hadn't sorted out day from night. She doubted Pixie got much sleep. 'Look, I'll go and leave you two in peace. Remember, I'm only next door. By the way, Gladys was out when I got home . . .'

'She's gone out with her landlord, that Siddy,' Bob said. 'She'll come home – or maybe she'll stay around his house tonight. Anyway, she'll be taking Sadie to the park tomorrow to feed the ducks.'

Rita told them not to bother to see her out. After all, she only lived next door. But as she opened the front door, visions of Joe with his arms about that girl came unbidden to her mind. She was glad she hadn't spoiled Pixie and Bob's happiness with her own misery.

Chapter Twenty-four

'I'm so glad you're with me.' Pixie hoisted the bag of baby things that she was never without, these days, on to her lap from the floor. Bob had George tucked inside his suit jacket, shielding him from the noise and cigarette smoke that swirled around the train's carriage. Immediately a space became available someone moved into it. The train was overflowing with servicemen. Some were sitting on rucksacks or kitbags, others standing, barely room for a pin between their bodies, and a few were parked on the floor among the litter and dog ends.

It was like this back in Gosport, Pixie mused. Something great was happening, and soon. The air held expectancy. She had no idea what was going on: even the daily newspaper hadn't explained why there were so many trucks, gun carriages, Jeeps and men at Elson. Yet still more servicemen were arriving on the south coast.

The train chugged along, the clickety-clack of its wheels on the rails soothing George and keeping him asleep.

And then they were alighting at Waterloo, going through the open barrier and into the main part of the noisy station, where even more servicemen were lounging on their kitbags.

As Bob guided her out of the side entrance and they found themselves on the street, Pixie was excited.

She was going to see a publisher!

Across Westminster Bridge, the Houses of Parliament and Big Ben looked like huge models. As Pixie glanced down into the murky waters of the Thames and smelled its dankness she marvelled that she was so far from her home. There were landing stages where boats plied their trade to visitors, offering sightseeing on the river. Amazingly, war or no war, life went on.

Bob had looked at a map while sitting at the kitchen table and he'd written down directions, deciding it would be quite easy for them to walk to Soames House in Bloomsbury.

So many people, thought Pixie. People from far-off countries, some brown, some yellow, smiled at her, making her blush. London was a lovely melting pot, she thought. It had taken the people of Gosport practically no time to get used to the different nationalities banded together to fight against the Germans. War changes so much, she thought.

A huge brick building behind an iron gate stood at the end of the small road. A café was on one corner, its windows streaked with condensation, and on the opposite corner a gentlemen's hat shop, its window filled with top hats, bowlers and cheese-cutters.

A wooden hut next to the iron gates practically concealed a dour man in a peaked cap, reading a newspaper. Bob spoke to him. Pixie handed the man the letter she'd received and he opened the gate, allowing them both to enter.

As he pressed a buzzer a tall girl came down the steps in impossibly high heels, clearly ignoring the wartime two-inch height restriction. 'Please come with me,' she said, after she, too, had glanced at the letter. Her posh voice made Pixie feel she had no right to be on such hallowed ground.

'I'm going to sit in the café,' Bob said, taking the big bag from Pixie's hand, delving into its contents and handing over her black handbag. 'I'll wait until you come and get me,' he said. He gave Pixie a quick kiss and left with George.

The young woman was waiting for her and held the

heavy door open so Pixie could go inside. The hall smelled of polish, and a huge glass chandelier hung down beside the stairway, which they began to climb. She marvelled that the building was still intact after the bombing London had taken.

Finally, the woman stopped outside a door with the name 'Simon Schultor' in gold lettering. She knocked but didn't wait for an answer before she showed Pixie inside.

'Ah!' a small man said. 'How lovely to meet you.' Rising from behind the desk he shook Pixie's hand and bade her sit on a leather chair. With the untidy desktop between them, he slid back on his own chair and smiled at her. He reminded Pixie of her old uncle, now gone, and she warmed to him immediately. She began to feel less agitated.

He made her feel comfortable by asking questions about her family and then they spoke of her writing. Eventually he told Pixie how much money he was willing to pay for her typed-up manuscript!

Pixie gasped. 'I can't believe you'd pay that much for something I've so enjoyed doing.'

'It's as much as I'm willing to give but . . .'

Pixie sighed. There was always a 'but' to spoil things. The money would certainly help to fill the pot for future schooling for Sadie and George. It also meant that she and Bob could afford a decent christening do.

'. . . I'd like to take your work up until 1943 and end the book there. Everyone's hoping the war will soon be over, but no one knows when. I'd like to commission you to go on writing until the war ends. We'll be able to bring out a second volume then.'

Pixie squealed. 'Will I get the same amount of money for the second book?'

He laughed and nodded furiously. 'Of course.'

Pixie wanted to scream with happiness. *Her name on a book cover! Just like Carson McCullers, Raymond Chandler and her favourite, Ernest Hemingway*. How wonderful was that? She wanted to get up from the chair and dance around the office but she didn't want him to think she was silly. As it was, he was giving her most peculiar glances.

'I take it you accept my offer?'

'Oh, yes.' Now all Pixie wanted to do was run back downstairs and share her news with Bob.

'In that case I'll have the necessary papers drawn up.' Simon Schultor came out from behind his desk and shook her hand. He pressed a buzzer. The tall girl came in to take Pixie back down the many stairs to the main door. She, too, gave Pixie a funny look. By the time they reached the entrance, though, she was almost friendly.

Pixie ran into the café where Bob sat in a corner with George asleep in his arms. In front of him on the oil-clothed table was a mug of strong tea. Pixie picked it up and drank gratefully. A waitress appeared and Bob ordered more tea while Pixie gabbled nineteen to the dozen about her book, Simon Schultor and, of course, the money.

Moments later, the young blonde waitress put down the fresh mugs of tea and handed Pixie some paper tissues. 'Don't let the boss see I've given you his precious serviettes,' she said. 'He'll go mad. But I had that trouble when my Alfie was a baby.'

'Thanks,' said Bob. 'The ladies' toilet is over there,' he said to Pixie.

Pixie glared at Bob, then stared at the waitress. What was the matter with them? Pixie could tell Bob was excited about her news, but why was she being told to go to the lavatory?

He put his hands over his chest and grinned at her. Pixie looked down at herself. She felt the heat rise up the back of her neck and spread to her face.

Oh, whatever had Simon Schultor thought of her? No wonder the waitress had offered her tissues. Her breast milk had soaked through her underwear and now covered the front of her blouse! Two huge circles darkened the material.

Pixie looked at Bob. She knew her face was practically

glowing with embarrassment. Bob was smiling at her. Such a lovely smile. She held out her arms for George who had just opened his eyes. 'C'mon, you,' she said to her baby. 'Feeding time!'

Rita crept along in the darkness of the Clayhall night. She was about a hundred yards behind Gaetano, who was scurrying down the long road past Haslar Hospital. She hoped he wouldn't turn suddenly and catch sight of her. There was nowhere for her to hide. She had to walk along as though she was intending to visit the newly built prefabs that housed families bombed out of their Gosport homes.

This morning at break Gaetano had pleaded poverty yet again. The same well-built man had treated him to a cuppa. Rita suspected that all was not as it should be.

As Gaetano worked the same shift as her, it had been easy to wait until he came through the main gate and follow him.

Why shouldn't he be a spy? The Italians had fought *against* the British, then *with* them. What if he was leaking vital information from Priddy's Hard to the Germans? What if, in his free time, he travelled to Stratford to that prisoner-of-war camp where the guard had hanged himself? It wasn't cheap to travel, was it? That might account for his lack of money. And if he was being paid to spy it was quite possible that difficulties arose in getting money out of Germany to England.

Rita thought about her boss and his trust in her.

Gaetano stopped, looking about him. Rita had no option but to carry on walking. The space between them narrowed. He looked up and down the road, saw her and began to search his pockets. Was he going for a gun? Or perhaps a piece of rope to strangle her with?

Her heart was thumping. She mustn't let her imagination run away with her. Gaetano was pretending to look in his jacket pocket.

Now she had to pass him. She could smell the sweat from his day's graft.

'Good evening,' he said politely, and took out a packet of cigarettes.

'Evening,' she mumbled and hurried on, her head turned away. The sweet smell of fresh cigarette smoke followed her.

How could she follow him when he was behind her? And had he recognized her?

It was quite usual to say 'Good morning' or 'Goodnight' when meeting people on a lonely stretch of road. It usually signalled good intent, didn't it?

Her high heels clicked on the pavement. No, she

decided he hadn't recognized her. Her hair, which was usually hidden by her work turban, was hanging down her back and acted as a disguise. Rita breathed more normally. When she reached the fork she would cross to Waterloo Road and allow him to pass ahead of her again. Rita prayed he wasn't going to Waterloo Road.

At the end of the street she approached a house with a for-sale notice. She closed the tall gate and stood behind it, watching and listening. He turned down the pathway between the prefabs. Thinking it was now safe to continue following him, she moved quickly, running lightly through the rows of prefabs. She was just in time to see him enter the side door of the end house.

Rita breathed a sigh of relief. He hadn't spotted her. Now she could find out who he was living with and what he was doing.

Suddenly the vision of Joe and that woman came into her mind. Why couldn't she stop thinking about him?

Perhaps it was her fault. Maybe it had been too early in their relationship to ask him to come down to Gosport for George's christening. Had she read more into Joe's kiss than was meant? She'd just assumed that no one else was in the background, hadn't she? She'd allowed herself to think their feelings had rekindled simply because they'd written to each other before he'd been wounded.

The idea that Joe could have met someone else inside the hospital had never entered her mind.

She knew a great deal of her unhappiness was caused by the abortion. It didn't feel right that she'd killed her baby. It never would, and Pixie's happiness with Bob and those two perfect children had made Rita see how alone she was.

Em, who deserved happiness, had found it with Sam.

And, of course, Lizzie was forever talking about herself and Blackie going dancing, or showing off some pretty trinket he'd given her. Even Gladys was chirpier now she was sleeping with her landlord Siddy: it meant she'd have a roof over her head for as long as the romance lasted.

Rita knew she could never have afforded to give the baby everything it needed. But that didn't stop her yearning constantly for it.

She tried to push away the thoughts.

She owed it to Rupert Scrivenor to find out why Gaetano's behaviour with money was unusual. And why the Italian needed to know about work at the bomb factory, especially when the newspapers were suggesting an invasion.

If Hitler knew the truth, *the actual landing sites*, he could win the war. If careless words were heard by the wrong ears, the Germans would squash us like bugs on a window-pane. Already there was talk of those V-1s, huge whistling bombs called doodlebugs, hurtling towards Britain. *Hitler had to be stopped.* And if that meant Rita following the Italian to find out what he was up to, she would do it.

Rita didn't have a love of her own now, but she had wonderful friends, who deserved to be protected to the best of her ability. Even Gladys's damned canary!

Chapter Twenty-five

A net curtain strung on wire that dipped in the middle was hanging at the prefab's kitchen window. Gaetano was taking his coat off while talking to a small woman with a child on one hip. The kitchen table was set for a meal for one. A large cloth hung to the side of the window. Rita guessed this was a makeshift blackout curtain. Dull light came from a bare overhead bulb. It was night and any moment the curtain might be pinned into place and Rita would be unable to watch what happened in the room. What she could see of the kitchen surprised her. A boiler, built in, next to a copper. Rita could see it was a copper, even though that, too, was built in, because the woman was now using tongs to stir steaming washing in the boiling water, the child still clinging to her. A cooker stood next to an enamel sink with two taps. It all looked very smart. But the kitchen furniture was make-do-and-mend: a small wooden table and three odd chairs.

Gaetano took the child from her, sat down at the table and jiggled the little one on his lap. The woman took a covered plate from the oven and placed it in front of him, well away from the child. When the little one was back in her arms, Gaetano began to eat. The meal seemed to consist mostly of potato.

Rita dodged below the window as the woman reached across the table, took hold of the length of material and pulled it across.

At the back of the prefab, creeping past the metal dustbin, Rita came to another window with a net curtain across it. The dull light inside lit an old sofa and a worn rug in front of a glimmering fire behind grated metal doors. A back boiler! She had noted the two taps at the sink, denoting hot and cold water. Just imagine, she thought now, hot water at the turn of a tap. What luxury! These newfangled prefabs were so modern. Here again, though, the furniture told of poverty.

In front of the fire, four children sat on the floor playing Snakes and Ladders. Aged from about three to six or seven, they were dressed in clean but worn night clothes. They seemed happy.

A water butt on bricks stood near the back door,

restricting her view. Rita moved closer to the window where the uneven hem of the curtain might allow her to see more. As she leaned closer, something furry ran across her feet.

'Argggh!' she screamed. She kicked out. The bucket beneath the butt's tap toppled and she fell against the back door. The door shot open and a hand grabbed her.

'I got you!'

Rita screamed again. Her ankle hurt. The children now stood in the doorway wide-eyed while she tried to hold on to the door-handle to rise. The hand clamped to her shoulder yanked her into the living room.

'What the hell?' The woman's face was grey with anger.

'I'm sorry, so sorry. The cat made me jump!'

'Ssh! Get inside. Marge, pull the curtain closed.' Gaetano's voice was blunt.

The woman placed the baby on the sofa and began to close up the room. The air smelled of stale cooking, yet the ancient furniture gleamed with polish.

'Who are you?' the woman demanded, one eye on the child kicking its legs in abandonment on the cushion.

'I know her. She works at Priddy's. Why you follow me?' Gaetano pushed his face close to Rita's and she tried to move away, but his grip was firm. 'Tell me!' His hand dropped. 'I would not hurt you,' he said, stepping away from her.

'I – I . . .' Rita stopped. She couldn't possibly tell him the truth, could she?

'I know why. You see me steal rolls of paper for the lavatory! I put them in my lunch tin. Paper costs money – we have not enough for nice paper. With newspaper, children make black their bottoms!'

He put his hands to his face and began to cry. Rita was confused. She'd never seen a man cry so easily before, used to the Englishman's stiff upper lip. Maybe Italians were more emotional. 'Oh dear!' he wailed. 'Now I lose job.'

'No, no!' Rita couldn't bear to watch him crying. The woman, her blonde hair straggling around her face, gathered up the child, who was busily scrambling down from the sofa, and hoisted it back across her hip. She, too, looked close to tears. Rita felt uncomfortable. Especially as the children were now huddled together, solemn-faced.

The Italian gave a big sigh and turned to the woman. 'You think, Marge, you can make tea? Or maybe I make it.' He wiped his face with the back of his hand.

The woman swung away but not before she'd whispered something to the eldest child, who marshalled the little ones into a crocodile. Then the children and their mother walked sedately from the living room into what Rita supposed was their bedroom. The door closed.

'I kiss goodnight later,' Gaetano called, obviously distressed at their exit.

Rita gathered her wits about her. Gaetano obviously thought he'd been rumbled stealing from Priddy's. This was a severe offence, and practically impossible with all the searches made on workers. He thought she was spying on him because of a couple of stolen toilet rolls!

Well, let him think that. Then she wouldn't have to explain her real reason for following him.

Gaetano sat down and put his head in his hands. Marge, the small child still clinging to her, returned to the living room. 'Don't be hard on him. I'll tell you everything. But first let me put Annie to bed.' The child now wore mismatched pyjamas.

Gaetano jumped to his feet. 'I make you cup of tea.'

Five minutes later they were sitting, mugs in hands, the atmosphere expectant. The woman looked first at Gaetano, who nodded.

'My husband was killed last year in France.' She put down her mug and tried to tidy her hair. 'I was finding it difficult to manage with four children and a little one on the way. My brother helps when he can but he lost a hand during the war and is now out of work.'

Gaetano broke in: 'I have nowhere to live and Marge, she take me in. Many times I ask for lodgings but people no want take me. I clean and pay but nobody want me. Marge and her brother very kind.'

He put down his mug and went towards Marge. He laid his hand gently on the back of her neck. She looked up at him and Rita saw the understanding in their eyes. It was obvious Gaetano was more than Marge's lodger. Their love seemed to reach out to her.

'He gives me almost all his wages.'

Gaetano said, 'Is not enough because her husband have many debts. People ask for money and we pay as much we can. Not correct to never pay debts. Her husband good man but foolish with money. My wages good but not enough. I no like to see little ones hungry.'

Now Rita understood why the Italian never had money to buy food at the tea wagon. The man who often treated him to a cuppa must know the situation he was in. But, she thought, that couldn't be why he was always asking about work going at Priddy's. Or could it?

'You ask for jobs for her brother?' She glanced at Marge. The Italian nodded.

'But surely you must know you're risking your own job for the sake of a toilet roll.' She drank some of her tea.

He looked sheepish. 'These little children are my life. I think maybe a toilet roll is such a little thing.'

'Oh, Gaetano,' Rita said. 'You're a lovely man but you're no use to Marge if you lose your job, are you?'

His eyes misted again. 'You are going to tell on me?'

This man wasn't a criminal. The theft of a toilet roll wasn't worth mentioning to Rupert Scrivenor.

Gaetano frowned at her silence, then got up and went into the kitchen, returning with an enamel bowl of water and a piece of clean cloth. He also had a small vial of iodine. He knelt down in front of her. 'I must touch you,' he said. 'Your ankle, it bleeds.'

Rita looked down and saw the blood. Gaetano took off her shoe.

He held her foot in one hand and dabbed at it with the wetted cloth. The smell of the blood was sickening.

'You want more tea?' Marge took her mug and, without waiting for an answer, disappeared into the kitchen, ruffling Gaetano's hair as she walked past him.

He smiled up at her, but said quietly, 'I think you didn't come for toilet roll. You know nothing of this. Why you really here?'

Rita, caught off guard, thought quickly. 'No, you're right.' She blanched as he dabbed iodine on the cut. What excuse could she give for appearing at his home?

'It's all right now,' he said, as he got to his feet.

'Thank you.' Rita thought quickly. The words rolled off her tongue. 'My mate, Gladys, found this five-pound note.' She sat back on the sofa wondering what to say next. 'She gave it to me because it wasn't hers. She found it in the tea queue.' She was speaking quickly now. 'We thought it might belong to you. She asked me to return it.' Rita hoped he wasn't going to ask her why she hadn't mentioned it when she'd passed him in Clayhall Road earlier and he'd stopped for a smoke.

Rita made a show of looking in her handbag and bringing out a folded note. She held it in front of her, a huge amount to her. It was tucked away in her bag because she'd intended to pay a taxi firm to collect Joe from the hospital and bring him to Gosport. She'd taken the money from her savings and had decided to ask the hospital to telephone a local taxi firm. Rita had wanted to surprise Joe . . . She gulped. He'd surprised her instead, hadn't he?

Gaetano looked down at her. 'That money isn't mine.' He was staring longingly at the folded note. 'Not mine,' he insisted.

Rita chewed her bottom lip. If he'd said the money was his, she'd have had to give it to him. It was obvious she was playing some kind of game with him. 'Not mine,' he repeated, his face grim.

'Right,' she said, thinking quickly. 'I'll get Gladys to hand it in at the office tomorrow.'

'Miss Brown.' He pulled her to her feet. Rita was surprised he knew her name. 'I honest man.' His dark eyes with their long lashes stared into hers.

Marge came back into the room with a freshly filled teapot. 'Everything all right?'

Rita saw how worn her hands were as she put the tray down. 'Fine,' she said. 'Gaetano has made a good job of cleaning my ankle.'

Marge laughed and her face suddenly showed some of the prettiness she'd once had. 'I can't remember the last time I wore stockings.' She settled herself on the arm of the chair. 'I've been listening while I've been making tea.' She sighed, as she reached out and put her hand on Gaetano's knee. 'Would you do us a big favour?'

Rita nodded. She'd do anything to right the wrong she'd done the little man.

'People think Gaetano is lodging here. We'd like to keep things that way. If it's discovered we're sleeping together people will make our lives, and the children's, a misery, even though Gaetano came here long before the war started. You know how the English feel about the Italians?'

'Not everyone,' said Rita, quickly.

'Most of them,' said Gaetano, equally quickly.

He'd been on the receiving end of insults and bullying at Priddy's, as Rita knew.

Marge picked up the teapot and went to pour tea in Rita's mug but she stopped her. 'You've got my promise,' Rita said, as the door opened and a little girl came in, dragging a threadbare teddy. She was the image of her mother.

'You didn't kiss us goodnight,' she said, sidling up to Gaetano's chair.

Gaetano jumped up, mock-penitent. 'I'm sorry. I come now,' he said. 'Perhaps a little story?'

The small girl was joined by her brother, whose pyjama bottoms had slid down over his skinny hips. The boy yawned. Rita's heart went out to them. 'I'm going.' She grabbed Gaetano's sleeve. 'I'm sorry,' she said. A look of understanding flowed between them. He nodded, then went to the children, and Rita saw how much the little ones meant to him: everything.

Marge picked up Rita's mug and put it on the tray. 'Any time you're this way, pop in.'

'I will,' said Rita. She put her hand on Marge's arm. 'You've lovely kiddies and a lovely home. I envy you. You've also got a man who cares a lot about you.'

Marge nodded. 'After all I've been through, I'm lucky to get another chance at love. He's a good man . . .'

As Rita walked along the paving stones between the prefabs, a tear rolled down her cheek. She regretted the loss of her baby. She hadn't known it would hurt so much and go on hurting with never a let-up. Marge had difficulties caring for her brood, but she managed . . .

Her fingers wiped the tear away.

In future she'd leave the hunting-down of spy suspects to Rupert Scrivenor.

Chapter Twenty-six

Blackie knocked loudly at the door of number fourteen Alma Street. He could hear the wireless playing a cheerful Glenn Miller tune so someone was in. He was looking for Rita but, unfortunately, it was Gladys who answered. Her smile lit up her face when she saw him.

'Come in, lad,' she said. The curlers in the front of her hair bounced as she stepped aside to let him enter. The rest of her dyed blonde hair was covered with a turban made from a scarf. She was wearing slippers with pompoms on the top, and a wraparound pinny covered her small, neat frame. 'Just having a bit of a clear-out,' she said. 'Double shifts at Priddy's don't leave much time for housework. Got to do it when I got the chance.' In the kitchen she stopped, turned to face him, then put her hands on her hips. 'I suppose you've come to see her upstairs?' She looked up towards the ceiling.

Blackie pushed back a curl from his forehead, tucked it beneath his tilted black hat and nodded. 'Rita's in, then?'

'She is. If I was you I'd go on up. She's done a double shift along with me and gone to bed exhausted.'

He grinned at her. 'You're a pal,' he said. Gladys was implying that if he shouted up to Rita she might yell at him to sling his hook. By going up unannounced she'd still tell him to push off but at least there was a slight chance of talking to her.

He clattered up the stairs and knocked gently on her door. If she refused to answer he would still go in, he decided.

She called, 'What do you want, Blackie?'

She must have recognized his voice, he thought. At least he hadn't woken her. He pushed open the door.

His heart did a triple somersault to see her in a flannelette nightie buttoned to the neck. She'd obviously washed her long hair, for her head was covered with tight pin curls. This was the way he liked Rita, all feminine and a proper woman, not dressed up to the nines in the posh dresses he used to buy her. But, then, he'd only bought her that sort of stuff because he'd thought it was what every woman wanted. When Rita wore a slinky dress she looked like a film star, with her hair all brushed to the side of her face. Ida Lupino, yes! She was just like her.

His Rita could have looked good in a bleedin' potato sack. There he went again, thinking of her as 'his' Rita. She wasn't his now, was she?

The bedroom smelled of perfume and Pond's Cold Cream. Without saying another word he sat on the end of her bed, took off his trilby and laid it carefully on the patchwork quilt. It was warm in the room and he was beginning to wish he'd left his overcoat downstairs. He daren't take it off now – Rita might get cross and he wanted to keep her sweet.

'I'll come straight out with it,' he said. The curl he'd brushed back had fallen forward again, once it had been released from beneath his hat. He ran his fingers through his hair. 'I'm going to Stratford tonight.' He saw she was about to protest. 'Yes, I know what the time is. But I wondered if you'd like to come with me. We could go dancing – you know how you love the Red Horse Hotel.'

He didn't want to sound as if he was begging but, well, he was! Damn, he missed her so much. He looked down at his hands, then lifted his eyes and stared at her when she spoke.

'It's nine o'clock. We'd get there about midnight just as the band is thinking of going home!'

'I know other places. The Rainbow Club in Birmingham

hardly ever closes. And we've got tomorrow night. A Saturday is always lively . . .'

'What about Lizzie?' Rita stared hard at him.

He wanted to scoop her up in his arms, pin curls, granny nightie, shiny face and all. 'I don't want Lizzie. I want you, Rita.' He paused, feeling silly that he'd bared his soul to her.

She made a tent of her knees beneath the covers, put her elbows on them and buried her head in her hands. 'It's too late, Blackie.' Her beautiful dark hair wound in its curls smelled of Amami shampoo. It hurt to remember that it was her favourite.

'We can be there in less than three hours if I put my foot down.' He was begging now.

She looked at him. 'No, it's too late for me and you. It's over. It's finished. We're finished.'

Blackie knew he was going to go on begging and he couldn't help himself. 'We could try again? Please, Rita. Lizzie meant nothing. She still means nothing. I ain't never stopped loving *you* . . .'

She put her hands over her ears. Tears glistened in her eyes. 'Stop it. No more, Blackie. It's nothing to do with Lizzie. I can't be with a man who doesn't think the same way as I do. You tread on people to get what you want, usually money.'

He was hurt but still she carried on: 'I hated it when you bought that load of stolen army coats and sold them on for a profit . . .'

He frowned. What did she mean? They were only overcoats. 'I got to make money, Rita . . .'

'See what I mean? They were *stolen*. They were meant to keep our boys warm while they're fighting for our country. The lads went without so you could make money!'

'I never stole the bloody coats!' Jesus Christ, what was she on about?

'You made money from them.'

'That's being a good businessman.' He'd got them off an American who'd driven away with a lorryload of army goods supposed to be shipped aboard a troopship at Southampton docks. Money had changed hands, of course it had.

'No! It's profiteering!' She seemed to slump in the bed. 'You don't understand how I feel and you never will.'

It hadn't occurred to him before that 'our boys' might go without. Now she'd pointed it out, he was hurt, angry and wanted to get back at her. 'You didn't mind taking the gifts that the money provided.'

He saw her crumple.

'I know. And that's what makes me feel so awful now I

realize what I did. You gave, I took. It was always about money with you. And now I hate myself for my part in it.'

He wanted to reach over and pull her into his arms. But he didn't move.

Of course it was about money. It was always about money. His dad kicking him when he was five years old and hungry and had asked for bread and jam. His dad telling him there was no money for new shoes and stuffing cardboard in his old ones. His dad drinking away his wages and his mother being knocked about for daring to beg his father for enough to buy a loaf of bread. Sitting in the dark, cold kitchen, frightened of the shadows because there was no money for light or coal. Yes, money mattered. He wanted never to have to ask for food again. He wanted never to be cold again. Never!

'Go away, Blackie. Just go away.' Her sharp words punctured his memories.

Rita put her face into her hands again and he could see this time she was crying. He wanted so much to enfold her in his arms but he knew that was the last thing she would allow.

He sighed, got up, picked up his hat and went towards the door.

He loved her.

But he couldn't be honest with her, not even now when he himself was sickened by what he'd done and would go on doing.

The under-the-counter buying and selling was only one part of it. There was the other buying and selling, where his *real* money came from. And he knew that, even if he promised Rita he'd finish his black-market dealings, he'd never be allowed to end the rest. He was in too deep.

His only way out was death.

At the bedroom door he looked back at the woman he loved, the only one he'd ever loved, and who was crying bitterly. Then he walked slowly down the stairs.

He paused in the kitchen doorway. Gladys was standing at the table spreading margarine on slices of bread. There was a tiny pile of shredded cheese next to the grater on a chipped saucer. She laid washed lettuce leaves over the bread. 'It was a shame to waste that tiny bit of cheese. Thought I'd make a sandwich for tomorrow for me and Rita. We're both doing extra shifts again.'

Blackie put his hat on and tipped it towards the back of his head. He thought of the boxes of French Camembert, rich and creamy, in his hallway at home and wanted to offer to bring some for the two women. Rita would hate him even more. He went to Gladys and put his arms about her. 'You're a good woman, Glad.' He let his arms drop, motioned towards the ceiling. 'So's she. That's the bloody trouble with her.'

The wipers weren't making a very good job of scraping the rain from the windscreen. He pulled a cloth from between the seats and rubbed at the inside of the window where the condensation kept building. He liked this car. With its top speed of ninety miles an hour, the Riley had some guts in her. Once he'd got used to driving with barely any lights it was easy, travelling as fast as he dared and sometimes even faster. Most drivers didn't like to be out at night during the blackout, so the roads were usually quiet.

He'd left Gladys's house and begun the slog to Stratford. He could have gone round to Em's and offered Lizzie the chance to come to the hotel with him. She'd have jumped at it. But he hated her prattling on about Frank Sinatra and going into mock-raptures about film stars and their private lives – stories about them were splashed all over the magazines for dimwits like her to read. Who cared about Esther Williams's new swimming pool? Who cared about the made-up life stories of the stars, some of whom were supposed to be descended from Russian counts or Austrian princesses, when in fact they were the same as himself? But the lies held glamour and fantasy for people with everyday lives. Lizzie had served her purpose. Dopey girl had unwittingly answered his questions about what was happening at the factory. Unlike Rita, who was as close as a clam-shell and hadn't been any use to him at all. There were even times when he swore Rita knew what he was up to. But, tight-lipped, she'd said nothing. Perhaps that was one of the reasons he loved her.

Aggie Fletcher from the council offices had buckled, though. Thanks to her, he now knew that all the factory overtime, spent on filling shells, was because England was about to invade France! Shore targets would be the first hit. The harbours floating in the Solent were to enable craft of all kinds to reach the shore. Radar would be jammed by bombers with anti-radar equipment. Flotillas of minesweepers would arrive on the Normandy coast. Air power would be assembled. Pre-dawn attacks were planned. All it needed was a break in the weather.

If he could pass this valuable information on to Irish Paddy at the camp, he'd be sitting pretty, with enough money for the rest of his life. Paddy's job was to radio the enemy or, in Blackie's case, his bosses. Blackie's job would soon be over. And who knew? Maybe, if he got some small knock-about job, and gave up the profiteering, he could fade into the background, prove to Rita he was like any regular chap.

Maybe England would be under German rule, but one country was much like another, wasn't it? German rule had to be good. The country was prosperous, wasn't it? Rather like England, with its museums and schools. And the Germans looked fat and healthy, didn't they?

He thought briefly about Aggie Fletcher. Forty years old! Thin as a broomstick. No lush breasts like his Rita who, no matter how he'd tried to wheedle secrets from her, wouldn't give them up. He'd worked hard to get the old trout into bed. She was the personal assistant to that new councillor with all the big ideas and the pretty young wife, and she'd welcomed him with open arms and legs after their meeting at the May Spring Ball. Aggie was brainy enough to keep her finger on the pulse of Gosport's part in the invasion and daft enough to spill it out beneath the bed covers in her Elson bungalow.

He shuddered to remember their lovemaking.

The silly cow had thought he wanted her. She was a virgin, for Christ's sake! A virgin at forty years old! The councillor's wife had been in awe of Aggie, had told him that Aggie, who used to be a schoolteacher, was as sharp as a razor when it came to council business and knowing what was what.

He'd taken her out to the New Forest, tea and cake in a little Lyndhurst café, and primed her, ready for his victory upon their return to Gosport. She'd wanted him to move in with her. Silly cow, he thought, and dismissed her from his mind.

His mission accomplished, Blackie was glad to be going back to Gosport. The rain hadn't let up and the roads were wet and slippery. It was very dark. No drivers about, except for the car following him that had been behind him for some time now. He looked in the rear-view mirror. It was difficult to make it out with the rain lashing his windows. It looked like a drop-head coupé. Yes, definitely a two-colour job.

Blackie thought of his reception at the prisoner-of-war camp. Boris had been cool but Boris never was a man to let anyone know what was really on his mind. Irish Paddy had met him at their usual rendezvous near the woods and Blackie had got off his chest all he'd learned since their previous meeting. Boris had kept looking about him, as though someone might be listening. Even more strange were the questions Paddy had asked: 'Did you come to Stratford with your girl?'; 'Is she meeting you at the hotel?'; 'Who knew you were coming to Warwickshire?' No personal questions had been put to him before. He glanced in the rear-view mirror again.

The coupé was coming up fast behind him. He was tipping seventy and the fool was closing in. If he had to stop he'd never stand a chance as the driver would ram him up the backside! He pressed his footbrake to let the driver know he was aware of his presence. Bugger! The other should have taken the hint and drawn back on seeing Blackie's rear lights flash. Now it seemed Blackie couldn't slow down even if he wanted to. Well, he'd have to outrun him. His speed went to eighty.

The coupé was on his tail, as though he was a mouse being chased by a relentless cat. It was no mistake: Blackie was definitely being followed. He was being played with.

The trees and bushes either side of the road spun by. It was now impossible for him to lessen his speed. If he slowed, the car might overtake and stop him. Or, more than likely, ram him. Damn! There wasn't even a side road along this stretch, or a lane he could swerve into that would serve as a hideaway, a method for slowing the following vehicle's speed.

Then he remembered the farmhouse. There was a gate to a field beside the farm. A forced stop might enable him to escape his tormentor. If only he could leave the car and run. His follower – who was it? And which side, England or Germany?

It clearly didn't matter, not now.

The farmhouse stood silhouetted against the night sky.

The gate was shut, of course it was. He turned the wheel sharply, felt the splinter and crack of shattered wood, then heard the scratch of bushes as he bumped across wet grass. Turning the wheel fiercely and putting on the handbrake, he slid, slewed and skidded in the mud to a stop. Then he was out of the car and running.

Behind him angry voices told him there was more than one and that his followers were close. Time didn't allow him to glance back.

Blackie could hardly feel his legs. They were merely pistons pumping, keeping his body on the go towards the edge of the field and the woods he focused on for cover.

Then he stumbled. He had stepped into mid-air where there should have been firm ground. He rolled, pain gripping his ankle and knee.

'He's down!' The words were clear in the night air. English!

Then hands were yanking him to his feet.

'Ouch! Mind me leg!' He cried out with pain.

'Last thing you need to worry about, cocker,' said a

brawny man. He, too, was gasping for breath. 'But better for us you can't run.'

'Who are you?' Blackie asked quietly, when he'd got his breath back. There were four men around him and he knew he was beaten, outnumbered. He was at their mercy.

One of the men left the group and seemed to be searching along the edge of the field. Blackie saw his foot slip into a rabbit hole. The man swore, regained his composure and went on searching. A rabbit hole had done for the pair of them.

He tried again. 'Who are you?'

The man returned carrying a huge lump of Cotswold stone. The strain of its weight showed in his face. A second man was now hunting around the edge of the field.

'It doesn't matter,' said the big bloke. 'All that matters is stopping you. Nice little business you've had going but it's over now. Doesn't even matter which side we're on, does it? Though as you won't be around for much longer I might as well say thanks for leading us to the crew who thought they might be able to stop our plans in the Solent going ahead. Your mates at the PoW camp have ceased trading and are no more. So cheers for that, mate.'

Blackie's heart was as heavy as the lump of stone

dropped near his feet. He moved back in alarm. What had happened in the camp? Was Irish Paddy still alive? It sounded as though this mob had stopped the information he had supplied from being radioed through. Had all his efforts been in vain? He feared they had. And now it was his turn to be . . .

'Oi!' he said. 'Watch what you're doing. You could have hurt me dropping that stone.'

Laughter was quickly muted.

'Sorry we can't use a gun on you. It would be quicker, but the sound travels.' The big man looked over towards the farmhouse. 'This is easier. Get on the ground and put your head on that rock.'

'You think I'm daft?' The second man had returned with an equally large stone.

The big man laughed. 'Daft enough to sell secrets to the bloody enemy!'

Blackie let out a big sigh. It really was all over. He thought of the money hidden in his house. No use to him now. But wait . . . 'I've got money. I'll pay you to let me go!'

'Letting you go would make us as daft as you. Unlike you, we bat for the right team.'

Down in the farmhouse lights had gone on. Voices tinkled across the night air.

'Get down.'

His mouth opened in a yell that was cut off by a callused hand.

Blackie struggled. A fist came from nowhere, stunning him, and he fell. He could feel himself being dragged and his head positioned on the cold, wet rock. He saw the big man take the other rock from the wiry man. Held down by unknown arms, Blackie couldn't move. He could just make out the bulge of veins on the big man's forehead caused by the weight of the rock.

He was being held so that he couldn't move his head from the stone, his body supine on the wet grass.

He was glad his Rita wasn't with him to witness his humiliation. The big man hoisted high the rock, then let it fall. Blackie heard the crack of his skull.

Chapter Twenty-seven

As Em handed Rita a sealed envelope, Gladys tried to read what was on the front of it. The wireless was playing 'As Time Goes By' and Rita stopped tunelessly singing to shout, 'Nosy!'

Gladys looked pained. 'I only wanted to know—'

Em laughed, 'That's what she said. "Nosy"!'

Gladys was waiting for Rita to open the letter. Instead Rita put it into the pocket of her navy-blue overall and went back to filling the bomb cases. 'I thought it might be something to do with that American.'

'Leave it, Glad. He wouldn't write me a note at work, would he?'

'I'm not stupid. You're walking around with all the worries of the world on your shoulders. I think he's given you the old heave-ho!'

'As a matter of fact it's exactly that, only it's me that's walked out on him. I saw him with another girl.'

There was silence, broken only by the rumble of machinery, the wireless and the mumble of other workers' voices. Then came the intake of breath from Gladys and Em.

Em had started to walk away but she stopped. 'Whyever didn't you say something?'

'I knew there was something wrong.' Gladys looked triumphant that she'd managed to worm out the reason for Rita's false good humour. 'You should never have ditched Blackie!'

'Oh, for God's sake!' Em looked as though she wanted to kill Gladys. 'Shut up about bloody Blackie.'

Rita gave a small smile. She'd kept her secret to herself long enough and now her words spilled out. The older women stayed quiet until she'd finished telling them how she'd seen Joe give the young woman a ring and hug her. By the time she'd finished, she was crying.

'I knew you cared about him, but I didn't realize how much,' Em said. She put down her clipboard and stared at Gladys. 'Don't you mention a word about that Blackie. He's not perfect, you know.'

Gladys stared haughtily at Em, then turned to Rita. 'So you've not spoken to Joe since that day?'

Rita shook her head. 'I feel like half of me is missing, though,' she said.

'You really fell for him,' Gladys said. Her eyes went all dreamy. 'But I also think you deserve to know why he was messing about with another woman.'

'Too true.' Em adjusted her turban. 'I don't understand how come you didn't know something wasn't as it should be. Blokes, as a rule, ain't no good at keeping secrets.'

Gladys nodded in agreement. 'So exactly how long has it been since—'

'A couple of weeks,' Rita interrupted. It felt like an eternity to her.

'And he doesn't know you saw him with that little tart?'

'No.'

Em and Gladys looked at each other.

'I was thinking of going back to the hospital and having it out with him,' Rita said.

'No!'

Both women practically shouted the word. There was a lull in the wireless music and the workers' eyes swivelled to the three of them. Rita felt herself redden with embarrassment.

'Look, love, if there's nothing wrong, he'll get in touch with you to find out why you haven't been to see him. You've asked him down for the christening of our George, haven't you?' Gladys said.

Rita nodded.

'Well, he's going to wonder where the hell you've been, isn't he?' Rita nodded again.

'If there really is another woman, he won't bother. If all this is some terrible mix-up . . .' Rita looked at Gladys as though she was mad. 'Mix-ups do happen.' Gladys frowned at her. 'Anyway, he'll use the christening as an excuse to get in touch with you, won't he?'

'She's right, you know,' Em agreed. 'If you go up there to that hospital now and start asking questions, you might get answers you don't want. Don't forget, he doesn't know you were at the hospital that day. Give him a chance, Rita. He'll not like it if he thinks you've been spying on him, especially if there really is a simple explanation.'

'Really?'

Em and Gladys looked at each other. 'Trust us,' they said simultaneously.

'In the meantime, throw yourself into having a bit of fun with the girls. Come down to the Fox.' Em grinned. 'It's packed almost every night with blokes.'

'But I don't want another—'

'We know that, but why sit at home moping?' Gladys said. 'You ain't the first girl what's been hurt and you won't be the last.'

It was an unfortunate choice of words and Rita began to cry again.

'If you don't want to go down the pub, come round and see George. You know how much he makes you laugh. Pixie swears he smiled the other day!'

Rita's heart melted. She'd love to be on the receiving end of one of those smiles. 'Pixie's busy these days, isn't she? Sorting out her manuscript, as she calls it!'

'Pixie's never too busy for you.' Gladys stopped filling a shell case and gave her a cuddle.

'Oi!' Em said. 'Get on with your work. We got a war to win.'

It was lunchtime before Rita remembered about the letter passed to her by Em.

In the lavatory she went into a cubicle and took it from her pocket.

Rupert Scrivenor wanted to see her. He suggested she visit his house on Gosport Road. It was a simple note with just the time and date for her to arrive by car. If she was unable to make the appointment he asked her to communicate via Em. That surprised her: she'd asked that no one should know about any contact between them. But when she thought about it, she realized that her overseer, Em, would be the normal channel of information between worker and boss. And the letter had been sealed.

Rita tore it up, threw it into the lavatory and waited until it had swirled away before she left the cubicle.

In the mirror she gazed at herself. Then she tucked her hair beneath her turban. She peered at the front. It was more dark gold than black. Damn, she thought. The pollution in this place was getting to her.

Lizzie came in, the door slamming behind her. She had a face like thunder.

Rita stopped thinking about the factory and stared at Em's daughter. 'You look like you've lost a quid and found a shilling,' she said.

Lizzie glared. 'I suppose you're going to say, "I told you so."'

Rita stared as Lizzie swung into the open cubicle. That door, too, slammed.

She decided to wait. When Lizzie emerged she'd been crying. She grabbed her, turned her towards the mirror and said, 'Look, two women with teary eyes. I bet yours are caused by a bloke as well.'

Lizzie smoothed down her grey dress. The bangles on her arms jangled. Presents from Blackie, no doubt, thought Rita. Still, she was Em's daughter and if Rita could help her she would.

'It's Blackie. He was supposed to collect me last Friday so we could go dancing at the hotel again. I waited all evening, but he never turned up. He'd told me he'd be going to Southampton at the beginning of the week and staying there for a few days. Something to do with the Americans, he said. "Bit of business." He had things to attend to for a couple of days, but I was to be ready on Friday night. He didn't turn up. I suppose he's found another woman. After all, he left you for me so it's logical he'd leave me for someone else.' She gave a huge sniff. 'It ain't you, is it? He still holds a torch for you.'

Her temper rising, Rita snapped, 'No, I haven't been dancing with him.' She shut her lips firmly together. There was no point in hurting Lizzie more by telling her Blackie had been round to see her at Alma Street. She tried to calm her. 'Look, one missed date doesn't mean anything. You know what he's like. I bet he's gone off to Southampton again or something, got involved in some scheme and not been able to get back. He's a businessman first.'

'I should have heard something by now.'

Rita admitted that was strange. She tried to placate Lizzie. 'Perhaps he's gone further afield. Does he always tell you where he's going?'

Lizzie shook her head.

'Well, that's the answer. I bet he's either waiting at the gate when you leave tonight or you'll find a note pushed through your door.'

'You really think so?' Lizzie was looking brighter.

Rita fumbled in her pocket and took out the bright lipstick that Lizzie liked.

'Have a borrow of this, make yourself feel better.' She watched as Lizzie filled in her lips, used a bit of toilet roll to blot them, then reapplied. 'I said borrow, not use the blinkin' lot!'

Lizzie laughed. 'Thanks,' she said, handing back the tube. 'And not just for the lipstick.'

It was just after seven when Rita went next door, hoping for a chat to ease her loneliness. Alone, her thoughts turned to Joe and made her depressed. She knocked on the door instead of pulling the key on the string. Now Pixie and Bob were married she reckoned they needed privacy.

Bob answered, looking harassed, and she could hear George screaming.

'Just in time,' he said. 'I want to get Sadie bathed and Pixie has to finish doing something with her manuscript.' The word came out through gritted teeth.

'She has to earn the money the publisher's paying her, Bob.'

'I know,' he said. 'But I've got to get some sleep within the next couple of hours or how am I supposed to get up early tomorrow to earn money?'

'D'you want me to go?' Rita turned away. 'I'll come back another time.'

He grabbed her shoulder. 'No!'

Rita stared at him.

'If you could sort out George, that'd be a help. Pixie's fed him, but he's got himself into a tizzy upstairs. I'll finish getting Sadie to bed. Would you do that, then buzz off so I can sleep?'

Rita laughed, walked over the threshold and straight up the stairs. She heard a sigh of relief, noted the light beneath Pixie and Bob's bedroom door, went into the children's room and scooped up the little boy, clutching him to her. 'You can stop that yelling,' she said. 'We know you're here. I can smell you're here!'

Almost immediately his cries slowed to a snuffle. Pixie shouted, 'Thanks, Rita,' and then near-silence descended.

Rita picked up a white nightdress, a white towel, tie-round vest, a nappy and a muslin square from the white-painted chest of drawers.

Her arms full of the baby and his clothes, she went

downstairs and into the kitchen. Sadie was sitting on Bob's lap and he was brushing her blonde hair. The room smelled of talcum powder. The little girl smiled at Rita and George. She was going to grow into a beauty. Shy, she cuddled into her daddy. She was Pixie to a T.

'Look, it's your daddy and your sister,' she said to George. She'd dumped the stuff on the table and was holding him up to see the kitchen. She saw his eyes focusing. Then his wobbly head turned to her and his mouth opened in a smile.

'He smiled at me! Bob, he smiled at me.' Rita was excited.

'George doesn't smile at everyone, so think yourself lucky.'

Rita could see the little boy was less stressed now. 'You don't know what it means to me,' she said. She wanted to shed a tear of happiness.

'I think I do,' he murmured. Sadie had her head against his chest and her thumb in her mouth. Her eyes were closing. 'She's going off now,' he said. 'I'll just put her upstairs to bed and if you start on his lordship, when I come down I'll put the kettle on.' He got up, the child in his arms, and went into the hallway.

Rita laid George on the floor on Pixie's rag rug. He'd

forgotten about crying and was kicking his legs and waving his arms. He was also very smelly. 'Another bath for you, Stinky,' she said.

The tub was outside in the scullery and she filled it with hot water from the kettle, then added some cold. She brought it into the warm kitchen and put it on the table. The clothes and towel she hung around the fire-guard to warm, then began to undress the little boy. She cleaned him up and sat for a while on the kitchen chair with him gurgling away. But then a stream of pee arced into the air, all over the pinny that she'd found on a nail in the scullery and put on. 'Ow!' she cried.

George's dark eyes surveyed her.

'You knew you were going to do that, you little monkey,' she said. His toothless mouth opened, his eyes crinkled and she was treated to another smile. Her heart almost exploded with joy.

She could hear Bob upstairs. His movements were quiet, as if he was taking no chances with Sadie – he really didn't want to wake her. Rita had George in the water and was soaping his dark hair. No mistaking this was Bob's child, she thought. He was the spitting image of his father. She heard Bob say something to Pixie and then he came downstairs.

Just as Rita was wrapping the clean baby in the white

towel and playing peek-a-boo with the corner of it over his head, there was a knock on the front door.

Bob must have gone along the passage to answer it for she heard the door open and shut and in came Marlene. It must have started raining hard for she was drenched. 'Let's have your coat,' Bob said. He took it into the scullery, followed closely by Marlene. She'd already glanced at Rita, then dismissed her before Rita had time to greet her. Rita could see from her tear-stained face that something was up.

Yes, something was very wrong indeed.

Chapter Twenty-eight

Rita could hear Marlene crying in the scullery, trying to talk between sobs. Bob's gruff tones were interspersed with the pop of the gas and the rattle of crockery.

She patted George dry, then powdered him, rubbing the talc into his damp creases. He smelled like Heaven to her and the bath had relaxed him so he was like a rubber doll, pliable and easy to dress in his nightwear. 'That's you out for the count,' she said tenderly. His cheeks were rosy and she'd brushed his hair into a quiff on the top of his head.

The voices in the scullery were now subdued, but Rita sensed emotions running high.

George's eyes were closing as Rita, holding him tightly, carried him upstairs to his cot. She pulled the patchwork cover over him. Pixie had made it and it was fashioned from pieces of cotton she'd cut from old dresses she'd picked up for next to nothing at jumble sales. A similar, larger, cover lay over Sadie's bed and the curtains at the window matched. The effect was one of brightness and warmth. Taking a last look at George and planting a kiss on his forehead, she ran her fingertips over Sadie's cheek, then pulled the door to.

She could hear the keys of Pixie's typewriter clacking away but decided not to bother her. Bob had had a few words with her when he'd put Sadie to bed, so she guessed that Pixie didn't need anything, only time and quiet to get on with her writing. Pixie had already explained to her that the manuscript needed some changes and she'd been asked to do the work as soon as possible.

Downstairs, Bob and Marlene had moved into the kitchen.

'I think I'd better go now,' Rita said.

Marlene looked at her. 'Not on my account.' Rita saw Marlene had dark circles beneath her red eyes. 'I'm waiting for Bob to say, "I told you so." He never did like Samuel.'

'You've a pretty poor opinion of me if you think I'm going to rub it in.'

Rita must have looked confused.

'The bastard's run off, taking everything I've worked for.' Marlene's mouth turned into a thin line.

Bob said, 'Don't go, Rita. You've not even had a cuppa yet. Besides, maybe you can think where Samuel Golden's gone, or at least come up with a way we can catch the bugger.'

Rita said, 'I take it you've lent him money and he's scarpered?'

'Not just *some* money. All I had, and I borrowed against my house.'

She sat down on the chair that Rita had occupied to bathe George. Talcum powder now clung to Rita's jumper and trousers and she spotted the dirty nappy near Marlene's foot. She bent to pick it up with the baby's discarded clothing. 'I'll get rid of this lot, then we can talk properly.'

Outside in the scullery she put the nappy and soiled clothing to soak. After wiping out the little bathtub she hung it in its place on a nail in the wall.

Back in the kitchen, Bob had poured tea.

'What about Pixie?' Marlene asked.

'Best not disturb her,' said Bob.

'I think she'll want to help,' said Rita. 'Pour her some tea.' She went to Marlene and gave her a hug, then ran upstairs and returned moments later with Pixie, in her pyjamas.

Pixie went over to Marlene and put her arms around

her. 'You don't need to worry about the house. If we can't find the man and get the money back, you'll still have your home. Remember what Bob said about paying rent? You can do that and we'll give you time to get over the shock of what's happened.' She moved away from Marlene but pushed a filled mug along the table. 'Get this down you. Then tell us everything.' She looked intently at Marlene. 'And I mean everything.' Then Pixie turned to Bob, who smiled to show he agreed with what she'd said.

The four of them drank their tea silently, then Marlene said, 'Samuel told me he owed money.'

When she told Rita the amount, Rita was shocked. Two thousand pounds was a great deal.

'He needed to pay for materials and a past debt so he could finish the houses in Queen's Road and go on with the sale of them.' She took another sip of her tea. Her hair, usually so vibrant, was still wet and hung about her face and shoulders like red rat's tails. The colour, darkened by damp, made her pale skin look deathly.

'I saw the houses were up for sale so I believed him. They'd been bombed and he'd put new kitchens and bathrooms in them. They'd be sold and he'd make enough money to pay me back. He promised we'd get married, have our honeymoon, and he'd replace my makeshift engagement ring with a proper one.' Marlene looked at her finger, which was now bare.

Rita knew exactly what had happened. 'You tore it off and flung it away, didn't you?'

Marlene sighed. 'Not even that simple. I took it off, as I did every night when I had a wash before bed, and put it on my bedside table. It's not there now. He must have taken it.' Fresh tears welled up and overflowed, running down her pale face. 'Stupid me. That ring was worth a few bob.'

'Never mind,' said Pixie. 'He'll get his comeuppance. What happened about the money?'

Bob's face was stern, his mouth tight,

'Everything Samuel said sounded so likely. And every time we went to an auction together he pressed money onto me to buy stuff I couldn't otherwise afford, but which made me a lot of money. So I simply offered to lend him enough to tide him over.'

'Which, of course, he took advantage of?'

Marlene nodded. 'I trusted him. I loved him.' Her voice was very small.

'Yes,' Bob said softly. Rita looked at him as if she'd forgotten he was there. He hadn't spoken for ages but had been sitting quietly, listening and taking it all in. 'I know you loved him,' he now said. 'What happened after that?'

'Well, I got the money together.'

'All two thousand pounds?' Rita couldn't get over Marlene having that kind of money.

'I went round to his flat in the Crescent and handed it over. I was just so pleased that I could help him.'

Rita understood perfectly that if you loved someone you'd do anything for them.

'He told me the whole thing – the remainder of the building work, sale of the houses and exchanging of contracts – was all ready to go ahead as soon as he paid over the money. Within a matter of days,' Marlene nodded, 'yes, *days*, he'd be knocking on my door with my proper engagement ring.'

'And you believed him?'

'You'd have done the same, Rita. He had money coming out of his ears, that man. And look at the places he took me to. I've been to villages and towns I never knew existed.' She faltered. Rita knew she was realizing now that Samuel had been buttering her up.

'Did you always pay him back for the money he pressed on you?' Bob asked.

'Yes, as soon as I made a profit. Sometimes the very next day.'

Bob nodded. 'He took you out in his car, bought you meals and spent time in bed with you in country pubs?'

Marlene nodded.

'And then took you for two thousand pounds?'

'You've been well and truly had,' Pixie said. 'A sprat to catch a mackerel.'

'A clever bugger,' agreed Rita. She stared at Marlene, who, eyes downcast, was crying again. Her heart went out to her. 'When did you find out he wasn't going to cough up?'

'Almost immediately. I stayed the night with him. When I woke – and remember, I had to get up early – he wasn't there. My ring was missing. I waited a week. Previously he'd said he had to go to Southampton for a couple of days on business and I thought he'd gone there. I made myself believe he'd left quietly, not wanting to wake me, and perhaps I'd only thought I'd left my ring on the bedside table. I thought he'd be overseeing the building work and checking up on his market stalls. Which, I know now, probably never existed except in his imagination. In my mind I gave him extra time to transfer the money he'd made from the sale into cash, to return it to me, and to make arrangements for the wedding and honeymoon. I know now it was all a farce. He was so apologetic that he couldn't take me abroad because of the ban on flights due to the war.' She faltered. 'Everything fitted. What didn't, I made excuses for.' Then she took a deep breath. 'I carried on working – well you know that,' Marlene looked at Bob, who nodded. 'But I began to wonder why he hadn't called round to see me. When you're in love, you want to be together as much as possible, don't you?'

Rita was staring at Bob and Pixie. They were so much in love with each other, despite all the setbacks they'd had. She was suddenly reminded of Joe, and pushed him from her thoughts. 'I guess you do,' she said to Marlene.

'I couldn't stand not seeing Samuel so I went round to the Crescent. He'd gone, left the day after I'd given him the money. When I'd woken and he wasn't there, that was exactly how he'd planned it.' Her lips trembled. 'I kept it to myself. Tried not to let you see I was worried,' she said to Bob. 'I've earned enough this week to give Mum the housekeeping money. You know she looks after that side of things and sees to my Jeannie while I work. But my stock's low and I have no money to get more. But, more importantly, I have no way to pay you back the money you lent me against my house.'

Bob got up from his kitchen chair and enveloped Marlene in a bear hug. Rita saw him hold her close with almost as much tenderness as he'd shown earlier to his little girl. This time there was no holding back her floods of tears. It was as if Bob's compassion had given Marlene permission to let herself go and cry out her pain.

Pixie got up, gathered the crockery, motioned Rita to help her and together they went into the scullery. With the kettle once more on the gas and flames shooting out from beneath, she said, 'What are we going to do?'

Rita began rinsing the cups beneath the tap, then dried them with the tea-towel. 'I've got some money,' Rita began. 'Not enough to sort her out, though.'

'I've got the advance coming from the publisher. Some of it's earmarked for the christening. Bob's already told her that as she got the money from him by handing over the deeds to her house we certainly won't throw her out on the streets. So her home's safe.' Pixie paused. 'Can you afford to lend her enough to see her through a couple of weeks with food and whatever she might need for her mum and the kiddie? She reckons she has enough for this week.'

'Yes.' Rita could do that.

'I'm going to suggest to Bob – it'll be all right, he'll agree – that we lend her enough to get more stock to tide her over until she starts to make a profit again.'

'She's done it once, she can do it again,' Rita said. She believed in Marlene. She smiled. 'The hard part will be getting her to agree to take the money,' she said. 'You know how bloody independent she is.'

Pixie nodded. 'We can't do anything about her savings, but it's a start, isn't it?'

Rita said, 'What about Em and Gladys?'

'What about them?'

'Should we say something to them?'

Pixie shook her head. 'It's Marlene's business. She's a private person. Best to keep it secret. If she wants people to know, she'll tell them in her own time. Would you want people to know you'd been conned?'

'Definitely not!'

'Well, Rita, what's been said tonight stays in my house. All right?'

'What about the police?'

'That's up to Marlene. But I reckon Samuel's done this before. He's too sharp and well-dressed to work for a living like a normal person.'

'You're right,' Rita said. 'But what goes around comes around. He'll get his comeuppance.'

'Let's get back in the kitchen in the warm. Bob will be getting worried. He's not at his best with weeping women.'

'You could have fooled me,' said Rita.

Pixie grabbed her arm, 'I haven't said thank you for changing George.'

'No need. It gave me a chance to think about something else besides Joe.'

'Everything turns out right in the end,' Pixie said. 'But in the meantime, I'm here if you need me.'

'Thanks,' said Rita. 'But neither me nor Marlene are having much luck with blokes. Come to think of it, Lizzie's lost Blackie too,' she said. She gave Pixie a quick rundown on the conversation she and Lizzie had had. Then she said, 'Let's talk this Samuel business through with poor Marlene, then I'll go next door. Your Bob was moaning about getting his sleep.'

Pixie looked guilty. 'He won't go to bed until he's sorted her out. You know how much he cares about her.'

Rita thought she was lucky to have such loyal friends. The image of Joe and the girl flashed through her mind. What a pity she, like Marlene, was no judge of character.

Chapter Twenty-nine

In her black dress with the padded shoulders, black high heels and her coat tied tightly around her waist, Rita walked down to the end of Alma Street. The large dark car was purring near the kerb alongside the greengrocer's on Forton Road. Rupert Scrivenor waved to her, and Rita walked quickly towards him as he got out and opened the passenger door for her. She didn't want anyone to see her getting into the car. The less people knew about her relationship with her boss, the better, she thought, as she slid along the leather seat.

'You look very nice,' he said. His eyes smiled, so she knew he meant what he said.

'Thank you,' Rita replied. What a shame he preferred men to women, she thought. He was so handsome – no wonder all the women at the factory fancied him.

He drove down Forton Road and onto Military Road,

where the naval barracks were, then out towards Lee-on-the-Solent, passing the HMS *Daedalus* air base. Above the pebbled beach, covered with barbed wire to discourage invaders, the road meandered towards Stubbington.

He was silent, but it was the kind of silence that was comfortable. Nearing the centre of the small village he announced, 'Here's where we live.' He drove straight up the long driveway of a large house facing the sea. In the distance, across the Solent, she could see the Isle of Wight.

They had a large garden, well set out with a lawn surrounding a marble birdbath. There was a pergola with wooden seats, and trees gave the house a secluded feel. It was nothing like the two-up-two-down where Rita lodged with Gladys.

The front door opened and a tall blond man stood smiling at the step. He ran his fingers through his fine hair, clearly nervous. Rita smiled. She felt a little ill at ease. She had met a few 'pansies', as Gladys called homosexuals. Those she had befriended on excursions with Blackie had been rouged and effeminate and Blackie disliked them.

The man welcoming her into their home was scholarly. Yes, she decided, perhaps a tutor of some kind. He looked bookish, his horn-rimmed glasses enhancing his amazing blue eyes. If he was a teacher, no doubt the girls drooled over him. What a waste, she thought again.

'You look nice,' he said, echoing Rupert's earlier words. He held out a hand to shake hers. Rita saw his nails were very clean. His smile was white and genuine.

'Rita, this is Lance,' said Rupert, introducing her to his friend. He ushered her into the parquet-floored hallway where he took her coat and hung it on a coat-stand. Then he divested himself of his jacket and led her along to a kitchen like none she'd ever been in before. Row upon row of expensive copper-bottomed pans hung from a long wall rack and another rack held kitchen implements. A huge white refrigerator hummed in the corner next to a gleaming sink that stood a little way from an Aga, which pumped out heat and a delicious smell. A Welsh dresser held blue and white crockery. A large window overlooked the back garden with an apple tree close to the house. Gingham-frilled curtains framed the windows and the blackout curtain was rolled up above.

'What a lovely room,' Rita exclaimed.

'Not my domain,' said Rupert. 'He,' he pointed to Lance, 'has a gift for colour co-ordination. I'll get him to show you the rest of the house, which, thanks to Lance, has the most delightful furnishings. He's also a gifted chef.' He paused. 'Lance teaches basic cookery at Hillsea

College to the little heathens, then comes home and tries out his latest concoctions on me.'

Lance looked at him in mock-disgust, raised his eyes heavenwards, then turned to Rita with a grin. 'He'll not be eating tonight, then?'

Rupert laughed. 'I'll ignore that and pour our guest some wine, shall I?'

Rita could see the couple were well suited. She decided on white wine and after one sip and a few moments' chat, she felt as though she'd known them both for years. The toing and froing of sarcasm between them made her smile and she felt they were letting her in on their happiness.

'Rita, I could easily lay the table in the dining room for you. We usually eat in here, but I could do it properly.' Lance waved an arm, encompassing the long scrubbed white table set with six kitchen chairs. 'If you wanted?' He was waiting for her reply.

'Oh, in here,' she said. 'It's such a . . . *happy* room.'

'Good. Then you can put out the cutlery,' said Lance, going towards a drawer and opening it. He passed the gleaming knives and forks to her and she began setting places for them.

'It's not very grand,' Rupert said. 'Coq au vin with rice. Though I'm pleased to report it's real chicken. The butcher in the village has his eye on Lance, which comes in handy as we often get an extra pork chop or two.' He laughed and dodged the tea-towel that flew towards him.

It was during the meal that the talk began to get serious.

'I'd like to thank you for keeping your eyes open and your mouth closed,' Rupert said. 'You may not be aware that I closely monitored your relationship with Blackie Bristow and was happy to see you had the good sense to realize he was up to something more than his wheeling and dealing . . .'

Rita wanted to tell him that her reasons for parting company from Blackie had more to do with the unfairness of him living high on the hog while ordinary people struggled for their country, but she kept quiet. Lizzie, of course, was another reason. But she didn't want to discuss her love life with her employer.

She was surprised when Lizzie's name came up in the very next sentence.

'Lizzie, one of our office girls, gave away information that he obviously couldn't extract from you. Tomorrow she'll be back on the line. We're not sacking her because she's a damned good worker, who was tricked into giving away secrets as pillow talk. We'd have to give a reason to sack her and, of course, she's my overseer's daughter, so it's better this way. However, the secrets she's been privy to will soon be divulged to everyone.' He took another forkful of the excellent chicken and continued, 'Mr Bristow was a businessman who went for the big money. His last trip to Stratford-upon-Avon involved selling secrets he'd gleaned elsewhere to an Irishman at the prisoner-of-war camp.' He took another forkful and chewed thoughtfully. 'Those secrets involved departure timings of what will be known as D-Day.'

Rita gasped. Then she realized he'd said '*was* a businessman', when referring to Blackie. What did he mean? She thought it better not to interrupt.

'Gossip's rife in Gosport,' Rupert said, 'about the troops and their possible landing sites across the water. But the weather, despite it being May and usually kind enough for sailors, has been rough and windy. This has held up operations.

'To cut a long story short, the work at Priddy's is highly confidential and it's up to me to make sure there are no leaks. Mr Bristow got to know more than was good for him and passed it on. His money won't do him any good now. There are no pockets in shrouds.'

Rita put her hand to her mouth. Her fork dropped to the floor with a loud clatter. 'You mean . . .'

Rupert nodded. 'He was a traitor.'

He seemed to be waiting for Rita to speak, but her

head was reeling. All she could think of was Blackie handing her yet another gift, then the feel of his body against hers beneath cool white sheets. She gulped and blinked away a tear that threatened to fall. So she'd been right all along. Blackie had never cared about anyone but himself. And now it seemed his past had caught up with him.

Her head was reeling. But Blackie a spy? How come she'd never known? Although the persistent questions he'd asked about what went on at the munitions yard had always seemed strange to her.

Rupert put his hand across the table and covered hers. 'You don't want to know what happens to traitors. I've let you in on this because I know you can be trusted not to speak to anyone. I'm saying he's been disposed of.' He gave a huge sigh. 'The local newspaper has been seeking his whereabouts. It's quite usual for us to put out a story like this. Young Lizzie probably believes he's moved on to someone new. You're close to her. Let her go on thinking that. Our overseer can be trusted not to give anything away, for the sake of her daughter. Probably better if nothing further is discussed.' He looked deep into her eyes.

Lance supplied Rita with another fork, then picked up the one that had fallen to the floor and smiled at her.

'I've managed to make a passable meringue, fruit from a tin, of course.'

The talk about Blackie was obviously at an end.

Lance picked up her plate and carried it with the other crockery to the draining board. 'War is so cruel,' he said quietly.

The warm, cosy atmosphere in the kitchen had chilled. In a passionless voice she managed to say, 'I love meringue.'

But the last word stuck in her throat and she began to cry.

Lance walked towards her chair and put his arms around her, bending so she was snivelling into his pristine white shirt. 'It's all right,' he said. Rita breathed in the cooking smells mingled with his spicy cologne. 'I lost someone . . .'

He left the rest unsaid, but finally he added, 'I've now found someone who loves me. You're a pretty girl. You *will* smile again.' He took out his clean handkerchief and gave it to her. Rita blew her nose noisily. 'Sorry,' she whispered.

'I think it's time we had pudding,' Rupert said. He was looking at Lance, grateful he had stepped in to comfort Rita. Meanwhile, he added, in a brisk no-nonsense tone, 'I need to tell you to ease up on the detective work. If you'd come to me first I could have told you our Italian worker isn't a spy.'

Rita felt herself blush.

'However, I commend you for your diligence.'

She shrugged. She knew she'd been overzealous about Gaetano and his lack of money. 'Do you know everything that goes on at the factory?' The words tumbled out before she could stop them.

'He doesn't miss much,' said Lance, taking off his glasses and cleaning them with a tea-towel. The two men looked at each other. Lance replaced his glasses, then came over to the table and set down a glass dish of a delightful creamy meringue pudding in front of Rupert. 'I know how much you like it so you can have the largest portion,' he said.

Then he placed a dish in front of Rita and passed her a spoon. 'Get your lips around that, darling girl. Men will come and men will go, but good food surpasses them all.'

The lightness and warmth in the kitchen slowly but surely began to return. Rita would have a lot to think about when she was alone in her bed later. She knew she would cry and her heart would ache for Blackie, for their baby, for what might have been. But for the moment the delicious meal needed her full concentration.

*

'Jesus, but it's windy and miserable,' said Em. 'I wish I'd brought in my flask.'

'Well, you didn't, so you'll have to queue for tea like the rest of us,' said Gladys.

'Oh, please don't start arguing,' said Rita. 'I really couldn't stand it.'

'You two are like a wet weekend in Brighton,' Em said. She moved up along the queue, Lizzie following closely.

'Well, I'm bringing in a flask tomorrow,' Lizzie said. She pulled off her turban and shook out her long dark hair. 'My money's gone down a notch now I've been moved to the workroom with you lot.'

'Couldn't hope to keep up that high-powered job, could you?' Dottie Benson blew cigarette smoke in Lizzie's face. Dottie was a force to be reckoned with. She had eleven children, no husband and a mouth like a sewer. Lizzie put her hand up to wave off the strong smoke from the Woodbines.

The women were searched for their cigarettes and matches before they went inside the building, and the first thing Dottie did upon leaving the workshop was to collect her fags from her locker and light up.

'Surprised you can even spell,' Dottie said nastily. Her second-eldest girl had requested an office job but had been refused.

Rita pulled Lizzie back before she clocked the trouble-maker's smirking face.

'Last in, first out,' jumped in Em. 'Too many typists and not enough important floor workers.'

Dottie sniffed loudly. She couldn't argue with the over-seer. Rita was glad Em had defused the situation. Her eyes scanned the people waiting.

At the front of the queue Gaetano was counting his money and taking ages about it. Rita elbowed her way through the dozen or so people in front of her, amid groans and shouts that she should get to the back of the queue. One man called her a bitch! She stuck out her tongue at him.

'I'll pay for that,' Rita said breathlessly, ignoring the crowd and putting the money for a cup of tea and a doughnut on the counter.

Gaetano stared at her. 'Is not necessary,' he said. He then lowered his eyes and Rita saw that she had embar-rassed him. She'd thought no more than to be kind. Out of the corner of her eye she saw the man, possibly Gaetano's friend, putting his hand into his pocket.

'I want to,' she said briskly, and returned to her original position in the queue, thinking what a mess she'd made of that.

'Make yer bleedin' mind up!' Dottie moaned, as Rita struggled past her.

'What are you playin' at, Rita?' Gladys frowned at her. 'Don't have nothin' to do with that Italian. They don't know what side of the war they're on.' Her voice was shrill.

'Shut up, Gladys,' was all Rita said. Em squeezed her hand in sympathy.

'Heard anything about Blackie?' Gladys seemed to have forgotten already that Rita had told her to shut up.

'No.' Lizzie tilted her face up to catch the sun that had suddenly appeared. She loved the sunshine and often sat in the back garden, in her halter-top and shorts. The last couple of days had been so changeable that it was more like March than the first day of June. 'I still think he's gone off with some woman. But he never cared for me as much as he liked you, Rita. I always felt I was second best.'

'I'm not getting into a silly row with you about Blackie Bristow.' Rita glared at her. 'Come on, move up.' The queue was thinning out and there were only a few people in front of the four friends now.

Rita watched Mick, Rene's business partner, fill the huge tea kettle via its spout and set it back on the Calor gas ring. It would boil in no time on top of those flames, she thought. By the time they reached the counter there'd be fresh tea brewed.

Em must have been reading her mind. 'I hope we get a strong cup. I don't want no pissy first-out-of-the-pot tea.'

'What you on about? The tea here's almost as good as ol' Tom serves down the Dive.' Gladys wiped her nose with her handkerchief. 'Pity it takes longer to pour, though!' She waved her hand at Mick. 'Look at the teapot. No wonder the queue's taking ages to get to the counter. That tea's only just crawling out of the spout.'

More people were queuing behind them now and the noise and cheerful banter were making Rita feel happier. She was trying not to think about Blackie's fate. It had kept her awake, as had her tears. She'd carefully dotted Pan Stik beneath her eyes to disguise the shadows. There was no one she could talk to about Blackie Bristow so she'd keep her thoughts to herself.

Joe wouldn't stay out of her mind, either. And today, no matter how hard she tried, his face kept floating in front of her. She decided the sooner the tea break ended the better. Much as she disliked filling shell cases, her concentration couldn't be allowed to wander towards Joe and that girl.

'Marlene wasn't at the market yesterday,' Lizzie said.

'A girl on line three wanted a present for her mother. Something a bit special, nice bit of gold, like.'

'I don't suppose she feels like facing people,' Rita said. 'She'll be all right. She's strong enough to get on top of things. She'll be back before long, mark my words.'

Rita didn't want to gossip about Marlene. She thought the girls knew as much as was necessary and didn't need to delve into everything that had gone on in Pixie's house that night. Marlene's house was safe and she had money enough to buy stock and groceries.

'Wasn't the first time that bloke had stolen from a woman.'

'Gladys? How d'you know that?' Rita frowned, moved along in the queue beside her.

'Marlene went to the police. Bob advised her to. That bloke wants stringing up. He changes his name and his hair colour and gets away with it. There was this woman down Glastonbury way who sold her house, gave him the money and moved into what she thought was his house, only to be asked for the outstanding rent after he'd pissed off with her money and jewellery.'

Rita held on to Em for support. The girls were open-mouthed at this new revelation.

'No wonder the poor cow needs a few days to recover,' Em said, then quietly to Rita, 'He's a bastard!' They both knew that the Crescent flat he'd told Marlene he owned had also turned out to be rented with the rent well overdue.

Rita nodded. 'Everything's so shitty,' she said. 'I wish this war would end.'

Gladys said, 'Mark my words, Samuel will soon be behind bars now the coppers know what he's up to. Yes, you mark my words!'

'No chance of that today, though, but there's every possibility of a cuppa at last.' Em was looking at the large enamelled teapot and its trickle of tea. Rita followed her gaze.

'I can piss faster than that,' shouted Gladys. 'Mine ain't so colourful, but it runs quicker.'

Rita watched the slow drip falling into a white enamelled mug. Earlier when the pot had been filled with boiling water, Rene had lifted up the half-lid, dropped in several spoonsful of tea onto the leaves already in the pot and poured on the boiling water. Now she waited a while, then went on pouring.

'I reckon there's something stuck in that spout,' Rita said.

'It's not usually as slow as this,' admitted Rene, putting the pot down and peering into the spout.

Rita threw her the spoon that was anchored to the leg

of the large glass sugar bowl by a long bit of string. 'Give the pot a stir,' she said.

There were mutterings of dissent from the growing queue.

'Stop messing about, Rene, and get on pouring the tea,' said Mick, about to put a tray of marge-spread currant buns on the shelves that held the last of the sandwiches.

Rene lifted the half-lid, put in the spoon and stirred vigorously. Rita, closest to the counter, saw she'd hit an obstruction. Rene lifted the spoon to examine her find.

'Agh!' Rita screamed. It was then a toss-up as to which of the girls was screaming the loudest. Draped over the spoon, its whiskers and long thin tail dripping with tea, was a dead mouse.

Rene dropped the spoon and the mouse fell to the floor of the wagon with a dull thud. She leaped back, careering into Mick. The currant buns flew about like tennis balls. Pandemonium reigned both inside and outside the tea wagon.

Gladys walked away. 'I'm definitely bringing in a flask tomorrow!'

Chapter Thirty

'You all ready for Tuesday?' Rita looked up as Em marked her clipboard. 'Our Lizzie's wearing a grey costume. Underneath she's putting on a white halter-necked top, so in the evening when the dancing starts she can just take off the jacket.'

'Where did she get the blouse from?' Rita asked. Even though material wasn't on ration any more, it was still hard to get hold of stylish clothes at a reasonable price.

'I am here, you know!' Lizzie spoke loudly enough for the whole roomful of workers to hear. 'It was a piece of parachute silk. Didn't take me long to run up the blouse. Actually, I got enough silk left to make you one an' all, Rita,' she said.

'I'd like that, but I wouldn't wear it when you was wearing yours. We look enough alike as it is without wearing similar clothes.' Rita tamped down powder in a shell. Lizzie had been very friendly towards her lately, when she wasn't moping about, missing Blackie. Lizzie was convinced that because Rita had refused to go to Stratford-upon-Avon with him he had finally given up on her and gone off to pastures new. Gladys had made a big thing about Blackie coming to Alma Street and begging Rita to go off with him. Em had told Rita that Lizzie had almost stopped mooning about over a bloke who didn't care about her: now she was going down to the Fox and having a good time with the forces lads.

'You heard from that American, lately?'

Rita stared at her. 'Don't rub it in, you know I haven't.'

'Shame.' Lizzie stuck her fingers under her turban. 'I'll never get used to this headgear. I thought by the way you was always going on about him that he could be the One.'

Rita continued staring at her. For once she was sure Lizzie was commiserating with her instead of being sarcastic. With Blackie out of the way, she was a lot nicer to be around.

The attack on Lizzie had left its mark, though. No longer did she walk home alone from dances or the pub. Em persuaded Sam to let her stay in one of the bed-and-breakfast rooms at the Fox if there was no one to take her home.

'You can use my place to change clothes for the evening,' Gladys piped up.

The christening was to be a late-afternoon affair at St John's Church in Forton Road, then a buffet meal with a band at the Sloane Stanley Hall at the Crossways.

'Funny day, a Tuesday,' Lizzie remarked.

'The Sundays were all fully booked and no one was more surprised than Pixie when she was told the weekday was available,' Rita told her. 'The vicar is working overtime burying people who've died in the air raids but he had a wedding cancellation.'

Lizzie said, 'I wish this war would end.' She had another scratch beneath her turban. 'Bleedin' thing,' she said.

Em said, 'Any of you lot coming in for a shift before the do?'

Both Rita and Lizzie shook their heads.

'Don't look at me!' cried Gladys.

Rita made a face behind Gladys's back. She'd been spending a great deal of time with her landlord, Siddy, just lately. Pixie said she thought something might come of it.

Em sniffed and moved down the line, muttering beneath her breath about workers not bothering to help their country when they were needed most.

'Em's having the whole day off herself, so I don't know why she's moaning,' Rita said.

'Are you sure your mum doesn't mind looking after the babies?' Rita passed Marlene a plate of sausage rolls to put on the table.

Marlene looked at the plate. 'These are more roll than sausage.' She smoothed a few crumbs off her dress. It was white cotton with sprigs of green flowers. The colour matched her eyes and showed off her mane of red hair to perfection. Rita was wearing her black dress, one bought for her by Blackie. She'd clipped her hair to one side hoping to disguise the scar. She forgot it at times – she was so used to seeing it every day. Occasionally, though, when a stranger noticed it she could see the horror in their eyes and it hurt her. That was something she knew she'd never get used to, but perhaps eventually she'd be able to ignore it.

She shrugged. 'Can't get proper sausage-meat,' she said. 'Still, they're better than nothing.'

The table was groaning beneath plates of food and at one end bottles of beer and Corona pop stood waiting with glasses. Bob had somehow managed to get a small barrel of ale and had tapped it, ready for the evening's festivities. Pink and blue crêpe paper had been cut and twisted to decorate the walls of the hall, and the blackout curtains fastened tightly because the lights were on.

'My mum isn't one for dancing and she complained this morning she had a bad headache, but she'd like to do something to help. She loves being with the little ones. Anyway, Ruth's baby girl, my Jeannie and little George are much better off with her to mind them in the quiet of Pixie's house than here. Wasn't George a little devil this morning?'

Rita laughed. 'When that trickle of holy water touched him he really let it be known that he wasn't havin' any.'

'Pixie was glad you managed to calm him. He set Sadie off – that little girl looks a picture but she can't 'alf scream.'

'She even threw Bluebell, her beloved doll, across the church,' Rita said. 'That christening won't be forgotten in a hurry.'

She thought of Pixie trying to calm a screeching Sadie, who, red-faced, was so angry that no one could hear the vicar. George had calmed the moment he was placed in Rita's arms. His eyes opened wide as soon as he felt her near and he immediately quietened.

'Pixie was right to put him to bed. Ruth's little girl is in her own carrycot. She was asleep the moment after Ruth fed her. That gives Ruth a chance to enjoy herself before she has to go back to Alma Street for the next feed. Her husband's coming along later, isn't he?'

'He was called to the aerodrome near Chichester, all very hush-hush.'

Rita saw her look around the hall, careful that no one had overheard her. Marlene had been very distant since the problems with Samuel, but now was slowly warming.

'You all right?' Rita asked.

Marlene squeezed her arm. 'If it wasn't for you and Pixie, I wouldn't be.'

Rita knew it would take her a long time to get back on her feet. She'd confided that she'd found it difficult going to auctions where Samuel had been. All the memories were practically killing her. She was out of sorts and cried a great deal.

'I can't believe Pixie used money from the advance on her book to help me out.'

'She wouldn't have done it if she didn't care for you,' said Rita.

Pixie had a two-book deal. The money wasn't a fortune, but was more than she'd ever envisaged getting from her writing. When the first book would be published was a bit of a mystery though, due to the paper shortage.

'And you, I can't begin to thank you enough . . .'

'Shut up, Marlene, and help me bring in some more stuff from the kitchen. This place is getting crowded now.' Rita wasn't surprised at Pixie's kindness. It was she who had insisted that Ruth and her husband attend the party. Although she was Cal's sister she was also Pixie's friend and had helped her through difficult times.

The band were unpacking their instruments and the hall was filling with people chattering and laughing. Some were still in the clothes they'd worn to the service, but others had gone home and changed into something a bit more glamorous.

'She's a live wire,' Marlene said. Rita followed her gaze to Sadie, who had discarded Bluebell, leaving her on the floor beside her underneath a small table. She was busy tying Mr Jones's bootlace to elderly Harriet Evans's. The couple were totally oblivious as they looked at photographs in an album, every so often laughing at past fashions and hairstyles while drinking their beer.

'Shall I go and stop her?' Rita didn't wait for Marlene to answer and started forward.

Marlene pulled her back. 'Leave her. Don't break her spirit. She's just full of mischief, that one!'

They giggled.

'Coo-ee!' Gladys had entered the hall on Siddy's arm.

Marlene and Rita waved back. 'Nice to see her happy,' said Marlene, and Rita agreed.

The band had started playing, so the floor quickly became full of figures dancing to Glenn Miller songs.

'Doesn't she look lovely?' Pixie drifted by in Bob's arms. Her floaty blue dress suited her blonde hair, which had grown quite long now. She'd pinned it up in a victory roll. 'She's a lovely woman,' said Marlene. 'How long have you known her?'

'All my life,' said Rita. 'We went to the infants' school together at St John's. She was my first friend and she's still the best friend I ever had.' She smiled at Marlene and thought of all the times she and Pixie had laughed and cried together. 'I'll be surprised if either she or Bob stays beyond nine this evening. She'll worry so much about George that neither of them will go the distance. There'll be plenty who'll stay on and clear up afterwards, though.'

The hall was filling with cigarette smoke, perfume and sweaty bodies. Near the door Rita could see Em being helped out of her coat by Sam.

'I suppose Milly's taken over for tonight at the Fox,' said Marlene. 'I expect the next celebration we'll have will be a wedding for them two.'

'About time,' said Rita. It made her feel good to see

Em and Sam dancing towards them. They looked so happy together. Em had on a black box-pleated dress that emphasized her curves. Rita and Marlene waved to the couple.

They gasped as the door opened and in swept Lizzie, looking very smart in her dark costume with the parachute silk blouse beneath it. Beside her was a tall, handsome American in uniform, upright but on crutches.

'Oh, God!'

Marlene grabbed Rita's arm. 'Is that . . .?'

Rita brushed Marlene's hand away. 'Yes, that's Joe.' She thought for a moment she was going to faint. But she quickly pulled herself together and moved between the dancers until she stood in front of him. He was in dress uniform with his peaked hat perched jauntily on his red hair. She marvelled that he now had an artificial limb that he seemed to be in perfect control of, instead of a pinned-up trouser leg.

Lizzie saw her descending upon them and said, 'Time for me to disappear.'

She gave Rita a hasty smile, then swept away to where Marlene was still standing near the food table, gawping.

'You've got a cheek . . .' Rita said to Joe. 'How dare you turn up here—' She couldn't finish the sentence for he had on that citrus cologne that made her legs feel like jelly.

'Have you forgotten you invited me?' His eyes twinkled. His American drawl made her heart sing. Why, oh why had she ever got involved with a man like this who could send her to Heaven at one moment then straight to Hell with his lies and cheating?

He used a crutch to move back. 'I could really do with sitting down,' he said. 'I'm not quite used to this contraption.' He looked down at his leg, then made for a table with a couple of empty chairs and eased himself onto one.

Rita had no option but to follow him. Her heart was still pounding. If Joe thought he could get round her after cuddling that woman, well, he had another think coming. She plonked herself down on the other chair, but before she could open her mouth to say anything, Joe put a hand across the table and held a finger to her lips.

'Listen to what I have to say first. Then you can talk.'

She stared at him, thinking how handsome he was, despite the scar near his eye and a square of gauze covering the wound, which was barely visible beneath his cap.

He took it off. A tumble of red hair fell forward. Rita

longed to put out a hand to touch it, but hesitated. This was the man who had hurt her deeply. She glared at him, still boiling with anger. Around them people were dancing and laughing but she was hardly aware of them. He'd put his cap on the table and Rita had to stop herself picking it up and throwing it on the floor.

'If Lizzie hadn't come to see me I wouldn't have known what the hell was going on.'

Rita stared at him. 'Lizzie? What's Lizzie got to do with it?' At his mention of Lizzie's name Rita's fury swelled. 'What—'

'Sssh!' he said softly. 'An unexpected visit from her, and she told me why you'd not been to see me, something ridiculous about me kissing and cuddling a nurse?'

'I saw you with my own eyes!'

'What you thought you saw was utter rubbish!'

'How dare you say that? I saw you cuddle her!'

He leaned forward and grabbed one of her hands. 'No! You saw me thanking that young woman for bringing back a ring that I'd asked my mother to send over to England. It was my gran's ring and she was of farming stock with big hands and fingers.' With his other hand Joe gently smoothed the back of Rita's hand. 'I wanted you to have it, as an engagement ring, but needed it to be made smaller to fit you. Ellie's hands looked as dainty as yours. She took it into the village jeweller's and had just returned it to me. If only you'd hung around . . .' His voice tailed off.

Rita could see the truth shining from his eyes. 'But . . .'

'Listen,' he said, pulling her towards him. 'You'd made yourself so miserable thinking there was something going on between me and that young physiotherapist that Lizzie decided to visit me, find out the truth and make it right between us.'

Rita was flabbergasted. She had no idea Lizzie liked her enough to do that. She turned to where she was deep in conversation with Marlene.

As though feeling Rita's eyes on them, both women looked over and waved. Rita felt ridiculous, the heat rising to her cheeks. 'I don't know what to say,' she said. She felt stupid she'd jumped to the wrong conclusion that day in the hospital grounds, and ashamed of believing Lizzie to be a selfish woman who cared only for herself.

'It's not nice to think the girl I love doesn't trust me.' Joe let go of her hands.

'I guess I caused myself and you a great deal of pain for nothing,' Rita mumbled.

Joe sat back on his chair, the worried look he'd worn earlier replaced by relief. 'I so wanted to come to Gosport and sort things out with you after Lizzie had visited me that it gave me the courage to get on with my life and try to walk again.' He gave her a small smile. 'So at least your mistaken anger did *some* good.'

Rita hung her head. 'I'm sorry I doubted you. I'm glad I was able to make you concentrate on getting better, though.'

Joe put his hand into his inside pocket and took out a small box. 'Here's the evidence.' He flicked open the top, and nestling in the ruby-red velvet was a gold ring with a glittering stone set in the centre of smaller jewels. 'This diamond ring goes back generations in my family. My mom's happy I've found a wonderful girl to take home after the war.' He leaned forward. 'That's if you'll marry me?'

Rita threw her arms around his neck. 'Yes, oh, yes!'

He disentangled himself long enough to take the ring from the box and slip it onto her finger. Rita wanted to stand up and shout that she loved him. Instead she stared at her hand with the ring on it. Joe stroked her hair and pressed his lips to hers. Rita returned his kiss, then pulled back.

She touched his beautiful mouth and then her fingers searched the broad lines of his face, running over his scars, then through his soft red hair, curling and winding it round her fingers. She looked into his clear, honest eyes, smiling now, and knew he was for her.

He had found her again. Joe wouldn't leave her and they would always be together.

A cheer went up in the hall, and Rita looked about her. Everyone was smiling at them. Neither she nor Joe had realized they had become the centre of attention. Joe started laughing. Then he shouted, 'Rita Brown, I love you.'

The hall erupted into cheers and clapping.

Until the shrill sound of the air-raid siren rent the air.

Chapter Thirty-one

'I must get back to George,' Pixie cried. She slung her coat over her dress and urged Bob, who had hold of Sadie, to hurry with her.

Rita saw a mass of people swarming towards the double doors of the Sloane Stanley Hall. Leaving Joe with a promise to return as soon as she could, she ran to help make sure the people rushing out to the nearest shelter didn't leave lights glaring out into the night's darkness. Safety was paramount.

Already planes droned overhead. A terrific bang made the wooden hall shake and dust fall from the rafters. Rita fell to her knees. Her heart was pounding. That was a close call, she thought. The sky outside was bright with searchlights. Ack ack sounds from ground fire returned the planes' firepower as the machines flew low over the area, dropping their loads. Soon the hall was filled with the smell of burning.

'Hit the lights! Shut the doors!' The noise in the small hall was horrendous as the crowd forgot their duty of calmness in the face of danger and instead were crying, screaming and still trying to run from the hall to the public shelters.

Every time Rita tried to get up, she was knocked off her feet again.

Mrs Harriet Evans, unhurt but cross after her fall, was sitting on the floor with her daughter who, grim-faced, was trying to free her mother's shoelace from Mr Jones's. He was laughing fit to burst. Of course, it was taking a long time as a certain little girl who had since left the hall had knotted them very tightly.

Some people decided they stood a better chance of survival beneath the tables in the hall.

A man pushed against the half-open entrance door and managed to get through. He pulled Rita to her feet, casting aside a beefy man, determined to leave, who was about to tread on her. 'You'll be no good to anybody trampled to death,' he cried, making space for her so she was able to catch her breath. People were still pushing and shoving around her. 'I'm looking for Ruth,' he said.

Rita noted his air-force uniform and fear gripped her. 'Nothing's happened to her husband, has it?'

'Oh, no! On the contrary. I've good news for everyone, and for Ruth, there's nothing to worry about.'

Rita took his arm, glad of his protection, and together they moved through the frightened people to where Ruth and Marlene were huddled beneath a table. Joe stood against the wall and a smile lit his face as he came towards Rita.

The man who had rescued Rita bent down and spoke quietly to Ruth, who at first, upon seeing his uniform, put her hand to her mouth as though fearful of any news he'd brought. After a while a huge grin appeared on her face and she crawled from beneath the table asking Rita, 'Has Charlie told you?' Rita shook her head as her friend continued, 'My husband won't be here, he's been delayed, but Charlie has some excellent information.'

Rita wondered what was going on. How could anyone have good news when bombs were falling outside and any moment they could take a direct hit? The earlier blast must have been extremely close to make the hall shake so much. She wondered where it had fallen. 'Tell them, Charlie,' Ruth urged. 'Shout it out!'

The man yelled, 'Quiet!' It took a further couple of loud pleas before he had the attention of the people remaining in the hall. He made an impressive figure in his smart uniform as he shouted, 'Listen, everyone! At one o'clock this morning, we jammed German radar. Airborne troops landed on the beaches at Normandy . . .'

A cheer started up but soon died away as the airman put up his hands for silence. He had their full attention now. 'At two o'clock minesweepers arrived. By five this morning Bomber Command had attacked Ouistreham in France using Lancasters, and HMS *Orion* shelled gun emplacements near Gold Beach. General Eisenhower's HQ has announced that our troops have landed on French soil. In the streets we're fighting Germans. I have no more news at present but it's straight from the horse's mouth, or rather Air Command . . .'

The noise eclipsed the sounds from outside as people whistled, stamped, clapped and cheered. Rita found herself pressed against Joe's body.

'We're on our way to defeating Hitler,' yelled Rita, as Joe kissed tears of happiness from her eyes. It was then she felt him trembling.

'Oh, Joe,' she cried. 'I forgot what all this noise could do to you.' His forehead was wet with sweat and his hands were clammy. His fingers gripped her wrist so tightly the pain was excruciating.

'Don't you dare worry about me,' he whispered,

suddenly releasing her hand. 'Time heals and I'm getting better every day.' He gave her a squeeze, then flinched as another bomb thudded to the ground nearby and exploded. People in the hall dived for cover once more.

'You'd think them daft Germans would be concentrating all their efforts in France,' Rita said, holding him tightly.

'We've been so good at keeping secrets from their top officers that I wouldn't mind betting that when everything started very early this morning they didn't believe we were doing it for real. So their bombing plans went ahead as usual.'

He stopped talking long enough to kiss her.

'C'mon, you two lovebirds,' said Em. 'Cut it out.' She prised them apart and took Rita to one side. 'I've got Ruth and Marlene practically wetting their knickers worrying about their kids in Alma Street. Come and talk to them for me?'

Things seemed to have quietened down again, though the flashing of searchlights still lit the sky and could be seen dimly through the heavy curtains. Rita squatted on the floor near the women. 'The babies will be in Bob's Morrison shelter. They'll be safe, don't worry. Bob and Pixie have taken their Sadie home so there's plenty of people there to look after them. And your mum,' she nodded at Marlene, 'knows more about looking after little ones than all of us put together. So I'm ashamed of you, Marlene, worrying like that.'

Marlene said, 'But that first bomb was so close . . .'

Rita ignored her. She didn't like to admit her first thoughts had been for George's safety as the planes arrived. As soon as Pixie had left the hall to go to her baby, Rita had felt relieved.

Just then they heard the all-clear.

Sighs of relief echoed across the hall.

Em squeezed Rita's arm. 'Thank God that wasn't a long attack.'

Lizzie said, 'Whew! Gets more nerve-racking every time.' Then, as she stood upright after crawling out from beneath the table, she added, 'Damn! I've got a run in my nylons!'

Marlene started to laugh but ceased when Rita said, 'Lizzie, I need to thank you for explaining things to Joe . . .'

'Don't start with all that rubbish!' Lizzie said, brushing her skirt down. 'It's me should be grateful to you for everything you've done for my family.'

Rita put out her arms and Lizzie melted into them.

Em, looking towards the sagging table and its burden of good things to eat, said, 'We've got all this food going to waste. Some of the people in this hall could be starving at home.'

'Charlie,' said Ruth, 'tell everyone to take some home with them.' She waved at the fast-disappearing crowd. Even the bandsmen were packing away their instruments. She looked at the rest of the girls to see if they all agreed and they were nodding frantically.

Charlie took a deep breath. 'Don't leave the food, you lot,' he boomed. 'Come and help yourselves. A bit of dust never hurt anybody!'

A little later Rita, walking slowly with Joe, stood looking at the huge smoking crater that had been cottages by the bus stop opposite the Criterion cinema. Rubble and cracked paving stones made it difficult for Joe to manoeuvre himself, so he had stopped to rest for a while.

The area was packed with ambulance workers carrying stretchers, and the WVS had set up one of their tea stalls. The air smelled of singed meat and dust clung to everything, including the workers scrabbling to find people in the rubble. Firemen were trying to put out the blaze in what remained of the end house. People were wandering about, stunned and mumbling.

In a space where a bus stop had stood, bodies lay on the ground in uneven rows, covered with sheets, blankets and even coats. People with nothing better to do were standing around, gawping and chattering.

The bomb had covered a wide area with many fatalities.

Rita's heart was heavy for the people who had died, for those remaining who would mourn them, and for those who might be scarred and disabled but would live.

'Thank God we Americans and you English are in France, hopefully winning this war,' said Joe. 'I don't know how your country has managed to survive,' he said sadly.

Rita couldn't answer. In the rubble at her feet was a doll. She bent quickly and picked it up. Her heart faltered. Bluebell had lost one of her arms. Rita tried to tell herself, as she turned the toy in her hands, that it wasn't Sadie's. Surely there were plenty of dolls just like this one. Of course there were. Many Gosport kiddies had similar toys, didn't they? She had been with Pixie when she'd bought Bluebell from Woolworths, and just imagine how many dolls that large store sold every day!

But the blonde hair on one side of the blue-eyed doll's head was shorter than it was on the other. She remembered the day that Sadie had given Bluebell a haircut. Rita clutched Bluebell to her. She knew then, without a doubt, that Sadie was dead.

A sob stuck in her throat. *That couldn't possibly be true.*

The doll had been dropped. Yes, that was it. Sadie had lost the doll walking home. No. Sadie was dead.

'This belongs to Sadie,' Rita said. Her voice was very small. 'Sadie's dead.'

Joe pressed her to him. 'Don't go jumping to conclusions—'

Angrily she pushed him away. 'Don't you tell me how to behave! Don't you bloody dare!' Rita rushed from him, tears prickling at the backs of her eyes. Stumbling over rocks and bricks she ran forward looking for someone she could ask. Despite the tears now streaming down her face, she saw a fireman bending to turn a handle partially concealed beneath a paving stone. Water, gas? She grabbed his arm.

'Watch it, missus,' he cried.

'Survivors? Where are they?'

'Steady on, missus.' His face was grimy, his eyes tired. 'You'll have me bleedin' arm out of its socket.' He let go the handle, stood up and rubbed his elbow.

'Survivors?' Rita yelled again.

'By the tea tent!' He went back to gripping the key-shaped handle, his face grim and muttering oaths.

The stench of the burned earth got into her throat and stung her eyes. But she had to find Sadie. Of course she wasn't dead. How could she be? It was only a short time ago the child had been tying shoelaces together.

Rita saw the tea tent. Some women had a stove going outside, boxes with tea things piled on them. The mugs looked curiously white after the grey of the dirt about them. The interior of the tent was practically filled with people. Sadie and Pixie would be inside having a nice cup of tea. Yes, that was it. They'd be shaken because of the bomb, like these other people. A lovely cup of tea would be just what Pixie, Bob and the little one needed. Sadie would be pleased to have Bluebell back. She must be crying her little heart out at losing her favourite dolly, thought Rita.

She looked at the people sitting on assorted chairs.

'Did you see a little girl?' Rita's voice was a breathless shriek. Nobody turned towards her. Perhaps she hadn't been heard above the noise about her.

She saw then that most of the people were glassy-eyed and shivering. Until one, a young lad who seemed more sensible than the others, tugged at her sleeve. 'It happened so quickly. Whoosh! And then there was fire and blood and—'

'A little girl with this doll?' Rita pushed the toy at him. The lad didn't look down at it. 'Tell me,' Rita urged.

'Please, I must know.' At last he opened his mouth to speak again.

'It happened so quickly. Whoosh! And then there was fire and blood . . .'

He and all these people were in deep shock. Her heart plummeted. She'd get no proper answers from them. Still carrying Bluebell, she ran from the tent, straight into a nurse.

'Whoops! Don't want any more casualties!' The nurse's friendliness was a relief.

Rita started to cry again. She grabbed at the woman's arm. 'Please help me. I have this doll.' She pushed Bluebell at the nurse. 'It belongs to my friend's little girl. She'll be so upset she's dropped it. I must find them.'

The nurse stared at her. 'Keep calm.' Her voice was soft. Rita heaved a sigh of relief and listened carefully as the nurse continued, in case she said something Rita might not hear properly. 'We're still looking for survivors. The film had finished and the queue at the bus stop was long. There were many people standing about, including a queue for the showing of the next picture.'

'But this belongs to a little girl. My friends were passing by on their way home.'

The nurse put her hand on Rita's arm. She stared at her intently for what seemed to Rita an eternity.

'Please help me find my friend.' Rita's eyes spilled over with more tears. 'She's got a baby at home.'

The nurse looked thoughtful, then said quietly, 'I shouldn't really do this but come with me.'

She turned and Rita followed, stumbling over the detritus of people's homes and lives. Rubble and bricks were still hot from the fires. Carefully they walked, ignoring items that had once been prized possessions. A ripped handbag, a broken umbrella, a half-burned shopping bag with a loaf of blackened bread protruding from it, a school satchel. The nurse paused near the sheeted bodies.

There were more lying on the ground than before.

'Describe your friends.'

'A blonde woman. A man, tall, dark, with glasses, and a little girl.' Rita tried very hard to be calm and for her voice to be clear.

Moving carefully among the bodies and gently lifting the corners of the covers so that everything was kept hidden from Rita, the nurse walked the aisles between the dead. Then she said, 'Had the woman put her hair up in a victory roll?'

Rita was stunned. It couldn't possibly be Pixie. The victory roll was very fashionable. She was suddenly turned to lead. But she had to know. Forcing herself to move, she walked carefully, trying not to tread on any of the coverings, nearer to the nurse. 'Can I see?' Without waiting for a reply, Rita peered beneath the raised corner of the sheet.

Pixie's pretty face. Untouched. Hair practically immaculate. She looked calm, asleep in her floaty blue dress.

Rita stared at her lifelong friend. Her heart was heavy. She nodded, but then she put her fist to her mouth and bit down on her hand. The sheet was lowered. She must not cry before she found out if . . .

The nurse moved on to the next figure. Bob was lying beside Pixie. Strangely, his suit jacket was gone and his shirt was ripped. There was blood on his hairy chest. The last time she'd seen his chest he'd been having a wash in the scullery at their home. Apart from the blood and his brown eyes being open, he was unmarked and appeared peaceful next to his darling Pixie. Rita nodded.

Sadie was by herself, lying near the hedge. There was a small cut on her cheek. Otherwise her little face, pale and lovely, was unblemished.

Rita, her head swimming, knelt down and kissed Sadie's cheek. It was cold, as if she'd been playing outside in frosty weather. Without a coat on or her knitted mittens, which she was always losing, or the little hat that Pixie had knitted for her.

'Please don't touch.' The nurse roughly pulled her away. But then her voice softened. 'I shouldn't be allowing this, but I know what it's like to lose someone and have to wonder where they are. You've identified this family and I'd be glad if you could give me their names and address. Sometimes it takes ages to find out who the dead are . . .' She put her hand on Rita's arm. 'I'm sorry, you must go. The death rate here is going to be high . . . I need to work.'

Rita let the woman's words wash through and over her as she laid the dolly, Bluebell, next to Sadie. The nurse pulled up the blanket.

As she stood upright, Rita felt the woman's arms go round her. The warmth of the nurse's body after the chill of the child's was incredibly soothing.

After a while she was aware of a second pair of arms. And a voice, saying, 'Thank you, ma'am, I'll take her home now.' Then Joe whispered to Rita, 'We must get away from here. Isn't there a baby?'

George? Rita forced herself to gather her wits. She looked up at Joe, then back at the nurse.

'Thank you,' Rita said. Her mind had again sunk to a blur when, seconds earlier, she'd managed to hold herself together long enough to give answers to questions and to explain the three dead were a family.

George. She had to find him.

'Are you all right?' Joe smoothed the hair back from her face.

Wearily, Rita nodded.

'D'you want to go on ahead to the house? I know it can't be far . . .'

Rita had forgotten that Joe had never been to Alma Street. 'Would you mind?'

She stared at him. She so badly wanted this night to be a bad dream. When she awoke, everything would be like it had been. She'd hear the wireless on in Pixie's house and Bob singing along tunelessly. Maybe Sadie would have one of her morning tantrums and Gladys would bang on the wall with the poker.

Only it wasn't a dream. Joe was talking again. 'Of course not. I'll follow at my own pace.' He looked so tired, she thought.

Rita gave him directions automatically. She tried *not* to think about the bodies beneath the sheets. The dead people she had loved so much.

She set off at a run, uncaring of the rubble that might twist her ankles. What was a minor accident when her best friend was gone for ever? She was hoping with all her heart that George was safe.

There was no need for her to knock on Pixie's front

door for it was wide open. The sound of Gladys wailing set Rita's teeth on edge. She heard voices trying to calm her, some familiar, others she didn't recognize.

Gladys sat in the big threadbare green velvet armchair in the kitchen. In the Morrison shelter three children, two babies and a little girl, were amazingly, despite the noise, fast asleep.

George was safe. Rita looked down at him snuggled beneath a patchwork quilt and said a silent prayer of thanks. Then she turned to Gladys and reached for her hand. 'You've heard . . .' Rita got no further.

Gladys turned her tear-stained face towards her. 'Mrs Tenant from number four was just coming out of the Criterion. The blast blew her back. She said Pixie and Bob and Sadie were walking down the road. When she looked again, there was just this big hole . . . I don't know where they are, Rita.'

Gladys had never looked so worn and old.

An elderly woman in a hairnet touched Rita's arm. 'I dunno what happened because I passed out. When I came to, there was a Red Cross lady bending over me.' She paused for breath. 'I told her, "Thank you very much but I'm all right an' them poor buggers over the road need you more." She left me then. But now we don't know what's happened to Pixie. No one seems to know.'

Her false teeth clicked as she spoke. Rita sighed. Gladys didn't know about Pixie, Bob and Sadie.

The noise in the small room was increasing in volume. Neighbours, well-meaning, had come to commiserate with Gladys but had stayed to chatter.

There was a sudden cry. Ruth's little girl had woken. Ruth appeared from nowhere to crawl inside the Morrison shelter beside her child. Rita watched as she turned her back on the noisy people and unfastened her dress, baring her breast to feed her baby.

Gladys was sobbing.

Rita thought it was time for her to take charge. She picked up a knife from the sideboard and rapped hard on the wooden tabletop. The canary, startled, hopped from bar to bar in his cage, his wings swishing like miniature yellow dusters.

'Listen, everyone.' The noise abated immediately, leaving the smell of cigarettes in the air and just a few whispered mutterings. 'Thank you all for your kindness in coming to sit with Gladys, but it's time you went back to your own homes.' More murmurings of dissent but within minutes the house had emptied. Rita walked down the passage and closed the front door.

Ruth was still feeding her baby. Marlene and her mother had begun tidying up. Marlene's little girl was still asleep, as was George. Lizzie volunteered to put the kettle on.

'Thank God the place is empty now,' Lizzie said. Her face was wet with tears, her eyes puffy. She said to Rita, 'Mum's gone down the Fox with Sam. She's no idea Pixie's missing.'

Rita stared at her as she began rinsing out cups. 'Where's Gladys's friend, her landlord?' She thought Gladys might like to be comforted by him when the women had left. *When the truth was known.* She would stay with Gladys if that was what she wanted but Rita needed to be by herself.

'Siddy's next door in your house waiting for her. Too many women frighten him, he said.'

Just then Rita heard Joe calling through the letterbox. Someone must have let him in because the next thing she knew was he was standing next to her. She'd completely forgotten about him! The deaths of Pixie, Bob and Sadie had eclipsed everything, except George. There was little room in her heart and mind for anyone else, not even the man she loved.

'Have you told her?' Joe murmured.

She shook her head.

'Told her what?' Lizzie's eyes travelled to Rita. She went quiet. Then: 'She's copped it, hasn't she? Pixie?' Rita didn't reply but she went over to the big chair and knelt on the rug in front of Gladys.

Gladys stared into her eyes. Then she looked across the room towards Lizzie. Then at Joe. 'She's dead, isn't she?'

Rita nodded.

There were gasps from the other women.

Gladys's eyes filled with fresh tears. 'Bob? And Sadie?'

Rita nodded again and pulled Gladys into her arms.

'You're wrong . . .' Gladys pushed away from her. Her voice had risen, shrill.

Rita shook her head. 'I identified them.'

'No!' It was a scream that stopped all of them in their paces. Even the scullery tea-making clattered to a halt. Gladys sagged against Rita and sobbed in her arms. 'My baby!' she cried out, again and again. 'My baby.'

Everyone in that kitchen knew Pixie was a grown woman, but to a mother her child, no matter how old, is always her baby.

Just then George woke. Gladys was now crying into the handkerchief that Joe had given her. She sniffed. Her eyes were red-rimmed.

After a while she said, in a small voice, 'Remember what Pixie and Bob wanted?'

Rita, still on her knees, looked up into Gladys's tearful face. 'What?'

'In church today, my daughter made you godmother of that little boy.' She looked towards the Morrison shelter where George was getting into second gear with his crying. 'But she also made you promise to look after him, didn't she?'

'Of course I'll help,' Rita said. Did Gladys think she'd walk away from George?

'No! More than that. I wasn't a good mother. You're the one with the love for that little boy. I'm too old and selfish.'

Rita saw fresh tears brimming.

'I remember what was said. But you'll think differently when the pain of Pixie's death lessens.'

Gladys gripped Rita's hand. 'It's what she wanted and what I want!'

Her red-painted nails were digging into Rita's flesh. 'Take this house over and bring him up as yours. It's what Pixie wanted.'

The sudden cessation of George's cries made Rita look round. Ruth had picked him up and was feeding him, holding his tiny head to her breast. Her baby girl was wrapped in her shawl and soundly sleeping.

'It seemed the easiest way to stop him crying,' Ruth said. 'Besides, I've got plenty.' Rita looked at her swollen breast, which George was happily sucking. 'I can provide for George while you get him used to a bottle and maybe try him with rusks,' said Ruth. 'My husband won't mind me staying a few days to help. Or have you forgotten we've landed on French soil? He'll be flying . . .'

Rita was shocked, not by Ruth's mothering, of course not, but by Gladys and the ease with which she was handing over her only grandchild.

'You know you love that little boy more than I ever could,' Gladys persisted.

She really did want her to take Pixie's child and bring him up as her own!

Rita's heart soared out of the pain that encased it. From where she was kneeling, she could see George's tiny fists folding and uncurling as he fed.

Then a shadow fell across her. 'There's nothing I'd love more. But I couldn't bear it if one day you took him back.'

'Are you mad?' Gladys put her hand on Rita's cheek. 'I'm offering you my grandson and you're worrying about me wanting to take over again? I don't think so! I've lived my life exactly how I've wanted for too long. There's a man next door waiting for me and I don't intend to turn my Siddy's comfort away. And,' she said, through more tears, 'you know I needs a man to comfort me. I never was one for the company of women.' Then she frowned.

'I'll make it legal, as long as you allow me to still be George's grandmother.'

Rita smiled, although she had nothing to smile about, with Pixie and . . . 'It's a deal,' she said. She felt like a caged bird that had been set free. 'I'll make sure George knows all about his mum and what a good person Pixie was. And I'll never allow him to forget Bob and Sadie.'

Gladys, now standing, embraced her. Rita was startled when a hand touched her shoulder.

Joe said, 'I need to get back to the hospital. I was only allowed out because I promised to be back for them to dress my wounds.'

Rita knew he must have overheard the conversation between her and Gladys. She could hear crying, the lowered voices of her friends and the rattle of cups in the scullery. They would be consoling each other for the loss of Pixie and her family. And this was where she and Joe had to part. For good.

He had asked her to marry him and she'd agreed, but men didn't marry women who had children to bring up. Most men wanted their own offspring, not another man's child.

She'd made her choice and, much as she loved Joe, it wasn't him she'd chosen. Joe *would* find another girl, one without the burden of a child. She *had* to let him go.

Rita, for the first time that night, was aware of the strain on his face. 'Oh, God!' she said. 'You came to Gosport especially for me and all I've done is cause you pain and practically ignore you . . .'

'I've got one of the hospital orderlies coming to fetch me in his car. It was all arranged.'

It was then she looked down and saw that his pale trousers were dark with blood where the prosthesis was rubbing against his flesh. He must have practised hard to walk, probably against his doctor's wishes, so that he could be as perfect a man as possible before asking her to marry him. His pain must be intolerable. She thought of him staggering over unforgiving, uneven ground to this house. Yet he had conquered it all *for her*. He'd stood by her tonight and what had she done? She'd shouted at him. Left him to his own devices while she'd searched for her best friend, and totally ignored him as though he hardly existed. She looked again at his bloodied trousers. He was a saint.

But now she had to tell him she couldn't marry him because, although he was the love of her life, so was George.

Her choice had been made.

Rita twisted off the ring and pressed it into Joe's hand. 'I'm going to bring up that child.' She looked towards

Ruth, who had wrapped George in a shawl and he was now sleepily gazing through the wire of the Morrison shelter. 'So, you see, I can't marry you.'

To stop her tears, she went over, bent down and picked up the baby, her baby.

The milky smell of him soothed her pain. The warmth of his small body comforted her. He opened his eyes and stared into her soul. Yes, deep down, despite her love for Joe, she knew she'd made the right decision. This little boy needed her and she needed him. She couldn't stop the tears that were falling on the white shawl.

She felt herself being twisted around and pressed against Joe's chest – gently, so that George wasn't crushed.

'If you think you're getting away that easily,' he said to her, 'you've got another think coming.' He looked down at the baby. 'Don't close your eyes, little man,' he whispered. His big hand stroked the soft dark downy head. 'The war could be nearly over and there's a big world out there waiting for you.' He held Rita's eyes for a moment before he smiled down at the little boy once more. Then Joe said, 'Aren't you going to say hello to your new pop, Georgie boy?'

ACKNOWLEDGEMENTS

Thank you to the many people at Quercus who have worked hard to make sure this book reaches my lovely readers. Special thanks to Jane Wood, Therese Keating, Hazel Orme, Sue Phillpott and as always Juliet Burton.